In the spirit of the best of American social commentary—think Sinclair Lewis or John O'Hara—Todd R. Baker's *Secrets of Men in a Lifeboat* follows the fall and rise of demoralized advertising executive and single father Luke Morrow, who fate gives a crack at the parallel life he has always wanted and believes himself to deserve. Carefully observed and cleverly plotted, Baker's tour-de-force is at once biting and poignant, both a commentary on the misguided values of our business class and a testament to the redemptive power of parental love. I cannot recall the last time I read a volume of this length in one weekend—at least, not for pleasure—and I entirely lost track of time in the process. The dialogue is as crisp and as authentic as any in modern fiction; the pages seem to turn themselves. In short, a first-rate novel that captures the pulse of its age.
—Jacob M. Appel, author of *Einstein's Beach House*

Tightly written and [...] adroit in its storytelling, *[Secrets of Men in a Lifeboat]* offers two finely drawn lives and a continuing mystery as to how they will overlap. The curious will wonder how it all ends [...] The novel should cause many readers to fervently seek [its] lesson.
—*Kirkus Reviews*

At a moment when America's adoration of its financial giants is approaching a unique level of madness, Todd R. Baker comes to remind us what dangerous heroes we have wrought. A timely morality tale, observed with an insider's fidelity.
—Robin Kirman, author of *Bradstreet Gate*

An inventive blend of fable and satire that expertly captures the complexity of the lives we lead.
—Lou Berney, *USA Today* best-selling author of *The Long and Faraway Gone*

Secrets of Men in a Lifeboat lays bare the warped narcissism of an unconscionable American billionaire, championing the redemptive antidote to him: a return to civility and basic decency. In the time of Donald Trump and garish Trumpism, *Secrets of Men in a Lifeboat* restores crucial faith in our most principled values: honor, empathy, and love.
—L.S. Bassen, author of *Summer of the Long Knives, Lives of Crime & Other Stories, Marwa,* Atlantic Pacific Press Drama Prize Winner

In the multiple incarnations of Luke Morrow, the hero of Todd R. Baker's tightly drawn debut novel, we are presented with life's many interpretations of success, love, and fatherhood. One man's oscillation between two converging worlds is what gives this novel its narrative drive, and it's worth holding on.
—Elliot Ackerman, author of *Green on Blue*

I found much to admire in the novel. Todd is clearly a talented writer, with a special gift for dialogue. I especially enjoyed the portrayal of the father-son relationship—tender, funny, and true.
—Lauren Acampora, author of *The Wonder Garden*

There are many tender scenes between Luke and his son… Luke's rise from despair [...] takes readers on a journey full of riches… A Faustian tale of a SoCal man given the choice between fame and fortune or his heart and soul.
—*IndieReader*

Secrets of Men in a Lifeboat is thought-provoking and unusual. It touches on difficult topics such as anxiety, autism, infidelity, divorce, depression, and suicide in a realistic manner and without stigma, which I found refreshing. I believe it will become a favorite of book clubs because it's packed with symbolism and issues ripe for discussion. Todd R. Baker has written a strong debut novel. *Secrets of Men in a Lifeboat* is haunting and unforgettable.
—*The Qwillery*

Secrets of Men in a Lifeboat

Todd R. Baker

Awards for
Secrets of Men in a Lifeboat

2016 HOLLYWOOD BOOK FESTIVAL

GRAND PRIZE WINNER

2017 IPPY AWARDS

SILVER MEDAL FOR COVER DESIGN – FICTION

5TH ANNUAL BEVERLY HILLS BOOK AWARDS

WINNER IN 3 CATEGORIES

LITERARY FICTION

NEW FICTION

BOOK COVER DESIGN – FICTION

2016 FOREWORD INDIE BOOK AWARDS

FINALIST – FICTION

11TH ANNUAL NATIONAL INDIE EXCELLENCE

AWARDS

FINALIST – BOOK COVER DESIGN

FINALIST – FICTION

Secrets of Men in a Lifeboat

By

Todd R. Baker

Greenwich Street Press

Published by Greenwich Street Press

Published in the United States of America
ISBN: 978-0-692-91916-3

First edition, Aqueous Books printing, April 2016
Second edition published by Greenwich Street Press, July 2017
Editing, book design, and layout: Cynthia Reeser
Text is in Adobe Caslon Pro and Penultimate Light
Cover painting by Cynthia Reeser. Used with permission.
Cover design by Matthew Revert.

GREENWICH STREET

PRESS

For Hut

PART ONE

1.

On his fortieth birthday, the man, unshaven and sleepless, unlocks a gun. As comets die overhead, he raises the gun, bruises blooming where cuffs had strapped him to a bed.

∞

Luke and the mom from Ocean Park stood on the beach, holding hands in the wind. "What are you thinking?"

"Nothing," he said.

"You can tell me anything, I promise."

He held her tighter and she was glad for it. Six years ago, she was twenty-four weeks pregnant when her husband left; six weeks later, she tried to kill herself. Now at thirty-two, she was safe in Luke's arms under the moon. Later, at home, she lit a warming fire and began shedding her clothes.

∞

"She's unbuttoning her shirt, telling me how women's breasts are never the same after having children, and I don't care, I want to be a good man. And then she says, 'Before we do this, are you going to make me a princess?' But there's already a lifetime of disappointment in her, and I don't know what to say." Luke is in a candle-lit home with two married couples bordering his age. Nearly forty years old with waves of russet hair, he's their link to the singles' world they envy and fear, but the dinner table is a hearth, and they want to hear his latest adventure.

So Luke's fable fills the canyon deep, and the women begin to drift away, wondering what it would be like to kiss another man after all these years, while their husbands will fantasize to Luke's story later that night, when their wives are sound asleep.

The husbands will figure Ocean Park Mom at half her age, and on their way to work, they will panic because their illicit toilet paper bunnies remain snuck under their beds. They will pray the nannies making the beds won't find them. Only nannies find everything, and the bunnies will be picked damp, and the dads and nannies will share an unspoken horror.

But there is tonight, when the universe is still whole, and the men can enjoy the Persian take-out without tomorrow's shame. And the women can dream, especially since Luke's 8-year-old son Trevor and four other boys have raced from the kids' table, leaving bitten pitas behind, which Barbara— a hound masquerading as a mid-century sedan—cannot reach.

That is, until the boys race in from the driveway, knocking bread off the table to Barbara, who drags it onto the porch beneath lightheaded moths. Before her master can shout, "No, not on your diet!" the boys are gone.

"Samurais on their way to slaughter the peasants."

"Game rated: Suitable for juvenile hall."

"Which one has the carjacking and the prostitutes?"

"Not until they're twelve." This from Keri, who lives wryly above the fray as a Smith-educated *beau ideal* to venture capitalist Bram Brask, the ever-sure parochialist across the table. Their son and Luke's son are buddies from school—that's how everyone met—and now Luke and Keri have this buddy thing going on as well, which they warm in a microwave set on defrost.

But their friendship shouldn't worry hosts Peter and Marnie Wessler; Luke and Keri have honor and won't attempt more than brother-sister, which is all Bram can sense, given his tenure as a powerful man to a blonder, engaging wife.

Peter says, "You didn't say yes?"

Luke says, "I couldn't promise."

Peter says, "What's so hard about saying you'd make her a princess? Right in front of you."

"Maybe she didn't really mean it." Keri bleeds for single women who get nervous on their dates, prompting them to say needy things she's certain they regret.

Marnie says, "What about her vibrator again?"

Bram says, "A girl with an implement. You can do better."

Keri says, "It hardly defines her."

Marnie says, "She cried when you left."

She did.

"Poor thing; she's crazy."

But Luke knew that the mom from Ocean Park was just being honest about her romantic dreams, which he kept to himself, along with the memory of his college professors, who published the paper, "Marginal Differences between the Sexes." These scholars—a husband and a wife—said it only mattered if a person were a man or woman when he or she wanted to make a baby.

Convinced that society's evolution had stereotyped the sexes into cultural roles, the professors asked their 5-year-old son to wear his sister's barrettes to school. They assured him, "It only matters if you're a boy or a girl when you want to make a baby, so who cares what you wear in your hair?"

And when the other boys pushed their son face-down in the snow, the professors chalked it up to commercials for Barbies and Hot Wheels—enforcers of self-fulfilling prophesies—because girls will play with trucks and boys will paint their toenails, if parents will just get out of the way.

But as time would tell, the differences between men and women proved unfathomable. For every woman thrilled to be successful in business, another seemed disenchanted with her hard-won lot. Unexpectedly, women grieved for the children they never had or couldn't be home to raise, and chafed at their husbands' slow, clumsy efforts to nurture and clean. There were whispers that wives were growing resentful of their husbands for not making more money, and stories circulated about men who anguished in silence, unable to wrest greatness from their ordinary lives.

So why blame Ocean Park Mom for wanting to be a saved on pedestal? Pine for a thwarted man in a ruthless economy? Bring on the king, with his castle on the sand.

"Decaf coming." Marnie brings cottura mugs, all with different patterns, each handmade in Italy.

Peter says, "We actually have a matching set, except these are more fun." Only he means the old ones were fine, silencing Marnie, and now their marriage, like the torte from the local bakery, is open for review.

Peter, mid-forties and hedgehog-out-of-shape, passes on non-fat milk carbs, trying to prolong his cable ad sales career. That's to pay for the five-bedroom house replacing the starter home with the scant ocean view. Add to that German cars, Deer Valley vacations, and the over-priced organic grocery, and it's a call for a casket.

Marnie, Pilates-petite with a tight brunette ponytail, is a go-getter PR girl turned enclave mom. And though she's thoughtful daily, she has nester's ambition, which means increasing the family's lifestyle every time her husband gets a raise. While Peter prays he won't lose his job, she has blind faith that he'll make the obvious choices to control their destiny. It's not like he's going to end up a janitor, right?

Luke wonders what would happen if Peter took a chance. Is Marnie in it for richer and not poorer? No, as long as they're a family, she'd happily live in a Winnebago. Wouldn't she?

Luke knows he's losing his ability to see in shades of gray. But the end of his own marriage has shaped him, and when Keri serves Bram a golden kiwi tart, Luke's cynicism comes into play: How come he never sees them touch?

"Any more Internet dates, Luke?"

The night before, yes. But the date was cut short; she was a responsible dog mom and had left her kid outside—and once it started raining, she needed to get home. The woman was also ten years younger than Luke and never married, which created questions: A friend, or a beautiful can of worms? Did she want him to call, or was she ready to fillet him after all?

Therefore, there was no point in sharing this date with his married groupies. Too anti-climactic; no prurient punch. Still, Luke couldn't resist. "You should read what some of these women write: 'The man I'm looking for must be financially and emotionally secure, comfortable in his own skin, and not afraid to show his true vulnerability.' Which is contradictory, because if you share your self-doubt with a woman, you're showing a lack of confidence and power."

"They probably don't mean it."

"They don't know what they mean."

"Maybe they're just looking for balance."

Marnie says, "It doesn't matter what they write; all men want is sex anyway."

Luke knows she's right but he says, "If that's the case, they'd just go to The Erotic Review,"—one website among many where consumer advocates using pseudonyms like Pussyluver and Famous MD can write provider reviews. The new facts unsettle the women—they didn't know a hooker could be ordered with a mouse.

Keri asks Luke, "Have you ever done it?"

Luke says, "I just read the posts—maybe I subscribed for a month."

Marnie says, "Men are disgusting."

Peter says, "Don't look at me."

"Bram?"

"An escort service? I have my beautiful wife." Bram gives Keri a kiss, and it's the first between them that Luke has ever seen. Keri absorbs the affection, Marnie waits in vain for a kiss from Peter, and Luke uses the opportunity to excuse himself from the table, thankful his story is over for the night.

∞

Luke leans into a bedroom, where digital gaming chains the boys. Thinking he's one of them he says, "How's it going in here?" They don't look up. "I said, 'How are you ladies doing?'"

The 11-year-old leader musters, "Fine, woman," and the others almost crack smiles, too busy to bother with a grown-up pest. So Luke bails downstairs to the living room deck. There, peering into the hillside, Luke hears animals crackling through the brush. But they're not possums or skunks; the great secret of Pacific Palisades is that it's overrun with rats. Don't tell anyone they're everywhere— scratching across roofs, poised to steal lemons off backyard trees. For the rats live well here, too, the western moon drenching them in shadows.

"Now my wife thinks I'm on it."

Luke's caught off guard and didn't hear Bram. "What are you talking about?"

Bram says, "The Erotic Review. You shouldn't have brought it up." Bram returns inside; he's buying women off the Internet and warning Luke to uphold the brotherhood of men. To spare Keri, Luke will, but Luke wonders how a man can be that dismissive and smug toward consequence.

"Dad, I'm ready to go now." Sidling up to Luke is Trevor, a little guy for eight years old with a ready, sly smile—a best friend to all the boys. Trevor has come around on cue, since he has always known himself when to call a play date quits, before a meltdown might wreck the fun.

Marnie says, "Leaving so soon?"

Luke says, "Sorry Nee, gotta get him to bed."

"Where did he just go?"

Trevor re-appears with Vans. Luke Velcroes them. "Where were they?"

"You know the baseball bat in the backyard?"

Luke doesn't.

"Has a magic marker skull on it."

Luke shrugs.

"That's not where they were."

"Did you say goodbye to the guys?" Trevor nods, and Barbara comes at him with her inexplicable woof. Trevor doesn't like that old dog and backs into Luke for safety— before the boy and man are out the door into the night.

∞

Luke lives in a one-bedroom oceanfront apartment with a monthly rent the size of a mortgage. And even though he should move somewhere cheaper, he accepts the expense because it keeps him close to Trevor, who spends most of the week one mile away on a coastal mountaintop with Luke's ex-wife, Lisa, and her new husband Mark Morello II.

To Trevor though, the apartment is a bear cave above the sea, and the bedroom Luke has given over to Trevor has everything. There's a maple bunk built with a full mattress on the bottom and a twin on top, allowing Luke room to join Trevor at story time.

Covering the floor and walls are toys and sports pennants, and on a corner stand, a burbling tropical aquarium. And if there is frequent fish mortality despite the hobbyists' concerted care, it's a small price to pay to have company in the house.

Trevor says, "Let's see if Fry French and French Fry are still alive."

"Okay, but it's time to get in your PJs."

Trevor is talking about the darting yellow baby bar-tailed platies, who suddenly appeared last week under the sunken sloop. "There they are. Tiger has not eaten them yet." Tiger is the four-inch vegan pleco—the big fish of this small pond.

"C'mon Trevor, we need time for our important conversation."

Trevor rises from the wavering hue and complies into the bathroom for tooth brushing that misses molars. Next, Luke administers medicines to ward off Trevor's allergies to dust mites, grass, and domestic cat pelt. Trevor doesn't mind the chewable pills, which taste like sherbet, but the liquid makes him shudder. Trevor gets in bed and Luke lies down next to him. Trevor says, "You know what Rachel R. said?" Rachel R. is the jazz ballerina in Trevor's second grade class.

"Tell me."

"She said cookies give you cancer. Then she wanted one because she forgot her snack."

"Rachel R. is unique."

"She has gray hair."

"She can't."

"Maybe it's blonde-gray."

"There you go. Listen Trevor, I've got some news for you."

"What is it?"

"Well, you know how I'm a creative director at work—well the head guys, my bosses—"

"I thought you were the boss."

"Well, I am for a lot of people, but these are the bigger bosses, and they're gonna make me Creative Director of North America."

"Do they pay you more bucks?"

"You don't need to worry about stuff like that. It's just that it's gonna be better for both of us."

"Ben told Archer he was his boss." Ben is Keri and Bram's son; Archer is Marnie and Peter's. "Archer said no, he was the boss of the boss. Then Ben said he was the boss of the boss of the boss, making him God."

"You guys drink too much beer."

Trevor says, "No we don't. Plus I can only have sips, because I'm allergic to yeast."

Then the two are quiet, absorbing. "Trevor, even with my promotion, you still remember what my real job is, the only important one?"

"I forget."

"My job is to love you. What's your job?"

"I forget."

"Your job is to be a kid. And you know what I say? The two easiest jobs in the world." Luke kisses Trevor on the forehead. "I love you. Goodnight."

Trevor rolls over, and moments later he's asleep. For fleeting seconds, Luke feels exquisitely happy.

∞

Sleep comes easily for Luke, but a bad dream follows hard. In the dream, Luke's ex-wife Lisa faces the mirror, removing a tortoise shell clip after a taxing day, letting dark tresses cascade over her flat-chested beauty.

To Luke's reflection, she says, "What kind of man are you, starting a business off of my back?"

Luke lowers his head in shame.

"Don't you understand? The man I want to make love to is powerful."

Luke battles himself awake, and when he's finally able to see, he finds himself overheated in Trevor's bed. He rises, fixing Trevor's covers. After a cold drink of water in the alley kitchen, Luke strips off his jeans and climbs onto the sofa. Aware for hours, Luke barely regains sleep.

∞

Luke says, "Too loud." Trevor is watching cartoons with the TV blaring. Luke serves him oatmeal, turning down the volume. Trevor raises the volume back up. Luke is about to snatch the control away and assert his rule, but the window is open to the street ten floors below and traffic is whooshing by. So maybe Trevor has a point.

∞

Luke eases his mineral-gray Cherokee from underground parking, with Trevor buckled in the back seat like a ventriloquist's puppet. Trevor says, "Dad, can you take my mind out of my head?"

"Can I what?"

"Can you take my mind out of my head?"

"If I have a jar to put it in."

"I don't want it in a jar."

"Then it should stay where it is."

Trevor says, "But my memory keeps coming back, and I can't make it stop."

"Is it a bad memory?"

"Sorta."

"Wanna tell me about it?"

"It's private."

"Okay, but you know our deal. You can tell me anything, even if you think it might hurt my feelings."

"It's just about this elephant song I keep hearing."

Luke is relieved that Trevor's memory isn't about the divorce. "Listen, the way to get rid of a bad thought is to think about something good instead. Can you try that?"

Trevor can. "I'll think about how it's good Tiger hasn't eaten Fry French. Yet."

Luke eyes his rearview mirror and meets Trevor's scandalous grin.

∞

The Jeep rolls to an estate call box. Luke reaches out to press the bell, but the gate is already giving way. He proceeds up the driveway to the two-story entrance of a glass fort.

Trevor looks expectantly out the back window, but he doesn't have long to wait, being that his stepfather, Mark, in a Yale polo shirt with collar up, is already opening the car's door. Mark unbuckles Trevor and waves, "Hi Luke," like, *Isn't it great how we share our son?*

Luke does his best to nod back at stepdad, a corporate attorney with a trust fund. Mark bends, "Welcome home, Bud," giving Trevor a paisan kiss on the lips, before leading the boy past a titanium Aston Martin and into the house. Luke drives on, fighting for forbearance under a leaden sky.

2.

The Venice headquarters of advertising agency Nicaida & Knight occupies a campus of wood plank buildings that once served as a cooperative dairy. Now, the white barns from the 1910s have pegged maple floors, halogen lights, and conference rooms with Aeron chairs. But the sun still flashes through the barns' clanking rooftop vents, like it did when Los Angeles was home to spotted cows.

Luke parks in his reserved space at Nicaida & Knight and heads for his office. Though the day has barely started, the pace inside is already rushed. Still, Luke comes to work with a sense of relief—his return to employment has been a difficult climb, and he is grateful for good luck.

Even better, he's being given his due. And it looks like he'll be able to promote his assistant into accounts. However,

Stacy is out until mid-morning on a personal matter and won't be around to hear the good news.

Taking a moment with his coffee, Luke reflects on his most recent work—storyboard mock-ups tacked to the wall. Luke mastered the campaigns and pleased difficult clients—a big win for all. Only, Luke's thoughts turn dark and suddenly, he's remembering the dreams that tricked him into The Bubble.

Brimming with ideas about Internet content, he had put his wife and son in jeopardy, hoping for a future as a captain of industry. Which didn't happen, and soon enough, Luke was a single parent. Worse, entrepreneurship expanded his ego, and he swore he would never work for anyone again. So when the First Great Internet Age cratered for him for good, Luke founded his own advertising agency. Except expenses exceeded income, forcing him to shut the doors. Still, he had led by fair example, and his Gen-X employees were philosophical, having taken their shot at building something better. And they asked him not to be sorry, seeing his hard times.

Then, despite faltering industry revenues, his employees found new jobs. Each one except Luke. He went to all manner of headhunters, but agencies were retrenching, indifferent to older creatives. Using a cutting-edge option,

Luke posted his resume online, but nothing worthwhile came back. Undeterred, Luke went back to the headhunters, offering to step down to a copywriter or a junior account executive. Except Luke was "overqualified," meaning that he might be bitter if hired.

And just when Luke was out of money, one stale connection led to Nicaida & Knight, a thriving agency with outposts in London and Sydney. The partners looked at Luke's past awards, took a risk, and eighteen months later, with profits up 20%, Luke was due to supervise multiple accounts, his standout work a pillar of the company's success.

∞

It's almost 9 a.m. One of the managing directors' assistants knocks on Luke's door. "They're ready." Luke nods, setting his coffee aside.

∞

Luke enters a glass-walled office with a polished concrete floor, where Tom Nicaida and Doug Knight rule behind industrial desks. Both imposing owners in their early thirties, they are remorseless bachelors, each wearing intentional stubble and Panerai watches—minimalist armor for bedding the daughters of Los Angeles.

Tom Nicaida says, "Close the door."

Luke does, sinking into a ten-foot couch.

"We're gonna cut to the chase. Doug and I aren't offering you a contract."

Luke takes it in, even-keeled. "No problem. No one really has a contract these days."

"If we don't have you under contract, we're not looking at the long-term."

There is silence, a slow-motion concussion.

Luke says, "I don't get it. I created the Nissan campaign; it went great." Now some fanfare toward the agency's entrance reception area catches Luke's eye. It's Jay Goble and Jamie Hoch of Goble & Hoch carrying in file boxes to welcoming employees. "What are they doing here?"

Doug says, "Nissan likes their ideas too."

Luke says, "They're in their twenties. They can't handle a $200 million account."

Tom says, "That's why they're selling."

Luke says, "I'll manage them."

"Too many bodies."

"Wish it worked out differently."

"Maybe if you had landed Mattel."

"And don't worry, we're not gonna fuck you out of any money. We'll pay you through the end of the month."

Luke says, "Ten days severance. Might bankrupt you."

Tom and Doug choose not to react.

Luke says, "Seriously, I've done amazing work for our clients. For which they've paid ungodly sums of money. And what about Stacy; what about her promotion?"

"We're assigning her to Goble and Hoch's desk."

Tom and Doug have nothing more to give, and Luke rises as expected. Except that can't be all. Luke stabs a finger. "You know, the only advice my dad ever gave me was: 'Leave 'em laughing.' But I don't think that's practical in this case, because you guys suck shit."

∞

Luke is removing his campaigns from his office wall when Robin, the queen of human resources, comes to his door, saying, "I'm putting your exit paperwork together, and don't worry about your stuff, we'll messenger it."

"I'll take it now."

But Robin lives for enforcing inconsequential rules. "The mock-ups stay here."

Luke says, "They're mine."

"Not according to the company handbook."

"You have triplicates."

"C'mon, time to go." It's the burly security guard, called in from the parking lot.

"Can I take the photos of my son? Or is that a crime?"

The guard's hand hovers over his pepper spray clip. Luke gathers up picture frames of Trevor. Robin and the guard follow Luke out, guarding the premises from theft. Luke drives away. He looks back once, only to see Robin trying to remove Luke's nameplate from his parking space.

∞

An unexpected Friday lunch at Venice beach. Benched, Luke eats doughy tourist pizza and drinks Hawaiian Punch. He shouldn't be having the punch, given that it contains 90% sugar and that rumored Red Dye #4. But Trevor would want him to have it—to cheer him up. Only the overhead sun quickly warms the drink, and Luke's uniform—dark jeans, black boots, and black linen shirt—heat him beyond comfort.

Tossing recyclables into a barrel, Luke sets out among the boardwalk entrepreneurs. For a while, he watches a sun-blistered artist, who makes a topless mermaid sand sculpture for coins. Luke donates two dollars, but the man—busy shaping the mermaid's knockers—doesn't thank him.

Luke walks on, remembering how, weeks after opening his own agency, he signed his first client—a small fresh juice company called Rainforest. Back then, the owners agreed to a one-year contract with Morrow Advertising, and Luke began positioning them for greater exposure, hoping to build a national brand.

And though there were other juice companies fighting for market share, Rainforest had the secret ingredient, acai—the chocolate-flavored berry from Brazil that is full of antioxidants. Revolutionary then but common now, acai would help Luke set Rainforest apart.

But as happens in advertising, annual contracts are swiftly over, and the juice company would not commit to renew, despite a 16% growth in sales. That's why Luke was willing to attend a cocktail party of the largest fresh juice company in the nation—a brand most people have heard of, though Luke will not identify it, per his attorney's advice.

All that happened was that Luke had a light beer with that company's executives, who had heard that he was someone to meet. He couldn't have known that one of them, the manager of marketing, would jump to the smaller juice company for a bigger title. And once that guy told how Luke met with the big company while still in Rainforest's employ, Luke was in trouble.

This did not occur until a year after Luke closed his firm, long after Rainforest left for an ad agency in San Francisco. And not until the big juice company began blending acai too, diminishing Rainforest's competitive edge.

Angered, Luke's former client accused him of violating his contract, which forbid working with competitors. Specifically, Luke wasn't working with a competitor; he never got the bigger account, and he did not tell the big company about acai.

He still got sued, with Rainforest demanding return of all fees paid to him on top of damages for sharing trade secrets. Except Morrow Advertising was history, with the corporation closed, sheltering Luke from harm. Moreover, according to Luke's lawyer, after years of depositions, the arbiter will finally be ruling in Luke's favor.

With renewed relief, Luke pauses at the boardwalk's hermit crab broker. Only, the upsell is hermit crabs need company, and he must buy two if he has a conscience. Maybe Luke will get one of the biplanes the blind man fashions from soda can strips, but the planes look really sharp, and Trevor would just cut himself.

So there's nothing to buy, and it washes over Luke that a few hours ago he had a job he enjoyed, and he looks to a Nissan billboard above and cannot make sense of anything anymore. Jay Goble and Jamie Hoch kings? What about his talent, his responsibility to succeed? Whatever, God, he thinks. On Monday, I'll find a better job. And tonight, I will appreciate being a father to my boy.

∞

The titanium Aston Martin whines into the circular drive of an apartment tower. Trevor climbs out of his seat to Luke. Luke shuts the car door behind him, and The Aston Martin growls away. Seeing a colorful box in Luke's hands, Trevor says, "What is it?"

"It's a whole collection of basketball cards." Luke gives the box over to Trevor.

"When did you get it?"

"Stopped at the card store after lunch."

"How many are in it?"

"I don't know. Twenty-four packs times eight each. Can you figure it out?"

Trevor says, "If I have a piece of paper."

Luke kneels down. "Listen, Trevor, you only get packs once in a while, when you help clean the fish tank and throw the trash away, right? But sometimes it's okay for a dad to give his son an extra special present just because he loves him. But it can't happen all the time."

"Okay."

Luke doesn't flinch, sternly eyeing Trevor, who figures it out.

"Thank you."

"Good boy."

∞

In his room, Trevor rips through the cellophane. "Shaq!"

"Odds of getting him are one in 288."

"How do you know?"

"It's a classic Laker jersey card. It's got an actual piece of Shaq's game jersey. The box says only one out of 288 will be like this, so it's very rare."

Trevor rubs the imbedded yellow swatch. "Is it very valuable?"

"Could be someday. Then you'll give it to your son."

"What if my son is a girl?"

"You'll give it to her."

Trevor tears open the remaining packs, a happy boy with riches. For Luke, watching his son revel in basketball cards is joy. Luke tells himself to imprint this memory forever. Then Luke says, "Have you ever had a lobster?"

"I think so."

"Think so or know so?"

"Know so."

"Do you think you liked it?"

Trevor says, "I only had a taste."

"So not a meal?"

"The meal was pasta."

"Where was the lobster?"

"In my mom's salad. After it got out from the boat and into the avocado."

"Now I'm understanding. But I must tell you that if a lobster isn't served hot with drawn butter, it's not official."

"I want to be official."

"That's why I'm proposing Red Lobster for dinner. A whole pound and a quarter lobster is on special for only $19.95."

"Is the butter drawn with a crayon?"

"You shall see."

∞

The waitress serves Luke and Trevor lobsters. Trevor says, "I can't eat him all."

Luke says, "Looks like a lot because of the shell. I'll help you. First what you do is break a leg off and dip it in butter." Trevor follows Luke's lead, unsure about the pluming gray shreds. "I think that's the gills but you eat it."

Trevor samples the gills. "Tastes like sand."

"Here, take the cracker and smash the big claw. That's where the meat is the sweetest."

Trevor takes the cracker.

"Squeeze as hard as you can."

"I am."

"Squeeze harder."

Trevor does, popping through the claw, squirting a loping rope of spoo onto the back of a woman's head. But the woman doesn't feel it, letting it be, fueling the boys' erupting glee.

∞

"No pajamas in your pack."

"I'll wear this." Trevor means his T-shirt and shorts.

"No, butter drips all over. How about these?" Luke is holding up long-sleeved pajamas from the dresser.

Trevor says, "They're too small for a long time, and it's a hot night."

Luke takes scissors, cutting the arms and legs off the pajamas. "There, now they're shorties."

Trevor slips them on. "They feel good!"

∞

Luke and Trevor lie in the bottom bunk. Trevor says, "Did your dad ever take you for a lobster when you were a boy?"

"He did, and that's the important conversation for tonight; it's about how we used to go to this place called My Favorite Inn for lobster, when lobsters were only $9.95—a lot of money in those days. But we stopped going."

"Why?"

"My dad found out black or brown people could not eat there."

"Why?"

Luke says, "The owner would not serve them."

"Why?"

"He didn't like black or brown people."

"Why wouldn't he like black or brown people?"

"He was prejudiced; I've told you about that before and it's wrong."

"Can black or brown people eat at The Favorite Inn now?"

"It closed down a long time ago."

"Did you ever eat lobster again?"

"Actually, Grandma Blessing used to get it for me. I really shouldn't tell you this story. I promised myself I would never tell anyone."

"That was before you had me."

"Yes, before I had a son who might understand."

"Tell me the story."

"Well, Grandma wanted me to have lobster for a treat, but Grandpa Phil—you know, my stepfather—he thought lobster wasn't appropriate for children."

"Why?"

"Well, it's expensive and he thought it was spoiling me. But on Wednesday nights, he always had a dinner meeting with his law partners—he was a lawyer just like your stepfather. Well, Blessing used to buy day-old lobsters and sneak them home, and we'd eat them cold with mayonnaise."

"Were they very tiny?"

"Why would they be tiny?"

"If they were a day old."

"No, they were grown, just not new, and live lobsters don't keep forever. That's why the fish store would boil them before they got too old to sell. But here's the thing: we would have to eat them as quickly as possible, because if Grandpa Phil came home and found us eating them, he'd be furious. So I had to keep a lookout through the window to make sure Grandpa Phil's car wasn't coming, and I had to tape the empty shells in newspaper to stymie the raccoons. Do you remember the word 'stymie'?"

"Mostly. But why did raccoons want those shells?"

"Raccoons love shellfish, and what if they got into the garbage at night? The shells would be scattered all over the driveway in the morning, and Grandpa Phil would see them when he left for work. Then there'd be hell to pay."

"What would happen?"

"I never wanted to find out, so I taped the shells in fifty sheets of newspaper, to make sure the raccoons could not bite through it."

"Did Grandpa Phil ever find a shell?"

"He did not. But sometimes I still have nightmares that just when he's opening his car door, a red lobster claw comes rising out of the snow where he can see it. I wake up screaming."

"That's weird."

"I added the part about screaming."

"Are you the Creative Director of North America now?"

"Not yet."

"I thought it was today."

"Well, it was supposed to be, but things never happen at the office like you think. And the thing is, it can be a double-edged sword for a dad to be too super-successful—a kid might worry about having to be bigger and better than his dad someday. And that could lead to self-esteem issues."

Trevor thinks about his dad hefting a double-edged sword against a tiger. "Who's the Creative Director of India?"

"They don't have one." Luke gently sings to Trevor, "I hope you don't mind, I hope you don't mind, that I put down in words, how wonderful life is 'cause Trevor's in the world." Trevor closes his eyes. Luke says, "Okay, I'm going to leave you now. And I'll just be ten feet away in the big bed. You know if you need me for anything in the night, you just call 'Dad! Dad!' and I'll be there."

∞

In the living room, Luke opens a brown mailer, removing a class book for his 20-year college reunion—a big waste of time since he will not go. Luke should put the book down, only he can't. He turns pages and sees: "Steve Barron (with wife Julie and daughter Brianna, 9), now a partner at Goldman Sachs," and "Fran Grant, home raising Chellie (10) and Andrew (8). A former attorney at Gerhard Simmons, she's married to Bill Thorpe, President of Thorpe Construction, an international builder of airports."

Good for them, Luke thinks, earning their American dream. He supposes that if he had just made the right choices, his family would be whole. Luke lowers the book to the floor and drifts into sleep. But the bad dream follows hard.

Lisa says, "You didn't take care of me."

"We take care of each other."

"You gambled your career, and your ship didn't come in. It was all on me."

"It wasn't all on you."

"I wanted to take my hands off the wheel."

Luke says, "We build a life together that demands two careers, but you get to let go? At eighty on the freeway?"

"Stop talking."

"That's why I took the chance, to find a way to buy your freedom."

Lisa says, "I can't hear you anymore. My body is floating away."

∞

Nick, nick. Trevor is on the couch's arm, switching off the lamp from the night before. Luke opens his eyes in the grainy light. "What time is it?"

Trevor checks his orange rubber sport watch. "Six o' four. Might be fast."

"Can't you sleep late like Archer and Ben?"

"No."

"They sleep till ten on Saturday."

"No they don't." Trevor is at the window screen, finger-painting fog droplets together. "I don't think it's going to be a sunny day." He takes a seat at the table, jarring Luke with cartoons.

∞

Trevor pours Froot Loops into a bowl. He adds too much milk, floating the cereal toward overflow. But this is how it goes every day, and he knows how to gingerly bring the bowl to the table, spilling milk and loops only after reaching the placemat. Then he says, "Why don't cartoons change their clothes?"

Luke is buried in the morning paper. "Time and money."

"For real or sarcastic?"

"Sarcastic."

"Tell me how Grandma Blessing wouldn't let you have Froot Loops."

"She wouldn't let me have Froot Loops."

"You could have Apple Jacks."

"Anytime."

"Why?"

Luke says, "She believed Apple Jacks to be apple, Froot Loops artificial."

"Why do you say my favorite food group is sugar?"

"Statement of fact."

"Why do you tell people in the elevator?"

"Making conversation."

"Could you have Lucky Charms?"

"No."

"You had a sad childhood."

∞

Trevor loads the dishwasher, placing cups on the bottom rack, ensuring that there will be no room for Luke's plates later in the week. Returning to the table, Trevor says, "What are we gonna do today?"

Luke draws his boy into an ebullient hug. "What are we gonna do today? We're gonna plant our own garden!"

"Why are we planting?"

"Because I've had it with our tree."

Trevor says, "Do you think there are more lemons?"

Luke and Trevor go to their living room balcony—an empty slab save for a spindly tree. Hanging from the tree is one tiny lemon. Luke says, "Everyone in California has a lemon tree. It's part of the dream, and everyone gets so many lemons they don't know what to do with them. You and me, all we get is this runt."

Trevor says, "It's a runt, alright."

"Shouldn't even be called a lemon. Maybe just 'lemonette.'"

"Yeah: lemonette."

"That, my good man, is why we're going to plant our own garden."

∞

Luke and Trevor are at the hardware store seed packet kiosk, which Trevor spins into a blur. Luke says, "What kind of vegetables shall we grow?"

"How should I know? I don't like them."

Luke halts the spin. "What about Sugar Baby tomatoes?"

Trevor says, "I'm allergic to tomatoes when they're stewed."

"How about Little John squash?"

"I don't think so."

"What do you think so?"

"Peas. Pinocchio Eyes."

"You like peas?"

Trevor says, "What about it?"

"Most kids don't like peas."

Trevor selects three other packets. Luke eyes them. "Lima beans, Brussels sprouts, and rapini. Your favorite food group is becoming vegetables."

Trevor says, "No—not a statement of fact."

∞

Luke and Trevor arrive at Santa Monica Community Gardens, where Luke has rented them sixty square feet for $60 a month.

Luke says, "Here we are, plot number twenty-three." Luke studies a seed packet. "Says here you plant each Brussels sprout eight to ten inches apart."

Trevor says, "What if you plant a Brussels sprout seven inches apart?"

"Could come up carrots."

Luke is about to break ground with a hoe when a one-legged homeless man in a wheelchair rolls up. He shouts, "Danger, black man approaching!" only he is a grizzled white guy in his early sixties with a satchel in his lap. Luke draws Trevor in, unsure what weapon the satchel might contain. "C'mon, man, acknowledge me! I'm a human being too!" Luke holds his ground, ready for child-saving evasive action. "Fuckin' motherfuckin' cocksucker!" The man wheels off.

Trevor says, "Did you see his stump?"

Luke did.

"He used the F-word."

Luke heard.

"What's a cocksucker?"

"Not sure. Might be French."

"Is he a Vietnam guy?"

"Probably."

"Was he a submariner?"

"Probably not. Listen Trevor, after we finish watering, what do you say we call Keri and see if they want to go to the dunes?"

"Okay. Can we get cardboard from the dumpster?"

"Yes."

"Can I climb all the way into the dumpster?"

"Yes. But why would you want to do that?"

"Because I'm eight years old?"

"Good boy."

∞

For kids, the Manhattan Beach Dunes are a wonder, except they're really just one steep dune, and it's not even on the beach, since it rises far from the water in a suburban neighborhood. Perhaps in the past, this grade was under an ancient sea, but now it's above a playground with a red slash sign warning that boogie boards are verboten on the sand. However, by some bureaucratic quirk, kids are still allowed to slide down the dune on flattened cardboard boxes. Plenty of fun.

Ditching sneakers, Luke, Trevor, Keri, and her sons trudge up the dune dragging cardboard sleds. But the uphill hike under punishing sun is worth the effort, considering the downhill slide is freedom of the highest order.

Once the boys reach the dune's crest, Luke says, "Stagger yourselves, so you don't plow each other over." But the boys all go at once, sliding safely to the bottom. Luke and Keri take their turns, only she cuts him off, sending him face-first into the sand.

Breezing downward, she says, "So sorry!"

∞

Luke and Keri drink Mountain Dews in the shade, while the boys play the dune. Luke says, "What's up for tonight?"

She says, "You guys are joining us for Spring Harvest at the club."

"Thanks, but you feed us way too much as it is, and it's not my night. Trevor is going to his mom's club, only they call it Spring Festival."

"Still no Jews allowed?"

"Unofficially."

"I hear they're making their hoods into napkins."

"Baby steps."

"Hey, I totally forgot—what happened with your promotion?"

Luke says, "Nissan wanted to go with this younger agency, but the founders didn't have experience, so we ended up buying their company for the account. Then I got fired to make room."

Keri doesn't believe him.

"True."

"That's unbelievable."

"I still have my health. But I can't pay you back the $5,000, at least for now."

"It's okay, don't worry about it."

"I pay too much living at the beach."

"It's great for him there."

"He doesn't know what happened."

"When you have to tell him, you will."

"He'll be disappointed in me."

"Jesus, Luke, he's your son. Children aren't disappointed in you—unless you don't love them."

Trevor approaches, his hairline braised with sweat. Surprised he hasn't been told about the chance for a soda, he says, "Hey, I like Mountain Dew."

Luke says, "When have you had it?"

"I don't know, but I like it."

Keri says, "It's got caffeine. Keeps you up at night." Luke hands the remaining Dew to Trevor, who drinks it down.

Luke says, "We gotta go, Monkey Boy."

Trevor says, "I need to wear a sport coat."

"There will be one waiting for you when you arrive."

Keri says, "Trevor Morrow in a sport coat? How handsome!"

∞

Luke turns his Jeep into the entrance of Trevor's country club. Trevor is quiet in the back seat, dressed fancy in new sneakers, ironed khakis, and a starched white shirt. As the car curves to a stop, Luke reaches back with an open palm and Trevor reaches forward with his, the man and the boy touching goodbye.

In an instant, the valet is opening Trevor's door. Through the side mirror, Luke watches stepfather Mark slip a blue blazer over Trevor. As Luke pulls away, Mark hooks a lacquered wood bow tie around Trevor's neck, matching Mark's own. Luke turns into traffic, warding off utter desolation.

∞

Dusk at Rigo's Taco stand: where bloggers and other undateable souls meet picnic tables for cheap dinner on Saturday night. Luke knows Rigo's is not the place to impress a girl, for this dive is sunk beneath a freeway underpass on a dreary stretch of Culver City. But then again, if a girl gets the Rigo's thing, Luke will never let her go.

Luke flogs this romantic thought while waiting in line for tacos and a sloppy tamale. That and how to beat the system at Rigo's, where cheddar cheese on a taco is an extra charge. Does he get one taco with cheese and apportion that cheese over two additional tacos, saving money, or should he graft cheese from the top of the tamale onto all tacos, saving even more, given that the tamale has enough cheddar to block a pipe?

More importantly, when he asks for one taco with cheese and two without, does the Latina taking his order get his ploy? Surely if he tips her for putting his order together, she won't take the time to ridicule him with her co-workers? Or will she?

Luke reaches the order window. "May I please have one taco with cheese, two plain tacos, and a small diet Coke?"

"Rice and beans?"

"No thanks, but can you please add a half-side of guacamole." Luke can justify the splurge, as Saturday night is for treating oneself. After a few minutes, Luke receives his food in a cardboard box. He gives a 20% tip, then squeezes onto the end of a picnic bench, joining Central Americans who understand the value of a homemade Mexican meal.

Luke looks forward to being among these people, because when he's without his son on a Saturday night, there's always an abiding sense of family at Rigo's graffiti-scratched tables. Gringo or amigo, Luke feels right at home, for he cherishes the little ones who cry for chips and spill their sodas: the night isn't so lonely when they do.

But then hatred invades Luke, for his boy lives most of his life in the home of another man who is not his father, and there is not a damn thing Luke can do about it, given that a custody battle in court would cost him thousands he doesn't have.

Luke looks into the kind glances of his dinner companions. Soon he takes comfort in their easy laughter, thinking again about his fortune. Because the story of immigrants is mostly about hardship; there are millions of parents who have left small children behind in distant lands, hoping to give their kids a better future. And many of those parents never get to see their children growing up, if they ever see them again, and that's unthinkable to Luke.

So as headlights above guide Westsiders to fine dining in town, Luke eats a taco under the freeway, nourished from a day spent sliding in the sand.

3.

Luke is sleeping but still aware that he has forgotten to wake Trevor; now Trevor will be late for school. Maybe if Luke would just rouse himself for his son's benefit, Trevor might still be on time. Only, Luke's comforter is a lead apron and the dawn is gray ice, and he cannot open his eyes.

But then he does, realizing that it's only a dream, since Trevor left the evening before. Luke falls back into sleep, knowing that he will spend the morning alone, prisoner of the coastal fog that socks in the shore.

Except an hour later, an eastern sun bombards Luke through his balcony window. And since he can't make sunglasses comfortable while sleeping on his stomach, Luke decides to face the day.

And critically, it's nine o'clock; the farmer's market is open across the street, and Luke wants to get to the crepe stand before the line replicates by mitosis. Wearing a baseball cap snug over his shades, Luke heads out to ply the market in deep, dark disguise.

∞

Luke opts for variety, buying a Heartbreaker Cajun Scramble from the organic sausage man. He eats on the steps of the Santa Monica Historical Museum, a restored clapboard Victorian. Spread out on the grass in front of Luke are families having breakfast. Amongst them, parents redirect free-ranging toddlers away from downhearted dogs, who are not allowed on the lawn.

Luke especially likes seeing the young parents so full of hope. He wishes them the best, and as he has his coffee, he knows that half of the families will end up divorced. It is just a reality, and he feels bad for what the families will endure. But for now, the fathers are buying their kids blue-dyed kettle corn, the moms are cooing to drooling babies, and fresh-picked Chinese broccoli is waiting at the Cambodian produce stand.

Luke heads for the stand, where he spies Jill and Jon Marron, a couple with whom he's had a tenuous past. It's not that anything bad happened between them—it happened between Jill and Luke's ex-wife. Lisa was once Jill's roommate in West Hollywood when the two were up-and-coming marketing executives in retail. Back then, the women were best friends, before some falling out when Lisa was promoted to Vice-President over Jill, which coincided with Trevor's birth.

Luke vaguely remembers that Jill failed to promptly visit Trevor when he was a newborn, or maybe it was that Jill seemed particularly ambitious at work while Lisa was on maternity leave. Either way, the former roommates ended up enemies, but since Luke wasn't to blame, he decides it's time he and the Marrons patched things up. That's why Luke steps in their way, making a special effort to praise their twin girls. "What cuties! I didn't even know you were pregnant!"

The homely toddlers are fussy in their double stroller. Jill says, "Jon forgot their bottles."

Jon says, "I guess I am a dummy." Which is Jon's way of reminding Jill again how he had convinced her father at the exact right moment to sell the family business, which printed album covers for the majors. This was just before compact discs caught on, just before record covers gave way to jewel boxes with cheap slips of paper. Then Jon invested the family's windfall in mini-malls on Ventura Boulevard, and when he and Jill were just into their thirties, they were able to buy a Palisades Riviera estate where Jill hung a chandelier of pale rose glass from a tree.

Jill says, "He doesn't care if they die of thirst."

Luke says, "The fresh orange juice guy is over there."

Jill says, "It's not pasteurized."

Jon says, "But she gives them sliced oranges at home."

Luke says, "C'mon, we'll go across the street." Jill looks at Jon like he should have thought of that, and Luke remembers how stressed couples can get when their children have simple, conquerable needs. They walk to Surf Liquor.

Jill says, "How's Trevor?"

Luke says, "He's what's right with the world."

"Third grade now?"

"Second, but we just had his conference, and he's reading at a seventh-grade level."

"Two smart parents."

Luke holds up his phone, scrolling through shots. Jill says, "Handsome boy," and "Does it bother you that he looks more like her?"

Luke says, "That's okay. He's got my soul." Luke enters the store, buying two Evians. Outside, Jill and Jon administer the water to the girls. Crisis over, Luke thinks, but the parents are still tense.

But then they rise, Jill saying to Jon, "What do you think about Alina?" Then she says to Luke, "Are you seeing anyone?"

"Not really."

"I'm throwing a forty-fifth birthday party for Jon on the eleventh. And I've got a girl for you. Thirty-four's not too old, is it?"

"No, of course not."

"'Cause some guys just want girls in their twenties."

"No, that's too young."

Jon asks, "Is there a deli up the street?"

Luke says, "Just the Omelette Parlor."

Jon faces Jill, trying to show concern. Jill says, "Fine, let's get them fed." To Luke, "It's at the house at eight; no gifts."

Luke is happy to reconnect. "Okay, I'll be there—empty-handed."

The Marrons head up the sidewalk, Jon cupping imaginary taa-taas for Luke's benefit, saying, "Alina: body like a stripper!" Luke gives a faint wave back, envisioning the rose chandelier glowing over Alina, who dives naked into the pool in the dark.

∞

Luke does the dishes from Saturday afternoon, rearranging the cups in the dishwasher, editing Trevor's efforts. In

Trevor's room, Luke scrubs algae from the fish tank, skittering the fish. But the fish get their revenge; as Luke withdraws his arm, he accidently knocks over their food, spilling a rainbow of flakes into the carpet. Luke curses at the mess; now he'll have to get the hand vac and hunt around for the brown extension cord.

But then again, when a man gets on his knees, he sees things, and it's only when Luke is bowed vacuuming that he becomes aware of Trevor's work. On the back of his door Trevor has taped a sign that says, *Luke Morrow Ad Maker's House*. Next to the sign is a color laser print of *The Idiot's Guide to Freshwater Aquariums* cover. On the page, Trevor has written, "Buy this book and get a PlayStation for free."

Luke wonders when the hell Trevor was using his copier, and just as Luke is about to buy the book out of pure joy, he sees that Trevor has also organized the basketball cards into a shoe box, stacking them between Lego wall dividers. Except one card, the Shaq jersey card, is on top with a sheet of paper that reads: "For my son or daughter, if she likes basketball cards. Love, Trevor."

Luke wedges the vacuum back inside the water heater closet. In the bathroom, he takes a long look at himself in the mirror, unable to arrest his welling fear. Maybe reading the Sunday *New York Times Book Review* will calm him.

But when Luke opens the review, his prayers are not answered; inside is praise for three new books that cannot save him. And it's not that Luke doesn't think Deepak Chopra, Jon Kabat-Zinn, and Marianne Williamson are wise; he has read their books and embraced their gods, meditating time and again for salvation. Still, The Truth never roots in his soul.

And then there are other self-help best-sellers, plus all the nurturing books to come—each saying that if one will just bring time-tested faith into his experience, he will be set free. But the road to spiritual peace is often impassible, and if the recipe for happiness can be answered in a book, how could that book justify its own sequel?

And why are there hundreds of other motivational books spawning at Amazon.com, when any one volume should conquer all pain?

Maybe it's just that Luke isn't good at changing his thoughts. Maybe if he had more willpower, he would receive God's gifts. Maybe if he listened to Tony Robbins' *Personal Power* more closely, his personhood would get what it wants. Luke rummages for Tony's *Lessons in Mastery* six-CD set, which his friend Peter Wessler gave to him.

Peter swore by *Personal Power*, only gravity still pinned Peter's life, and when Luke listened to Tony's exhaustive bark, the superabundant surefire advice seemed impossible to implement, ending up like TV screen snow falling on a headache. Today though, if Luke can be more open-minded, Tony Robbins will transform his life. Luke finds *Personal Power* pitched high on a shelf. He jumps ahead to disc six and hears Tony launch a rocket on how to anticipate market forces. According to Tony, if a person can just figure out how the business world will change in advance of that change, he will be a winner. If he can just figure out when paradigms are shifting, he won't be left behind in a stalled career.

But wasn't Luke on the ground floor of a worldwide paradigm shift when he left advertising and founded his Internet company with thirteen others, twelve of whom were brilliant PhDs in computer parallel processing? They had cutting-edge technology for Luke's humanistic applications, so why would Luke hang around in old economy advertising? No, Luke was going to change the world, never guessing that the First Great Internet Age would implode.

But if ambitious men had just listened to Tony Robbins, they would have intuited that the actual paradigm shift was away from the technology paradigm shift sweeping the globe, and back toward the predictable trades of yore. Then those men wouldn't have invented foolishly, since brave men who risk but fail often spend the rest of their lives recovering from burnt dreams. But let's not talk about that, or the infomercial might not sell.

Maybe Luke should just turn to faith. After all, he is a thinker who has studied The Sermon on The Mount, Paul's Letter to The Corinthians, *The Talmud*, *The I Ching*, assorted psalms, and the gnostic gospels, on top of going to yoga once. Still, The Son does not speak to him.

This is too much thought for a Sunday afternoon, all promulgated without pot, something Luke never smokes owing to his child. Hence, he'd better get to the gym and make something of himself.

∞

Luke finds a lucky parking space in front of Gold's gym in Venice. However, it is not all good news; the one-legged homeless man in the wheelchair is headed his way. Luke wonders what it will feel like to be stabbed when the knife flashes from One Leg's bag.

But One Leg just has a simple question for Luke, who grips workout gloves. "Hey man, you got an extra pair? 'Cause my hands are all torn up from wheeling around." Luke sees how scabbed One Leg's hands are and how no man's palms should bleed. Luke opens his Jeep for his old, worn gloves.

Luke says, "Try these."

"Thanks, Man."

"They're pigskin. They make these new ones from nylon, which isn't as good." One Leg cinches the worn pigskins on in struggle with his swollen hands, only that's okay, because now he has gloves. Luke asks, "What happened to your leg?"

"Aw man, I got some diabetes; there was some problem with the blood flow, and the doc said he had to take it off. I'm okay as long as I got insulin."

"You serve in 'Nam?"

"I was an engineer in a submarine. After that, I was a brilliant programmer for ARPAnet." One Leg pulls a tattered composition book from his satchel with a four-color pen clipped to it, showing Luke code scribbled in blocks of red, blue, green, and black ink. "I'm a genius at algorithms. A guy like me comes along once in a generation. But all the thinking finally made my head pop."

Before Luke can say sorry, One Leg says, "That's just the way it is, man. But I'm grateful for this chair." One Leg leans his chair off the curb into the street, nearly causing a three-car collision. He gives the bottlenecked cars a peace sign for not hitting him before wheeling away into his day.

∞

Luke bench presses 220 pounds in sets of twelve—a respectable weight for a trim 5'10" 170-pound man. Luke likes the way the big forty-five pound plates look on the barbell, showing that he's strong and desirable, and he hopes that the Hawaiian beauty on the elliptical trainer is liking his determined strength too, even though Luke has been too shy to talk to her for a year.

Later, Luke increases the weight to 180 pounds on the Hammer Strength lat pull machine—impressive by any standard, which explains why the trainer with the hefty implants and Celtic tattoo above the small of her back crack is making eye contact with him. No doubt she wants his body once she breaks up with her Mr. USA runner-up boyfriend, who drives the puny white truck.

After weights, Luke climbs 150 floors on the stair climber, heating himself into a perfect endorphin sweat, and it's not until he's cooling down on the stretching mats that he feels the pinch of shame. Luke wonders why he didn't just give One Leg his new gloves. He could get another pair; they're not much at the pro shop. And he didn't even ask him his name.

Luke half does some sit-ups but soon leaves the gym, driving all over the neighborhood, hoping to find One Leg, hoping to give him the better gloves. But One Leg is nowhere to be found.

∞

Again the fog comes, shutting down the airport, shrouding the city in mist. Only Luke doesn't know his flight would be cancelled, if he had one to catch, because he's dreaming that he's in his house with his former wife—past midnight in their chef's kitchen, where she's sitting on the floor in the corner. Lisa says, "I went into *emergency*."

Luke says, "You didn't have to. It's not like I'll never work again."

"You're panicking all the time; you're not stopping."

"I'm doing my best. I'm trying to conquer it."

"It's not what I signed up for."

"I'm sorry I burned through the first round of money. It couldn't be helped. Now the investors are on my back 24/7. Thirteen good men are gonna lose their jobs."

"You asked if I disappeared. Just like when I was six, when my dad went to the hospital."

"There's a big difference between his mental illness and my anxiety."

"You don't know who I am anymore."

"Of course I do. You're my best friend."

Lisa says, "I feel like I've been locked in a basement for a year."

∞

Monday morning and it's 6 a.m. with nowhere to go, and Luke feels the confounding weight of being useless. Then it's 6:50 a.m., and Luke senses he should get out of bed and force himself back to the gym. Now it's 9:50 a.m., and everyone is at work. Luke goes snow-blind staring at the white wall, until a loud knocking startles him. He opens his apartment door, revealing six boxes on a dolly and a messenger who says, "From Nicaida & Knight."

Luke tightens, signing for his things. After the messenger leaves, Luke dumps the contents of the boxes down the garbage chute. Then he butchers the boxes into the chute with a bread saw. Because he's an executive and recycling to Level A? No fucking way—slammed today.

∞

Course of action: the vague pang of thought hanging over an unemployed man sunk into the couch at 11 a.m., after depleting himself of chi twice in twenty-five minutes. Course of action—begin to understand how one could have gotten into such a bad spot, especially since one's personhood once graced the sandstone halls of an elite university, earning top grades, including an A+ in Baroque Architecture.

The choice is Luke's. Go from couch and DVD player toting a roll of toilet paper and Nivea Creamy Moisturizing

Oil, to his bed and his more obsolete but functioning VCR, and he will end up shaky, unable to give his due to Western civilization. Or Luke can revisit his self-help best-seller, apprehending that he who is joined with the living has hope.

∞

Equanimity: a pleasant state of existence, achievable if Luke can just be happy for his fellow man. Which Luke can, shoving off manganite shoulder chips, freeing himself to applaud those who succeeded in the Internet, like the builders of the California Unemployment Compensation website.

To a sold-out Orpheum, Luke praises the programmers, saying, "A) the site is very well-designed, B) the interface buttons are right where one would expect them, and C) a man can fill out his sob story about how he got fired in just a few minutes, clicking himself forward to six months of poverty-level wages that cannot bounce him back on his feet."

"But this is not something you need to hear any more about," Luke tells the nation's plutocrats. "You've earned your niche. However, in case the Justice Department cleaves you from your golden parachutes, know it's not that bad. The State of California will simply sign you up for a mandatory job training lecture, where an Education Employment

Development counselor will give a harebrained presentation on how information technologies are creating jobs for you to pursue. It's all very upbeat, and there will be sexy, unemployed women in the classroom, and you can gaze at them under fluorescent lights, and none of them will ever suck your dicks because you are unemployed."

∞

Luke reads old emails sent to headhunters, revisiting how headhunters wrote back saying, "Best of luck." Still, past is not always prologue, and there is no guarantee every conversation will go like this: "Armin Zames' office."

"Hey, it's Luke Morrow. Is he there?"

"Who?"

"Luke Morrow."

"Does he know what it's regarding?"

"He knows me."

Then a beat, leading to, "He's actually in a meeting. Can he get back to you?" But he won't get back to Luke, because Luke is calling him, making it clear that Luke is no longer an employed piece of talent that Armin can place at another agency for more money.

And that means Luke is just another guy begging on Armin's doorstep, when ad agencies only want sizzling manpower contracted to rivals. So that's why Luke should take a hike, because if he thinks headhunters are there to help him, he is sadly mistaken.

∞

Luke should not be at Home Depot on Monday morning, because executives do not shop there until Saturday morning at the earliest. Luke guesses that most of the floor staff at Home Depot were once white-collar workers whose employment ceased in their late fifties. And it's not lost on him how the men are now sixty-four and ages like that, and how they're doing what they can to survive. Somehow, they buck up wearing orange aprons while tracking down drywall screws and 18-watt bulbs. Or white resin chairs in the garden pavilion, where there are mini versions for children.

For that bit of grace, Luke rejoices. He pays for a big chair and a little chair, then gets the hell out of Home Depot, where on Monday morning, he feels lost and illogically afraid.

∞

Garden Plot #23. Luke waters Trevor's seeds and arranges the chairs. He sits in the big chair with a sense of accomplishment, inasmuch as he has helped the seeds. And it's okay shooting the shit with himself, plus he's not really alone when private jets from Santa Monica airport are streaking overhead into greatness.

Luke expects the jets are Gulfstream Vs, even though he doesn't really know the difference between a Gulfstream IV or a V, except that the Gulfstream model matters when it's parked in full view. Luke wonders which powerbrokers are on board, knowing that if any had to brave the lines at LAX, it might harm the nation.

And really, having money and power does not always equal talent, so maybe Luke has the big boys beat after all. But what is Luke's talent anyway? The ability to write one-liners about a new ciabatta sandwich at Jack in the Box? The facility to feel things deeply to no apparent end? Why be cursed with ideas and emotions but have no ability to forge them into anything but boisterous thoughts and swirling pain? Because creativity can waylay Luke from boring things like selling cement, which, despite his pretension, can provide food for his kid.

But since Luke has always believed that imagination is a terrible thing to waste, he stubbornly ventured into creative fields where he tried to be an artist and a businessman. Except he was neither, owing to God, who made him medial—neither talented enough to create lasting works, nor shallow and aggressive enough to single-mindedly pursue money.

Consequently, Luke has spent his life manic, torn between his desire to create something meaningful and his dream to be rich. Only he isn't getting either, because he is not a gifted artist or a leading businessman, because he is sentenced to half of both.

∞

It's nearing lunchtime and Luke wants to cut costs. Solution: shop 99-cent stores, where he can buy Smiling Seas canned octopus, Yum Yum brand peanut butter, and chocolate Swiss Rolls, which are Ho-Ho quality even though they are wrapped in plastic.

Some will say canned octopus is gross, since they have Westside-itis, meaning that they can afford better at Huntington's premium market, where there is baby octopus salad for two and one-half times minimum wage per pound. Learn though, because Smiling Seas octopus is quite al dente, and if a hungry man drowns it in balsamic, he's got a meal fit for a squire.

∞

Luke tries to make the best of his free time at Gold's Gym after lunch, knowing that afternoons off won't last forever. But he feels anemic in his shorts and is tormented by the question of how the body builders working out at the gym in the middle of the day make a living. Luke stares into the weight room mirror, hating himself for being translucent like non-fat milk. Who does he think he is, loafing about at 2:30 p.m.? Get a fucking job.

∞

Luke picks up his voice mail at 2:45 p.m., and—shocker— it's a call from headhunter Armin Zames. Luke dials back.

"Armin Zames' office."

"Hey, it's Luke Morrow calling."

"Hold on, Luke."

A rush of happiness warms Luke, now that the assistant is putting Luke through, now that Luke is manpower. But what is the opportunity? Luke will accept any number of senior positions, but the companies better step up. He is Luke, after all; Nissan loves him, and don't even think about asking him to share a secretary. "Luke, he's just getting off a call." Luke holds. "Armin, you're on with Luke."

Armin, fairly mistaken for a Minotaur, says, "Hey, kiddo, are you available?"

"Of course. Wow. What's up?"

"You'd better have your A-game."

"Always."

"Doesn't pay much, but you'll be thanking me with a new mountain bike anyway."

"Whatever you want."

"Goble and Hoch are hiring a stable boy for the Nissan account."

"But Armin—I mean didn't you hear—I just left Nicaida & Knight."

"Then this one isn't for you, is it?" Armin jumps to another line, onto the next. Tears flood Luke's eyes, blurring the text message that has just come in. But then Luke steels himself and reads: "hey morrow, back in town 4 awhile maybe dinner tomorrow night? srry late notice. meg ;)."

Meg—the responsible dog mom with the sea glass-green eyes—who shook his hand goodbye in the rain, never to be seen again. Luke's heart skips and he thumbs back: "gr8 2 hear from u, will b available." He watches his phone for one minute until her response silently appears, and he is astonished to have another chance with Meg, because she could be everything to him.

4.

Luke waits outside a trattoria on Abbot Kinney, a bent boulevard where no one came when it was run-down, save for artists, who came when it was run-down like them. Now Abbot Kinney has pricey restaurants and swish galleries, and Meg is happy to meet Luke there, as it's a romantic place to have dinner with a nice guy.

And when she emerges from her Mini Cooper right on time, she kisses him. "Hey, you!"

Startled, Luke says, "Ladies and Gentlemen, Megan Wendle."

∞

The host seats Luke and Meg in a rustic courtyard under flowering vines and stringed lights. Suddenly shy, they both look down. Luke says, "Hope your dog isn't outside, because it's supposed to snow."

"It's not gonna snow."

"And sorry I referred to him as 'your dog,' but you never told me his name."

"Pursey. As in, little purse under my arm."

"Except he's a boy."

"My niece named him—pretty clever for a 6-year-old, don't you think?"

"Yes, but wouldn't he feel more confident being called Spot?"

"Can't change his name for you or my brother's ex-wife."

"Uh oh, now I'm not in good company. How long were they married?"

"Seven years."

"The length of the average marriage."

"How long were you married?"

Luke says, "Six years, ten months."

"Was the divorce hard on your son?"

"I guess. I'm not really sure. The worst is over."

"My brother misses my niece a lot during the week, and even though he and my ex-sister-in-law say it's amicable, they're still fighting."

Luke understands, and as the waiter tells them the specials, Luke senses Meg has an understanding too. And he sees more than ever how bright she is and how hard she works repping handbags till she can launch her own line.

After dinner, over coffee, she says, "You promised to tell me about your Internet company."

Luke says, "It's kinda technical slash boring."

"Stop, I really want to hear."

"Okay; you know how parents go to work in office buildings for twelve hours a day and never see their children? We built this company that installs webcams in the den, nursery, or wherever, so the parents, on their office computers, can watch their kids playing at home—so their kids' childhoods don't pass the parents by. I just thought the whole thing was very humanistic."

Meg furrows her brow.

"Uh oh, your silence is terrifying."

"I'm just thinking of the possibilities, and you don't have to apologize for anything. You came up with something really good."

"Who knows?"

"I don't even know you and I'm proud of you."

"Listen, there were lots of people sharing in our delusion; venture capitalists gave us money, but then my partners from

Korea—these Cal Tech PhD candidates—couldn't crack the right algorithms to make the technology work. So looking back, the whole thing was very risky."

"Don't beat yourself up for it. Maybe you can get it going someday when the timing's better."

"No, it's for other guys now. I can't go through it again. But you and your fashion empire—I'll say I knew her when."

∞

Meg is snug in Luke's arms under a lamppost, the din from the gelato place up the street melting into the past. He says, "Now that I think about it, Pursey is a great name for a guard dog."

"Shut up and kiss me."

∞

The valet arrives with Meg's car outside the restaurant. Luke says, "Friday night, 8 p.m., Morrow Mansion West. I will prove I can cook."

"Is this the surest way to a woman's heart?"

"You will decide." Luke tips for them. Meg gives him a parting hug. Then she's off, downshifting up the street. Luke watches her disappear where Abbot Kinney bends toward the beach, and it's not until the valet nudges, "'ey, hombre," that Luke climbs into his car.

∞

Wednesday at last, Trevor is with Luke, and if anyone has been confused about the custody so far, that's understandable. It's not one weekend on and one off—it's Wednesdays starting after school, one whole weekend a month, scattered Thursdays, a few Fridays, which came to pass a long time ago when both Luke and Lisa had corporate jobs and conflicting obligations. An inequitable schedule skewed toward mom and carved in stone, unless Luke can get Lisa to change it, which she will not do, even if he crawls through broken glass.

∞

Luke serves Trevor a sloppy joe face made from ground turkey breast placed on toast circles cut with an aperitif glass. Five rounds make the mouth, three rounds make the eyes and nose, and vertical green beans are the hair.

Trevor digs in. Before Luke joins him, he slides the window open to the sea. Toward China, Luke shouts, "Good people of Xinjiang, I love Trevor Morrow!" Trevor breaks into a smile because homemade dinner is even better when you're deeply loved by your dad, a known crazy.

∞

Luke has fallen asleep in the lower bunk, condemning himself to a night of repeated thoughts: if he turns over, he might accidentally whack Trevor in the face. In Luke's dream, his errant elbow opens a deep gash under Trevor's eye, leading to a scramble for a towel to staunch the wild bleeding, before a desperate drive to the ER where Trevor will shake as an intern sews stitches.

Not to mention what Lisa will say, because Luke's ex-wife must be notified immediately of any emergency, meaning Luke better grab his cell, although an urgent call to Mom will only fuel Trevor's spiraling fear. Therefore, Luke doesn't roll to his stomach, and when he finally wakes at dawn, he has a crimp in his neck—a small price to pay for Trevor's safety.

∞

Luke and Trevor are in the Jeep, Trevor squinting into loud, blowing air. Luke says, "Put it up already."

Trevor says, "When my wind bath is over!"

"Do you know what's happening soon?"

"WHAT?"

"I said, WHAT'S HAPPENING SOON?"

"WHAT?"

"If you don't put that window up so you can hear me, I'm gonna put the safety lock on till you're a teenager."

"No you're not." Trevor raises the window, just in case.

"As I was trying to say, we'll soon be on our Spring Break adventure."

"What kind of trash are we gonna be again?"

"White trash. But I apologize again for saying that. It's pejorative to people who camp on the sand."

"It's prejudiced."

"That's right."

Trevor says, "What color are the ATVs?"

"I don't know."

"I hope yellow."

"How far are the dunes?"

"It's gonna take a few hours."

After a beat, Trevor says, "You know why Archer always has to poo after we're in the car?"

"Remind me."

"Tradition."

"Good boy."

"Are we going to camp on the beach with the trash?"

"No, we're staying in the canyon in Santa Barbara."

"What about rattlesnakes?"

"If you don't stay on the paths."

Trevor says, "Who do you like better, squirrels or chipmunks?"

"Neither. Squimunks."

"What the heck?"

"A cross between a chipmunk and a squirrel, with fangs. And we may go on a squimunk hunt in Santa Barbara to catch one. If you want to."

"Can I use my courage?"

"You can." Luke eases the car past cyclists. "Trevor, there is something I wanted to talk about for our important conversation, except we fell asleep."

"What is it?"

"I've been thinking about moving us to a new place that's less expensive."

"Is ours expensive?"

"It is. And we need to save money."

"Why do we need to save money?"

"For college, for starters."

"But I like where we live."

"I'm not saying it's gonna happen, but a move might be necessary for a while."

Trevor stares out the window. "Okay, because I'm moving to Martha's Vineyard anyway."

"You mean you're going to Martha's Vineyard on vacation with your mom."

"No, my mom said I'm moving there."

"Trevor, it must be a change of plans—the Vineyard instead of Hawaii." Luke steers the Jeep into the drop-off lane at Trevor's private school.

"Dad, are you going to the benefit Saturday night?"

"I am."

"Are you gonna buy something?"

"I'd like to help out. Only, the stuff in your school's catalogue—I mean who needs the fancy yellow diamond necklace or that vacation in St. Bart's?"

"Yeah, who needs those things." The SUV reaches the head of the line and Trevor climbs out. "Sorry about the chimp in your neck, Dad."

"Thanks, boy. Me too."

∞

Luke parks at the Temescal Canyon trailhead, tapping dollars into the honor system parking box. He hikes up the mountain, reminding himself that a walk is good for clearing one's head, even when one's head fills up again back home.

Luke wonders if he is like John the Baptist, or more like Moses, except that Luke has only been in the wilderness seven years since his career collapse and divorce, and to be righteous with Moses, Luke would have to spend thirty-three more years lost.

That thought is relief for yards, until Luke comes to a fork in the path. Suddenly Luke understands why he is there—it's that road less traveled bit from high school English. Thirty-three years less wandering than Moses and twenty-three years since he was seventeen, pontificating on a poetry quiz. And since one path leads to Chumash Meadow and the other to a waterfall, which way will make all the difference?

∞

Luke lies down under an oak in the meadow. For a moment, he is at one with the coastal prairie, but then he asks why, when he has prepared for favorable outcomes, the answers are *no*. Like when the agency board told him no, when he was overdue for a partnership at Nicaida & Knight.

So Luke quit the agency to make his fortune in the Internet, because "You never get rich working for someone else." But when his company needed a second round of capital to survive, it was a no, from at least fifty venture funds. Then when Luke asked for forgiveness and begged for his marriage, the answer was, "No, it's over." There was the bank loan for the founding of his own ad agency, which was a "Yes," but too many companies said no to Luke's pitches, and when he needed to renegotiate the loan, the bank said, "No, that's not way it works." And then there were no jobs and no one would help him, but providentially, there was one last "Yes"—a chair at Nicaida & Knight. But then after his hard work, what about that promotion to Creative Director of North America? No.

Now new *no*s are piling up—unreturned calls from headhunters are *no*s whether it seems like it or not, and Luke starts to think that this is the *Meditation on No* that no one wants to hear. Because Americans are taught to Never Take No for an Answer. Except *no* is often still a *no*, no matter what a man does, and if he persists, he may wear out his welcome and become a pariah, because those in power will eventually pound him with, "What part of *no* don't you understand!"

However, there are people who never take no for an answer who find great success. Because they didn't stop at *no*, or because they were lucky? There's really no such thing as luck because, You Make Your Own Luck, and The Harder You Work, The Luckier You Get, and Luck Happens When Preparation Meets Opportunity.

Except what would happen if Luke worked exceptionally hard, but his company imploded under the weight of its own lies, and he was a middle-manager family man toiling far away from the corruption? In this case, the harder he has worked, the unluckier he has gotten.

What about preparation? What if Luke prepared his whole life until he invented something really cool, only to discover that someone else had applied for his patent days earlier? Suddenly the opportunity would be theirs, since no one would fund his invention when the applicant with the patent pending would be bound to sue. In this case, Luke would not have made his own luck but his own devastation, because no matter how smart he was or how hard he worked, Everyone Needs A Little Mazel, which is old-school Yiddish for Luck is Random. This is Luke's *Reverie on Luck*; act now, one payment—$6.95.

Luke rises, knowing he must persevere. But before he goes down the mountain, he pauses at a cluster of green sage. Only the bush hardly rustles, its purple thistles clothed in the wind.

∞

It's noon at the Brentwood Country Mart, where the drill is: order chicken tenders and a mound of fries and eat around a fire pit. Except Luke is not a mom, nanny, or toddler who crowds the red barn mall, he is a grown man who should be bridling the economy at a business lunch.

But watching kids being silly is fun, and what would that mom look like naked, and if Trevor were here, he would dip his chicken tenders into ketchup and barbeque sauce, even though he's allergic to both.

∞

Luke could have ordered coffee at the mart, but he instead crawls in traffic to Starbucks on Lincoln, where he purchases a vanilla ice blended. He would like to sit—he has been on his feet for three minutes—but customers perusing newspapers have all the seats mid-afternoon. Nice to be heirs, heiresses. Moments later, an elderly woman decamps on her walker, clearing the way for Luke to nab her club chair out from under a pest control man, who thinks he got there first. But he didn't, and Luke stares him down, causing the man to glare back, "Spray you with dioxin."

But then the man departs without further conflict, only to give Luke an enraged finger while slowing his truck past the window. Luke shouts, "Fuck off!" in response, startling folks around him. Then his cell rings.

"Luke, Steve Kahn."

"Steve."

"Listen, Buddy, I've got some bad news—the ruling went against you."

"What?"

"The judgment just came in. The award is for $168,000."

"I don't understand."

"When you borrowed money from Luke Morrow Advertising—"

"I only did it twice, Steve. It was my own money. I took it for groceries!"

"You never paid it back."

"You said wouldn't matter!"

"I said it could go either way, Luke. That's what I told you. I'm sorry, but they pierced the corporate veil, so you're on the hook. The arbitrator faulted you for meeting a competitor while under contract, but cleared you of sharing acai."

"Which I never did!"

"She's agreeing. Look, it could have been worse. You only have to return the money Rainforest paid you—plus attorneys' fees."

Luke flushes, growing damp.

"Luke, you there?"

"I don't have the money. I put it into the agency."

"You'll earn it back."

"What about your fees?"

"You can pay us in installments. You'll be out from under in two years."

"They're gonna come after my cash."

"I can't advise on that."

"But you'd tell me to withdraw it if you could. I only have $14,000 in my checking account—all my money in the world."

"Get to the bank before it closes, Luke. Don't leave it for tomorrow."

∞

Inside the bank, Luke is dizzy with fear, while the teller counts $13,800 into a fan. Luke fumbles the money into an envelope.

"Sure you're alright, Mr. Morrow?"

"Fine, I just need to lie down."

"Feel better, and I'm glad I don't eat sushi."

"You're smart. Food poisoning, no fun."

∞

In *The Los Angeles Times* classifieds, Luke finds a cheaper apartment—except the ad says 'LARentals.com, Agency Fee.' So he skips that one until he finds a studio that is 50% less than his current rent. But at the bottom of that listing, it says, 'LARentals.com.' Luke moves on, locating a third apartment. And if he wants that one, he'll have to pay a fee too, seeing how LARentals.com swings all the keys, and he will have to submit to another's Internet success even if it kills him.

Luke heads to see a flat at the foot of the freeway, but when he arrives at The Pico South Seas, sorrow washes over him. However, he is not a potato famine farmer and that thought medicates him long enough to complete the lease for the only available unit—a first-floor studio facing a crumbling alley. And although The Pico South Seas is yellow stucco smirched with soot, Luke's unit luckily has bar-covered windows, for Luke cannot have Trevor stolen in the night.

∞

There are only three packing boxes in the recycling bins on the B level, and Luke regrets wasting the Nicaida & Knight boxes that could have made nine. Then again, nine boxes will not hold the contents of two lives anyway, and Trevor has lots of toys, and he will be broken-hearted if important ones are left behind.

At Public Storage, Luke buys two stacks of moving boxes, and after returning to his apartment for the night, he is struck that this was his house for five years and that it was good to him after he was no longer welcome in his own home. He must honor the one-bedroom, thank it for its care, and say goodbye. Then, long into the night, he packs his belongings, and it isn't until 5 a.m. that he crawls into Trevor's bed for a few hours of sleep.

5.

Friday is a new day, bright and hot over the sea. Luke, freshly shaven in a suit and tie, heads out the door at 8 a.m. He stops at the Shoreline Towers leasing office, telling them that he will be gone by Tuesday. In turn, they will return his security deposit, barring any damage to his unit.

Then Luke heads to fill out a job application at Nordstrom, listing his previous employment as a non-profit office coordinator, knowing that if he says he was an executive, he'll be threatening to the men's furnishings manager.

Afterwards, Luke steps onto Westwood Boulevard, where he sees a McDonald's up the street. But Luke will not apply there because when he said he would flip burgers if he had to, he was a lifetime away from the moment of truth.

∞

Luke knows about hedging his bets, so he drives to The Valley and fills out an application at The Great Indoors, where he meets the director of human resources, who is just back from a luncheon at the Marriott. She is an efficient women in her fifties, and she asks Luke if he would like to take the employee aptitude test right then and there.

Luke says why not, and she says, "Just do your best. It shouldn't take more than thirty minutes." And that's how it came to pass that Luke took a multiple choice test for the first time in twenty years.

∞

Luke has somehow lost the Post-it with the moving company numbers, and since his phone battery has died, he stops at Ocean Park Library, which still has phone books. Inside, homeless people occupy all of the seats. Most of them are napping, and Luke wonders if this is a pleasant day for them and whether he will end up homeless.

More pressing, who shall earn the job moving his stuff? Gentle Giant or Starving Students? Luke memorizes the number for Three Brutes and a Big Rig, because their ad promises 'Lo Lo Rates'.

Luke leaves the library, closing his eyes in the sun, wishing he were in Kauai with a woman to love. Which suddenly reminds him: Meg is coming over for dinner, everything he owns is in boxes. How will he explain?

∞

Luke waits in line at Santa Monica Seafood, since he has decided to make Vongole alla Napoletana—sautéed clams. He has never made the dish before, but when he skimmed *The Tuscan Kitchen*, the recipe looked producible. Back home over his pan, Luke samples the Roma tomato broth, pronouncing it "Magnifico!"—which is embarrassing behavior, even when you're alone. Then lobby security calls. Luke says, "Send her up."

Luke rushes to the window and sees Meg ten floors below heading back to her car with a parking pass. Which gives him a second chance to check his appearance in the mirror. Is his black T-shirt too tight, making him hetero-suspicious?

Luke rips it off, rifling through his closet until he finds his black linen button-down dry-cleaned in plastic. He hasn't worn it since Nicaida & Knight fired him, so it's time to cut with superstition. Then there is a knock at his door. Luke waits for an extended beat to seem like he was not there waiting. He opens the door and Meg leans in with a kiss, saying, "Hi, Spot."

Luke says, "Where's Pursey?"

"I didn't know he was invited."

"You're kidding? I have dinner for him." Luke presents a jerky pig ear.

"He loves those!" She takes it, stepping inside. "So this is Morrow Mansion West."

"You don't have to take off your shoes—this time."

"I'm honored."

"It's usually 'No shoes in the dojo,' but since the carpet is being replaced Monday, what's the difference?"

"The carpet looks fine to me."

"No no, it's threadbare. The new Berber will be better."

"It's a big job, huh?"

"You have to pack everything in boxes and move them all out before they'll put the new stuff down."

"I feel bad. We should've gone out."

"I promised I was cooking. Hope you're hungry."

"Starving. I barely had lunch."

"Then you are The Princess and you're to put your feet up until dinner is served." Luke leads Meg to the dining table, where he puts her legs across a chair. "After dinner, if

you would like, I will give you a peppermint foot massage—
because you've had a long day."

"Your depravity is safe with me, probably."

Luke pours her a glass of wine. Tasting it, she says, "Very
nice."

"Ninety-one points on the card at Costco."

"What are you making? It smells great."

"Vongole alla Napoletana."

"Sounds wonderful. What is it?"

"You will learn. And you look very beautiful tonight."

∞

Over dinner with the pig ear for the table's centerpiece, Meg
talks about how much she admires her dad, a great provider
and the orthopedist to the Golden State Warriors. Then she
asks, "What happened with your meetings?"

"They went well."

"Anyone would be lucky to have you."

Luke says, "Not everyone has a Clio and a One-Man
Pencil."

"It's your self-deprecating confidence that's intriguing,
and what about that spearmint foot thing?"

"Peppermint."

"Whatever, I'm yours."

∞

Sundaes subside in bowls while Luke finishes rubbing Meg's feet. He's worried that he's cheesy for breaking out the pink lotion so fast, but Meg says, "I'm so relaxed. How can I ever repay you?" Luke wipes her feet dry with a towel, and Meg comes over to lie on top of him. Soon, she's asleep. Luke holds her tight, cherishing her peace.

∞

An hour later, Meg wakes and leads Luke into the bedroom. There, they curl on the comforter until the question comes up, as always. She says, "What are you thinking?"

He says, "Nothing."

"C'mon, you must be thinking something."

"No. I'm just glad you're here."

"Thank you so much for dinner."

"More to come."

"I'd like to meet Trevor. Does he ever he wish for a brother or sister?"

"I'm not sure."

"Bet he'll get one someday. The way your face lights up when you talk about him, I'm sure you'll have another kid."

Luke says, "I don't know, sometimes I think I don't want to share him. I don't want to give him short shrift."

"My mom says when you have a second child, you grow a second heart."

"I guess if that happens, I might have another, if it's with the right person."

Meg says, "Well it has to be with the right person, but if you think you don't want more children, I guess we better talk about that sometime."

"Okay, but no need to tonight."

"But when the time is right, I need to tell you about this guy I was with for this whole last year who was a good guy, but then he tells me he never wanted kids in the first place, and I can't waste another year again."

"I understand."

"It's fine and everything, having a career for a while. But I don't want to be a businesswoman forever, and eventually, I just want to be home, because I'm not having some stranger raise my kids."

"The nanny thing can be a problem."

"It's just that my mom didn't have to work, and I don't want to end up like a lot of the women I know. They have their independence, but deep down, a lot of them are miserable."

"I know some of those women too, and I don't blame you. But what if you're living in a small apartment and your husband is doing his best, only things are hard? I mean what if you had to work, because it takes two incomes half the time?"

"If I needed a job, I'd get one. I really do believe things work out for the best. And you're just living here until you buy a house, so nothing's forever."

Except sometimes in life, some things are forever. Meg's online dating profile suddenly swarms over Luke: "A guy is fine but a man is so much better." "My partner in crime will be inspired and successful in his work." "My soulmate is always comfortable in his own skin."

Luke doesn't think he's any of these things anymore, and he isn't sure he ever will be again, and how can he live up to Meg's father's care? And then he fully realizes how deeply he's lied to her, and how she doesn't know he's moving to an apartment under the freeway. So Luke goes cold when Meg needs a strong man most, and after a short while, they're off in their own dark worlds. Then it isn't long before Meg gets off the bed and lets herself out the door.

∞

Alone at his dining table in the dark later that night, Luke conjures a willing audience. Onstage delivering his viral TED talk, Luke says, "Now as it turns out, what women suspect but can't confirm is that most men would prefer sex without strings attached. And even if that's not exactly true and an exaggeration of comedians worldwide, women should know men still hope to have girlfriends to guarantee sex on a regular basis—as every regular guy knows how rarely he gets it."

The audience, of women and men of all races and socioeconomic demographics, nods knowingly.

Noting average guys in the second row for impact, Luke says, "See, if you're a man without compelling power, you're basically expendable. There is no good reason for a woman to pull down your pants and make you see stars, since your middle-class career is hardly an aphrodisiac. And it's not that kind women don't appreciate an afternoon bike ride and a casual bite out. But this pales to meeting a man with a soaring income, who commands legions."

The average guys agree, shaking their heads in fond dismay.

Luke presses his points. "Now, it is true that women need sex too, though that is often difficult for them to express, except, maybe, sometimes on girls' night out, right? However, making love with the same person regularly means you're probably heading toward marriage—a good thing, assuring you of predictable conjugality.

"Only it doesn't work that way in real life, and neighbors would be surprised how little sex married couples actually have. No sex in marriage is society's secret, because every couple will tell you they have it, even if it's only four times per year. No one talks about this, and the studies saying that most married couples have sex all the time are wrong, since nobody answers those questionnaires truthfully, as people are often untruthful with themselves.

"Clearly, if you're only going to have sex every other month or go without it for seasons at a time, especially when you have small children, there must be a better reason to be married. And that is companionship, the safety of couplehood, and the marital contract that you will love and care deeply for each other.

"Unfortunately, a lifetime of devotion toward another person is a responsibility few endeavor to understand. Love and care are wholly separate things, and if you're unable to care for someone the way they expect, their love for you can fade.

"So, if you're a married man, you'd better provide for your wife; not many women want to financially take care of their husbands, and if you can find the ones who do, you are mining them from Mars. For the majority, across all classes of society, men must still be the successful hunters, especially if their wives have powerful jobs.

And if you are an enlightened woman who disagrees, your words are deeply appreciated.

"But if you are like most and honest with this world, you instinctively feel that *he* better step up. Far worse, you do not see that what you expect of him is not always possible, because a perfect destiny is not always within his control. And for that, he is forever sorry."

Luke bows his head, concluding. "So take a man like me and give me some strength, because I will not tempt a woman's heart unless I can shelter her from want. I'm here to admit that I've dated my share these last lost years and I've had my way with good, kind souls. But I was insincere and unfair to all of them and I will never go there again. Thank you."

The audience rises, applauding and whistling their appreciation for Luke. But then everyone is gone, behind black vapor blanketing the sea.

∞

Saturday morning with a relationship that died in its crib. Luke hasn't even put his contacts in and he's already throwing the pig ear down the chute. And it's not going to be a sunny day. Luke stands at his open window, where rain is streaking across the rattling screen. It's coming down steadily now, and who knows if it will ever stop.

∞

How to move Fry French, French Fry, and the other fish without them croaking? It's way harder than most might think, given that a tropical fish tank is a fragile ecosystem. A yeoman could suppose, "Just put the fish in a bag with water, empty the tank, move the tank, refill the tank, and add the fish." But that would be a big mistake, and shortly, all of the fish would be dead. That's because fish secrete ammonia and ammonia is poison. Luckily, a fish tank naturally cycles ammonia, growing ammonia-eating bacteria over time in the water and on the gravel.

So if a fishkeeper wants his fish to survive, he needs to save their old water and gravel, because those contain the colonies of bacteria that keep the fish alive. It's just Fish Tank 101, and it means a big, crappy job for Luke.

∞

Luke nets Trevor's fish into a Tupperware bowl with water from the tank before using a hand pump to drain the remaining gallons of water into six empty, plastic, two-and-a-half gallon spring water containers. Then he scoops the thirty pounds of scummy gravel from the tank into assorted cooking pots.

It takes six trips to carry the containers and pots from the tenth floor down to the car. Upstairs one last time, Luke puts the Tupperware bowl inside the tank with the sloop and other tank accessories. He takes the tank down to his front seat, where he can blast it with the car's heater. He heads for his new apartment under a thundering downpour.

∞

Luke parks in the alley behind The Pico South Seas. He lifts the tank to his chest and backs toward the building's rear door, not needing his key, because the landlady is there holding the door open. He enters, stamping his feet. She says, "There's no pets allowed."

She is gowned in a bathrobe with cherry lipstick clinging to her teeth. But that doesn't mean Luke can't appeal to her humanity.

He says, "I know, except these are just fish, and they're very well-behaved."

"What if the glass breaks and floods the carpet?"

"The tank is acrylic. It's indestructible."

"If I make an exception, I could lose my job and my home. So unless you want to share your bed with me, be on your way."

∞

Luke pops the Tupperware open inside a pet store in Santa Monica. The slacker behind the counter studies the fish and says, "Looks like this one has a tumor." He's talking about Neptune, the neon-blue Gourami.

Luke says, "That little brown speck? A birthmark."

"Sorry Homer, that's cancer."

"How about the tetras and the pleco?"

"Naw man, we really stopped taking fish from people's homes. They come back diseased and our tanks get infected."

"C'mon. Except for Neptune here, they're all tip-top."

"Those guys look lethargic."

Luke says, "The bar-tailed platies? They're just born. They need Ritalin, for God's sake."

"Where are their parents?"

"They passed a couple months ago."

"We can't risk contagion."

Luke re-seals the Tupperware and brakes across town to West Hollywood. Once he reaches Beverly Tropical Supply, all will be fine; they always adopt unwanted fish.

However, when Luke arrives at the store, he discovers it's closed down.

There's a redevelopment bulletin in the window, and the flashing neon angel fish sign is off. Apparently, it's another venerable Los Angeles business gone without a footnote. Luke heads home.

Except, after reaching The Pico South Seas, the fish are barely living, listing on their sides in the Tupperware. And it's not like Luke hasn't read the chapter in *The Idiot's Guide To Freshwater Aquariums* on euthanasia; the advice is if someone must end his fishes' lives, quickly is best, and best is to throw them hard onto the sidewalk, killing them instantly.

Luke takes hold of Tiger and flings him onto the pavement, but Tiger flops in agony. Luke scoops him back into the bowl and hurries inside, because the other method is to "Put your fish in a bowl of water in the freezer, which leads to hypothermia and death." Luke shuts the freezer door on the bowl, leaving Tiger and the other fish cold in the dark.

∞

Under a hot shower, Luke tries to psych himself up for the evening's auction. An auction sounds like fun, especially with trays of mini crème brûlée and an open bar. Except Luke is a broke father facing Westside royals. That, and he is a single, divorced parent without a date, and no married couple wants such a person around, because what if that divorce thing rubs off?

To be fair, there are two single mothers with children in Trevor's grade. One is a lesbian banker who, artificially inseminated, had a bespectacled son, and the other is a party girl turned cosmetic surgery display case, who told an NFL backup quarterback that she had an IUD when she did not, garnering her a daughter and MVP child support.

Both women are witty and sarcastic, and they huddle with Luke at school events, where they make fun of the married couples. Only, the two women aren't at the auction tonight, and Luke cannot find them, no matter how many times he scans the gym.

Just as the auction is about to begin, Luke spies Lisa and Mark yukking it up with others at a nearby table, and he hopes they will see how powerful he is in his black linen shirt. Finally, they do notice him, nodding over bouncy hellos like, 'Hey it's the father of our son.'

But if the benefit chairperson could finally have everyone's attention, there are terrific items for sale. And don't forget, the money goes for a good cause: the school must pay for the swimming pool stadium it constructed, as well as the new six-story parking garage that houses students' cars in the shade.

Without further ado, how about the seven-day vacation on Costa Smeralda, Sardinia at the Hotel Romazzino? Valued at $20,000, it sells for $35,000, and there's plenty of buzz for the sockless, boasting father in Gucci loafers who gamely steps up.

Second up for bid is a once-in-a-lifetime ride in a Soviet-era jet, which closes for $3,850, before another dad lowers his paddle triumphantly, having secured his 10-year-old son a boxing lesson with Sugar Ray Leonard. Next it's on to the fine wines, and wouldn't you know it, a bottle of Paul Autard Chateauneuf-du-Pape La Côte Ronde goes for three times its asking price.

All of these items are beyond Luke's reach; he cannot be a big shot here, and he wishes he could bid on the sports memorabilia for Trevor. But that is out of the question until Mark raises his paddle, bidding $500 for Shaquille O'Neal's signed sneaker, size 18. The sneaker is set in a Plexiglas box, Luke realizes Mark is buying it for Trevor, and all Luke has ever bought Trevor is the Shaquille O'Neal jersey card, meaning Mark Morello II must be stopped.

Luke raises his paddle, bidding $515. A general "Huh?" goes up; everyone knows Luke and Mark are rivals by circumstance, and Mark is not about to let Father, Jr. best him. He offers $600. Everyone squirms, hoping this showmanship is for the school's greater good. It's not. Luke says $800. Mark says nine, and it's going once, twice, and remembering how Mark has Trevor calling him "Babbo"—

Italian for father—despite Luke's objection, Luke offers $1,000.

Mark goes up to $1,500 because that's what Lisa expects, and Luke jumps to $2,000, seeing how Mark always shows up uninvited at Trevor's school conferences, imposing his opinions about Trevor.

And why is Mark now bidding $2,500 for a collectible that retails for $1,000 on the Internet? Four thousand is Luke's next bid, before the gavel comes down—"Sold!"—and before Luke has time to understand that Mark has quit. Suddenly, Lisa is at Luke's side congratulating him, reminding him that she, Mark, and Trevor are leaving the next day for the first half of spring break in Hawaii.

Within seconds, Luke is giving his maxed out credit card to the auction attendants, who do not see him puke afterward in the parking lot for what he has done.

∞

4:15 a.m. Luke eyes boxes towering over him, which will bury him if there's an earthquake. Better for him to get out of bed, anyway: Three Brutes and a Big Rig will be there in a matter of hours and the kitchen packing isn't finished.

And besides, it's not too early to call his kid sister in Chicago, where it's 6:15 a.m. on this Sunday morning. She will certainly be awake with Kit, her 5-year-old daughter.

But Sara answers the phone from another world; her household is dead asleep at this ungodly hour.

Luke says, "Hope I'm not calling too early."

Sara says, "Are you alright?"

"No, everything's fine. Guess what? I've got clients in Chicago, so I thought I'd fly in tomorrow and maybe spend some time with you. Would Kit like that?"

Sara says, "Hard to say. Where are you staying?"

"At the Four Seasons on Wednesday, but can I crash with you first?"

"Okay, but we still have See's suckers from last time."

"Then I won't bring any."

"Pack warm pajamas—the furnace is on the fritz."

"I'll be fine."

"If it's 66 degrees like yesterday. Except they're saying it might freeze."

"Snow in April? When are you moving to California?"

"Never."

"Sure about that? Because our schools are awful."

"I'll get you at the airport."

"I'm renting a car and I'll be at your place around six. Then I'm taking everyone to dinner."

"If you're delayed, it'll be too late for Kit. I'll just make something at home. And Luke—you have to be patient with her. It's never what you think."

"I know. I love her no matter what."

∞

At 9 a.m. the movers show, and they look like they did time with the Aryan Brotherhood, except Luke learns over the course of the morning that they're just working men from the hard side of San Bernardino. They pack the truck with purpose, don't break anything, and expertly dismantle Trevor's bed with their own Allen wrench when Luke's can't be found.

Then the sky winds forward and Luke finds himself in his first-floor bachelor apartment with the bunk reassembled three feet his from his couch. After tipping the movers who gave their Sunday, it's done, and Luke must dig through his boxes for sweat pants—because he doesn't own pajamas, and what if it really is cold in Chicago?

6.

Luke and Sara would like to say that they're close, only she's twenty-nine, making them eleven years apart. And she is his half-sister, actually, and did not live under the same roof with him growing up, since their father left both their mothers for other women. FYI—Sara's mom was the other woman to Luke's mom.

Sara feels guilty about being the affair child, while Luke is numb to what went down in the past. Old wrongs are water under the bridge, as they say. Who really thinks twice about that swaggering guy—that marketing consultant for Pitney-Bowes and IBM—who checked out of the suburbs to party with his second bride? Like nothing ever happened.

But what happened is this: Luke's mom never saw her husband's infidelity coming. She had to work six days a week in the stationery shop at Old Orchard Mall just to keep the house, because her ex-husband cried poor, hiding his money from the judge.

Then again, it was all just so much elemental suburban psychodrama, and one day, Luke's mom remarried. To Luke's stepfather Phil, who wore his mother down. Those two have now passed on, along with Luke and Sara's brain-clotted father, who divorced Sara's mom, Francine, when Sara was three. This happened after their dad met a stewardess for American Airlines, and it was devastating to Sara's mom, who later married the furrier, Walt. Walt wasted their money betting at Arlington Park, then lost his fight with cancer like the rest.

Now there's just Francine, and while a living mother can be a great gift, Francine is an alcoholic who used to beat Sara with a shoe. If you ask Sara, she will say that Francine still uses the shoe over the phone from Boca Raton.

If all this seems distressing and complicated, it is, and it cannot be changed, as it is historical. A person can, however, have compassion for an almost 40-year-old man and his 29-year-old half-sister, who have three dead parents between them but little else.

∞

Sara, her husband Michael, and Kit live in a modest brick house in Evanston, Illinois north of Chicago, with two bedrooms and a crawl space attic that's great for keepsakes. There is a small, balding yard behind the house with a picnic table that gives splinters, and the budding peonies in the mud-chunk flowerbed are covered with ants. The house is particularly sweet at Christmas, when Sara and Michael cover it with winking lights. Luke especially likes the plastic Santa Claus table lamp in the living room that blinks on and off in the dark.

Sara is embarrassed about her house's small size, but she shouldn't be. It's biking distance to the graduate library at Northwestern University, where Michael is an assistant librarian, plus it's not too long a drive to the Erickson School for Early Education, where Sara is studying for her master's in childhood education. The neighbors are peaceable, it's very multicultural, and Luke would consider living in Evanston, except that he can no longer afford a modest brick house.

∞

Luke's plane departs its Denver stopover on schedule, and when he arrives at Sara's, he's on time for dinner. There, next to the house near the garbage cans, is brother-in-law Michael, wispy with unbrushed red hair. Luke offers a handshake hello, saying, "Don't get up," because Michael is on his knees next to a stack of redwood planks.

Michael says, "This pen better keep the raccoons out." He fishes around for a bolt. "How was your flight?"

"Fine, except the people next to me talked the whole way. Price for selling your own jet."

"Really, what jet is that?"

"My Gulfstream IV. I'm on the waiting list for a G-V."

Michael nods. He's never liked Luke's California sense of humor.

"Can I help?"

No, he cannot.

"I totally get why you're building the pen, by the way; in Highland Park, the raccoons always spread our garbage everywhere. It was bad because there was a chance there'd be lobster shells in the driveway." Michael keeps working. Luke continues, "You know my stepfather, he thought lobster was spoiling me, so my mom used to sneak it home to me, and I always had to hide the tell 'tail' signs."

Michael thinks, *lame*. "Well, we don't get much lobster on a librarian's salary."

"They're not as expensive as you might think, if you buy them a day old."

Michael nods toward the door. "Sara's inside making dinner."

Luke heads up the stoop. "Smells good!"

Sara shouts, "In here!"

Luke leaves his carry-on in the hall and joins her in the kitchen, where she is naturally pretty as ever, her wavy blonde hair in a ponytail like when she was little. Luke puts a brotherly arm around her and she links an arm around him, offering him a taste of sauce. Luke blurts out, "Magnifico!" and, "Did I just say that?"

"Embarrassing."

"Where's my niece?"

"In her room. Don't annoy her."

"It's her or you. Take your pick."

"Her."

Luke goes up the narrow staircase to Kit's room, where she is arranging colored beads into rows on the floor. Luke smiles at her with compassion, for she is a blonde ponytailed cutie just like her mom, except she has an Autism Spectrum Disorder. He says, "Hey Kit," but she prefers the task at hand.

Luke looks around the room. It's filled with colored beads, all lined up on book shelves and nightstands. He reaches into his backpack and pulls out a new Bratz doll, even though he knows Sara might not like Kit getting a doll with a bare midriff. He offers the doll to Kit, but Kit does not notice the gift. Luke sets the doll down and joins Kit on the floor.

"Those are beautiful beads, Kit. Every one a rare jewel."

Kit keeps at her work.

"Hey, can I show you something?"

Kit peers up, seeming to appreciate Luke's efforts.

"What if we put a red bead first, then a blue bead, then a purple bead, then a red, blue, and purple bead again to make a pattern?"

Luke rearranges Kit's beads into his pattern. She stares at the change. Suddenly she's in tears, pushing away from Luke to her rocking chair, where she starts screaming so loudly she has to cover her own ears. Sara and Michael come running. Sara reaches Kit first and Michael stops short at the door.

Cocooning Kit, Sara hisses, "What did you do!?"

"We were just playing with beads."

"No, don't ever touch her beads!"

Luke looks to his brother-in-law, but Michael steps away in disgust.

Sara says, "Don't touch her stuff. It's very disruptive."

"Can't you tell her I'll put everything back?"

Sara cannot—and it wouldn't do any good anyway. Then Sara says, "And I don't want her having that doll."

∞

In the breakfast nook, Sara takes Michael's hand. Together, they close their eyes and begin saying grace. Kit sits between Michael and Luke, but her dad does not take her hand. Luke inches his hand toward Kit's, grasping her tiny palm. Kit does not protest, and Luke closes his eyes in prayer as well.

When grace is finished they say, "Amen," and Kit says, "Amen" too. Only an expert would say that's mimicry and don't be sad when it's never mimicked again.

Kit knows to eat dinner and she receives organic, wheat-free pasta instead of rigatoni, since medical experts suspect that wheat gluten promotes ASD. That's also why Kit gets fruit juice instead of milk; milk has casein protein, and that may cause ASD, too.

Keeping Kit on a wheat and dairy-free diet is a challenge for Sara and Michael, and sometimes they run out of ideas for what to feed her. But if all else fails, there are plenty of gluten and dairy-free waffles in the freezer, and Kit likes them with honey.

Midway through dinner, Michael speaks. "Who's your client downtown?"

Luke says, "A publisher of Pokémon manuals."

"Is that a big business?"

"Getting to be. Pretty soon, you'll be stacking them next to Faulkner."

Michael nods as if to say, 'Regular comedian.'

Sara says to Michael, "What about the children's symphony tomorrow?"

Michael says, "What's the program again?"

"Famous symphonies and movie scores."

Luke says, "Sounds like *Jeopardy!*"

Michael says, "I'm sure they're sold out."

Sara says, "I can't imagine; there must be tickets online."

Michael says, "How much?"

"Thirty dollars apiece?"

"Waste of money. Last time at the ballet, she had a fit."

"Okay, but we need to try again."

"She won't know what's going on."

"Don't say that in front of her."

"She doesn't know what we're talking about."

"You don't know that."

"Yes I do. So do you!"

"Stop it!"

Luke says, "Hey, I'll pay for the tickets."

Kit says, "Hey I'll pay for the tickets!"

Michael says, "If anyone's paying for the tickets, it's me!"

∞

At Orchestra Hall, there's discordance from impatient kids, stressed parents, and an abridged Chicago Symphony tuning up onstage. But it's not long before the assistant conductor makes his entrance in black spandex. With rubbery pomp, he launches the symphony into the hit, "Twinkle Twinkle Little Star." Only, the orchestra plays "Twinkle" in a progression of sad keys, happy keys, and grumpy keys, while the conductor's booming narration tells how a few simple notes of music can make people grumpy, happy, or sad, depending on how they're played.

Kit stares ahead, and that's moment-to-moment relief for Michael, who is sure she's going to snap. But she doesn't, through samples of *The Magic Flute* and Vivaldi's *The Four Seasons*. When the conductor announces that Bernard Herrmann's score to *Psycho* is next, Sara and Michael freak, thinking that the screeching violins will undo their daughter, except Kit just listens and soon enough, kids and pleased parents are milling out of Orchestra Hall, into the morning gray.

∞

Lunch in Greektown at The Greek Islands, and it's Luke's secret pleasure to have given the maître d' his credit card in advance. Luke loves the noisy restaurant with the plastic sunflowers. The Greek Islands has been in Chicago for fifty years, and he figures it's where the FBI wiretaps the Greek mafia. Only there is no Greek mafia, per se, but nobody acknowledges that because it spoils the fun. Luke orders a Shirley Temple for Kit—the first she's ever had. And isn't it great how she likes gyros too, since most 5-year-olds will not eat spicy meat.

Then, before they know it, lunch has gone off without a hitch, with Sara and Michael sharing baklava for dessert, now that he's been forgiven for last night. Because Sara and Michael love each other, and they are coping the best they can. And they are a nice family with a few broken dreams, just like everyone else.

∞

It's Luke's idea to take Kit to the park for the rest of the afternoon, where Luke places her on a swing. Michael and Sara aren't sure about this, since they don't know if Kit will hang onto the chains. She does, and Luke begins pushing her higher, until her pealing laughter fills the sky. Luke, Sara, and Michael begin pealing with laughter as well, for Kit is happy like a regular kid.

But as things go when a kid is like Kit, life changes quickly, and what was once fun and affirming can become frightening without explanation. Kit suddenly bursts into tears. As Luke quickly takes her from the swing, Michael winces as if to imply that Luke is to blame.

Luke feels like the goat once more, and why won't the kids on the jungle gym stop staring with morbid concern? And what time is his flight back to California, where he can be safe and unknown?

At 5:45 p.m., Luke is at Hong's Café picking up take-out. Hong's has been up the road in Glencoe since 1960, and they are among the last folks in America to make Chicken Subgum with peas and carrots. The dish is a time-warp classic, and Luke orders it, along with shrimp egg rolls, pork fried rice, and two whole lobsters in black bean sauce.

Back in Evanston, Luke is glad he ordered plenty, being that Michael has thirds of lobster, including both big claws. As for fortune cookies, Luke's says, *Avoid taking unnecessary gambles.* But that one doesn't count, and if any other down-and-out foodie got it, he'd probably say it doesn't count either. And late at night after everyone's asleep, he might crack open a second or third fortune cookie just like Luke, until he finds: *All is not lost, yet.*

∞

Michael and Luke clean up from dinner, while Sara supervises Kit in the tub. Soon, Michael is back upstairs without thanking Luke for dinner, but that's just Michael's treatment of an imposition.

Alone in the living room with a popsicle, Luke longs for a night when he can have important conversation with Trevor again, and it's not until Sara returns to the living room that Luke stops feeling sad. Sara asks whether Luke is dating anyone, and he says there are so many women out there that his head is spinning.

But then guilt flares through Luke, because he cannot ask Sara for money, which is why he really came. For Sara needs every penny she has for Kit's ongoing care, and it's not Sara's fault Luke blew the 200 grand he inherited from their father on failed companies.

And it's wrong of Luke to regret the expensive last-minute ticket to Chicago; outside of Trevor, this is the only family he's got, and he will say goodnight to all of them now, since he's leaving at dawn for his business breakfast downtown.

Kit is already sleeping when Luke goes upstairs. He kisses her on the forehead, and she is hugging the Bratz doll, with Sara smiling at uncle and niece from the bedroom door.

Luke waves goodbye to Michael from the hall, saying it's time to turn in, and Michael says take care, it was good having you here. Luke and Sara hug goodnight, and there are tears in her eyes, because she does not know her brother either.

Luke shivers in his sweatpants, and who would bet it would drop thirty-six degrees overnight in the spring. At 6 a.m., Luke rises and lets himself outside, where the ground is covered with a dusting of snow.

As he pulls away, patches of red catch his eye in the broadening light. The patches are lobster shells strewn across the driveway. Raccoons have managed to get into Michael's cans, despite the pen.

Luke stops the car and gathers the shells back into the garbage, as red lobster claws on the driveway are evidence that he has been spoiled, and that is a secret he must take to his grave.

∞

Luke heads north to Highland Park, past turn-of-the-century Tudor homes to Braeside Elementary School, designed by a disciple of Frank Lloyd Wright in 1928. There, the original 1930s ice rink warming house still stands, reminding Luke of an Indian summer that turned to snow when he was six, when his dad moved away.

Driving past Edgewood Middle School, Luke finds himself trying out for his junior high basketball team. And when the coach tries him at small guard and cuts him last,

Luke wishes once more for his father, but Dad says, "See ya soon. Gone again until next June."

Luke drives on toward Highland Park High School but, weary from his past, he detours to Starbucks on Central Avenue, joining sociable fathers buying coffee for the commute downtown. Luke notes condensation on the store's windows and suddenly, he cannot breathe. He bolts for the frozen curb outside, because these are the shores of Lake Michigan, where he is a ghost.

∞

Luke waits in line for breakfast at McDonald's at the airport. The line moves briskly, there's playful teasing between the Filipina employees, and Luke thinks that maybe spending his life inside in the fast food business wouldn't be so bad after all.

Soon he is taking his seat on the plane, where the sun flaring through the window warms him, reminding him that he is heading home to his son. And before he knows it, they'll be riding ATVs and drinking Cactus Coolers, and Luke will finally be able to forget how he upset Kit's beads.

∞

At baggage claim, Luke checks his voicemail. There is one message from The Great Indoors. He returns the call in his Jeep at long-term parking, and when he's connected with the human resources director, she compliments him on receiving 100% on his test. Luke says he's surprised people miss questions, but she says they do, making Luke's candidacy shine. Luke will meet with her again later that afternoon, and he thinks, What has become of me—thrilled for minimum wage?

Luke goes straight to Santa Monica Community Gardens, where he finds Plot #23 baked dry. Hustling with the watering can, he gently soaks the soil like a Mennonite pioneer. And he prays: Please, seeds, don't be dead. Bring forth your great goodness from God's earth.

But the buried seeds don't talk back, and as cars rush by on Neilson Way, Luke brims with fear by rote, for his job interview is less than an hour away.

∞

Luke waits in a suit and tie for Carole, the human resources director, until she invites him into her windowless office, where he takes a seat on her cut-rate couch. The couch is low, Carole is high behind a Formica desk, and Luke wrests the possibility of throwing up from his mind.

Carole says, "So tell me—what *don't* you like about our store?"

"No Pizza Hut café."

"Well then, we'll have to get one! Now, where do you think you should start?"

"Probably learning the business from the bottom up. What about the stockroom?"

"We need a delivery coordinator. Would that interest you?"

"Is it in back?"

"I'm afraid so. You might get bored because you won't be dealing directly with the customers. But the delivery coordinator is critical to their satisfaction."

"I'm your man."

∞

The human resources director introduces Luke to Wayne Garcia, the stocky store manager with grandiose cologne, who says, "Welcome aboard," but who is noncommittal and busy with responsibilities in his head.

Or maybe it's that turnover is a fact of retail—average hires leave in less than a year—and maybe Wayne already knows that Luke is chafing to be outta there. So Wayne, who is in his mid-thirties, only reminds Luke that the dress code is black pants, black shirts, and black shoes of any kind. Then he turns Luke over to Brenda, the African-American sales supervisor in major appliances.

Brenda is 5'9" with beaded braids, a high butt, and perfect French nails, and Luke would think she'd have men clowning all over her, except she's single and bitter. She immediately lets Luke know she was a flight attendant for American Airlines before pursuing her singing career, and Luke is already worried about her because she's thirty-seven and time has meandered around her dream.

Brenda shows Luke the employee locker room, which has vending machines, no lockers, and doubles as the command center for deliveries. Against the back wall is a steel desk with a computer and phone. Brenda explains that this will be Luke's office.

Now Wayne Garcia sends in Lance, a chinless sales associate who must plod the earth resembling a rubber chicken. He quickly confides to Luke that he's applying to Cal Arts and that he will be an animator at Pixar, as soon as he can find a connection. Does Luke know anyone? Luke doesn't, and Brenda doesn't roll her eyes because she already asked Luke if he knows anyone in music.

Lance and Brenda show Luke how to set up deliveries, which is quite simple, especially if a man is computer savvy. Luke is, and he would tell them he was the founder of a seminal Internet start-up called Tribal Fire Networks, but maybe he'll save that for happy hour at TGI Fridays.

After a few practice orders, Luke thanks Brenda and Lance for their mentoring and they depart, leaving him alone in his formal attire. He isn't expected to start till tomorrow, so he takes a breather in his new office, where there are no brilliant advertising campaigns due yesterday. For a moment, Luke feels splendor at home indoors.

∞

Luke curses Los Angeles traffic at rush hour, even though it now takes an hour to get anywhere in town, at any hour of the afternoon. At the Century City Mall, he buys black chinos and black polo shirts, then finds a pair of black patent vinyl high-tops on sale.

The Reebok Afronauts are a bit showy, but Luke will hardly be seen, and he's been hankering for basketball shoes for quite some time. He purchases them and drives home to The Pico South Seas, where he places them on his pillow, because he has fly new dogs that he loves, and he will sleep with them in his bed to gain prowess from them throughout the night.

∞

Luke breezes into work on Thursday wearing his Afronauts. He says a joyous "Mornin'!" to Wayne, Brenda, and Lance, who follow his brash sneakers with their eyes. No matter—

Luke settles down at his desk to a stack of orders. First, two Miele dishwashers must travel to a domicile in Bel Air.

Second, a Viking Professional refrigerator/freezer comes to the plate, ready for expert installation in the Hollywood Hills. Only, no one tells Luke that he has to ask the right questions. So while the deliverers show up at the correct address on time, they can't possibly get the monstrous appliance up the steep, winding walkway, frustrating the customer, who has Trader Joe's mochi that must be freezered immediately. Mostly in life, one learns by doing, and by the time Luke sends out a crane, the ice cream has melted.

At one o'clock, it's time for lunch, and Luke accepts Lance's invitation to Taco Bell, where they eat outside on stools. Lance notes Luke's burrito and says, "Grade D beef."

Luke says, "Nothing wrong with Taco Bell."

"The government says that meat's good enough for students or prisoners."

"That's bullshit urban legend."

"No, it's the last meat on a cow's skull. They scrape it off with a rake."

"You're gonna make me blow."

"Want to know the real USDA scale? It's prime, choice, select, standard, commercial, utility, cutter, and canner. What's your taco?"

"I don't care."

"It's canner. By law, it can contain testicles and skin."

"Jesus, Lance!"

Lance looks around. "There's a trick pad around the corner. You can't tell from the outside."

"Good to know, but is it okay if we just eat without talking? I've got to figure out my schedule with my son for the next couple of days."

"Family first—cool, you have your priorities straight. But when you're ready, I'll tell you which bitch swallows."

∞

Luke and Lance dash across four lanes of traffic returning to the store, and Lance is dying to share more, but Luke is remote and will not look at him, since Lance's entire personhood is a reminder of how far Luke has fallen.

So Lance goes back to selling cabinets, and Luke heads to his office corner, where he processes thirty more orders, completing his work an hour early. Luke thinks, Quality is Job One, and wouldn't the room be more comforting without the fluorescence and his high-tops?

He knocks off the lights and kicks off his sneakers and soon, he's staring at his computer screen imagining he's the captain of a navy destroyer. Until the store manager, Wayne

Garcia, opens the door, tossing on the lights. "Why is it dark in here?"

"It got hot, and I can see with the screen."

"Overheads stay on for everyone. Turning them off is self-aggrandizing. And put your shoes on. What if a customer came back here, or someone from OSHA?"

Wayne Garcia departs. Luke thinks, Someday you'll be working for me, Wayne Garcia, just as Brenda appears at the door. "Sold the last Jenn-Air. You need to tag it and enter a floor model pick-up."

Luke nods and heads out onto floor, where he finds the Jenn-Air oven. He tapes the delivery address on it, and he's all set to return to his hideaway when he hears, "Luke?" It's Jill Marron coming around the stoves with Jon and the crabby twins. "What are you doing here?"

Luke says, "Shopping for a dishwasher."

The Marrons look at his all-black outfit. Jill says, "Dishwashers are over there."

"Thanks—now I know why I can't find them."

Jill says to Jon, "I'm not sure the six-burner Viking is big enough."

Jon says to Luke, "We're hiring a private chef three days a week. He has to have eight burners, right honey?"

"What if he caters, Jughead, and we have 400 people?" To Luke, she says, "You'll be at the party?"

Luke nods, and sourcing enthusiasm for the toddlers, he says. "They are so bitchin' cute, and way bigger than when I saw them last."

Jon narrows his eyes. "You saying they're fat?"

Jill says, "Looks girls, Unckie Luke!"

The girls scowl. Jill and Jon study Luke again as if to say, Sure you're not working here? But Luke is shopping, and realizing he's run out of time, he backs away, cupping imaginary taa-taas for Jon's benefit, saying, "Tomorrow's the big night, but no 'body like a stripper' for you!"

Jon says, "Her ass is sick!"

Jill says to Luke, "Please give him all the details, so he can live vicariously."

Luke heads out of the store, skirting the parking lot to the store's loading dock. There, he hoists himself back inside on his way to his post offstage, where a working stiff can take his life's bow.

7.

It's not just women who have fashion crises—men have them too, and if anyone thinks getting the shirt-jeans combination correct makes a metrosexual, they can fuck off. This is what Luke thinks while trying on numerous shirts for the Marrons' party, none of which properly deploy his alpha male. There is, however, his black linen shirt, and it does favor his broad shoulders, and it's pristine once again in plastic from the cleaners. So on it goes above black jeans, after a body spritz of cologne to fascinate Alina.

Luke stuffs dollars into his pocket in case the Marrons don't have a complimentary valet. Then he heads west to the Palisades, vowing to be happy at the Marrons' house, where his Cherokee is the only American car in their circle drive. Luke wonders what it would be like to drive a roaring

Bentley coupe. Wouldn't he be landed gentry in the Range Rover Sport? Imagine coaxing an actress home at 2 a.m. in the 600-horsepower SLR McLaren.

Luke climbs the marble steps into the foyer, where servers bearing trays appear, and he will have a baby lamp chop, except what's he supposed to do with the bone once he's done? There are no trash cans anywhere, so the chop goes into the powder room waste basket, and when the Marrons find the gnawed bone later while cleaning up and it makes them gag, they will know next time to properly plan for their guests.

However, if highborns have a big yard, they may not need trash cans, since their friends can pitch what they don't want into the bushes. That's what Luke does with a gristly duck taco, which becomes unsuitable in his mouth. Then Luke walks deeper into the yard through the milling crowd, past an R&B cover band. He's on his way to peruse the pool house, where he's startled to find Jon Marron sharing a water bong with two couples. They are behind a lemon tree sagging with fruit, and Jon is stoned but gracious, saying that Alina should be down shortly, leaving Luke wondering down from where.

Luke excuses himself in a hunt for the bar, where he accepts a flute of Cristal. Luke has a sip, pretending to be at ease and in enjoyment of this sophisticated event, and it's only a moment later that Jon's arm lands heavily on his shoulder. "Having fun?"

"Wonderful time, and that pink chandelier—it makes the whole backyard magical."

"I think it's gay. See that guy over there? He pioneered phone cards and made 200 mil. Then he bought a 20,000 square foot house in Holmby Hills."

"Wow."

"And that guy over there, he's about to build Asia's largest mall in Macao."

"Does he have a nice house?"

"Two acres in Brentwood Park with a private bistro."

Impressive, as everything in Jon's life is celebrating how much money the big boys have and how Jon is one of them. But Luke is not one of them—he can't even afford a hammered wife like Jill, who drapes Jon with a dreamy 'I love our life' hug. She says, "Howdy Unckie Luke," and, "Don't choo worry, Alina's done with the girls." Now Luke understands that Alina is the Marron's nanny, and can she really be his destiny?

Luke says, "Has she had any serious boyfriends?"

Jill says, "Dated sports agent What's-His-Hoozy. Made her get the boob job." Then Jill says to Luke, "Think I can sneak him upstairs?"

Luke says, "Worth a try."

Jill thinks better of it, slurring to Jon, "You'll get your BJ later."

Jon raises his glass to Luke, "Cheers," before he and Jill stumble down the stairs, Jill barely avoiding a wipeout in the fountain.

Seconds later, Luke has Kevin McNally at his side. "Luke Morrow." McNally is better-dressed in Brioni, with his hair shorn short for power. He is the Managing Partner of Unite and Conquer—an advertising giant with clients like Tag Heuer, Dell, and Ducati.

But McNally wasn't always powerful; when he and Luke were junior executives at storied Croesus Advertising, most thought McNally stupid. However, Kevin kept to his knitting, which is business-speak for a steady worker less imagination and courage. He could play golf, and he did an excellent job of organizing networking luncheons at the Century City strip club. Eventually, McNally was in the right place at the right time, as sometimes happens to pieces of shit. He says, "I heard you left Nicaida & Knight."

Luke says, "That's the rumor."

"They will fail soon enough."

"I'd mark your words, but I doubt it."

McNally says, "Fuck 'em anyway, 'cause I'm looking for a new creative. You should come in and meet."

"Really?"

"Why not? Let's explore."

"I'm on vacation with my son the first part of the week."

"Just set something up." McNally's cell rings, and he steps away for the call. With nothing better to do, Luke heads back into the house, where he tries to comprehend himself in the game room mirror. Then he heads back to the patio, where a brown-skinned beauty waits by the balustrade.

She wears a simple black dress with diamond stud earrings, and if there were ever a body to be naked in the sand, it's hers. Only she's not a waif, for this woman is structured like a 5'7" terra cotta vase.

"Alina?"

"Ay—Luke."

"Are the princesses finally asleep?"

Alina says, "They couldn't settle down for nothing. The music so loud."

"It must be hard caring for two at once. I mean, one son is enough for me."

"Ay, c'mon, they're my babies, and it's good practice anyways—for when I have five of my own."

"Five?"

"Just kidding. But I do want at least three kids someday."

Luke wonders if that means Trevor and two more, or Trevor plus three more, for a total of four.

"You do advertising?"

"Attempt."

"What do you do for fun?"

"You know, mostly hang out with my son."

"I like a good father. Does your son live with you?"

"Part-time."

"You like dancing?"

"I guess."

"Do you like Club Prey?"

"Haven't been."

"Their mojitos are the best."

They smile over the party, where Luke sees the Brasks and the Wesslers sharing a table below. "My friends over there—they're members of the Bel Air Bay Club with Jon and Jill."

"You come with them?"

"I didn't even know they were invited, so I'd better say hello to them before they get mad at me. And we should talk some more." Alina says sure, trying to hide that brave look one gets when someone doesn't want them like they should. But Luke will not take up her precious time, because she deserves a good man who can take care of her babies. And Alina is a partier, while Luke is sober for his son, should his ex-wife die in a hit-and-run.

Below, Keri says, "Luke Morrow—the man, the mystery, the legend."

Luke puts his hands on Bram and Peter's backs. "Hey, guys."

Bram says, "I didn't know you knew the Marrons," meaning why would they bother.

Marnie says, "Where's your date?"

"No date."

She announces to others nearby, "You should hear his Internet dating stories."

Luke says, "Oh God, no."

Too late—a married woman at the next table says, "Tell us one!"

Peter says, "He'll have you rolling on the grass!" Now other married couples have overheard, and they'd like a tale too.

"Yeah, tell us!"

Suddenly, Luke is on the spot with all eyes upon him. So, trying to do his best, he says, "Well, okay. There was this one woman who was a real estate agent at Prudential, and you know, she got so drunk after she came back to my place that she threw up all over my bed. Then I put her head over the toilet, and when I came back to check on her a couple of minutes later, it turned out that it was also ladies' time, because there was blood everywhere and you know, some feces too, and she was just sitting in all of it, wallowing! So I kicked her out for good into a cab, and from that day forward, my friends and I referred to her as Placenta Girl!"

The crowd sits in stunned silence. Then one of the women throws up in her plate. Luke puts his hands up like, 'Last encore over and goodnight,' while making a hasty retreat from the backyard. His car can't come soon enough, and when it does, he stuffs a fistful of cash into the hand of the valet who ran for it. It's not until he's leaving the long driveway that Luke finally sees a 'Gratuities by Host' sign receding under the moon.

∞

Luke unpacks Trevor's bedding from Hefty lawn bags at The Pico South Seas and makes the bottom bunk. He lies down and closes his eyes, wondering about the millions of particulates from freeway cars invading his windows. How can he subject his son to such horrible pollution, and if that isn't failure as a father, what is? And: Luke has forgotten to email his new apartment address to Lisa, per the custody stipulation, so he'd better do it now. The sooner that she sees his struggling street, the sooner she can scoff, affirming her solvent world.

Soon, Luke will have to explain to Trevor why they must live in less, and how: "A house is not home; a home is built on love alone." Only, that bromide will not silence Trevor's heart; he will still worry for his dad, and no kid should have to do that. Luke hears distant sirens and muffled tramping above, and again, he wishes to die, which he keeps to himself every time; if he tells a therapist something like that, they must report him to The State.

Luke thinks about his gun. But don't think the gun is accessible or known to children; it's in a tackle box with a Master lock securing it. Plus, the box is stored in a large fireproof safe, which has another combination the secret police will never get out of Luke, even if they torture him. The safe is hidden high up on the shelf, and not even a blow from a giant's sledgehammer can bust it open.

Now all that's left is the question of believability, because how can a kid from Chicago's North Shore grow up into a suicidal person standing in a gun shop in North Hollywood?

This is something Luke cannot readily answer; the explanation might be as long as a book. But when his businesses have crashed and his broken marriage is a riddle of rubble pondered in circles, he thinks about teaching God a lesson, as in: My death will be on your conscience.

Luke wonders why he isn't a phone card king or a mogul of Macao. Which begs the question: Is he trapped in his cocooned milieu? Luke prays, *Please God, help me to appreciate what I have.*

And all through the night, Luke asks God to send him to Darfur so that he may witness the horror of genocide. But that doesn't happen, nor does Luke find himself hostage in the wilds of Islamabad with his head severed, as is his desire. He will not feel what it's like to perish in Banda Aceh—sudden waters will not drown him—and he will stay in Trevor's bunk until his cell phone buzzes him awake the next morning.

Keri says, "I can't believe you told them about Placenta Girl."

"Why? You guys laughed the first time you heard it."

"Let's just say: If any of the couples last night were contemplating divorce—they're not anymore."

"Glad I could be of service. Now can I just go camping already?"

"How does the Great Indoors feel about your taking time off?"

"They knew I had plans before I was hired. I might be done there anyway—I've got an ad agency job offer."

"There you go. It was just a matter of time."

Luke says, "Exactly, because no one's unlucky forever."

∞

At 5 p.m., Luke checks Trevor's flight online—a welcome activity, since Luke has passed the day dehydrating on the couch. But how can a plane's departure be ninety minutes late out of Maui? What if there's a mechanical failure that isn't licked and the aircraft spins into the sea?

There's only one answer: Trevor will slide safely onto a yellow life raft, moments before sashimi fisherman complete his rescue. Yes, Trevor will survive the crash because he has to, and he will not be afraid, bobbing in the ocean, knowing that Luke's wings are over him wherever he goes—what Luke has told Trevor many times during important conversation.

Luke looks to the bright side of divorce, which forces a physical separation between a child's parents. If Lisa and Mark are thrown from the Airbus and eaten by hammerheads, Trevor will still have one parent to love him. And do not think Luke wants Trevor to lose his mom, even if Luke has considered her passing of late. Because he knows Lisa's death would mean a lifetime of devastation for the boy, and Luke would never want Trevor to bear that unimaginable loss.

So it's time to know that the good people at American Airlines are just replacing a cowl, and Luke will wait patiently for a call telling him when to arrive at Lisa's house to get their boy. He guesses that will be around 6 p.m., which is perfect for his latest plan.

∞

Luke can't pick Trevor up until 7:45 p.m., due to a glitch at baggage claim, where the ground crew took their sweet time delivering Trevor's boogie board to the oversize carousel. Luke and Trevor's frustration over this delay lifts when they see each other, and Trevor cracks a broad smile: Luke is his dad and his dad has come.

Mark, on the driveway behind Trevor, stiffens as if to imply, 'I'm supportive and happy to have you enjoy quality time with my wife's child.' Luke shifts into park, and Mark loads Trevor's backpack into the car. Trevor climbs into his seat and begins to buckle himself, but Mark finishes the buckling, because stepdad's hands-on parenting must be always be shown. Mark says, "Have a great time." Luke nods sarcastically, as if to say, 'Super.' Mark says to Trevor, "Give me a kiss goodbye."

Trevor does, and it's on the lips again—their way, enraging Luke once more. Is Luke the only one who thinks that a stepfather insisting on a lip kiss from his stepson is inappropriate?

Or maybe Luke should just be grateful Mark cares. Or…maybe Luke should bolt from the car and pound Mark senseless for having the emotional intelligence of Peter Brady. But then again, that might result in the police arresting Luke for assault, and the whole thing will just be a stain on Trevor's memory.

So Luke sucks it up, pulling away. Catching glimpses of his son in the rearview mirror, he thinks, Damn I love this boy, and considers how much he's grown since he saw him last.

Which was only a week ago, but any divorced parent will say how much their child changes to them, even when they've only been apart for days. To Luke, Trevor's kid-countenance is that much more mature, and for a moment, his boy seems almost preppy, even though the only change in Trevor is his sun-shined hair.

Trevor says, "What are we doing tonight?"

"It's a surprise, Surfer Boy."

"Is it a new surfboard?"

"Is it your birthday?"

"No."

"Then a more plausible guess."

"I can't think plausible."

"How are your hungry bones?"

"I can feel them." Luke parks the car at Santa Monica Community Gardens. Trevor says, "Why are we here?"

Luke says, "We're visiting our plantation. Disembark, please." Luke removes a lunch box cooler and a grocery bag from the passenger seat.

"What's in those?"

"You will see. Carry this." He hands the cooler to Trevor, who pries it open. Luke says, "No, not yet!" Trevor is startled and slides the cooler shut without seeing, out of respect for procedure. Then they head to Plot #23 where Luke says, "What do you see?"

Trevor looks up. "Planets?"

"The first two of the night. But that's not it. Take another guess."

Trevor looks again. "Cars?"

"There are cars in the vicinity, but you're not being a good looker." Luke nods downward, a direct hint.

"The rapini has sprouted!"

"And the peas, lima beans, and Brussels sprouts."

"When where they born!?"

"Without time lapse photography, hard to say."

"They look thirsty."

Trevor uses all his might to tip the watering can. Two big glugs of water splash out, and if that continues, the seedlings will wash away. Luke says, "Let me help." He lifts the can with Trevor, dispersing gentle rain on the leaves. Luke sets the can down as a Honda Accord with a Dagwood's Pizza sign rolls up. Now Trevor realizes it's a pizza party.

"Can I see what's in the cooler?"

"You may." Luke pays for the pizza while Trevor holds up two ice cream bars. The Honda drives off, and Luke removes tea lights from the grocery bag, placing them around the plants. Luke helps Trevor strike matches and light the candles. Then Luke and Trevor sit in the big chair and the little chair, sharing pizza under the stars.

∞

Luke loads Trevor into the back seat, since the flight against the jet stream plus dinner outside has turned Trevor into a lolling boy doll. And Luke regrets not saying what he should have said sooner, but they needed time to become a family again, and he can't always have important conversation when it's best. Luke says, "I have something to tell you; I've been meaning to tell you all night."

Trevor says, "What is it?"

"I'm sorry I didn't tell you earlier—it was wrong of me—but I've moved us to a smaller apartment. It's actually called a 'bachelor,' but a single woman could live there too."

"I don't want to move."

"I know, but sometimes grown-ups have to recalibrate their lives to save money. I needed to do it now for both of us."

"Didn't you get Creative Leader for the Continent?"

"Actually, it didn't work out, and I no longer work at Nicaida & Knight. But it's not how many times you get knocked down, it's how many times—"

"You get knocked up."

"Close enough, good boy."

"Did you have another fight, Dad?"

"No."

"What happened?"

"Trevor, you're so wise and I think I can tell you some very grown-up ideas, because I think you can understand them. Sometimes in life, things don't go like we plan, and no matter how hard we try to understand why that is, there aren't always answers. But I'm going to get a new job soon enough."

"Where is the bachelor?"

"Not far away on Pico Boulevard, near our favorite Taco Bell."

"Are the fish waiting?"

"No, that's the only bad part. We don't have the fish anymore."

"Did you forget them?"

"At the new building, they don't allow pets."

"Fish are not pets."

"I agree, but the landlady said no."

"Where are Fry French and French Fry?"

"I tried to find people to adopt them, but then I ran out of time, because the movers were on the way."

"Are the fish dead now?"

"They are."

"How?"

"In *The Idiots Guide to Freshwater Aquariums*, it says if fish are sick and dying, it's best to help them end their lives quickly. That's called euthanasia."

"The fish were not sick or dying."

"I know; it was not fair to them, but I followed the book's directions to be as kind as possible."

"What were the directions?"

"I put the fish in a bowl of water, which I put in the freezer. The fish go to sleep from the cold and die without even knowing. I put the frozen fish in the dumpster and soon enough, the garbage men came and took them away. What I did is the most humane way to deal with fish that can no longer live, though some people say if you throw them hard on the sidewalk, they will die instantly."

"Did you throw any of the guys on the sidewalk?"

"No, Trevor, that method doesn't work. I'm sorry about what happened, and my heart is breaking for you. But someday we'll get a huge tank that we can fill with a whole school." Then Luke says, "Are you angry and sad about the fish?"

"Yes."

"Do you want to cry about them?"

"Yes."

Trevor leans over and buries his face in Luke's chest, crying ever harder, about a lot of things. Luke hugs his son. "I'm proud of you forever."

∞

Luke carries Trevor into their home at The Pico South Seas, and they are hushed while Luke sets Trevor on the bed, helping him out of his clothes and into his shorties. Luke says, "We won't be here long, son, I promise."

Trevor's eyes are closed, wanting sleep, and he whispers in faith, "I know," for they are in a run-down flat facing a derelict alley, and sometimes a dad and his boy can't pretend they're in a bear cave above the sea, even if they try.

8.

The first photons of light soften the sky, waking Trevor.

He says, "The sun is up."

Luke says, "The sun is not up."

"The sky isn't black anymore."

"Is it navy?"

"Yes."

"Go back to sleep until it's light blue."

"Are we going to DK's?"

"Yes."

"Because it's a tradition?"

"We always buy donuts before our camping trip, and I'll be your best friend if you go back to sleep."

"You're already my best friend."

"Although I can't be your best friend and have you obey me at the same time."

"Since when?"

"Grandma Blessing said it's inappropriate to try to be both friend and parent to your child; I believe most psychologists agree. Now go look in that box by the lamp."

Trevor goes to the cardboard box, removing its top and sliding the Plexiglas case with the signed Shaq shoe onto floor. "When did you get it!?"

"I bought it at the auction. It's yours."

"How do we afford it?"

"We purchased it as an investment. In ten years, it will be more valuable."

Trevor jumps onto the sofa bed, ringing his arms around Luke's neck. "Thank you, Daddy!"

"Don't mention it, Pajama Boy. I always wanted a Shaq shoe myself."

∞

When a man is not feeling accomplished, he needs to get his ass to DK's Donuts by 6:40 a.m.; when he is freshly showered in the stifling sugary air there at dawn, it feels like he has places to go and people to see. This stupid advice fills Luke's head, while Trevor chooses a dozen donuts from the case behind the counter.

Back at the car, Luke places the donuts on the floor mat under Trevor's feet, in case the saturated oil bleeds through the pink cardboard box. Then Luke tries to slip his forefinger under the box's tape seal, but Trevor says, "No, not yet!"

Luke stops, reprimanded. "Just wanted to see what you got."

"Not until Ben's."

"Okay, but dads get first choice."

"No, little boys get first choice."

"Since when?"

"And we get two donuts each."

"Leaving two to split between parents?"

"Plenty enough for slivers."

Slivers are right, for few Westside adults ever eat a whole donut at once, and those who do know that it takes 200 sit-ups just to burn off the glaze. But if only a single wedge is snacked at a time, with the remaining wedges consumed over a period of thirty minutes, then the donut is less caloric than eating the whole thing at once.

This is Luke's theory, which he shares with Keri, Bram, Marnie, and Peter, who divvy up the remaining donuts while gathered in the Wesslers' kitchen. And they are all chiming in, saying, "Yeah right," with Marnie sighing, "Can I just say I love DK's?"

Peter says, "We'll camp out more often."

Keri says, "Staying in cabins with Jacuzzis is not camping."

Marnie says, "Who came up with this plan anyway?"

Bram says, "The decision was made to leave our ivory towers and be among the people."

Peter says, "To be in touch with our inner NASCAR."

Marnie says to Keri, "They're gonna get their asses kicked."

Keri says, "While we're at the Canyon Ranch getting ours massaged." She and Marnie bump hips with snapping fingers—a hapless display.

Peter says, "Have a lovely time. Put it all on my credit card."

Marnie says, "Oh I will."

Peter says, "See how she loves me?"

Bram says, "You know what they say—those who marry for money earn every penny."

Marnie says, "Where's his money again?"

Peter says, "Nice."

Marnie squeezes Peter's cheeks together before giving him a punim kiss. "Oh honey, you know I conditionally love you unconditionally."

Peter quips through the squeeze, "Hello? 1-800-Divorce?"

∞

The boys play a furious game of Knockout with basketballs flying everywhere, while Luke, Peter, and Bram finish loading the cars. Then Bram says, "Okay, big guys ride with us." The 11-year-olds clamber into the back seat of the Volvo SUV. Trevor, Ben, and Archer follow into the Cherokee.

Luke says, "Has everyone made a pit stop, 'cause if you gotta go, do it now." The boys blink back. Luke says, "Archer, that means you."

"I went."

"It's over a two-hour drive, and we don't wanna have to stop this time."

Archer says, "I said I went."

Peter says, "He's good to go."

Archer's brother says, "Yeah, good to go diarrhea!" The other boys crack up because they are boys.

Marnie nods to Keri, "Lotta testosterone."

Keri says, "We want some girls!"

The boys boo. Peter and Luke start their engines. Marnie and Keri plant smooches on their sons through open windows and wave the cars goodbye, long after they have disappeared.

∞

Twenty minutes up the road, Archer says, "I need to crap."

Luke dials Peter. "Your son is sneaking roughage behind your back."

Peter says, "I gave him a bowl of cabbage before we left, to spite you."

"See you at the next exit."

"Where I might leave a big pile myself."

"Wonderful. Glad you're not on the speaker."

"Put me on speaker. I want the whole world to know!"

∞

After a mini-mart stop, where the boys have urinal sword fights and Archer makes a filbert in the toilet, it's back into the SUVs for another hour. That's until the fathers have the crowd-pleasing plan of getting In-N-Out Burger take-out for lunch, forgetting they're driving fine autos.

So when lunch is completed, stray French fries are squashed on leather seats, meaning that Luke's placing the donut box on his floor mat that morning barely mattered. Luke lets his frustration at the mess go as he must; it's only a car, and they are on an adventure to California's enchanting central coast, where his luck might change forever.

∞

Oceano State Vehicular Recreation Area. Formerly Pismo Dunes, this sand dune complex of 18,000 acres is geologically unique and provides an impressive playground for off-highway enthusiasts. Specifically, nearly two million visitors come to Oceano every year, and nearly all camp on the beach between the dunes and the Pacific, and Luke has never seen so many RVs and motocross bikes in one place at a time.

The same goes for sunburned beer bellies and tattooed breasts in halters, and if Luke were ever wondering where a good 'ol boy would wear his souvenir wife-beater from the Daytona 500, he is wondering no more.

Additionally, while Luke and the gang are riding ATVs over the dunes, flattening the nests of snowy plovers, the staff at Oceano Dunes wishes them and the other 5,000 people crowding the beach a safe stay. But understand that sand grains blown over the dune crest tend to accumulate high on the leeward slopes, causing tons of sand to slide down. For this reason, the leeward slopes are called slipfaces, and slipfaces can collapse. Also, campers might like to hear how the first European explorers traveling through the dunes were members of Don Gaspar de Portolá's overland expedition of 1769. And every kid might as well know that in September of that year, Portolá's men killed *un oso flaco*—a skinny bear. This is interesting because the lake at the southern end of the park takes its name from the incident.

Also, during the 1930s, the dunes were home to free-thinking people, including mystics, hermits, and nudists, who called themselves The Dunites.

This is Luke's history lesson to Trevor, Ben, and Archer while they wait in line in the Jeep to pay for parking. But the 8-year-olds do not want to be Dunites; they don't grasp the benefit of being a mystic, and hermits are strangers offering candy. Not to mention, the boys will not be nudists, because girls might see them.

But the ocean dead ahead is achingly blue and the sands rise high, and the inland Manhattan Beach dune where they once slid on cardboard boxes is forgotten. Trevor says, "Where do we rent the ATVs?"

"Ahead at Arnie's."

Archer says, "Do they have dune buggies?"

"We'll see."

"If they have one, can we get it?"

"No."

"What about tomorrow?"

Luke says, "How about we just get through today."

The boys hop out, running for the rental lot, where Trevor suddenly has a crisis. It seems the other boys are big enough to ride red Kawasaki 82 cc's—all except Trevor, who appears too small to control even the next size down, a yellow 49 cc.

Trevor doesn't want to be the only guy on a little yellow ATV; it's not a good color anymore, and he doesn't understand why his 8-year-old buddies are big enough for the ten-and-up machines. Trevor climbs onto a red 82 cc, but he can't reach the handlebars with his feet firmly planted, so the bigger ATV is dangerously out of the question.

Now Trevor feels even more ashamed of his size, and he is not going to have fun ATV'ing, having to ride a baby's four-wheeler. Luke also knows that it's Trevor's first time operating a gas-powered machine, and that Trevor needs practice to be safe. Luke says, "We'll let them go ahead, and you and I'll warm up together—till we get the hang of it."

Trevor says, "I don't need any hang of it."

Peter, Bram, and their sons don helmets and motor off for the dune's entrance, leaving Trevor and Luke behind, who practice going forward and back in the sand next to Arnie's.

Soon enough though, Luke and Trevor head up the beach, Luke on a big black ATV trailing Trevor on a little yellow one. Trevor wears a bulbous red helmet and his protective goggles are giant on him; he can barely hold the thumb throttle down. But other four-wheelin' freaks are giving Luke the thumbs up from inflatable beach chairs.

And Trevor is more than determined to succeed, except he hasn't the strength or maturity; he's more like a circus monkey gripping the back of a St. Bernard, and zooming motocross bikes cut in front of him or narrowly pass him from behind, forcing Luke to berate: "Use the brake!" "Look for traffic!" "Pay attention!"

It's all too much for Trevor, and he is fighting back tears, until he and Luke finally reach the wide-open dunes. There, they begin zagging across desolate sands, and Trevor does get the hang of it, beginning to feel free out there upon the moon. And it isn't long before he and Luke find their friends on the larger dunes, where the bigger boys are taking turns riding ATVs down a slipface.

At the top of the grade, Trevor says, "I want to try."

Luke looks down the hill and says, "I think it's too steep for you."

Trevor says, "Aww," in frustration, as Ben and Archer have already gone down it.

Without giving Trevor approval, Luke says, "Let me try first." Luke positions his ATV at the edge with Bram on his

ATV at Luke's side. Luke applies the throttle and goes, fighting to control his ATV's fat tires.

For a split second, Luke almost falls, and when he comes to rest at the bottom of hill, he cannot believe he did something so risky and stupid. He could have broken his neck, as the sharp descent is treacherous.

It's at that same instant that Luke sees Trevor and the yellow ATV pointed at the edge above, as Bram has given Trevor the go-ahead. Before Luke can yell *stop*, Trevor is sinking down the slipface, only Trevor can't dominate his vehicle. Sand collapses under his wheels, and suddenly Trevor is thrown from his seat, with the 300-pound ATV rolling over his tiny body—end-over-end down the slope.

Luke screams, "*NO!*" and throws off his helmet, rushing to Trevor, who can barely breathe. A nearby dune buggy tour guide urgently radios for rescue.

A moment later, Bram reaches Luke and Trevor. Certain nothing bad has happened, Bram says to Trevor, "On a scale of one to ten, how bad are you hurt?"

Trevor manages, "Three."

And so Trevor does not die on this day. Everyone waits in concerned silence for the dune ambulance, while Trevor cries, "I don't want the ambulance. I don't want to go to the hospital!" But it's all established procedure.

When the paramedics arrive, Trevor must walk twenty paces forward and back under the blazing sun to prove that he's okay. Then Luke must fill out an injury report before he and Trevor can ride back to Arnie's through the buzzing off-road traffic—for Trevor has had enough of these dunes.

Back at Arnie's, with their ATVs turned in early, Luke and Trevor sit in the shade under the rental office awning, drinking Cactus Coolers. They are silent, and it isn't until years later that Luke reads an article in the *Los Angeles Times* about how risky the Oceano Dunes are for children, and how one doctor at the emergency room in Arroyo Grande is campaigning Sacramento to ban children from riding the sands, as he's seen more than his share of tragedy.

∞

At the El Capitan Canyon cabin campground, the fathers and boys eat pizza for dinner at the resort's country store café. The boys are free and easy on stools at the wooden counter inside, while Peter, Bram, and Luke sit at a tree-trunk table outside, where butterflies flicker in the wind.

Later, at the campsite, the boys roast marshmallows in a steepled campfire. Overhead, bats intercept the night, stars are spilled for splendor, and then the day is done.

The boys climb into their bunks, and not long after, Peter and Bram are sound asleep, too. But Luke is still awake on top of his bed, replaying his son's accident. Luke watches the ATV rolling over Trevor, killing him, and Luke will replay the scene over and over until morning sun whitens the sky.

∞

Bram is in charge of breakfast. Magnanimous, he pulls out a Kellogg's Variety pack, except he has forgotten milk, stumping the boys. How are they supposed to eat cereal without milk? Bram says just eat it dry or with orange juice.

Peter says he'll get some milk at the country store, and clearly the price of that milk will be jacked, and any decent dad would hop to and say, "No stay here, I'll get it." Bram doesn't; dry cereal is good enough for the children, since he wants coffee and a bran muffin.

Ten minutes more and Peter returns with a carton of milk and six orders of turkey sausage. Then it's 10 a.m. and time for a dune buggy ride—except Trevor won't go. Bram encourages him, saying, "Don't worry, the buggies only flip once a day." But Trevor doesn't think that's funny, and when Luke says, "C'mon," Trevor bursts into tears, crying bitterly at Luke, "Stop pressuring me!"

Luke says, "Okay, not a big deal, we'll just hang out here." The others turn to go, and soon, Trevor is happy in the cabin bunk bed having important conversation with

Luke. Luke says, "I like that you feel you can stand up for yourself. Telling me to stop pressuring you was very mature of you."

Trevor says, "It wasn't you who was doing it, it was the other grown-ups."

"I don't really care about a buggy ride myself."

"Do you like Bram?"

"Well, he doesn't always say the right thing."

"Can we hunt a squimunk now?"

"We can."

∞

Hiking up a trail, Trevor says, "Dad, tell me about The Bubble again."

"The Bubble—that was the two-seater speed boat we got to drive at Camp Shewamegon, if we were at least eleven years old."

"Tell me how you gave them the finger again?"

"I didn't give them the finger. I was driving The Bubble when I went past a boat house on the lake near the camp, and I gave the people on the shore a thumbs-up like, 'Isn't The Bubble cool?'"

"They said you gave them the finger."

"I gave them the thumbs-up."

"They called the camp director and told on you."

"They did."

"How did you get punished?"

"I could not drive The Bubble again."

"Tell me about the second time there is no justice?"

"You mean the crayon fight?"

"When that hand grabbed the back of your neck."

"That hand was Mr. Philbin's. He was the principal of my junior high, and we were throwing crayons in the stairwell between classes."

"You got in trouble."

"Me and another guy."

"Mr. Philbin made you stay after school and pick up garbage on the field."

"He did."

"Why not the other kid?"

"A puzzle to this day."

"I like your stories. Can I have another?"

"Why don't we enjoy the quiet of the hills for a while?"

"Okay, because there aren't any hills in Martha's Vineyard."

Luke drops to a knee, spinning Trevor around. "You know, that's the second time you've mentioned Martha's Vineyard."

"Because that's where we're moving."

"You're not."

"That's what my mom says."

"Then I'm going to give her a talking to right quick!"

Trevor's eyes widen with fear. "If you say so."

Luke says, "Back to the campsite!" Luke leads Trevor down the mountain without speaking. And after Luke has given Trevor a PB&J sandwich and carrot sticks, he leaves Trevor to his own devices with a whiffle ball and bat.

For the rest of the afternoon, Trevor does not to dare approach Luke, for Luke has gone away into the cabin, and it isn't until the others return hours later that Luke comes out.

Then Trevor and his buddies have races in the El Capitan pool, with Luke timing the heats on his watch. But later, while the boys thrive on the carefree evening's bluegrass band and the tri-tip barbeque, Luke is alone on a boulder, overcome with hate.

"You gonna eat?" It's Peter, scarfing sliced meat.

Luke says, "I'll get a plate."

"Did you see the MILF over there?"

"Missed it."

Peter says, "Chunk in the trunk, but still fuckable."

"Go for it."

"One teenage daughter. They're staying in a creekside double."

"How do you know?"

"I talked to her for you, Buddy. And she's okay with you having an average cock, because when they're too big, they're uncomfortable."

Peter gives Luke a hand up, pulling Luke to his feet. Shortly thereafter, Luke holds a plate of corn, steak, garlic bread, and fresh-baked brownie. But Luke cannot eat, the arrival of fireflies at dusk means nothing, and he can't be amazed when a skunk the size of a hyena strolls through the campsite, blasé.

Worse, the drive home the next morning along the Pacific is war in traffic, though few cars are out, and the boys' expansive banter in the back seat is harsh dissonance. When Luke and Trevor are suddenly back at The Pico South Seas, Luke is crushed, having only minutes left with his boy.

Trevor says, "When is my mom coming?"

"Soon."

"Why can't we play all week?"

"I have to work, and I'm sorry about the transitions. I know it's hard sometimes. But there's still time to have important conversation before you go."

"What is it?"

"I've been wanting to show you this box. I've been storing it away. It has letters in it to your grandfather."

"Did you write those letters?"

"No, his best friend did, during World War II."

"Who was his best friend?"

From a frayed blue cloth, Luke removes a 6-by-8-inch oil portrait of a young man. He's a kid really, a youthful 20-year-old in a tan military shirt and tie, with a groomed hedge of brown, parted hair. Luke says, "This is Hershey Resnikoff. Grandfather painted him from memory in 1944." Hershey, rendered against a blue Van Gogh sky, smiles back, wry and light-hearted.

Trevor says, "Was he friends with grandfather from kindergarten?"

"No, they started at the University of Illinois together in 1941, and when grandfather went to the South Pacific to fight in the war, Hershey joined the Army Air Corps. He was stationed in South Dakota, learning to be a pilot."

"How do you know?"

"I've read the letters. They wrote each other back and forth across the oceans for eight months. There are almost fifty letters here, so you can tell the importance of their friendship."

"What else did they write about?"

"They spoke a lot about girls."

"Why?"

"It's something you do when you're twenty. They also had great hopes." Luke removes a letter from on top. "This is the one that means the most, and here's what Hershey wrote: 'Dear Funny Face—"

"Funny Face?"

"They talked differently back then, and many of the words we use today will seem corny someday too. 'Dear Funny Face, I now have twenty-five hours of stick time on an L-5. Nothing to this game of flying. Of course an L-5 is a far cry from a P-51, the fastest pursuit ship in the world, and the strongest, the B-24. But it is the first step. I can really buzz that job around. Even did a loop, a barrel roll, and at least five stalls.

"'God, how I love to fly. After the war, I will take you up in The High Blue Yonder for a couple of thrills, yes? Yes! You must learn how to fly someday. Nothing like it, take my authoritative word. Even for an atheist, it takes one right up to the gates. No dirt, no petty bickering, no deceit, no slander up there. Peace of soul and mind, blue sky, speed, recklessness.'"

"What the heck?"

"He's just saying how great it is to fly planes."

"What are those numbers?"

"The L-5 is a beginner plane, the P-51 Lightning is the fighter plane that helped win the war, and the B-24 is a bomber, and it was a very sturdy plane.

"Now, Hershey and your grandfather had a dream, and here's what Hershey says about it. 'Concerning that projected trip across the oceans and continents, may I say that I give hearty approval to its principle: that's why I went to California—I had the wanderlust, and I still have it, and I'll always have it.

"'I have built mighty dreams of the day that I'd take off and see the world, everything in it—its mores, religions, people, countries, etc.—and in my own way, that is taking my damn sweet time, going where I wanted, when I wanted; working when I needed cash, roaming when I had cash, boarding and working freighters, roaming the streets of Paris, Cairo, Moscow, Berne, Hong Kong. Also, Honolulu, New York, Glasgow, Beonus Aires (pardon spelling)— always observing, always seeking, always wanting.

"'I'd sleep when I wanted to, and I'd explore when I wanted to. There would be no one to tell me to dry the dinner dishes or to run down to the store for a bottle of milk.

"'In different words, I'd be free, uninhibited, with no trammeling chains, and no dependents. I'd own the world, and I'd search and wander over my possession until I had sated myself with knowledge, wisdom, and contentment.

"'But yesterday and today I tore at my heart because such an expedition could not be. This war, this dastardly war, cut across my schemes, and I'm a soldier.

"'Yes, I'll see the world now, at least part of it, but not in the manner that I wanted to. I'll see it under the direction of Gen. Marshall, that medal-embellished tactician who never was in a battle, yet who now directs the fiercest battle of all time. But everything is deeper and more intricate than I'd like it to be, so I'll leave it here for now. Hershey.'"

"When was he in California?"

"I don't know."

"Did he ever go to the world?"

"No Trevor, Hershey died in the war when he was only twenty-one. He became a B-24 pilot, and he was shot down over Germany."

"I thought you said a B-24 was sturdy?"

"They were, and even though they were called Flying Fortresses, they were also slow and lumbering, and sometimes they were sitting ducks for faster German fighters."

"Where does his letter say he died?"

"It doesn't, but your great uncle in Chicago found out about Hershey's death first, and he wrote grandfather in New Guinea telling him the terrible news. That's in this letter."

"Did grandfather cry when he found out?"

Luke holds up another letter. "We don't know. All he wrote back was, 'Too bad,' and that, 'Hershey was a good kid.' But clearly, Hershey meant way more to him than that, because grandfather took the time to paint this amazing picture of Hershey on this broken piece of an ammunition box, which grandfather carried all the way home from the South Pacific after the war.

"Do you think you know Hershey from the painting? Look at the gleam in his eyes. I think my dad had talent as an artist, and he perfectly captured Hershey's happiness."

"Is my mom here yet?"

"We'll see. But Trevor, do you think Hershey had a good life? I mean, I know it's kind of an adult question."

Trevor shrugs.

"Well the thing is, Hershey died very young, and that is very tragic, but I think that even though his time on earth was short, he was really glad for it because he was an idealist. Have we ever talked about idealists?"

"I don't know."

"In his case, it means he was open to the world being good, and that he could be good in it. I think he was pleased with who he was, and that's one of the things that made him a great man. So my point here is that all you ever have to do to make me proud of you is just be you, okay? Whatever you become, whoever you are, it's fine with me." Luke looks out the window and sees Lisa's car pull up. He leads Trevor down to the front of The Pico South Seas.

"Bye, Dad."

Luke kisses Trevor on top of the boy's head, handing his duffle over to Lisa. Then Luke is left alone, on the curb.

∞

Luke puts on his black linen shirt, dark jeans, and boots, projecting confidence. And because he cannot be late for his 3:15 p.m. appointment, he will leave an hour ahead for the 30-minute drive.

But when he gets to Unite and Conquer's tower in Beverly Hills, it's only 2:40 p.m.—way too early to wait in the lobby. So he drives to a residential street south of Wilshire where he can park for free.

Upstairs on Unite and Conquer's twentieth floor at 3:10 p.m., Luke marvels at the reception area, which is vast and white, with mod couches and molded plywood chairs.

At 3:40 p.m., an assistant appears, leading Luke up a cascading staircase to Kevin McNally. Luke steps into a 1,500 square foot corner office with a wave to Kevin, who is distant at his desk, finishing up a call. But then Kevin rises to meet Luke in the office's living room.

Kevin says, "How's your son?"

"Great, thanks for asking. Your kids?"

"Knock on wood. Now where do you see yourself?"

"I have great relationships and I'm ready to lead."

"How many One Man Pencils do you have?"

"One."

"We have fifty and we just signed Mattel."

"Wow, congratulations! You know what I can do."

"You don't have to sell me. I'll email you a contract."

In seconds, Kevin is back at his desk re-headsetting, and Luke is back in the elevator. And, touring through Beverly Hills on his way back to The Pico South Seas, Luke at last acknowledges God's hand, saying, "Please make me your vessel for good." For Luke knows that within days, he'll finally be working at Unite and Conquer, where he belongs.

9.

isa is home when Trevor returns from school. Trevor is fortunate to have a mom there to make him a snack; Luke's mom worked until dinner time during her son's childhood years. That meant there were only Pop Tarts after school in the cupboard for Luke, but that's a minor sadness compared to Lisa moving Trevor away—and Luke is ready for Lisa when she answers the phone. Luke says, "Where is he?"

Lisa says, "Excuse me?"

"Where's Trevor?"

"At a play date."

"What's all this about Martha's Vineyard?"

"We're moving there when school's out."

"No you're not."

"The movers will be here Fourth of July weekend."

"You can't take him out of the state without my approval."

"We'll see about that."

"This is insane! You can't be serious!"

"Mark is taking over his firm's Boston office, and he's going to commute on weekends."

"Retreating to the family compound just like the Kennedys. You are royalty."

"He's always planned to return home."

"But not with my son!"

"He's our son, too. And we're going to do what's right for our family."

"What about my family?"

"Why is everything always about you, Luke?"

"When am I supposed to see him?"

"You only care about how you'll feel."

"What about him?"

"He'll see you on vacations. Children do it all the time."

"I will fight you to my last penny."

"Do you even have a penny, Luke? That I have to see Trevor living in that broken-down apartment. My heart is breaking for him all the time now, because you still can't keep your head down."

"What are you talking about?"

"News travels fast, Luke. Instead of doing your job, you have to show Nicaida & Knight you're smarter than them. You're M.O. as always."

"That's not even close to the truth. The judge will never let you take him."

"I've been told otherwise. You can't even afford to feed him."

"Fuck you, prick!"

"Nice. Now we can share your abusive behavior toward me with the judge, along with how Trevor almost died on the camping trip, on your watch."

Luke presses the line dead. It's no use arguing with a granite obelisk, and how can any mother's heart be a chunk of glass?

Luke dials his divorce attorney, Ellen. She says, "Lisa will have to prove why it's in Trevor's best interest to move. As long as the psychological evaluations show a healthy bond between you and him, she'll have an uphill battle."

"I don't have a job now, Ellen. I mean, I think I'm getting a good one, but she can show I'm unemployed."

"They're looking for the emotional bond, not how much you make."

"But what if I don't have any money, and I can't support him?"

"The judge looks at what's in the best interests of the child."

"I thought it was about the bond."

"It usually is. Having said that, the judge has discretion."

"So then there's no law in California."

"The truth is, we never know what will happen in court."

"What's it gonna cost me?"

"Somewhere around five thousand dollars, if there's one hearing. But if it turns into a full-blown fight, seventy-five thousand is not unreasonable."

"How do poor people do it?"

"I try to do pro bono work whenever I can. It's very sad."

∞

Whatever the cost, Luke will fight to stop Lisa, if he can only find the money. And luckily, minutes later, Kevin McNally sends the email that will spell out Luke's generous new salary.

Perfect in its bold-faced, unopened state, the email is pure salvation, and Luke quickly clicks on it, reading: "thanx for stopping by. good to catch up with u. and while it would be good to work with someone who is smart, your (sic) a friend so I'm not going to bullshit you, and I think your (sic) out of the loop. thanx again."

"Thanx." Whenever people write the word spelled with an x, a man can be sure he is crossed off their list, and if anyone actually thinks they're being polite, he's not getting it, because thanks with an x means: Do me a favor, don't notice that I just shit on you. And since I'm wiping you from my conscience, don't follow-up, because I don't want you becoming a burden.

A man being told that he is "out of the loop," however, is the real death knell, especially from a friend. But Kevin McNally is not a true friend, and how many of those does an executive really make in his business life anyway? Just to be accurate, Luke was never totally out of the loop after having been a creative director at Croesus—he knows more loops than most will ever know.

Plus, he had the courage to start his own technology company from scratch. And venture capitalists gave him a first round of funding to fulfill his dreams, and when that money was gone, he picked himself up and started Morrow Advertising in the worst ad-buying climate in decades. He did his job well at Nicaida & Knight, he held his own against meaner minds, but now he is out of the loop?

No, McNally is out of the loop, for Luke diagnoses him with a degenerative disease that suddenly makes McNally fail. So when McNally begins confusing the names of his clients to the stupefaction of his partners, Luke will think, I guess McNally's kinda falling out of the loop.

Then when McNally can no longer identify television networks on his wall-sized TV, Unite and Conquer orders him to a specialist, putting him on sick leave, and he is unofficially out of the loop.

And sooner rather than later, when McNally is wasting away in hospice and can no longer tell a banana from a nut, Luke shoots him an email saying, "how does it feel being totally out of the loop? thanx!"

Then, in weeks, McNally's body is too stupid to know that the glucose dripping into him is food, forcing him to take his last death-rattle gurgle, sending him finally out of the loop. And while McNally's casket lowers on squeaky pulleys, Luke thinks, Oh well, just another man come and gone, for you should know all men eventually end up out of the loop in this life.

But revenge daydreamed never serves, and Luke should know that, except he needs a scapegoat for his devastation, and that scapegoat will be the spindly lemon tree outside his window. He should have tossed that sad-sack tree out long ago, but he told Three Brutes and a Big Rig to put it on the truck, as it's hard to throw worthless things away when he has nothing.

Luke glares through the barred windows at the tree's single, puny lemon. Out into the alley he goes, ripping the lemon from its branch before kicking the tree over for dead. One pump with the bread saw, and the lemon is halved. Luke chokes a tablespoon of juice from the lemon into a jelly jar, then adds tap water.

Because when life gives lemons, make lemonade, and how can it still be bitter after half a pack of Splenda? Luke downs the juice, tossing the empty jar into the sink, where it cracks. Only, he does not hear it breaking, because he has blacked out on the floor.

∞

Thought hurtling backwards slams Luke into consciousness, and he has no idea how long he has been down, but the day's light is vanishing and a soft breeze is clattering the metal blinds, and maybe it has only been minutes. He rises with his mind racing, and all he can see are thousands of numbers and letters somersaulting in his head.

He cannot make the calculations go away, so he reaches for a pen, forcing them onto printer paper, until he has furiously covered a ream with endless equations, all nonsensical.

But if he were Byung-Jun Kim or one of the Korean parallel processing PhDs from his Internet start-up, he might see he's onto something big: visionary algorithmic code. Only he cannot comprehend what he's writing, and after six frenzied hours of uncontrollable scribbling, Luke's hand is bleeding.

Starving, he tries to chew a slice of bread, but it's too stale. He must get to sleep—it's 1 a.m., and he's supposed to be back at The Great Indoors tomorrow, except the numbers and letters keep flooding his head, and now that he's out of paper, why not just type it all into the computer?

But that means rationality, and Luke's only reasonable thoughts are: There is a legal judgment against me, a string of failed businesses behind me. I've spent all my money foolishly betting on myself, and despite my best efforts, God somehow gives Lisa the power to take my son away, and here I am—a man visited by madness!

Which is true; Luke's insanity is real, and how could mental illness suddenly overtake a person? Now Luke is reaching for Hershey Resnikoff's letters, writing all over them until he's ruined fifty historical documents. Holy shit—it's 5 a.m., and Luke is grabbing Trevor's childhood artwork off the refrigerator, sending Pokémon magnets flying. By 5:30 a.m., Luke has destroyed Trevor's drawings with jumbled scrawl.

At 7 a.m., Luke has covered the walls with notations. And as he sits contained on his sofa for a spell, he's afforded the thought that he better get some help.

Luke phones the therapist he saw during his divorce, leaving an emergency message. She calls back within twenty minutes, as empathetic women in their late sixties are up at dawn themselves. He tells her that he is not hearing voices, meaning it may not be psychosis, though there is a strange calculus springing from his hand everywhere, and maybe she'd better refer a top psychiatrist pronto.

A half-hour later, after smashing the Plexiglas box and inking theorems all over the Shaq shoe, Luke is on the phone with psychiatrist Dr. Gellar, who says, "We'll start with Valium to calm you down, then come see me at 2 p.m."

Luke careens to the pharmacy, where he picks up his prescription. But even after he's home and taken twice the dosage, he has not calmed down, because the Valium has no effect on him, and how this could be is beyond science.

So he continues to vandalize his walls, and he will not answer Wayne Garcia's call at 11 a.m., and after never phoning Wayne back, he will be fired from The Great

Indoors, though he will never know about that. At 12:30 p.m., Luke reaches Dr. Gellar, saying, "I'm going out of my mind. Please help me!"

Dr. Gellar says, "Go immediately to Cedars-Sinai and sign yourself in. I'll meet you there."

∞

At the psych ward, Luke struggles to sign himself in, given his hand wants to desecrate the admittance forms with computations. A nurse eases his pen along, then leads him into a private room. Moments later, Dr. Gellar arrives, giving the thumbs-up for olanzapine. Luke swallows a dose, and the nurse encourages him to lie back on the bed, where he should start to relax, since an anti-psychotic mixed with Valium is a potent cocktail.

Another technician takes a blood sample, and Dr. Gellar says it's first a matter of getting the meds right. The nurses depart, and Dr. Gellar agrees that Luke has been under quite a lot of stress. He says sometimes coping people can snap, and when he looks at the math scratched on Luke's paperwork, he can't make any more sense of it than Luke.

But that's the mystery of a nervous breakdown; no one knows how it will manifest itself, and the suggestion that lemonade could bring one on is fantastical. Dr. Gellar departs, saying, "Don't worry. You're safe in this hospital.

You're probably just suffering from a temporary situational disturbance. Not as uncommon as you might think."

Luke tries to calm himself over the next half hour. Only, the spinning numbers in his head are implacable. He finds the black Sharpie he stuck in his back pocket at home, and he goes to the wall, slashing technical code on it.

There's a camera mounted in the room's corner, and the monitoring nurse sees what he's doing. She summons two orderlies. They enter Luke's room and ask him to desist. He looks at them with desperate eyes.

The orderlies and nurse try to lead him by his arms toward the bed, but Luke resists in a struggle for control, with Luke landing a wild right across the nurse's brow. She goes down as the orderlies tackle Luke, slamming him onto the bed, where they pin his wrists and ankles in restraints.

Luke is choking for air and grievous, saying, "I'm sorry, I'm sorry, I'm sorry," but it's too late for that; he will be shackled until his blood chemistry levels. It's for his own good, and Luke succumbs, agreeing, "Okay, okay."

The orderlies attend to the nurse, who wants to cry, but is professional about occupational hazard. They leave Luke alone in his room, unaware that the doctor's diagnosis will never be correct, and that Luke's trauma is far beyond theory and experience.

And they do not hear him suffering to himself in the restraints, "All this on my fortieth birthday. Didn't anyone pick that up from the chart? If you'd just check the custody agreement, you'd see that Trevor is always with me on my birthday to celebrate. Which of you is going to tell Trevor that his dad is locked up? Who can explain something like that to a kid, anyway? What special birthday dinner would Trevor like tonight, since I won't be staying here?"

Luke fights against the restraints, and how he is able to bust through them is the seventh of the infinite components of a miracle. He rights himself, undoing his ankle ties.

He strides into the lobby, where he tells the nurse and the orderlies that he is signing himself out. It's his right, as he's committed no crime beyond being uncontrollably upset.

The staff can only watch him go; they have no actual jurisdiction, and another altercation with him might threaten their safety even more. But they will follow procedure and call Dr. Gellar to convey the worrying news.

∞

Home at The Pico South Seas, Luke reads an email from Lisa telling him that Trevor will be dropped off at 6 p.m. Then Luke stands on a chair, encoding the ceiling. At 5:50 p.m., he checks his voice mail, deleting messages from Dr. Gellar. Ten minutes later, Luke meets Trevor in front of the apartment building. The Aston Martin coupe departs, and Trevor says, "I get to be with my dad on his birthday!"

"Aren't you lucky?"

But Trevor doesn't know that his father is overwrought and says, "Can we go see the vegetables?" Luke turns down the hall for the apartment. "Did you water today, Dad?"

The seedlings haven't been watered since before the ATV trip. Now, more than ever, they need to be saved. Luke says, "Too bad, they've slipped my mind."

Trevor says, "How can they do that?"

"Stop asking questions."

"We better water them, Dad."

"Fine! Fuck it!" In the alley carport, Luke throws Trevor's backpack into the car, crossly buckling Trevor into his seat, and Trevor does not know what he did all of the sudden to be a bad boy.

They go to Santa Monica Community Gardens, where the seedlings have grown into beautiful green plants. And the soil around them is dark and moist—someone has watered in Luke's place. Luke reads a note written in green ink that is stuck through one of the stakes. "I saw your plants drying up so I gave them a drink. Thanks again for the skins. Sidney Newton."

Trevor asks, "Who's Sidney Newton?"

"The homeless man with the stump."

"What does he mean about the skins?"

"I gave him my old gloves."

"Why?"

"He needed them."

"Is he your friend now?"

"No."

"How come?"

"Because this is my fucking garden! Who the fuck does he think he is, trespassing on it! And I don't need anyone's fucking charity! Do you fucking understand?" Trevor blinks, frightened. "Answer me!"

"Daddy!"

"FUCK THESE PLANTS! I DON'T WANT THEM ANYMORE!"

Luke starts kicking over the plants, destroying them row by row.

"Daddy, No!" And when the second grader tries to save his last vegetable by clinging to Luke's leg, Luke violently rips him off, whacking Trevor with an errant elbow, opening a deep gash under Trevor's eye.

Stunned, Trevor cries, "I want my Mommy!" but he will not get her because Luke shouts, "Get in the car!" Indifferent to the blood spiraling down Trevor's cheek, Luke manhandles Trevor into the back seat saying, "We're going home to order a pizza for my birthday!"

"I don't want a pizza for your birthday!"

Luke drives to The Pico South Seas, where he jerks Trevor down the hallway back into the apartment. Inside, Trevor's terror deepens when he sees that the walls and ceiling are covered with graffiti. "I want to go home! I want my Mommy and Mark!"

"Okay, I'll take you to your fucking house. And take your fucking shoe!"

Luke throws the ruined Shaq shoe at Trevor, before hauling Trevor to the Cherokee. Trevor vomits in his seat, blood streaming all over his hands and knees, and when Luke pops the locks at Lisa's, saying, "See ya!" Trevor screams, "I HATE YOU!" Then the boy runs for his home's front door, and when Lisa answers in a horrified puzzle, Trevor falls unconscious into her arms. But Luke has already driven away.

∞

Luke holds still in the dark with his eyes closed and his palms flat before him on the table. His cell phone rings and he answers. From the emergency room, Lisa says, "You bastard! His cheekbone is shattered, his skull has a hairline fracture, and he lost so much blood that he could have died. So the police are headed your way, and by the time the judge is done with you, you will never see him again!" The line goes dead. In the distance—an approaching siren.

Luke climbs onto his chair, removing the safe from the shelf. He opens it, removing the tackle box. From the box, he takes out his gun. He loads the gun with bullets. Then he takes his Sharpie and begins scribbling on the wall again, only this time, he wants God to know how painful it can be for a man, in his time and place, to be cognitive in this world.

But Luke is aware that what he's writing is churlish, and does any of it really hold universal truths? And why leave pathetic frustration behind for others to dismiss? So Luke blackens out the *Dear God*s and the ramblings and steps to the window for the final sign.

The sign is there, for perishing comets are lighting up the sky, and Luke knows all is lost and that he cannot save himself, as he will always feel too much, to the detriment of others.

Luke does not point the gun at his temple; everyone knows he can end up blind if he's off. Instead, Luke puts the barrel to the roof of his mouth while thinking, Now I will know what it feels like to have a hot bullet through my brain.

He squeezes the trigger. There is a loud bang.

PART TWO

1.

The bang is a trap door slamming over Luke, who cartwheels through it onto a deserted plain that is windswept to infinity. Landing with a thud in the dust, grimacing but whole, Luke struggles to his feet and faces The Roar. And to say it sounds like an oncoming freight train is an understatement; the 100-foot wall of water shuddering toward him has a timbre all its own. Down comes the curl, an unbounded bomb, crushing him into the sand.

Luke surfaces in a lifeboat, churned toward a tossed buoy. If he can just leap onto the buoy, he might be saved; it has the world's last pay phone and 911 might answer. Luke's boat keels, but he can't grab hold of the buoy—lobsters swarming all over it are pinching his hands.

Luke drops to the depths, and it would be his end were it not for the sushi fishermen who hook him onboard. They have a fine vessel decaled with Hokusai woodcuts, and are not expecting the suddenly crashing and burning American Airlines jet, whose tail shears their boat's bow. Donning goggles and caps, the fishermen strip to their shorts and plop into the sea, and what happens to them, their ship, and the Airbus, time will never tell.

Luke dives for safety too, into a vortex that drags him to the ocean floor, where the South Equatorial Current pushes him forth across the globe, until he finally settles in river shallows, where an outfit of nippy yellow bar-tailed platies finds him quite the curiosity.

∞

Waters recede into terra firma. Luke awakens on a bed of moss under a canopy of birch in upstate New York, and how this could happen is only the ninety-fifth of the infinite components of a miracle. He rises to see what is in the forest behind him, but he finds a clearing instead, with a forked road branching out from it.

On the right fork, through a narrow iron gate, is a trail twisting steeply skyward—a harrowing way into foreboding mountains, dying lightning, and rumbling avalanches of rock and snow. Down the left fork is a solid 24-carat gold gate, and it is wide and unlatched, beckoning him. Beyond the wide gate, bay trees bloom. Luke looks toward the narrow gate one last time.

He steps through the golden gate onto a two-lane highway that drops under bluest sky. The gate's latch slams shut behind him, releasing from the clouds a hand greater than the temple mount—a Da Vinci meteor hewn from Michelangelo's stone, and if it is the hand of God, who can really say.

The giant hand hurtles toward Luke's heart, but Luke will not wait for impact; rather, he passes out in a slurry ditch, where a glass marble, lucent with blinding white light rolls from his shirt pocket. Then all is black, spinning silence.

∞

A liter of water emerges from woolly light and is offered to him by a boyish man in a tan military suit and a tie. The man is almost twenty, has a heartening smile, bushy eyebrows, and a hedge of brown, parted hair. He props Luke up. Luke takes a sip from the bottle. The young man says, "Your color is coming back."

Luke believes he is in a dream and says, "When I wake up, my shoes won't be covered with mud." At the edge of the road above them is an idling SUV limousine on carbon-22s. Luke offers his hand. "Luke Morrow."

"Hershey Resnikoff."

Luke wonders at the inexplicable.

"Everything under the sun is possible, Luke."

In a flash, Luke and Hershey are barnstorming the steppes of South Dakota, fanning grasslands in a pup of a plane, a blue Air Force Stinson Ghost Squadron L-5 Sentinel, top speed 130 miles per hour. Hershey pilots the plane as an 8th Squadron tyro with only 100 hours in sky, and he will never fly a P-51 Mustang or Grumman P-47 Hellcat, since he will die a bombardier over Germany in a B-24 Liberator.

But the Sentinel is a worthy, single-engine forerunner of the weekend Cessna, and in its past, it directed artillery attacks from a ceiling of 15,000 feet, bearing a ferocious shark's mouth painted on a Chihuahua steel nose. Still, with its windows slid back and throttle thrust, the L-5 delivers a ride, and Luke whoops for joy in his seat. He shouts, "Are you sure this baby will hold together?"

"Don't worry! You're behind a Lycoming O-435 flat six-cylinder, air-cooled engine. Very reliable!" Hershey lifts an aileron, sending the craft into a barrel roll. "Also, it's plenty sturdy—they cut the wings from solid wood!"

Down toward the cottonwoods they go, Hershey leveling the plane just above power lines, and when the Sentinel comes to a bumpy stop on its donut wheels, Luke is more than ready to bail. He drops from the plane to the ground, wobbly in airman's gear. Hershey hops out to Luke's side and says, "The High Blue Yonder, yes? And now you don't have to take my authoritative word: no dirt, no petty bickering, no deceit, no slander up there. Just peace of soul and mind!"

Luke nods weakly, retching in the weeds.

Hershey says, "I blew my first time too."

Luke sleeves his mouth. "At least this isn't for real."

"Oh it's real, alright."

Luke says, "Right, real enough for a dream, but this will be over soon, and I'll be telling it to Trevor."

Hershey peers into the wind. "No Luke, that's not how it's going to go. Shortly, you won't remember him being your son."

"That's funny, Hershey. You are a good kid."

"And a good parting gift to you as well."

"A parting gift to me? Hershey Resnikoff? For what?"

"For your life."

"Really, that's very kind of you, and it's nice to meet my father's best friend. But unlike you, I'm not dead."

"So you say. The thing is, you're going to forget your past life if you haven't already, and you're going to be an entirely different person now with a different path and past.

Unfortunately, you don't get a forum to discuss the upshot, since we have to be going—because you're needed on Wall Street by 4 p.m." Luke turns, and he's suddenly standing on a tailor's stool facing a fitting room mirror, wearing a Brioni suit and Panerai watch, his russet waves of hair now shorn short for power. Hershey, now wearing a business suit as well, says, "If you don't like the tie, we can stop at Barney's on the way."

Luke says, "The tie is fine. What is going on?"

"What is going on is: you're getting the life you wanted, the one you deserve."

Luke gets into the limousine. Hershey shuts the door and steps behind the limo's tailpipe, where ribbons of blinding white light radiate from a wood plank crate on the ground. Hershey hoists the crate, securing it in the limo's rear.

In the driver's seat, Hershey says over his shoulder: "Also, you need to be sharp, and since you've been through a lot, you probably should rest." Luke is not expecting the mask that drops from the map light panel. Hershey says, "It's a mild laughing gas."

The mask grips Luke's face. Luke inhales before he tries not to, as the window separating the passenger compartment from the driver seals Luke in his sleep. The limo heads swiftly down the meadow, toward distant mountains shrouded in storm.

∞

The 22s spin through thunder and hail and abruptly curb. Hershey opens the back door, holding salts under Luke's nose. "Rise and shine."

Luke tries. "Today is your last day."

Hershey offers more water. "In another continuum, maybe, except I don't work for you, and no one can see me anyway or hear us talk, and even if they can, they'll just think I'm your intern, so they'll ignore me."

Luke rejects the bottle. "Do you know who I am?"

"Tell me."

Luke says, "I'm the Chairman and Chief Executive Officer of Tribal Fire Networks!"

"You are, indeed. And no one will be surprised that your entrance is down to the wire, and you will wonder why they can't just push things back for you. Now get out of the car: your company has just gone public, it's 3:58 p.m., and you are closing the day's trading. And when you do, you will be a rich man."

Hershey opens an umbrella against the Atlantic drizzle. Luke steps forth beneath it, at the steps of the New York Stock Exchange.

∞

Luke and Hershey advance through tapering pandemonium across the Big Board floor, entering an elevator leading to the balcony. They emerge into a sellout of executives, where the Stock Exchange CEO is already back-slapping Luke, saying it's a terrific day to have Tribal Fire on the NYSE, and a credit to Luke's strong leadership for not buying into volatile NASDAQ—it shows he really cares about shareholder value.

Luke nods, though he only cares about how much his stock will be worth within seconds. Luke pounds the gavel, there is life-defining joy all around for Tribal Fire's soaring IPO, and Luke is posing for photos, telling Hershey that ten million Class A shares times a closing share price of $87.50 is $875 million.

"That's right, Luke, you're almost a billionaire."

Luke says, "Not a surprise. Even if I don't know how I got here."

Hershey will help. "Let me show you your future. And your past."

∞

Luke and Hershey stand in a hangar before the world's finest private plane, a Boeing Global Express X-10000, fifteen stories long. Painted across the gleaming fuselage in giant magenta letters: *The Defensible.* Hershey says. "This will be yours."

"I'd like to go inside."

Luke and Hershey view the cockpit, an absolute realm of technology. Hershey says, "Range is 21,600 nautical miles—once around the earth—on a single tank of fuel. Plane can land on speck of an island strip, stopping on a dime. All jets to come will attempt the same feat, but will end up in the sea.

"Boardroom table inlay is Qing Dynasty mother of pearl. Seating for thirty, onyx Capra Hircus cashmere cushions, which may also be used for flotation devices. IAF Hatzerim Dov anti-missile system installed under the wings.

"Mile-high master suite. Custom expanded California King mattress with Sferra Milos 1,020 thread count sheets sleeps a man with two women, retractable Baccarat crystal wall separating his and their showers. Caiman leatherwork and rare Timorese wood, courtesy of Bentley Motorcars, Crewe, England.

"Walk-in Lebanon cedar humidor, 1,000-bottle wine cellar stocked with Quintarelli Amarone, true sky bar with satellite connection to Wynn Casino Sports Book."

Hershey points a keychain remote toward one of the sky bar's oval windows, popping the limo's rear hatch outside of the plane. Technicians step forth and remove the wood plank crate, before conveying it to the X-10000's hold. Luke watches, concerned, for the blinding white light is streaking through the crate's boards. "What is that?"

"Not for you."

"It says 'Hazardous Materials'; it's going on my plane."

"You're about to receive enough money for 500 lifetimes. That box is to be stowed away and forgotten."

"I expect to know."

"Take my advice and stay away from it; you don't get everything in life." Hershey checks his watch. "Uh oh, the reception has begun."

"I don't want to leave."

"It's an amazing aircraft, Luke. You will live to see the day."

∞

Hershey leads Luke into Daniel Boulud's Bistro Moderne, West 44th Street, New York City. The maître d' ushers them to a private dining room, where power suits crowd the bar.

Hershey says, "Your hosts from Goldman Sachs, your Latham and Watkins attorneys, your Deloitte & Touche corporate accountants, a veritable hall of fame of venture capitalists and fund managers, all here to pay homage to your newfound success.

"And you will have a meal for the ages: Maine lobster salad with grapefruit gelée, Kobe burger stuffed with braised short ribs and foie gras, pommes soufflés, and a dessert of pear tarte Bourdaloue." Then Hershey says, "It's a rare man who can create something worthwhile, let alone receive a fortune for his efforts. Minimum, you're one in ten million."

"I worked hard."

"Others as well."

"They didn't have my vision."

"Then it is a meritocracy."

Luke surveys the room. "Many important people need to know me."

Hershey says, "It wasn't always that way."

∞

Luke and Hershey stand over a 29-year-old Luke, who is wrapped in a sheet before dawn on a mattress on the floor. Hershey says, "Your home when you were a tenant." The shadow of a hunchback moves outside. Hershey continues, "You're about to become your younger self because he becomes you, and you will not see me or think of me again until it happens."

Luke slides out of his bed in the bungalow, his future and Hershey Resnikoff vanished. Peering through haphazard blinds, Luke spies wheelchair-bound, scab-handed One Leg rummaging through the garbage can. Luke dials 911 emergency. "I'm calling from Electric and Abbot Kinney. There's this mental patient outside trying to break in." Through the pane, One Leg contemplates Luke anew, before withdrawing from the alley into fairy tale fog.

∞

Luke showers in a crummy stall. He wrestles with the bath's swollen window, finally shoving it open. Cold air swoops in on sunrays; Luke closes his eyes, embraced. Outside in the alley, an LAPD Interceptor bounds over stony potholes.

∞

Wearing a black suit and blue dress shirt, Luke sails past his assistant.

She says, "Good morning, Stacy."

From inside his office. "Coffee."

∞

Luke is behind *Advertising Age* with his feet up. Stacy brings him his cup, saying, "You're supposed to be giving Becker and White 'a good pounding.'" Luke puts the magazine down, remembering.

Luke knocks on a frosted glass door, opening it without care for the answer. Inside are Becker and White, a copywriter and art director team. Luke says, "You're two days late on the dress rehearsal." Becker and White blink back, continuing their Nerf basketball game. Luke snags the ball, stepping to ad campaign mock-ups. "Why are these in sketch phase? What's here isn't even close."

Becker says, "If that's what you think, then maybe you have some suggestions."

White says, "Yes, valued input from the account executive."

Becker says, "He's been demoted from prison guard?"

Luke says, "Maybe if you guys would get in first thing in the morning instead of all this epic procrastination, we might actually keep the account."

Becker says, "The client is happy—last I heard."

White says, "However, maybe if we were at our desks bright-eyed and bushy-tailed like Babbitt here, we would be more productive."

Becker says, "When you punch the clock, great ideas birth."

White says, "Perfect summary of the creative process."

Luke says, "I'm the one out signing clients every night, putting my reputation on the line for you—for what?" Luke leaves, dismissing the basketball into the waste basket. He heads past Stacy, who says, "Did their noses grow again?"

Luke disappears into his office, saying, "They are my Pinocchios, foolishly carved from blocks of wood."

∞

Luke pushes sand back and forth with his Zen desktop garden rake, watching the clock tick to 5:51 p.m. He opens his door, spotting a college kid Xeroxing. "Daniel the Intern."

"Sir."

"Meeting out of the office."

∞

Luke and Daniel are at Chaya Venice restaurant, where they fantasize about waitress Lisa, whose dark tresses fall over her flat-chested beauty.

She says, "What can I get you?"

Luke says, "My Chief of Staff would like, what?"

"Corona Light."

Luke says, "I'll have a Johnny Walker Blue on ice."

The bar manager eyes her. She says, "I kinda need to see your IDs this time."

Luke pulls out his license. Looking it over, Lisa says, "I'm older than you by three months—who knew."

Daniel says, "I'll just have a cranberry juice."

She says, "No, don't tell me you're still in school."

"Part-time internship. But I'll be twenty-one in June."

"You could have gotten me fired twice already."

Luke says to Daniel, "I'll give you a teaspoon taste of mine." Then, nodding over at a woman who is bottle-feeding a baby boy, he says, "Don't you think it's wrong to bring him here?"

Lisa says, "Aww, he's so little, he doesn't know."

Luke says, "Babies are sponges, and all these beers going around—they're bound to make an impression. Also, just so you know, I don't ride my motorcycle without a full helmet. So if you're into that Third Reich bad boy thing, it's not me."

Daniel says, "You really should go out with him already. Major account executive next door; his prospects are excellent."

Lisa shakes her head, *no way in hell*, again. But she is smiling from his persistence, and it looks like she's starting to cave. 'Sensitive or jerk? Pretty cute. Successful. Sharp dresser. Pray no hair on butt.'

∞

Slingshot under the sun, Luke guns his Harley down a country road, with Lisa hugging him from behind. Soon the motorcycle blusters into the Ojai Hot Springs' parking lot, where Lisa shakes out her mane from under her helmet. Holding hands, she and Luke head into the timber spa toward a woman with blonde whiskered armpits. The woman says, "Mornin', how's your Valentine's?"

Luke and Lisa already have an understanding. He says, "Actually she wants me to ignore it."

Lisa says, "Too forced and commercial, but maybe that's just us."

"Okay, then happy anti-Valentine's Day. Name?"

"Morrow."

"That's two massages at eleven, brunch at one, Hot Tub C ready and waiting." To Lisa, the woman says, "Not even one red rose?"

"What can I say? We're a match made in heaven."

∞

Luke and Lisa step out of their changing rooms, bashful in towels. They enter Hot Tub C, a private, raftered stall with two coopered tubs on a wood platform. Slowly, they drop their towels, revealing his board shorts and her bikini. They climb into the sulphurous hot tub. Adjusting to the broiling water, Lisa says, "Next time, we'll probably go naked."

Luke says, "Promises, promises. When you're ready, we'll dunk in the cold one."

"How hot is this tub again?"

"Three hundred degrees?"

"I'm ready already."

Luke and Lisa climb out, lowering into the cold tub. Lisa says, "It's freezing!"

"C'mere." Luke gathers her up. "Hold still and let the heat of your body warm the water around you like a shield."

They hold still in the cold plunge, Lisa starting to shiver. She says, "Can we get back in the hot one now?"

"On the count of one." Luke and Lisa hop back into the hot water, splashing into a long-awaited kiss.

∞

A waitress serves Luke and Lisa eggs Benedict and mimosas at the spa café. Starving, they dig in, until the question comes up. She says, "What are you thinking?"

Luke says, "Nothing."

"C'mon, you must be thinking something."

"I'm thinking how relaxed I am after that massage."

"Ask me what I'm thinking."

"Okay."

Lisa says, "I'm thinking this has been a pretty perfect morning and that you're a very charming guy—but I don't exactly know you yet."

"You say that like it's a bad thing."

"Not a bad thing. It's just that I've only had a couple of long-term boyfriends, and I'm a really bad dater and when I like someone, I tend to get emotionally involved. So I just want to know, before I go too far…that you're open to a relationship—at least the possibility of it. There, I said it."

Luke takes her hand. "There's nobody else in my life now. If you weren't right for me, I would tell you."

∞

Luke and Lisa return to Lisa's West Hollywood apartment. The motorcycle's headlight throws shadows across the courtyard window, where a miniature husky pokes her face past the curtain. Lisa slides off the bike, handing off her helmet. "I had a great time and I'd invite you in—"

"What about Damsel in Distress?"

"She can meet you from the stoop, but just know she's very protective of me." Lisa unlocks the door, and D.D. jumps kisses all over her and Luke. Lisa says, "She likes you!"

Luke says, "What's not to like?" He tussles with the dog, unzipping a jerky pig ear from his pocket.

Lisa says, "I was wondering what smelled like bacon!"

"Boy scouts are always prepared." He grants D.D. the pig ear, after she bites for it, ladylike.

∞

Lisa throws D.D. out of the room. On the bed, Lisa helps Luke lift up his shirt, before racing to undo his buckle. Unzipping his pants, she says, "Oh my God, I don't think it will fit!" Luke flips Lisa over, undoing her jeans, yanking them down, before taking hold of her hands from behind. Lisa closes her eyes and bites her lip, succumbing in the moment to a sexy, confident guy.

∞

"Vitamin pack?"

"Yes."

"Waiting."

Stacy delivers the cellophane packet to Luke in his office.

"What is it now?"

Stacy isn't budging. "You have your review in ten minutes. I've been here eighteen months, and you've been promising to talk to me for three weeks."

"I told you, as long as I keep giving you things to do, you're doing a great job."

"What about my promotion into accounts?"

Luke checks the clock. "I will fight for you with Bennett Reign."

∞

Luke arrives at the door of Bennett Reign, the Croesus ad agency's managing partner.

Leigh says, "C'mon on in."

Luke takes a seat across from Bennett and Shelley, the VP of Human Resources.

Bennett says, "We appreciate your ongoing work with Rainforest Juice. As you know, there are two tiers of raises—3% and 5%—and we're awarding you the top tier, same as last year."

Shelley says, "You'll see the increase reflected in your next paycheck."

Luke says, "Are we entering into talks with Electronic Arts?"

"We are."

"I want to make our case."

"Have you worked with Neal Hill? He'll be front and center."

"He knows me."

"Let me give it some thought."

Luke says, "Thanks. When you cut my veins, they bleed Croesus."

∞

Luke walks past Stacy into his office. Stacy gets up, joining him. Luke says, "I wanted to make your case, but there wasn't time."

Fighting back tears, Stacy returns to her desk, saying, "Lisa called. She's making dinner at your place and wants to know when you'll be home."

"Tell her to be ready for me by seven."

∞

Luke opens the door to his home, where Lisa is popping a cork, saying, "Happy three-month anniversary!" She pours champagne into glasses.

Luke says, "You're a loon. Is that the shower?"

"It is, and by now it's hot."

∞

Under a steaming shower, Lisa draws Luke's face to hers. Then Luke eases her around, pressing her against the tile wall.

∞

Dressed in sweats at the bungalow's garden table, Luke and Lisa eat beneath a lemon tree that's zizzing with bees. He says, "Any time you want to make Tuscan Chicken again..."

"I'm so glad you like it."

"What's for dessert?"

"Homemade tiramisu—if you'll tell me what happened today."

"Nothing to say. They gave me the usual shit raise, and when I asked for a better account, the managing partner said he'd have to think about it—when I've already been there for five years."

Lisa says, "A raise is still good news. I'm proud of you."

"Whatever; they're A-holes."

"You'll jump ship soon enough."

"Great—leave one set of problems behind for another. Genius advice."

"What's that supposed to mean?"

"Working for other people sucks, Lisa. Get that through your head."

"Everyone works for somebody in the end, and please don't talk to me that way."

"You know, by your logic, Lisa, you should have never have left retail."

"I didn't leave because I had a boss. I left because it was soulless."

"But you still want a house and vacations."

"They're not everything."

"Just be more supportive, okay?"

"I am supportive. Who just made you dinner?" She rises, clearing plates. She will not come back, and Luke will remain under the lemon tree long after the bees have retreated from the night.

∞

Luke and Lisa sleep apart on the mattress on the floor in the morning dark. But One Leg is spry, and he's making his breakfast run. He's tipping Luke's garbage can to see what's inside. Lisa wakes from the incongruous sounds, and when she glimpses One Leg glaring at her through the window, she gasps. Luke leaps from the bed and races out the door with an eight-iron, but One Leg is gone.

Luke comes back to bed, hugging her, finally whispering: "I do care about you, Lisa. More than anything. And we can get a place together, if that's what you want."

"You have to want it, too."

"I'll have Stacy call Shoreline Towers."

"It's not safe for me down here at night or leaving early."

"I know, and they allow pets, so you won't have to leave D.D. for the night."

Lisa says, "You're a prince."

Luke reaches between her legs, except Lisa is faster, scissoring her legs together. "Never!" she says. But she can only hold out so long, and after twenty minutes of goofing around with Luke on the bed, she is unscissoring and trembling all over him in a welcome, sudden surprise.

∞

In a Shoreline Towers apartment, delivery men set up a king-sized bed, while Luke and Lisa gaze toward the Santa Monica pier from the living room window. Luke says, "The Ferris wheel is solar-powered and stays lit all night. On a clear day, we'll be able to see Point Dume."

Lisa holds D.D. in her arms. "We love it!"

A strong gust of wind rises off the sea, causing Luke, Lisa, and D.D. to squint in the bowing screen.

∞

Under summer sun, Luke and Lisa play beach volleyball against another couple. Lisa sets the shot, and Luke spikes it home, winning the match. They high-ten into a kiss.

∞

Halloween gales lambaste a hay-bale ziggurat outside Shoreline Towers. On the hay—an FBI's Most Wanted lineup of Jack o' Lanterns carved by tenant kids who are tucked in their beds before dawn, when the only ringing phone is ten floors up. Luke answers the phone. A middle-aged woman's voice says, "Oh, I apologize, I must have the wrong number." Luke rolls over to hang up, but the woman says, "Wait, that must be Luke. Luke?"

"Yes."

"Pat and Stan Hudson." The Hudsons are in their early sixties.

Luke says, "Good morning."

Pat says, "What a surprise to find you there."

"I just came over. We're going for a hike."

Stan says, "The reason we're calling—we're off to Santa Fe and we wanted to make sure we're on for Thanksgiving."

Luke says, "I'll be coming back from New York that Thursday, probably mid-morning. And Lisa is gonna fly into San Francisco at the same time to meet me."

Stan says, "We thought she was coming Wednesday."

"No, she has to work that night to get the holiday."

Pat says, "They work her to the bone."

Stan says, "Becca's driving in from Berkeley. We're planning dinner at the Four Seasons in the city to keep Pat off her feet this year."

Luke says, "Let me walk to Lisa and give her the phone." Lisa is waving Luke off like it's way too early in the morning to deal with parents. Luke says, "Actually, she's still sleeping."

"Okay, just let her know we called."

"I will."

"We just wanted to confirm before we left."

Luke says, "Looking forward to meeting you. Have a great trip. Me too. Bye."

Lisa says, "They totally suspect, don't they?"

"Odds are they're onto us. You think your sister told them?"

"She would never."

"Maybe it's time to tell them."

Lisa says, "Hmm—must ease them into it."

∞

Twenty-five days later in a Four Seasons bistro booth, Stan, Pat, and Becca anticipate Lisa and her new boyfriend. "There they are!"

Luke and Lisa make their way over, Lisa giving her fair-haired, zaftig 26-year-old sister a kiss. "Hey, you." Lisa gets hugs from Mom and Dad, and Luke receives a paternal handshake and welcome-to-the-family kisses. Then Stan says, "Shall we get some grub?"

∞

Stan and Luke are at the turkey-carving station. Stan ventures, "Getting cold in New York, is it?"

Luke says, "I always forget my coat liner. You'd think my assistant would remind me."

"What was the nature of your trip?"

Luke lowers his voice. "I went to meet a headhunter."

"After a new position, are you?"

"Laying the groundwork for starting my own company."

"Lisa hasn't said anything about that."

"It's not for broadcast. But most of the agency partners left early for the weekend, so I took advantage."

"Did the headhunter have some ideas?"

"I gave them to him; I'm looking for creatives who are undervalued and hoping to join me for equity."

"Anyone possible at your current firm?"

"There is this one team, Becker and White, but I would characterize them as habitually lazy and not up to my standards."

"I've had a number of employees like that over the years."

"In hospital administration, I can imagine." Luke ladles cranberries. "I'm not big on these, but they always end up on my plate."

Stan nods. "Sounds like you know where you're going. Best of luck to you."

∞

The Hudsons and Luke eat with intention. Becca says, "Seriously, we're pigs at a trough."

Stan says, "We should take a break and rekindle our Thanksgiving tradition."

Becca tells Luke, "We used to have Indians over for popcorn and smallpox."

Pat says, "Becca!"

Lisa says, "She's the unfunny one in the family."

Becca says, "Whatever, let's get this over with. I'm grateful for sweet potatoes, my loving family, and that after two years, my boss has promoted me to associate mortgage broker."

Stan says, "Wonderful, why didn't you tell us?"

Pat beams, 'Super kid!' to Lisa.

"It just happened. I wanted it to be a surprise."

Lisa says, "Becca Hudson, future millionaire."

Becca agrees. "Because you're my sister, I'll only charge you a point."

"Because you're my sister, I'll shop your quote."

Becca thins her eyes.

Stan says, "Lisa, your turn."

Lisa sighs, "Other than her, I'm grateful for my family, and I can honestly say I'm the happiest I've been in a long time—because I've met Luke."

Pat and Becca say their *awws*, and because it's a saccharine moment that must be broken, Luke says, "On that note, I'm grateful that you've invited me to share this day with you—and not that you should cue violins—but it's nice to be with family, especially since my mother and father have passed. So thank you for your hospitality—and for your daughter Lisa, who is the best girl I've ever met."

Stan says, "The best girl I've ever met too."

Becca says, "Daddy!"

Stan says, "Just being truthful."

Pat says, "Stan!"

Becca says to Luke, "I want a new father."

Stan says, "C'mon, I love both of my daughters equally, and I'm forever grateful for my beautiful wife, who has put up with me all these years."

Pat says, "I'm grateful that you're grateful." To Lisa she says, "And I'm especially glad that you found someone honorable; I've got a good feeling about him."

Becca raises her glass. "To the lovebirds." Luke and the Hudsons clink wine glasses, cinching the future.

∞

Luke and the Hudsons fork the last of dessert. Their waitress steps in, offering more coffee, but Stan says, "Just a check, I think." The waitress returns the bill to Luke, with his credit card already run. Stan says, "Hey you're our guest!"

Pat says, "Lisa?"

Lisa shrugs to her family, 'He's a good guy. What can I do?'

Stan says, "C'mon, give it over."

Luke says, "I crashed your party."

Pat appeals to Stan not to allow, but it's done. Stan says to Luke, "We'll have to make it up to you."

Luke says, "Just wheel me off to bed and we're even."

Pat says, "The guest room is all made up. I hope you'll be comfortable."

Lisa blanches. "Okay—but Luke and I, we're actually staying at The Fairmont tonight. Luke reserved a room for us. With his miles."

Stan and Pat say, "Oh."

Becca says, "Oh dear."

Lisa says, "I thought I told you on the phone."

Pat says, "No."

Lisa takes Luke's hand. "And—" she says, "we've moved in together!"

Stan and Pat struggle to bear it. Luke smiles placidly at Stan, as if to say, 'Yeah Stan, I am fucking your daughter. And she likes it.'

∞

Lisa spoons Luke in their hotel bed, while distant foghorns roam the bay. She says, "You asleep?"

"Almost." Then, "Lisa, you need to let go—they're from a different generation."

"I know. But there's something else I need to tell you, too."

"Tell me in the morning."

"Pat isn't my mom. I mean she's my mom, but not my real mom."

"Since when?"

"Since my real mom left when I was one. My dad married Pat two years later and she adopted me."

"What happened to your real mom?"

"She left my dad a note saying she wasn't happy, and all I can say is, what kind of a mother leaves her daughter behind? I mean, what kind of a person can do that? And my dad, he could never talk about her again. But that's why I was in therapy in college, just trying to understand."

"I wondered why you and Becca don't look alike."

"Half-sisters. Mystery solved."

"But there's more of your dad in you anyway."

"Wonderful—a girl who looks like her father."

"No, Lisa, it just makes you a handsome woman."

"Now you're really digging your own grave."

Luke says, "All it means is you're going to age like a fine wine. You'll be even more beautiful in your forties."

"So what about you? Any dark secrets?"

"Me? I'm an open book."

∞

Luke enters Chaya Venice at lunchtime with a colleague and clients.

He presses forward to the hostess, who says, "I got you with Lisa." She seats them, as Lisa efficiently approaches.

Luke says, "Neal Hill, Lisa Hudson."

Lisa says, "Good to finally meet you."

Neal says, "Uh oh."

Lisa says, "He's only said great things: Croesus Creative Director genius, resident whiz kid."

Neal says, "It's all true."

Luke says, "Tom Newton and Kurt Clarke of Electronic Arts fame."

"Welcome. Can I start you off with drinks?"

The Electronic Arts guys pause.

"Iced tea for me."

"Same here."

"Iced tea."

"Me too." Then Luke says, "And Pellegrino for the table."

Lisa nods and departs. Tom says, "Beautiful girl."

Kurt says, "You're a lucky man."

Luke says, "I count my blessings every day. She insists on pulling her own weight, and she's committed to the Chrysalis Foundation, which helps the unemployed get jobs."

"If Electronic Arts fires us, we'll know who to call."

Luke says, "Believe me—me as well."

∞

Lisa sits on a bench with a cup of hot chocolate at New York's Rockefeller Center ice rink. Luke races past on skates. She shouts, "You don't want to kill a kid on Christmas!"

Indeed, Luke is flying past little tykes, shouting, "Zermatt Olympics! Short track champion!" Then he leans into an ice-spraying hockey stop in front of her. "Wins the gold by ten seconds!" He falls back on the bench, blades up.

Lisa hands him her cup, saying, "Here's what you get for 100 lessons." She glides onto the ice, skating into simple spins and junior jumps. "Fourth place, Santa Clara Middle School Invitational." She skates off the ice. Luke gives her the cup back, saying, "I love New York on New Year's. Everyone clears out, so you can really enjoy the city."

Lisa pauses, elsewhere. "Listen Luke, I've been doing a lot of thinking, and if it's okay with you, I think it's time for me to stop working at Chaya."

"Fine."

"I mean it's kinda humiliating waiting on your clients, plus I really owe Chrysalis my full attention."

"Quit."

"Okay, but I need to know what's happening. Because I won't be able to contribute much rent with the non-profit pay, and you know, if it's not gonna work out between us..."

Luke takes her hand, stopping her. "Lisa, I'll do anything for you. You won't have to worry about anything ever again. Just give me a little more time to sort things out with the agency, and we'll move this whole thing forward."

∞

Luke and Lisa land first-class on American Airlines, sugarcane and ochre soil reaching up from below. Luke says, "The best part of Hawaii is when you first step from the plane into the humidity."

Lisa says, "What about lying around the pool?"

"Way down the list."

∞

"The second best part of Hawaii is when you pull up at your hotel and they give you chilled juice." Luke and Lisa climb from their airport cab to a muumuu-gowned hostess, who offers them glasses of juice. Luke says, "Even if the juice is canned."

∞

"The third best part of Hawaii is having lunch at the swim-up bar, eating Mahi-Mahi sandwiches and these corkscrew pickled peppers you don't get on the mainland."

Lisa says, "When do I see what's in there?" On the bar stool next to Luke is a tied plastic shopping bag.

"Eat a good lunch and I will consider."

∞

On a coral sand beach, Luke opens the bag. "Reef shoes."

They slip on the rubber shoes, and he leads her onto a lava flow that stretches into the sea. Way off the beach, they stop and look back at the jade mountains. Lisa says, "Thank you for bringing me here."

Luke says, "Someday, I will buy you this island. But first: Will you marry me?" Luke is offering Lisa a blinding two-carat diamond ring.

"Oh, my God. Yes. Definitely yes!"

"You won't regret it, Lisa Morrow."

"I love you!" Then, "I want to call my mom!"

∞

Luke and Lisa stand before a minister under an arch of white roses at the edge of a Sonoma canyon vineyard. Behind them: the Hudsons, Luke's half-sister Sara, brother-in-law Michael, and 100 guests, all gilded in the sun. As the minister speaks, Lisa dreams into her husband's eyes, but they do not betray his innermost thoughts: Hold on, be calm. Soon you will be ripping off your monkey suit and partying!

Her vows uttered, Lisa wonders fleetingly if her husband understood what he just said—to have and to hold, for richer or poorer, in sickness and in health.

∞

Luke and Lisa leave their white-splashed Santorini hotel on a Vespa scooter. Speeding down a mountain pass, they force a shepherd and his sheep to the side of the road. Among the scattered sheep is one coal-black lamb. Luke shouts to Lisa, "Now you know where the phrase comes from!"

Shouting gleefully back, Lisa says, "Keep your eyes on the road!"

∞

Luke and Lisa feast on roast chicken at a seaside taverna. The whole chicken is surrounded with lemon halves and French fries, with two empty, king-sized Heineken bottles nearby. The waiter brings a third frosty bottle and soon, the newlyweds are sleeping on the beach under a pitched umbrella.

Only Luke isn't asleep, because these are the Grecian Isles where women are topless, save for Lisa, which is fine because Luke will not have Bulgarians in Speedos leering at his property. Later, with the soft splash of the Aegean below, Luke and Lisa make love, their honeymoon aerie level with the moon.

2.

arketing director Tom Newton and brand manager Kurt Clarke give Luke Morrow and Neal Hill a tour of Electronic Arts' campus south of San Francisco, where Luke is amazed at the 700,000 square feet of office space. Here, there is a fully-appointed gym and a healthy cuisine cafeteria, both free of charge to Electronic Arts employees.

And it's important for the employees to feel at home, since they're programming computer gaming for the world 24/7. Moreover, once the new millennium comes, dial-up will be dead, and does Luke have DSL? Because gamers will be spending billions of dollars playing each other across the globe. Luke does not have broadband but says he does, further adding that because he's so addicted to Electronic

Arts' *Madden NFL*, he might need to check himself into the Betty Ford Center, even though Luke has only tried *Madden NFL* once before, on Becker and White's PlayStation.

But as long as Luke can turn gleaned information into relative knowledge, he can sell the EA'ers, all the while wishing he were the founder of Electronic Arts—a man on his way to imponderable riches.

∞

Neal Hill heads to wine country with his wife, freeing Luke from having to stay on point during the flight home. Suddenly footloose at the airport, Luke loads up on magazines, but he is not reading *People*, *Spy*, or *Cigar Aficionado* for pleasure. Instead, he buys *Red Herring*, *The Industry Standard*, and *Business 2.0*, for the Internet age is now, and the whole world is transforming, and if a man misses the train, he will be left behind with his horse and buggy.

At baggage claim in Los Angeles with his perk limo driver, Luke reaches Lisa on her cell. She says, "I'm heading home soon. I haven't been feeling well all day."

Luke says, "Do you have a temperature?"

"I don't think so. But can you stop and pick up some chicken soup and seltzer water?"

"Okay, except I won't be there for an hour. My car is still at the office."

The Chrysalis receptionist stops at Lisa's door and says to her, "Can you see one more?"

Lisa shakes her head no to the receptionist and then says to Luke, "I miss you, okay? Hurry home if you can." Luke will try. Lisa leaves her desk for the restroom.

The receptionist watches her go before turning to a man in a wheelchair. "Sir, our apologies, but the counselor you were going to meet with had to leave unexpectedly. Can you come back tomorrow?" The man in the wheelchair is One Leg, hoping for a job.

In the restroom, Lisa is shaking her head in disgust, having suddenly vomited.

∞

Luke sets his suitcase and bag of groceries down on the hall floor and opens the apartment door. He heads for the bedroom with D.D. arfing at his feet. He kisses Lisa hello on her head.

She says, "I threw up twice."

He reaches inside the grocery bag, holding up a box of Lipton chicken soup mix. "I couldn't stop at the deli, so I got you this."

Lisa says, "Maybe just some seltzer."

Luke looks into the bag. "Forgot it."

"What else is in there?"

"Captain Crunch and Stouffer's French Bread Pizza."

"I can't eat that."

Luke says, "It's for me. And guess what? Before I got on the plane, I bought *Red Herring*—you won't believe how thick it is. At least an inch, and there are more ads in it than the fall issue of *Vanity Fair*." Lisa rolls over, weak and dizzy. Luke says, "Think you'll stay home tomorrow? Because then they can come and install DSL."

"I guess."

"Great. Now this cowboy is gonna take a hot shower." Minutes later, standing alone in the tub with the lights off, Luke climaxes against the slippery tile.

∞

Luke removes a tray with untouched soup from the bed, where Lisa and D.D. are asleep. He puts the tray in the kitchen, then channel surfs in the living room, stopping at an infomercial starring Tony Robbins, who vends into the night.

∞

Lisa wakes before dawn still ill, and Luke brings her tea, although he needs to get out the door for his busy day. At 10 a.m., Luke's assistant, Tracy, phones Lisa to tell her Excite@Home will be installing DSL between 1 and 4 p.m.

Meanwhile, Luke is poised to strike at his desk, watching the stock ticker on CNBC. At noon, Luke and his stockbroker act, buying as many shares as Luke can afford, because if an American isn't accumulating CMGI, JDS Uniphase, and Metricom, he's an idiot and deserves to be poor.

∞

Luke returns home at 9:45 p.m. after a business dinner. Lisa is in bed with the covers to her chin. Luke kisses her hello and sits where D.D. was before he cleared her aside. Lisa says, "The guy didn't come until five, and he couldn't get the modem to work for an hour."

"Did you try it out?"

"I went on Amazon and ordered a cookbook."

Luke says, "I can't believe that guy Jeff Bozo is gonna make it. Wait till B. Dalton gets up to speed." Luke goes to the bedroom computer and starts clicking away on Netscape. "Blazing speed. Pretty soon, I won't even have to stop for food. We'll just have WebVan deliver."

"I'm pregnant."

"How is that possible?"

"I forgot my last two pills."

"You criticize me for forgetting seltzer water, but you just forgot your birth control?"

"I'm sorry, it happened."

"'It happened.' Great."

"God, Luke."

"I guess it's settled then. We're having a kid. In the first year we're married."

"I know it's sooner than we planned. I know we said we were going to travel more, but we can take the baby with us. I mean people in Europe, they take their babies with them at the drop of a hat."

Luke goes to the window, looking out over old Santa Monica. "Feels like you've trapped me here."

"Trapped you? I'm your wife." Lisa gets out of bed, grabbing her keys. "D.D.!" She leaves with the worried dog, slamming the door behind her.

In her absence, Luke surfs the Web, until he chooses to find his wife in the parking garage at 12 a.m. He taps her Jetta window but she will not lower it, despite D.D. pining for him from inside the car.

"Not a very good dinner, now that you're eating for two." On the seat next to Lisa is a half-eaten bag of popcorn, a York Peppermint Patty wrapper, and an empty bottle of seltzer water.

Luke goes around to the driver's side and says, "Please, can you just see your way to forgiving me?" He opens the unlocking door and gathers her up in his arms, carrying her into the elevator with D.D. underfoot. Inside the apartment, Luke lays Lisa on the bed and says, "It's just a big shock Lisa, that's all. And maybe it's good that I'm going to New York tomorrow. Gives me time to get used to the idea." Lisa turns away, a tear breaking to her pillow.

∞

Carat USA will buy ad time for Electronic Arts, and it's an art deciding how to spend EA's $30 million dollars. But Saryn Shafer is the 28-year-old media supervisor for Carat on the EA account, and she will capably chart major ad play on ESPN for maximum exposure at reasonable rates. Armani-clad and the only woman in the room, she says her game plan is obvious to all, with a wink that indicates great minds think alike.

For the guys, it's a pleasure watching her busy, slender hands, and each man envisions their slide inside her, into the initial moment of wetness. But that's not going to happen—she's their professional link to television viewer bounty, and she would be horrified to know that she's their fantasy, every 180 seconds.

After a marathon meeting battening down ad placements, during which lunch and then iced-blendeds are ordered in, the team is burnt. However much is accomplished—given Tom Newton and Kurt Clarke are satisfied that their company's marketing money is on track, and not an hour too soon—they have a plane to catch to Tokyo. Neal Hill must get going, too; he and his wife have tickets to the Philharmonic.

So the principals depart, shaking Saryn's hand until next time. Then while she and Luke pack their papers into briefcases, she says, "Do you have plans for dinner?"

Luke says, "I think I'm gonna crash with room service."

"First flight tomorrow?"

"Pretty much."

Saryn says, "C'mon, let me take you out. If I don't show expenses, they freak out."

"Okay, but I can't stay out too late."

"Don't worry, I'll have you in bed by nine."

∞

Luke and Saryn toast their collaboration with Chinese food and cold beer at Shun Lee, as a waiter unloads five dishes. She says, "I think we ordered too much."

"You'll take it home."

"Thank you, Carat USA—food for a week."

Luke pauses, "So what's up with your social life? Stop me if I'm prying."

"Actually Morrow, I'm sorta out of a long-term thing. It would have been three years next month."

"Sorry to hear that. Shafer."

"You have to believe it's for the best."

"Who was he?"

"A lawyer downtown. But you know, he had his place, I had mine; we never moved in together, which says it all."

"Sounds like an amicable split."

"Well, not exactly. We weren't officially broken up when I went to Club Med."

"Don't tell me: You had an affair with a wind surf instructor?"

"Worse. A law student from Duke—a baby, really."

"Cradle-robber Saryn Shafer."

"Spilled my guts out of guilt when I got home, and then it got ugly. I can't believe I'm telling you this."

"It's okay, you're human."

"Except I feel like a machine—all I do is work, and the next guy I meet...it's gonna be rebound central." Again aware of Luke's wedding ring, she says, "Are you and your wife planning kids?"

"Funny you should ask. She's pregnant with my first."

"Oh my God. Why didn't you say something?"

"Well, the whole thing was very unexpected. I mean, we're practically newlyweds."

"But you're gonna make a great dad."

"Any baby would be lucky to have me. Here, let me make you a pancake." Luke fills a mu shu pancake, folding it into an unfolding lump. "Hope you don't mind my fingers."

Feeling a sweet warmth below, Saryn thinks, Too bad he's married; a man like him is almost my type.

∞

Luke settles into first class on American Airlines Flight #1, studying the others up front with him on the marquis flight between New York and LA. Luke wonders about the fifty-something man seated next to him—a big, tanned ego in pinstriped Zegna, slumming commercial while talking stock prices with his employee.

The employee, who is hedgehog-out-of-shape, says, "How'd your Agilent do this week?"

The boss says, "Up $14. I'm buying a buck fifty more."

The employee says, "What do you think of etoys?"

The boss says, "Maybe worth 2,000 shares. Diversify."

Luke reaches for *Forbes* in his seat pocket, nonchalantly dropping, "I'll stick with Metricom."

The boss says, "What's Metricom?"

Luke says, "Wireless networking in the major cities. Paul Allen is behind it with almost a billion invested. I bought $20,000 worth. Now it's worth $80,000."

The boss says, "Decent return, but my protégé here just joined us and he already has holdings of a million nine."

The employee says, "Okay, it took twelve months. But he's got sixty to seventy mil on paper."

The boss adds, "Plus or minus five."

Luke says, "What do you guys do?"

"Venture capital."

The employee nods in deference. "The Managing Director."

The boss holds out his hand. "Bram Brask."

"Luke Morrow."

"What's your business?"

"Advertising account executive in charge of Electronic Arts for Croesus. I just spent thirty million dollars in one hour buying TV ads."

Bram says, "Before I rescued him, he sold airtime for ESPN."

Luke says to the employee, "You're kidding—we're pouring money into ESPN."

"Peter Wessler."

"Luke Morrow. Small world."

Bram asks, "What do you think of the banner-ad model? Are pure content plays the future?"

Luke says, "Just look at TheGlobe.com. Its stock has rocketed, which is proof that traditional media is dead. My Replay stock is already up 30%; viewers are fast forwarding through commercials, and the only way you'll aggregate eyeballs is on the Web. Twenty-five percent of our Electronic Arts buy is targeted for Netscape, AltaVista, and Excite, so you have to be out front to survive." Luke pulls out his card. "There's no better executive to handle your portfolio."

Bram says, "I'm not sure our companies are big enough for you."

"Yet. But we're taking stock in hot start-ups in lieu of fees. You keep money in the business, we get equity down the road."

Bram offers his Camden Capital card. "Maybe we'll have occasion to talk in the future. You on the Westside?"

Luke says, "I'm about to buy in the Palisades."

Bram says, "He just bought a new house."

Peter says, "We had a small ocean-view but we needed more space. He's building on an acre in the Riviera."

Luke says, "Beautiful," raising his orange juice glass. "To the stock market."

Bram and Peter raise back. "To low-hanging fruit."

Peter says, "To the Dow at 30,000. Next five years."

∞

Luke reaches baggage claim and finds his driver holding a "Mr. Morrow" sign. And, though Luke returns to Croesus in Town-Car comfort, his frustration mounts, for Bram Brask is on top of the world, while Luke is trapped in amber.

At his office, Luke hauls his suitcase down the corridor chafing, past Becker and White, who are playing broom hockey with a tennis ball in the hall. Becker says, "Make way for the brain trust."

Luke says, "Spend your lives working for a paycheck—fuck if I care."

Luke reaches Tracy's desk. She says, "How was the flight?"

"Met some heavy hitters, worked 'em over with body blows, and now they're putty in my hands."

But at his desk, Luke can't concentrate, because a bald man is becoming a billionaire at Amazon.com, after summoning the dull inspiration to sell books online. But not Luke—he's stuck on a hamster mill, while the genius founders of Wine.com, Furniture.com, and DrKoop.com burnish The Street.

∞

Luke finishes a memo for upper management, then decides to leave at 4 p.m., as it's Friday and he's done plenty for them. He departs with his back to Stacy, saying, "Did everything get delivered?"

She says, "They confirmed."

"Are you sure?"

"I told you they said yes."

Luke detects indignance in Stacy, and thinks, What the fuck is her problem? It's not like she had to get up at the crack of dawn and catch a plane. And then, for his five-minute drive home to Shoreline Towers, Luke thinks, Kiss my ass, fat bitch. You're lucky to have a boss like me. And stop looking at me like I owe you. Maybe if you'd stop chowing bagels from the meeting platter, you'd have a date!

Luke pushes his apartment door open with his suitcase, finding D.D. hopping at him and Lisa standing in the living room with three dozen roses in vases. Next to her—the finest white Bellini bassinette made. Luke says, "I meant what I said in the card."

Lisa goes to him, burying her face in his shoulder. "I'm so sorry about how I acted, and that I didn't understand at first. And I just want you to know that you're not the only one who's scared."

He puts strong arms around her. "Shh, I'm here."

"I'm just so emotional; my hormones are going crazy."

Luke says, "Hey, do you know how to make a whore moan?"

Boorish old joke, but Lisa can't help but sniffle a laugh. "Shut up, weirdo." Then she asks, "Could we go down to the beach just to talk?"

"I'm beat."

"Please? The ginger ale's chilled." She motions toward a champagne bucket with Canada Dry on ice.

"Can I at least get changed?" Meanwhile, D.D. is pawing at the front door, sure she heard "beach." Luke shakes his head at her. "Forget it; you're not going. No dogs on the sand."

∞

Luke and Lisa spread a blanket on a berm above the sea. Lisa pours ginger ale and they sip, watching the slipping tide. After a while, Luke says, "So what's wrong?"

Toward the setting sun, Lisa says, "I'm stopping the Xanax."

"What did the doctor say?"

"There's a chance it could hurt the baby. He's not really sure."

"So you'll go off it."

"My anxiety will probably return."

"You don't know that."

"I need to conquer it on my own anyway. And Sherri agrees: If I can just get over my fear of losing control, and make peace with my childhood abandonment issues, I'll be cured."

"I hope so."

"Except I keep having dreams I'm gonna be a bad mother, like I'll feel the same way my real mom did about me. But I could never hurt my child, ever. Sherri says I'm a lioness, and that I'll protect my cub to the end."

"She's your therapist; she knows best. And I would just add that, as usual, you're thinking too much."

"I'm stuck with that part, unfortunately."

"It's just a matter of controlling your emotions once and for all. It's not good for anyone having intense feelings. You need to be a happy person, like me."

∞

In the bedroom, Lisa and D.D. sleep on top of the covers with the television flickering on mute. In the living room, Luke opens two UPS packages. One brown mailer contains his college class book, inviting him to his ten-year reunion. Except Luke won't go. He can hardly remember anyone there making an impression on him.

Still, Luke opens the book, finding Fritz Fell smiling on a Scottish golf course with the caption, "Fritz enjoying the good life, after retiring as a Microsoft Millionaire." Then it's on to a photo of Susan Wolfe and her husband, Chuck, in Patagonia, saying how ten years selling at Cisco helped her to buy their freedom. And that's enough for Luke. He dumps the book on the floor.

Now he opens a thinner mailer, containing Tony Robbins' six-CD set, *How to Use Your Personal Power to Create an Extraordinary Life*. Impatient, Luke jumps ahead, putting disc six into the CD player. Listening, he becomes exhilarant, because Tony knows the secret to life.

If a man can become a trend creator and a paradigm shifter, and if he can anticipate and solve human pain on a massive scale, then he will succeed beyond his wildest dreams. Simply ask the questions no one has had the courage to ask, create products that comfort and enhance the quality of life for humanity, and never take no for an answer.

Luke stops the CD, wracking his mind in the dark. How can he save humanity; how can he turn prescience into gold? And then it finally comes to him at 12:50 a.m., in a flash.

∞

Three Brutes and a Big Rig movers finish near sunset, folding moving blankets on the street. Inside the master of their three-bedroom stucco house, Lisa unpacks books from boxes. Luke calls for her from downstairs, and when Lisa appears in the front hall, Luke introduces architect Stewart Ebenhoch and designer Wendy Kendall. Then Luke says, "Let me show you the kitchen." Stewart and Wendy assess the space; it's all about moving walls and installing Viking appliances. Peering into the bathrooms, Stewart and Kendall begin suggesting imported Bisazza tile.

Outside on the canyon slope, Luke shows Stewart where he wants the infinity pool, and Stewart says it's no problem; all you have to do is sink caissons thirty-five feet into the rock to support a retaining wall. Then Stewart asks to take pictures, since that will help him and Wendy price their proposal. It's not until Stewart and Wendy have gone into the kitchen with their camera that Lisa is able to say, "What are they doing here?"

"Neal Hill used them."

"I thought we agreed the house was fine for now."

"You said you didn't want construction while you were pregnant. Doesn't mean we can't draw up plans."

"We stretched for The Bluff Streets, we just leased my Volvo wagon, and you're still gonna have to get a new car in a few months."

Luke says, "My car is fine."

"You're not driving the baby around in a Porsche."

"When we take the baby, we'll go in your car."

Lisa says, "What if I'm out running errands and I want you guys to meet me? How's that going to work?"

"I'm not giving up my car."

"Okay, then we're not throwing money around here either. I don't need perfection."

Luke says, "It's not about perfection. It's about my being able to have clients over and the house looking great."

"What happened to 'All we need is a solid starter house for our baby?'"

"Your words, I believe, and in the unlikely event we need cash, we can always tap into your college trust fund—which you've never used."

"That money is for emergencies or our child's education, or maybe I will go back to school."

"Exactly. My money is your money and your money is your money."

"Enough with that—such bullshit!"

"Right, and if someone would just knock some sense into you, you'd realize that you have the best husband in LA."

"Well, we got what we need." Stewart and Wendy have returned from inside. Luke, Lisa, and D.D. escort them out the front courtyard, Luke thanking them for coming on such short notice.

Stewart and Wendy step through the gate, making way for a Vittorio's Pizza boy. D.D. barks expectantly and Luke says, "That's right, you shall beg for sausage." To Lisa he says, "Happy Valentine's Day, anyway." He pays for the surprise pizza, which he custom-ordered in the shape of a heart. But Luke points out that if you turn the pizza around, it also resembles a saggy bosom, which causes Lisa to laugh despite herself.

Caving, she kisses Luke, saying, "You're a piece of work, you know that?"

"You too."

∞

Lisa sleeps on Luke's chest on a chaise lounge on the deck outside their bedroom, and they are wrapped in blankets against the night air. On a teak table nearby—the remnants of the valentine's pizza. Below the table is D.D., snuffling in a ball. Luke tries to sleep too, but he can't because crackling in the chaparral below is annoying him. As the sounds become louder, Luke says, "Did you hear that?" But Lisa doesn't stir. Luke tries to rouse her. "I better put you to bed."

He helps her rise, guiding her into the darkened room, where she waits patiently in shadows. He helps her lose her bra from underneath her tee, and she shimmies out of her jeans. He lays her down, tucking her in.

Returning to the deck, Luke squints into the brush toward the crackling. There, under a spare moon, he glimpses a rat making its way onto the property. The rat sniffs at Luke, before it jumps the trunk of Luke's lemon tree and snatches a lemon twice the size of its head.

Luke dashes downstairs. At the edge of the canyon, Luke chunks a brick in the rat's direction, causing a trickling of dirt and rocks downhill in the dark. Luke returns to the bedroom, herding D.D. to her inside mat. He lies down next to Lisa, only now there's rude scampering across the roof. Luke opens his eyes, vengeful, for the Palisades' rats are mocking him, and he will not rest until they're dead.

3.

Lisa is sixteen weeks pregnant, and she and Luke will see if it's a boy or girl today via ultrasound. But learning the baby's sex is always up for debate, and the blonde woman who shares the waiting room with them has decided not to find out. She already has two sons and hates to say it, but she wants to prolong the dream of having a girl. The woman is Keri Brask, and she has a reassuring way about her as she discusses her and Lisa's pregnancies. Still, in the middle of the conversation, panic rakes Lisa.

Luke, blank to his wife's unease, is reading *Vanity Fair*'s "New Media Power 100," angry at his lot, knowing that he will never make the list. And he will never know that Keri is thinking about how lucky Lisa is to have a supportive husband like Luke. Keri's husband Bram is on yet another plane back to Wall Street and is always able to leave his wife when business calls. That's the contract Keri made—being a younger, engaging wife to an older, powerful man. And when the Morrows are finally called into the examining room, Keri wishes them well, saying, "Being a parent is the greatest gift."

∞

Dr. Yellen is hands-on, performing the ultrasound herself. In a minute, the news is it's a boy, and there is general excitement until Lisa suddenly starts to pale. Dr. Yellen props Lisa up, saying that blood pressure can suddenly drop during the second trimester. But Lisa's consciousness is emotionally ruled, and she does not confess her anxiety disorder to Dr. Yellen out of embarrassment; instead, Lisa tries to staunch the panic right there. Then, for no apparent reason, the worst is past, as Lisa regains a tenuous hold of herself. Ten minutes later, chilled from cooling sweat, she leaves the office with Luke and a printout of their son.

∞

Luke and Lisa ride in silence to Orso restaurant, where they receive a garden table. They order bottled water, and by time the bucatini arrives, their marriage is barren in the heat of the day. And that is more than Lisa can bear. She becomes hollow and nihilistically scared, which forces her from her chair to the restaurant's entrance, where she blacks out.

Luke finds her, and there's much kneeling commotion about her condition. A moment more and she's coming to, sipping water, while Orso's manager wants to call an ambulance. Lisa pleads no, that she just got overheated, and soon she is on her feet, shaky. Luke drives her home, tears of shame filling her eyes.

∞

Luke brakes the Porsche into their Palisades driveway, saying, "What are you going to do now?"

"I'll be okay. I have to finish a report for the board, and I'll try to rest."

Luke nods. Lisa gets out. He revs away. Inside the house, Lisa goes to the second bedroom that will be the nursery. The room is empty, save for a white crib and D.D. nosing around in shopping bags. Lisa gets to work hanging a wallpaper runner of cows jumping over moons. Outside, Lisa plants giant sunflower seeds in buckets, telling D.D. how she hopes the stalks will grow tall, so the flowers will bloom through the baby's windows. Calmed, Lisa thinks that maybe she can go to yoga. Yes, she has to get out and stave off thoughts of agoraphobia. She pets D.D. farewell, then bravely drives to YogaWorks on Main Street for an intermediate class.

Jittery that fear will seize her again, Lisa begs her mind to concentrate on deep breathing until she finally relaxes, eight minutes before the class comes to a close. Grateful with thoughts that she can function, she shops at the organic vegetable market up the street, then makes a pleasing purchase of wild salmon at Santa Monica Seafood. Returning home, she calls Luke from her cell. "I'm fine now. I went to yoga."

"You should go every day."

"What time can you come home?"

"Not till late."

"I have artichokes, and I'm going to barbeque salmon."

"Neal Hill and I have to meet Tom and Kurt for dinner, then I've got to get back to the office to write a production schedule."

"What time will you finish?"

"If it's before eleven, it'll be a miracle."

"I really wanted to cook for you tonight."

"It's okay, you enjoy it."

Ninety minutes later, Lisa steams an artichoke and grills the salmon with rosemary from the garden. She eats alone with D.D. on the canyon patio, where a final burst of cold sun dips behind the ridge.

∞

Lisa and D.D. alternate taking bites of an ice cream bar while watching Antiques Roadshow on the bed. At 8:15 p.m., the phone rings. Lisa races to grab it, hoping it's Luke calling, saying, "Hang in there, Sweetie, I'm coming home early." Only it's not Luke on the line; it's Neal Hill.

Neal says, "Sorry to call you at home. I just have a quick question for Luke."

Lisa tightens. "Thought you guys were having dinner?"

"Not that I know of."

"Then he's probably at the office."

Neal says, "I already tried."

"On his cell, then. He's not here."

"How've you been feeling?"

"A lot better. I'm starting to get my energy back."

"How long will you stay at Chrysalis?"

"A couple more months, at the most."

"Well when you're up for it, let's all get together again."

"Sure, of course. Would love to see you."

Neal says goodbye and Lisa hangs up, not remembering a word he said. And when Luke crawls into their bed reeking of Boucheron at 1:30 a.m., Lisa is wide awake with her eyes shut tight. And it isn't until Luke kisses her forehead that she feels the full dose of devastation.

∞

Lisa never falls asleep, the guillotine of betrayal annihilating impure truths, until morning light seeps into the hills. Luke yawns out of bed and takes a long shower, before rubbing Lisa goodbye. He tells her to stay in bed since it's Saturday, and that he will call her from San Francisco after his meeting.

In the garage, Luke slings his suitcase into his Boxster, but as he starts the engine, he sees he's not alone. Lisa, vagrant in T-shirt and panties, is fixed on him from the back hall stoop. Luke powers down his window. "I should be home by noon Sunday."

Lisa holds up his dress shirt. "Where were you at 8:15 last night?"

Luke will tell. "Okay, I won't lie. Neal and I went to a strip club and had a lap dance. It was spur-of-the-moment."

"To blow off some steam."

"Exactly." Luke heads out with a wave, but Lisa has already disappeared into the house.

∞

The New Economy is permanent—unless a man's brain-dead head is in the sand. And he cannot believe the thrill of a weekend lunch in Palo Alto under gentle winds. Inside Il Fornaio, Luke is in his right time and place among the world's best and brightest. Seated across from him is Eric Duncan, dressed like everyone else in black cotton slacks and a blue button-down shirt.

It's miraculous how Eric has gone from a failed investment banker to head of business development for the venture capital group for Excite@Home—all within eight months. But that's how it works—arrogant Old Economy horses rear, and before a flunky can feel his broken neck, he's got an amazing new job with millions in stock.

And, as fortune always shines on Stanford University alums, Eric is a former fraternity brother of Luke's, and is forever remembering Luke, who led the plunder of a San Jose flower farm one immortal night, when the brothers needed leis for their spring luau party. Over pizza margheritas, Luke continues his pitch, praising Eric's exemplary intelligence. Eric is receptive; his job is to bundle the next revenue-producing enhancements for broadband, and he's actually had similar ideas himself.

So Luke is onto something big; people do miss their children and pets, and with simple webcams, they can view their families over the Internet from anywhere. Imagine an Electronic Arts programmer creating into the night, never seeing his baby. Now, from his computer, he can watch his wife nursing.

But will the innovation become viral? Will people pay for the service on top of DSL, and at what price? Can Luke guarantee sticky eyeballs? Understand that the venture group doesn't want to be in the installation business; the cameras and software have to be plug and play, and what exactly is Luke bringing to the table, except his ideas?

Luke says, "Ten years of marketing experience from Croesus," but more importantly, he has a compelling, humanistic story to tell—one that will appeal to millions across the globe. He says, "Make me head of the start-up under your umbrella, and we'll figure out the business. Don't cede the future to others!"

Except he can't fund a new company without technical know-how. Can Luke meet with a group of programmers who've already made an appeal to Excite@Home? They are Cal Tech PhD candidates in parallel processing who are proposing a live video email service, though Eric says there's no money in that. But maybe if Luke married his ideas to their ability to send full-motion video packets across the Internet cloud, there might be a chance.

Writing on a napkin next, Eric says, "Here's their number in Los Angeles. Join forces with them and come back to us with a business plan and a white paper." Luke will, hearing, 'Return organized and we will fund your team, pushing the envelope to a record-breaking IPO.'

After lunch, Eric chats it up at the valet with various Internet CEOs, all under thirty, and Luke cannot believe their camaraderie. When Eric introduces Luke as the potential founder of a new Excite division, Luke feels like a rock star, since the others are looking at him like, 'How come we don't know you yet—another visionary?'

After Eric pulls away in his waxed Range Rover, Luke strides down University Avenue, a king in the making—even though he has no idea what *video packets* or *Internet cloud* or *white paper* mean. Before heading to his motel, Luke stops at the Stanford Shopping Center, where he stocks up on black pants and blue button-down shirts.

∞

Lisa can't eat, but she must not allow trauma trim to harm her baby. For her child alone, she scrambles three eggs, forcing forkfuls down. Then the phone rings; it's her sister Becca, at last.

Lisa says, "I want to die."

Becca says, "You will survive this."

"Why did he do it?"

"Do you know who she is? Have you listened to his voice mail?"

"I don't have the password."

"I'll break in."

"What am I gonna do?"

"You're gonna take care of your baby, and you're gonna start saving moving money."

"Mom doesn't know."

"I'll tell her."

"But not Dad, not now. Why did this happen to me?"

"Because your husband is a fucking asshole, that's why."

∞

Women have game plans too, and a cheating man will never know when their strategies are in motion. Devastated women needing to survive can act like nothing has happened at all.

∞

Mid-morning on Sunday, Lisa's husband returns home. She has brunch ready and waiting. On the table are homemade waffles with imported French preserves and applewood bacon, like they serve at the Auberge du Soleil in Napa. Hazelnut coffee too, served in one-of-a-kind Italian pottery cups, from their wedding registry at Cottura in the Century City Mall.

The big food makes her hubby happy. He says, "I'm leaving Croesus and putting an Internet company together."

"The agency is finally giving you a long-term contract, and you're walking away?"

Gorging, Luke says, "My shot at the big time."

"What about the Electronic Arts guys—Neal, and whatever her name is from Carat?"

"Saryn Shafer."

"I thought you said they were the best group you've ever worked with."

"They are, but I'd rather make $100 million."

"Okay, but we're about to have a baby, and we have a new house that we can barely afford. What if it doesn't work out?"

"Okay—you have no imagination. At all."

He rises from the table and leaves the house, and he does not return until after dinner, when he walks right past Lisa, going straight to bed. And while he is sleeping scot-free, the call comes.

Lisa says, "How'd you get it?"

Becca says, "Men are so basic. You want their voice mail code, just try their birth date or their social security number."

"What is it?"

"His birthday."

"You're amazing."

"Don't listen to them, Lisa. There are over twenty old messages. You just need to make your plans. Promise me you won't listen to them."

Lisa promises, but at 3 a.m. she does listen to them, and they are: "Hi, it's me." "I'm at baggage claim." "I'm almost at the hotel." "I'm under the covers naked for you."

∞

At 10:49 p.m., Lisa becomes exactly seven months pregnant, and the next morning at 11 a.m., she is in a conference room in Beverly Hills meeting her new divorce attorney. Two billing hours later, she and her attorney have agreed on a plan. Lisa will endure her fucked-up marriage until Luke's Internet company is formed. He hatched the business during their marriage; half his granted stock will be hers, and 50% of nothing could be worth a shitload someday.

∞

Luke meets the Cal Tech PhDs for the first time at Koo Koo Roo Chicken, where they can safely talk under the lunchtime din. But the three PhDs aren't minted yet; they are Korean engineers on student visas, supporting their studies programming for DARPA—the Defense Advanced Research Projects Agency. What they're actually doing for the U.S. government is top secret, and has Luke ever had bulgogi wood barbeque, because there's a place they'd like to take him on Western Avenue, where he'll be the only Caucasian.

After cookies at Mrs. Field's next door, Luke and the Koreans are partners—that's how fast new companies gel for the Web. Byung-Jun Kim, a stout, mousse-spiked 27-year-old with a sardonic wit, will be the Chief Technology Officer. Francis Oh, silent and courtly at thirty-four in a wrinkle-free blazer and grandfather slacks, will be the Chief Operating Officer. Joey Wook, twenty-one and bony with Japanese couture bifocal rims, will be the Chief Scientist, reporting to Byung-Jun, since only Byung-Jun knows what the youngster is talking about. Luke announces that he will be Chief Executive Officer, and the Koreans accede, insecure about their English.

Now all that's left is a contract between them, which Luke will have a lawyer draw up. A tentative time is set to sign the partnership agreement at Luke's house in a week, but until then, they exchange joyous dap because they are the founders of MyWorld.com.

∞

Lisa is on the second story landing of her house, straining to hear the heated talk below. She feels debased by spying, but her divorce attorney says she must ascertain MyWorld's value—for her and her unborn child.

In the dining room, the Koreans are fraught, given the contract before them is a stunning squeeze. That's because Luke has given himself 70% of the company. And when everyone's stakes are further diluted for the law firm, taking two points in lieu of up-front fees, Byung-Jun, Francis, and Joey's shares are less than 10% each. Byung-Jun says, "This is crap. We're equal partners with you!"

Luke says, "Okay, but the problem is, you have no meaningful application for your technology."

Byung-Jun says, "We have VideoEmailPopster.com!"

"There's no money in that. Without my ideas, you're dead in the water."

Joey says, "Without our algorithms, you're dead in the water!"

Luke says, "Ideas that can be monetized rule. Eric Duncan is backing my concept, and if you force his hand, he'll just go to India for programming, for me."

The Koreans share grim looks.

Francis says, "You're a very tough businessman."

Luke says, "I negotiate for my company like I negotiate for myself. You'll be lucky having me as the boss."

∞

With the signed partnership as his first step to fame, Luke wants to celebrate. He tells Lisa, "Let's take a drive," and she is game, keeping up appearances as a benchmark wife. Off they go to Ojai Hot Springs in the Boxster, but Lisa won't sit in a hot tub there—it's bad for the baby—and she will forego a massage, not wanting to be handled in her bloated state. No matter; she will read *What to Expect While You're Expecting* in the shade until brunch.

Free, Luke takes a hot tub in his assigned raftered stall, and in its planked privacy, he takes hold of himself until his climax is left for others—a strand of poached egg swirling. During his massage, he loses his spa towel, flipping to his stomach, so that he can show off his big dick to the hippie-chick masseuse. Then it's time for another climax, leisurely in the shower, before brunch with his wife.

∞

Outside under an umbrella, Luke and Lisa silently regard the menu. And when he downs a second mimosa without notice of her, Lisa can bide her soul no more. She says, "So Saryn Shafer's your girl, isn't she?"

"Yes."

∞

On the drive home, they don't speak, now that Lisa is dead inside. Curling back onto the freeway, Luke offers, "This whole fatherhood thing—it's a suit that doesn't fit me."

"How do you afford yourself that luxury?"

The car presses onward in traffic, solemn into the haze.

4.

The judge's order is: Luke may not be in the delivery room with Becca, and Luke is outraged at Lisa's bitter request, as it's his baby too. The day-old ruling should be challenged before the Supreme Court, and Luke would appeal the injustice for fathers everywhere, except Lisa has been induced and the baby is just hours away.

Stranded in the waiting area when he's the father, Luke can't look at either Pat Hudson or Stan Hudson, who said he would shoot Luke if it were legal. But it isn't, Stan, Luke thinks, and I'd shoot you first anyway.

Stan smiles weakly over at Luke, trying to blunt the fuse. "Should be anytime now."

"Yup."

Pat smiles with unraveling worry at Luke; now she has an ex-son-in-law who hates her, and what if he prevents her from seeing her grandson? Calamitous—a ruined old age.

∞

At 4:30 a.m., the boy is born. He is five pounds, barely, and he will be Trevor Morrow, a name haggled out between plaintiff Lisa and respondent Luke. Further to the stipulation, Trevor is to be placed within fifteen minutes in his father's arms outside of the delivery room for at least five minutes, but not more than twenty, should the baby have no complications. Trevor has none that he knows of yet, and when the nurse fixes him in his daddy's arms, the baby opens his eyes for a worldly peek before sinking back into slumber.

Luke takes in Trevor's teacup face, and as the boy definitely looks more like him, that's enough for Luke, for now. Luke returns Trevor to the nurse after one minute, and she is startled at the hand-back, but he's not the first new confused father. Luke quickly departs the hospital for his and Lisa's house, where there will never be an infinity pool.

∞

When the house sells in the divorce, Luke will happily take half of the Hudson's wedding present down payment—thanks again, Mom and Dad. And maybe the dollars he's spending now are a treat from those proceeds, since the girl

Luke selects from The Erotic Review charges $250 for a sensual massage.

The call today is Amber, a Marina-based alley kitten who was born in Ohio but lived a whole six months in Britain, which explains her archduchess accent. Soon Amber is at Luke's door; she had no trouble finding the place at the crack of dawn, given she's been there before, when Lisa was planning Trevor's baby shower with Becca on a weekend away in Berkeley.

Up to the master bed Luke and Amber go, and she is a solid eight for looks, though other, less-exacting reviewers like FAMOUS MD give her a ten. But she's only a seven across the board for performance. By The Erotic Review's definition, that suggests a well-executed hand job or Hot Time, further indicating Amber doesn't provide oral (8—Went the Extra Mile), intercourse (9—Forgot it Was a Service), or anal (10—Once in a Lifetime). But a seven is better than a four (She Just Laid There) or worse, two (Barely Worth the Effort). Luke is pleased to be her first of the day, i.e., she's baby powder-fresh.

Off comes her Dress for Less Pucci top and white capri pants, revealing a shiny purple G-string that she dangles to the floor. Now Amber gives Luke a two-minute, no-effort back rub.

He turns to his stomach, ready, and she drizzles oil from on high, showing dark roots in her henna part. Alabaster ass grazing his brow, she strokes him while Luke applies oil to his forefingers, which he strokes between her thighs. But she snaps, "No, lavender doesn't agree with me!" Chastened, Luke immediately stops, wanting to show that he understands R.E.S.P.E.C.T.

When his climax comes, she backs away, not wanting it on her where he's aiming. But that's forgiven, after she wipes his belly puddle away with Lisa's face towel. And as Amber slides the nightstand money into her macramé purse, Luke luxuriates on his bed, feeling exquisitely happy, like he has before during some profitless past. When Amber lets herself out downstairs, Luke briefly thinks, I have a son, before he ascends into a gorgeous sleep.

∞

Luke wakes at 8:30 a.m. He dials Neal Hill to tell him the good news, saying, "It was all very last-minute. Lisa went in for another ultrasound, but there wasn't much fluid, so the doctors induced her. I left her for an hour, came home for some clothes, and eighteen hours later, the baby was born!"

Neal congratulates Luke and says, "Enjoy your week off."

He shall, but not how Neal Hill thinks. Luke does not say anything about his impending divorce, and he will continue to wear his wedding ring when he returns, because why explain inconsequence?

Luke hangs up and begins his second life. Act One starts with an express check-out of his Palisades house, where he has lived in the den for weeks with Lisa enraged around him, especially during chance meetings in the kitchen.

This occurred because they could not agree on a temporary custody arrangement for their impending child until the final hour. Because if Luke left on his own accord, the state of California might say he abandoned his unborn baby, and Luke will not have Lisa painting him evil.

The resulting custody decision is that Luke may visit his son every day for forty-five minutes in the morning and forty-five minutes in the evening with Lisa somewhere present, and Luke has to give her a one-hour warning before he arrives. But Luke won't have time to come around when his son comes home from the hospital, because he must travel.

∞

Vases of flowers from Neal Hill and Tracy arrive for Lisa, but they topple over on the stoop in wind with no one to receive them. And Tracy is so upset that Luke didn't phone her about Trevor's birth that she officially begins looking for a new job. Becker and White messenger over a Tiffany child's comb to Luke with a card that reads, "In case your boy is hairy like you."

But the comb goes missing, carried off by an opossum that night, and who cares? Luke will not write thank-you notes to his co-workers anyway, given his commencing plan. Which is to find a crash pad before jetting to Chicago to raise capital for MyWorld.com.

∞

Luke loads his suitcase into the Boxster before returning to Shoreline Towers, where he swiftly rents an ocean-facing penthouse at top dollar, which is only fair since the frozen marital asset decree says he is entitled to the same lifestyle as Lisa. Then it's off to short-term parking at LAX and an upgrade to first class, where Luke hones his speech to the investors who anxiously await his arrival.

∞

When Luke's sister, Sara, sees him emerge from baggage claim at O'Hare, she hastens from her Toyota Corolla, throwing her arms around him, holding him dear. Luke remembers to appear devastated, and he pets her hair in gratitude for her empathy.

"Thanks for picking me up."

"Of course."

"What about Kit?"

"She's with Michael. They're picking up Chinese food from Hong's."

Luke sighs as if shell-shocked. "Time heals all wounds, right?"

Sara nods as if to indicate yes, that's what they say.

On the toll road, Luke stares ahead, conveying clinical depression. Until he says, "Why did my wife do it?"

"Oh, sweetie."

"We're married less than a year and she starts an affair with Tom Bowman. While she's pregnant!"

"She's sick."

"Maybe because Tom is powerful—with his millions in Electronic Arts stock."

"You're better off."

"If it weren't for Trevor, I would smash her head on a rock."

∞

Michael and Kit are in the driveway, just coming home themselves. Michael sets the Chinese takeout on his minivan hood, welcoming Luke with brotherly back pats and words of sympathy. Kit looks up, wide-eyed, at her uncle, and Sara says, "I think she's hoping for See's."

Luke says, "See's?"

"Don't you always bring See's suckers?"

"I do?"

Michael says, "I bought a double-order of lobster in black bean sauce."

Luke says, "That's too expensive."

"Sometimes you gotta splurge, plus I saved a pretty penny collecting overdue fines." Luke nods; he's never liked Michael's Chicago sense of humor.

Sara says to Luke, "Why don't you take Kit upstairs so she can show you her beads." To Kit, she says, "Your uncle is gonna play with you now. How about that?" Kit goes up the brick steps into the house, and Luke follows his autistic niece with a last, doleful look back at his siblings, that they would take him in.

∞

Upstairs, Kit begins lining up her beads by color. Luke stands at her bedroom door, bored out of his mind.

∞

At their breakfast nook table, Michael and Sara close their eyes for grace, Sara joining hands with Luke. But Luke is trying to ignore Kit, who stares at him, transfixed. He could clasp her tiny palm, but maybe she's putting a hex on him, and will she ever speak? Weird little goblin.

Luke heaps lobster on his plate, taking both big claws. Sara and Michael are just grateful he's able to eat, given what he's been through.

Finally Michael says, "Must be really tough on you, being here the same day your son is born."

"It is, but the witch's family is with her at the hospital, and I can't be around those trolls after what she's done. I just thought it was best to get away for the night, to begin 'the healing.'"

Lisa says, "Probably not good for a newborn anyway, all that tension."

Luke says, "Believe me, my thought too. I'm trying to act in Trevor's best interests—until he can get to know me in peace, not pain."

"Are you sure you won't stay another day? We're taking Kit to the Children's Symphony and Greektown for lunch."

"I wish I could. It wouldn't be right. I have to get back."

Michael says, "Truth be told, we never trusted Lisa from the get-go. At your wedding when we were leaving, I kissed her goodbye and said 'Good luck,' and she goes, 'Good luck—what do you mean by that?'"

Sara says, "As if he was saying: 'Good luck—odds are you'll end up divorced.' It was really awkward. He only meant her well."

Luke says, "Apparently one never really knows what's under the hood until it's too late." He looks down as if he might cry.

But Michael helps stave off Luke's tears. "So, we've given more thought to your enterprise."

Sara says, "We like the name."

Luke brightens. "MyWorld.com—it works."

Michael says, "We think it's got a good premise."

Luke says, "So obvious; go to a browser on your computer at the library and see Kit anytime."

Michael says, "We've batted it around, and we're thinking $5,000."

"Five K? No, if you want to be an early-stage investor, it's $75,000 per one-third point. What I told you on the phone."

Sara and Michael are pure nerves. Michael says, "Look, we want in."

Luke says, "If you owned $10,000 worth of Apple stock at the beginning, you'd have like $18 million today. So you can't be afraid, or you'll be punching a clock the rest of your life."

Michael knows he's in over his head, but how can he pass up unimaginable riches? "Can we just think about it a little more? We won't hold you up."

Luke says, "Take all the time you need, although my tech guys are bringing in angel money as we speak, so if you wait too long, there might not be room."

∞

Luke and Kit sit on opposite ends of the couch eating popsicles, the television tuned to CNBC. After Michael and Sara clean up from dinner, they make their way into the den. Putting an arm around Sara, Michael says, "We really appreciate your flying out here and taking the time to talk about your ideas, and even though we know it's a chance to get on the ground floor of what you're doing, we think we'd better take a raincheck."

Luke says, "Because what—you don't believe in me?"

Sara says, "That's not true. We think you're totally brilliant, but with all of Kit's special needs, it's just too risky. I mean—we're just making ends meet, and we're still saving to fix the broken furnace."

Luke says, "What about your inheritance from Dad?"

Michael says, "I'll drive you to the airport in the morning. What time should I set the alarm?"

"Don't bother. I'll take a car."

Sara says, "Please don't be angry, Luke."

"I'm not angry. Just sleep in. It's the least I can do for your generosity."

∞

Luke shivers all night with no heat in the den. Then when the livery's high beams pierce the dawn, Luke hurriedly escapes the house, stepping over lobster shells strewn across the driveway.

∞

Luke curses at the jam in his world at O'Hare airport, and maneuvering through the crowded terminal, he chafes, 'Stuck behind the two-thirds of Americans who are obese,' and 'Bet you're all hoping for fried Twinkies in your Bistro Boxes, aren't you?'

That, and 'I will survive my start-up costs without you, Sara and Michael—many thanks for wasting my time.' Starving and too early for his flight, Luke waits in a crawling line at McDonald's, and if the Filipina yentas manning it would stop idly chatting with each other, imbecilic to their required speedy service to The Customer, he might get his Egg McMuffin.

An hour later, Luke finally calms in first class, when the married stewardess says, "Mimosa?"

Sure, and as she hands him back his drink, Luke says, "The last time I had a mimosa in Ojai, my soon-to-be ex-wife spoiled it for me." The stewardess smiles supportively, even though that's way too much information.

Luke has three more mimosas in quick succession, and sundering into sleep, he thinks, You know you want it on the galley floor, American Airlines MILF. But she cannot see into his dreams, where she's on her back for pay all the way to LA.

∞

The 1950s Park La Brea apartment complex rises over 167 acres east of the Westside, boasting a Miracle Mile address. But to Luke, the eighteen thirteen-story concrete towers are a dreary Soviet gulag, imprisoning the city's middle class.

Still, a Park La Brea two-bedroom apartment is a serviceable space: the rent is reasonable, and don't tell the leasing office the unit is being used for a business or they will kick MyWorld.com out.

Luke rings the 50-year-old ding-dong bell from the linoleum corridor, then pounds on the cracked varnish door of 9E, Tower 11 for over a minute until Joey Wook answers, wiping Mr. Sandman from his eyes. Luke says, "It's 11 a.m."

Joey says, "We're up all night."

Luke enters the apartment for the first time, where leftover Yoshinoya Beef Bowls compost on windowsills. And on the conference card table—a dozen Styrofoam cups of expired, cold coffee, since no one can ever remember which one is theirs. Luke says, "What a pigsty. Don't you understand I'm footing 70% of the bill?"

Joey gathers the cups, "Yeah, so we keep one-third a dump the way we like."

"Funny. The other très stooges?"

Joey points. "Your office."

Luke tramps to a bedroom, where Byung-Jun and Francis are cadaverous on futons, sandwiched between piles of dirty laundry. Luke says, "Might you be getting to work sometime soon?"

Byung-Jun cracks open an eye. "We didn't go to bed till 6 a.m."

"For your information, I was up at 5 a.m. in Chicago on the company's behalf, and I came straight here from the airport. So the company's first rule is: we're keeping regular hours."

"And second rule is: not how we work." This from Francis, who shields himself from the sun as Luke yanks back the curtains, saying, "And this is my office."

Byung-Jun says, "You want an office, use the other bedroom."

Luke heads that way, but it's filled floor-to-ceiling with computer servers, boxes of programming books, and code printouts. Luke returns to Byung-Jun and Francis, saying, "Okay, the head of the card table will be my office."

Byung-Jun says, "Now you're acting like a start-up CEO."

Joey says, "Chief Technology Officer rules, third rule."

Francis says, "Bulgogi brunch?"

Luke says, "God help all of you."

∞

By the crack of 1:37 p.m. after a bulgogi run, MyWorld.com is a juggernaut, firing on all pistons, as they say. Byung-Jun, Francis, and Joey have brought in other Korean computer wizards, and now there are twelve countrymen total. They are swigging Red Bulls while debating algorithms on dry erase boards. But the boys speak in a strange tongue, and Luke has no idea what they're saying, though it's surely game-changing and on the fringes of possible math.

At the head of the card table, Luke savors his leadership, having struck a second hard bargain: Byung-Jun, Francis, and Joey must dilute their 9% shares to give ownership to the programmers they've hired, since the triumvirate originally said they could do all the work themselves. But Luke will continue to make a 70% contribution for office supplies, which is the least he can do.

Moreover, Luke is always worth his weight in gold, given he's writing a stellar business plan. And creative selling is second nature to Luke; he admires every page he constructs. See how perfectly he crops photos from the Web, showing a businessman at a computer screen, with arrows to pictures of the businessman's wife and children, indicating MyWorld's connective power.

At 4 p.m., Luke's head is pounding, plus he has an important reason to cut out early. He says to his partners, "By the way, my son was born yesterday."

Byung-Jun, Francis, and Joey look hurt. Byung-Jun says, "Wow, congrats. But why didn't you tell us?"

"Thought you would have remembered to ask."

"What's his name?"

"Trevor—my first choice after Luke, Jr. Also, Lisa and I are separating." With no more light shed, Luke takes his backpack and heads for the hall. But sensing his partners' concern, he turns and says, "It's nothing; it's amicable, don't worry." Only, Byung-Jun, Francis, and Joey will worry after the door bangs shut, for who is his wife, really, and what will happen when Lisa has a 35% say?

∞

Luke swings by the Bel Air Hotel to get Saryn, who is in a Los Angeles meeting with the NBC marketing group. The

Boxster knifes through traffic, banking turns on Sunset Boulevard to Luke's Palisades house.

Remaining in the car wearing a Princess Grace scarf and Gucci shades, Saryn gets her first glimpse of Lisa, who confronts Luke at the front door. Lisa says, "What's she doing here?"

"Don't worry, she doesn't want to come in."

"How dare you."

Luke says, "It's not like she hasn't been inside before. Now let me in. You've had fair warning."

Lisa lets him pass, as she must. On his way upstairs to the bassinette, Luke says, "Where's your mother?"

"She left with Mariela for an hour. Please be gone before she returns."

"Note to file: Lisa needs to work on irrational anger."

"Fuck off. Fucking hell!"

Luke goes to the crib, where Trevor naps. Luke stands over him a moment, then sits in the rocker. A minute more and Luke's on his way downstairs and out the door.

Lisa says, "Where are you going?"

"Shower for two, then room service."

"Despicable. Couldn't even spend ten minutes with your son."

"Not much to do at this point."

"How about change a diaper?"

"Oh, here we go. I'm a chauvinist pig. You know, Lisa, most women would be thrilled to have a nanny. Try showing some gratitude." Lisa slams the door, then claps the plantation blinds shut.

In the Porsche, Saryn says, "She's a classic woman scorned."

Luke says, "I told you she was psycho."

∞

Standing lithe in their hotel lair, Saryn reaches around Luke from behind into his boxers. Luke says, "I could hang a wet beach towel from it when I was fifteen."

Saryn presses her cheek against his back. "Hmm, then I am lucky, aren't I?" Through the window, framed with fiery bougainvillea, a hummingbird whirs away and Saryn goes for a ride—gonzo cowgirl. And she is thinking, I love my new man. He is going to be huge in business too, and his wife was too stupid to know what she had.

∞

Luke leaves Saryn at 2 a.m. She needs the rest anyway, as her breakfast with NBC is only six hours away. But Luke's power is a strong aphrodisiac, and she must pleasure herself once more before she can fall asleep.

Inside Croesus at 2:45 a.m., Luke copies his computer rolodex onto floppies, then sets his miniature Zen garden in a file box. Pictures of Lisa go plunk into the trash on Luke's way to human resources, where he slides a letter of resignation under the door. On the way out, Luke collects Becker and White's brooms and tennis ball, pitching them into the parking lot dumpster.

∞

Luke sleeps supremely until his cell buzzes at 10:30 a.m. On the other end is his divorce attorney, Ellen. She says, "I just got a fax from her lawyer. They're filing a stipulation to prevent you from leaving your job."

"A waste of time and money. I'm inches away from my own Internet company."

"What will be your compensation?"

"Up front, a third of what I made."

"The judge can say you took the job to avoid paying child support on your old salary basis."

"But that's a fucking lie."

"Okay, but it's still likely he'll make you contribute according to what you used to earn, even if you're not earning that anymore."

"Let me ask you a question, Ellen. Do you believe in equality of the sexes?"

"Luke—"

"No no, keep with me here. If women want to be equal to men, shouldn't they pay the same amount for their child?"

"The judge won't see it that way."

"Make him see it that way. That's why you get the big bucks." Luke picks up call waiting.

"Luke Morrow, Eric Duncan."

"What's up, brother?"

Duncan says, "I need your white paper and business plan by noon tomorrow."

"Uh, okay—but I thought we had two more weeks."

"We got forty-eight proposals sitting here, the door closes at fifty, and we're picking the best three. Get in the pile before it's too late."

"We'll be up all night."

"You should have been up all night since we met."

"Well my tech guys have."

"Dude, this is the Internet. If you don't like the pace, move on."

Duncan hangs up, leaving Luke exploding from the bed.

∞

Written urgently on the dry erase board: THESE ARE THE TIMES THAT TRY MENS' SOULS, and IMAGINE YOUR MILLIONS!!! Below the words, a mad scramble as the Koreans' hands clack across keyboards, trying to explain sure-fire technology.

They are saying, "Here's MyWorld's proprietary Bandwidth Broker, an algorithmic wonder that, coupled with The Video Agent, forms an efficient heterogeneous parallel processing architecture for guaranteed levels of service for multimedia streaming.

"It's all quite simple: video streams are trafficked through either The Greedy Algorithm, The Best Fit Algorithm, or The First Fit Algorithm. Any variable bit rate traffic is assigned a maximum bit rate. As each connection is established, either constant bit rate or assigned maximum bit rate is consumed by the connection. This allows for a limit to be set on any new connections requesting the link.

"When a connection is terminated, reserved bandwidth is de-allocated and additional allocations can be assigned. Got it?"

Luke battles to refine the Executive Summary. Make it short, make it sweet. Now it's brilliant. Read it and weep:

> MyWorld's mission is to lead the world in delivering personal, secure, live webcam video to the masses.

MyWorld installs webcams in homes or businesses, and sends private, live, password-protected video feeds to MyWorld's server and website. Customers can then view their personal feeds on a subscription basis from wherever they log on to the Internet.

MyWorld's connectivity reduces feelings of loneliness, homesickness, and guilt. MyWorld makes family bonds stronger, work more pleasurable, and life more fun.

MyWorld's installation teams and Website server service will make having personal webcam views commonplace (and a snap to use) for millions of average Internet users.

But refining technical processes takes hours, and the pressure to clearly chart The Cluster Organization, The Local Recipient Scenario, and The Network Protocol Stack obliterates the afternoon, and cries of "Where the fuck is dinner?" become desperate as one of Byung-Jun's underlings is delayed fetching bulgogi.

By 11:39 p.m., only half the white paper is written, and that's when Byung-Jun and Joey lose it, and no one is exactly sure who threw the first punch. Now Joey is storming to the elevator screaming, "I don't care! I don't care!" and Byung-Jun is trying to explain to Luke how Joey is wrong about which algorithms in the bitstream decoder actually work. Luke says, "I thought you had this down!"

Byung-Jun says, "Yes, but it's never been tested!"

Francis says to Byung-Jun, "Better apologize to the youngster—he's the only one who can save your ass."

"Fuck him! I'm the Chief Technology Officer!"

Francis says, "Without the Chief Scientist, the whole thing is over!"

From the enclosing elevator down the hall, Joey hollers, "I'm Byung-Jun Kim—the biggest asshole known to man!"

∞

Joey angrily sucks a flaring cigarette in the plaza courtyard below, where Luke finds him. Luke says, "C'mon Sir Wook, live to fight another day."

"Blow me."

"Um sorry, I choke on small bones."

Joey almost laughs at the stupid old joke. "Why do you get so much of the company, and I'm down to 8%?"

Luke says, "You're gonna make $50 million, what's the difference?"

"$437.5 million to you, at full valuation."

"You did that in your head?"

"B.F.D."

"Haven't you heard? Money can't buy you happiness."

"That's bullshit. If that were true, you'd give yours up."

"I'm going to give it up. I'm going to donate it to worthy causes."

"The worthy causes will be you."

"Don't be so sure. Now how about when we go public, I buy you a new Porsche outta my share?"

Joey says, "What color?"

"Midnight-blue metallic."

"Okay. But not one for Byung-Jun."

"Agreed."

"What about Francis? He knows what I bring to the party."

"Francis—I'm gonna buy him an all-you-can-jizz happy finish at the Ginza Spa."

Joey stamps out his cigarette. "You're a cool dude. Might even be a friend."

∞

Upstairs, Byung-Jun and Joey soul-shake a grudging apology with the Korean team encircling them. After Red Bull chugs, it's back to the computers, and when the sun rises, searing over Park La Brea, it's still a dire race to complete the work.

But finally, at 11:58 a.m., all is well. Luke emails PDFs of MyWorld.com's perfected white paper and business plan to Eric Duncan at Excite@Home. Then everyone goes their separate ways, to wait.

∞

Miracle Mile midday swelters under ninety-one degrees, and Luke, drained from the night, has earned his keep. At the Ginza Spa, he puts $150 cash and his driver's license down by rote for the kimonoed mama-san, who files both in a recipe box. Then she unlocks Room B. "Please undress. Make comfortable."

Luke does, hoisting himself onto a rickety massage table with dingy yellow sheets. Legs dangling over the side, Luke contemplates his toes, like a kid waiting for the pediatrician. Only the room isn't medicinally clean; it's moldy and moist with frayed, unpadded carpet and chipped Formica paneling.

Li-Po politely knocks on the door and enters at the same time, wearing camouflage carpenter pants and a pink orchid tank top. She is mid-twenties to mid-thirties, Japanese-Thai, with frosty pinot eye shadow and baby seashell teeth. She takes Luke's wrist, placing his hand on her crotch, verifying his need.

He nods and she puts fingers to his chest, pinching his nipples. Exhaling her breakfast's garlic, she takes down his boxers and tries to mouth a regular condom over him. "Big boy, like all way."

He says, "Suggestion box: get some Magnums already." Directing, he puts auteur hands on her humid hair, and she rises from her knees in response, nudging him onto his back. After her up-down squats it's over, and a polite knock-knock later, she's gone into Room C. Ray-Ban incognito, Luke returns to alley parking, where he maxes out the A/C, before driving home to the ocean, tremendously carefree.

∞

At Shoreline Towers, Luke sunbathes poolside, marmaladed in Bain de Soleil. Action junkie, he deletes old voice mail messages. First to go: quavers from Saryn—"I miss you. Call you from the gate," and "The NBC breakfast went great, if anyone's asking." Plus one from Tracy, fumbling, "So best of luck anyway," meaning, 'I can't believe I fell for your promise to take me with you.'

But what does Tracy know about the Internet anyway? He can't spend his life bringing a dumb secretary up to speed. Then there is a speech from Neal Hill saying how he understands Luke's desire to do something entrepreneurial, but where was the heads-up, after Neal went to bat for Luke's contract?

But Neal Hill is just thinking about himself, and Luke can't call back now anyway, because Saryn is beeping through from New York. She says, "Where ya been? I left two messages."

"You did? I better call Verizon. Things have been insane. Got a last-minute deadline from Excite and had to pull an all-nighter."

"Was Croesus upset?"

"Would you be if you were them?"

Saryn says, "They won't be able to replace you."

"That's what I'm hearing."

"I wish you were here."

"I know you do, but the funding's on the way."

Saryn says, "Can I just tell you how much I appreciate you? All I want to do is stay home tomorrow in bed with you and watch old movies."

Luke thinks, Okay, but who said I was your boyfriend? "Stay home anyway."

"I only want to with you!"

"Let me see how things are going. I'm about to go under in parking, so I'll probably lose you. Hello? Hello? Saryn?" Luke disconnects, moving towels to a lounge in the shade, where he begins a long-deserved nap.

∞

Six hours later, Luke edges forward in line at Rigo's Taco stand. Finally reaching the window, Luke orders three tacos with cheese, a cheese tamale, rice and beans, a large Coke, and a full side of guacamole. When he receives his food, he pockets the change, because who says a Mexican girl should get tipped for placing food in a box?

Luke spreads out at an outdoor table, and when hopeful Nicaraguans approach with three small children, Luke spreads out even more because the table is his and why share it with dirty-cheeked kids who cry for chips and spill their drinks?

After enjoying his meal, Luke returns to his ocean-view bed, where he reclines with his hands behind his head, watching the Santa Monica Ferris wheel light up the sky. After a while he sighs, knowing he's one of the best to come along in a long time. He closes his eyes for the night, regent of the bay, commander of crashing waves.

5.

Luke drives to Shutter's Hotel for breakfast seaside, where he taste-tests all four midget jellies. When he receives his check, he tips 25%; the meal is expensible, since he overheard the party next to him discussing their dot-com business plan.

Eighteen minutes later, Luke is at his Palisades Bluffs house, bounding upstairs to the master bath, where Lisa, nanny Mariela, and grandmother Pat Hudson are bathing Trevor. Luke says, "Hey guys!" The women look at him, aghast. "How's my Hall of Fame quarterback?"

Lisa says bitterly, "Thanks for the call first."

Luke says, "It's a ridiculous requirement and you know it."

Lisa, Pat, and Mariela just leave, Mariela handing Trevor to Luke with a bottle filled with formula. Luke sits in the rocker and tips the bottle to Trevor, who sucks the shake down. Then Luke sings to Trevor, "I hope you don't mind, I hope you don't mind, that I put down in words, how wonderful life is 'cause Daddy-O's in the world!"

∞

Luke strolls into work at Park La Brea near noon, finding the Koreans huddled around a monitor. Joey says, "Check it out."

Luke squeezes forward to a series of photos of an Asian girl slicked, post double-pump.

Joey says, "BangkokSluts.com."

Offended, Luke says, "That's disgusting. Look how scared she is."

Francis says, "She look happy to me."

Joey says, "You know where MyWorld will make its fortune—people setting up webcams in bedrooms and having virtual fuck."

Luke glares, "Okay, we're not looking at porn in the office anymore. MyWorld stands for family, and if it's otherwise, I won't be involved."

Byung-Jun says, "Ease up, Dude. We're just jokin'."

Luke says, "Really? How would your wife feel if she knew you were looking at porn?"

"She doesn't care."

Luke says, "What about you, Francis? What if your wife found out?"

Byung-Jun says, "Leave him alone."

Luke says, "I'm not going to tell her. Francis can screw his life up on his own."

Byung-Jun says, defending, "Make yourself useful. Call Eric Duncan and follow up."

Luke says, "I'm sure he'll call when he has some news."

Byung-Jun says, "What about your email?"

"He's not gonna email his response."

"Have you checked?"

To prove otherwise, Luke goes to his desktop. The others gather around.

There is an email to lmorrow@myworld.com from Eric Duncan at Excite@Home. Byung-Jun says, "Sent two hours ago!"

Luke says, "Fuck me!" and opens the email. Eric writes, "we appreciate your submission of my world's materials, but after evaluation, we've decided it's not right for us at this time. thanx."

Joey says, "Bastards!"

Luke says, "I'm calling right now!" Luke dials on the apartment's hard line, warning the rest not to breathe while they listen on cordless extensions. When Eric Duncan comes on, Luke says, "Hey man, so I just opened your email."

Eric says, "Didn't want to hold you up."

Luke says, "Okay, but I thought we were close with you. I thought, you know, it was just a formality."

"A formality? To get a million dollars of funding?"

"I just thought you were on board."

"I've had similar ideas. But our Chief Tech Officer didn't like your white paper."

"Didn't like it?"

"He said it was boilerplate, and those 'greedy algorithm' things—he thinks your calculations are way off."

"Let me have my CTO and chief scientist talk to him. They're Cal Tech PhD candidates for Christ's sakes. I'm sure they can explain."

"Dude, the work has fatal flaws. How much clearer can I be? My CTO has a double PhD in Physics and Computer Engineering from Princeton. And he was Bill Gate's right-hand man at Microsoft, overseeing the perfection of Windows 95, so I think he would know. We're simply not going to invest in a business that sends subpar images across the Internet. Plus, my other colleagues don't believe parents will allow video streams of their children to be broadcast on the Internet anyway."

"Broadcast? It's all password protected on our proprietary network. No one can see the pictures but the subscribers."

"What part of no don't you understand?"

Luke says, "Hey, c'mon, what about those flowers we stole for the luau?"

"You have our answer." And that's it—the call ends.

Luke faces the Koreans. "Get out of the lease, whatever computers and supplies I've paid for, I'm keeping 100%."

"Hold up, we can submit the paper elsewhere."

Luke says, "No Joey, it has fatal flaws—in case you weren't listening. If you continue to put your name on fucked-up shit, word will get out, and one day, when you somehow graduate Cal Tech, no one will hire you." Luke sweeps the leftover beef bowls onto the floor. "Motherfuckin' pigsty!"

∞

But all can't be lost now, and when Luke guns his Boxster from Park La Brea, his cell rings. He answers.

"Luke? Armin Zames. Know why I'm calling?"

Luke says, "You're returning my call from two years ago?"

"Guess again."

"Someone said I was looking?"

"Who gets called who's looking?"

"Uh..."

Armin says, "This isn't on the street—you're their first choice."

"I am?"

"You're major on the radar. Electronic Arts is hot, and since you're their account manager, you're white hot. So how'd you like to be the global manager of the Nissan account at Nicaida & Knight overseeing Goble and Hoch?"

"I'd need equity in the company."

"Offered, with a four-year guarantee and a 65% raise on your current base."

"Kick in a Titus Super-Moto bike out of your commission and I'll sign."

"What color?"

"Copper anodized."

"Done. You'll have a draft of the contract by 9 a.m. tomorrow."

"Pleasure doing business, Armin."

"I only work with the best!"

∞

It's about time his talents were recognized, and when his Porsche screams into the parking lot at Nicaida & Knight,

Luke finds the human resources VP, Robin, and a burly security guard trying to hang a Luke Morrow nameplate in front of his space.

They beam 'Welcome to the company,' one-fifth of a second before the Porsche nearly takes out their knees. Luke nods, 'Thanks for executing your duties hanging my sign.' He heads for the building, too busy for bonus chat. Inside, Luke strides into a corner office past his assistant, because a new copper-colored mountain bike with a gift bow is waiting next to the couch.

"It came first thing."

Luke raises a deigning eye to Daniel the Intern, who has been promoted to Luke's desk from the mailroom at Nicaida & Knight. Luke climbs onto the bike, bouncing on the tires, testing the bike's mettle. Luke says, "When I'm out, arrange the rake, pebbles, and sand in my Zen garden like they were at Croesus."

"Yes sir."

Luke stares him down.

"Dear Leader, Sir."

"What's with the watch?"

Daniel says, "It's a graduation present from my grandmother."

"Day-Glo orange rubber?"

"It's a Tag Heuer."

"I don't give a fuck, I don't like it. What time is lunch?"

"Twelve thirty at Chaya. I confirmed with Goble and Hoch."

"Make sure the hostess seats them with their backs to the room." Daniel hustles from his seat, right on it to earn his stripes, while Luke dismounts to check his email.

On his screen is another string of Saryn Shafer missives: "I left two messages for you again." "What's up with Verizon?" "I'll get my belly button pierced like you want—if you take me to Paris/just kidding/lol."

Luke calls Saryn in New York. "Listen, you can't keep bombarding me."

She says, "What are you talking about?"

"All the emails—I'm busy."

Saryn says, "Just tell me what happened with Excite@Home."

"How about I didn't get a dime. My chief technology officer's paper sucked, and Excite@Home passed."

"Where are you now?"

"I'm heading the Nissan account for Nicaida & Knight. They backed up the armored truck and I took it."

"Wow, what a shock. I can't believe that about MyWorld. But Nissan—it'll be amazing for you!"

"Glad you're psyched."

"It's proof that when one door closes, another one opens!"

"What are you taking, happy pills?

"Are you serious?"

"The question requires a simple yes or no."

"Why are you treating me like shit all of the sudden?"

"I don't know. Why are you being a bottomless pit all of the sudden?"

"What's wrong with you?"

"Hmm, I have a newborn to care for? I'm going through a divorce? My Internet start-up just cratered? And if that weren't enough, I heard I'm starting a new job."

Luke hangs up, and he will never call Saryn again. And he thinks, Who cares about her trained kegels anyway? Every time I go down there, it's dead bass on a rock.

As he hops on his mountain bike again, he cannot envision Saryn picking up her pieces on Madison Avenue, for months, and there's no need to, especially since Nicaida & Knight works with ad buyer Universal-McCann. And neither he nor Saryn will ever grasp that a leopard can't change his spots, and that no woman will ever get a better Luke.

∞

It should be a triumphant return to Chaya restaurant for Luke, only it's not. He's borne back ceaselessly into advertising, and now to make a buck, he must oversee Goble and Hoch. And they despise him on sight, after Nicaida & Knight told them they'd have endless freedom to manage Nissan if they'd just sell out.

Now, with their shop shuttered, Goble and Hoch have become employees again—a disastrous career move—especially with Luke Morrow on their ass. Gritting their teeth in a window booth, they wait for Luke, knowing in an hour they will have a smirky victory after filling him out of the loop on their upcoming Nissan campaign.

But Goble and Hoch's resentment is sunny compared to that of Becker and White, who occupy the first table facing the room. When Luke enters the restaurant in rushed relevance, they imagine him indicted; who else would have stolen their prized brooms and ball? As Luke passes them in his black linen shirt, Becker says, "You're welcome for the Tiffany comb, fuckhead."

Luke stops short.

White says, "And we've written a play about you."

Becker says, "It's called *The Peter Principle*."

Luke says, "That the best that you can do?"

White says, "For the two seconds we spent. Also—your bridge with us is burned."

Luke says, "Damn shame, having to step through a puddle." Luke continues to his booth, where Goble and Hoch give him strained hellos, sure he's thrilled with his world. But while the waitress runs down the specials, Luke's consciousness becomes a toxic sky, and his self-loathing could detonate TNT: he is a failed Internet entrepreneur whose dreams are dead.

∞

Lisa answers her phone. It will be challenging to talk, with Trevor wailing colicky over her shoulder. Luke says, "I'm buying a bike rack for my Porsche."

"And you're telling me, why?"

"Can't you pass him to the nanny? It's hard to hear."

"What do you want?"

"I'm just notifying you that once the rack is installed, I'm going back to my office to pick up my bike, so I should be there at my house that you get to live in fifty-eight minutes from now."

Lisa hangs up. For the next hour, she rocks her son, trying to soothe him, but he is still crying when Daddy-O shows up.

Luke says, "Ply him with those colic tabs from Canada."

"They don't work, asshole." Lisa transfers Trevor to Luke, who relaxes in the rocker. Lisa goes downstairs into the garden, leaving Luke with Mariela, who is changing the bedding in Trevor's crib. Luke selects *Vogue* from a pile of magazines on the floor and begins flipping pages with his free arm, while Trevor continues to bawl. But maybe Trevor has had enough for now, and fighting somethingness has exhausted him, because he soon heaves a big sigh into sleep.

Luke winks at Mariela, "I've got the touch," before handing Trevor off to her. While she puts Trevor in his crib, Luke slips into the master bath with *Vogue*, which he uses for enhancement. And just when he's about to climax, he notices there's no toilet paper. But he follows through anyway—serves Lisa right.

Outside the house a minute later, Luke finds Lisa watering the sunflowers. He says, "I'm the baby whisperer."

"You're so talented."

"You need to be cordial."

"I should have known, don't you think? I should have seen the red flags."

"You spend too much time blabbing with your girlfriends."

"At least I have friends. Who are yours, anyway? You don't even speak to your sister."

"Really. I just came back from Chicago."

"Because your father left you, you're cold and mean."

"Stop with the psychologizing."

"And when you first met my mom at Thanksgiving, she was about to have hip surgery, but you never even asked how she was feeling."

"Didn't I take everyone to dinner? Let's replay the tape."

"You had no interest in my dad's business. You spent the meal leering at my sister."

"Don't be jealous of her rack."

"Get the fuck out!"

"On my way, soon as you know the truth."

"You're incapable."

"Really? How about I never loved you."

"Oh that's great, Luke. Then why did you marry me?"

"Felt right at the time, but now I don't want all your emotions—they make it too hard to relax."

"Just leave, please."

"Next time I'm here, I want you gone, because I won't have you harassing me while I'm caring for my son." Luke gets into his car and floors it, the wheels on the mountain bike spinning in the air.

Backed against the stucco wall, Lisa lowers her head, her white picket fence gone forever.

∞

Luke stares at his office monitor, watching The First Great Internet Age implode. But he won't sell his Metricom, etoys, or CMGI; he will ride them to the bottom because only motley fools sell their holdings in a rash rush; everyone knows quality stocks bought and held long-term become candy mountains.

Still, there is revenge: Excite@Home's stock is free-falling too. Luke never owned one lousy share, and ouch, Eric Duncan, your ten million on paper is history. And FYI, SoftBank Tokyo is calling in your chips; now, without investment capital, your power base and job are gone.

But don't worry, Eric, WaMu Bank is looking for part-time tellers. And that's the best you will do; other venture capital firms are folding their tents too, and there will never be lift under your wings again because the New Economy is dead.

For everyone, including "Bun Fun." Luke shouts into the intercom, "What the fuck are you talking about?"

From his assistant's bay outside of Luke's office, Daniel tries to recoup and identify his mistake. "He's on the line for you."

"It's Bee-young-yun, not Bun Fun."

"It sounded like—"

"Shut up! If you're not sure, ask!"

"Should I put him through?"

"Come with me!"

Daniel says into the phone, "He's actually getting off another line, can you hold?" Daniel parks the call, Luke looming over him.

Luke says, "Get up," ushering Daniel on a forced march into the men's room.

At the first toilet stall, Luke says, "Give it."

"What for?"

"Take it off."

Daniel undoes his orange Day-Glo Tag Heuer watch and hands it to Luke, who flushes it down the toilet. "I told you, don't wear it."

Back at his desk, Luke picks up the line. "Byung-Jun Kim, to what do I owe this honor?"

Byung-Jun says, "I fixed the algorithms."

∞

Luke checks his own stainless steel Tag Heuer at Kun Lai Suk Bulgogi Barbeque in Koreatown, where he is the only white person. Finally, Byung-Jun appears, wending his way through the brewing wait. Luke says, "I've interrupted your beauty rest."

Bed-headed Byung-Jun says: "Try this—very mild." Luke declines Byung-Jun's offer of Gochujang pepper paste. Then Byung-Jun removes a floppy disc from his briefcase. It is titled, "A Distribution Methodology for One-to-One Multimedia Streaming on the Internet." Byung-Jun says, "As chief technology officer, the buck stopped with me."

"Was Joey right?"

Byung-Jun says, "Yes and no. I was the same."

"Have you shown him?"

"He agrees with the changes. But he's pulling double duty now, working for DARPA and trying to finish his dissertation."

"Francis?"

"He went to Malaysia."

"What about his studies?"

"His wife got down on him, said he was becoming a professional student. So he took an offer from Singapore Airlines doing route analysis."

"You?"

Byung-Jun's eyes well up. "My wife said she wants a divorce—unless I get on track. I borrowed too much money from her brother to start Video Email Popster, and now she says a real man knows when to cut his losses and take care of his family. So who needs a PhD, anyway? Half are them are unemployed."

Luke says, "There's no money out there anymore. We had our shot."

"Maybe you'll try again and not take no for an answer." Byung-Jun edges the floppy forward. "I need $12,000 dollars for my student loans. Then I'm going back to Seoul to work in my uncle's drapery manufacture."

"Are you sure the programming is right?"

Byung-Jun bows his head. "All I ask is, if you get the company going someday, you bring me, Francis, and Joey back to let us share in what we created."

Luke says, "With the market crashing, I've lost nearly two-thirds of my net worth. If I take your word on something that may not work, you'll have to sign over the rights to make it worth my while. And if something comes of it in the future, we'll re-open things then."

"I know you are a man of your word."

"Thirty-five hundred dollars—dumbest check I'll ever write."

"Ten thousand."

"Three thousand six hundred fifty, best and final."

Byung-Jun wipes his eyes backhand. "I insist on paying for lunch, then. Please have whatever you want."

∞

The food poisoning must have come from the sushi, except Luke actually had the charcoal short ribs platter, though no one at Nicaida & Knight will ever be the wiser. And it's possible he will have to stop at the emergency room; please tell the bosses he'll be out for the rest of the afternoon.

Daniel, ever-loyal, does as told. Home at Shoreline Towers at 3 p.m., feeling just fine, Luke emails the corrected white paper to the tech lawyers representing MyWorld.com. And let them earn their one point eliminating Byung-Jun, Francis Oh, and Joey Wook from *Tribal Fire Networks*—Luke's new name for the company.

By 6 p.m., Byung-Jun has signed and faxed away all rights to the algorithms. At 7:30 p.m. at the Coffee Bean in Beverly Hills, Luke hands Byung-Jun a check for $3,650. They dap fists goodbye, Byung-Jun's future beyond the bend.

Sequoia, Kleiner Perkins, and Accel—venture capital titanic might—are the Holy Sees of Silicon Valley. A salesman never knows until he asks, and Luke will, in an electronic blast to them and their foes: Benchmark, Redpoint, Mayfield, Battery, Flatiron, Polaris, Idealab, Sand Hill Partners, and ninety others around the globe.

And Luke must attempt to make it stick, only how does he throw his invention against the wall when half the powerbrokers don't give their emails online or take unsolicited calls? Answer: safe crack. Example: John Doerr, the Kleiner Perkins czar investor behind Amazon and Sun Microsystems. Email his elevator pitch to: *doerr@kpcb.com, john@kpcb.com, johndoerr@kpcb.com, john.doerr@kpcb.com,* and all other possibilities, since the address that doesn't bounce back is the combo in.

Repeat for every venture capitalist ever mentioned in *Red Herring*, *The Industry Standard*, *Business 2.0*, *Wired*, *Forbes*, *Kiplinger's*, *Fortune*, *NYT*, and *Wall Street Journal*—if, according to their company websites, they're in his space.

Luke emails feverishly through the night and will continue to work until dawn, until the Tribal Fire business overview and white paper attachment are sent to 200 men and two women venture capitalists who can give "Yes" for an answer. An example, to John Doerr:

Subject: Cal Tech PhD Candidates Introduce Tribal Fire Networks Attachment: TRIBAL FIRE Business Overview, TRIBAL FIRE White Paper

Dear John,

I'm the founder of Tribal Fire Networks, a start-up with wholly owned proprietary technology that prevents the current, unacceptable degradation of video streams across the Internet Cloud on a person-to-person basis.

Tribal Fire's Video Agent and Bandwidth Broker Technology, coupled with Tribal Fire's Distribution Network, will guarantee the quality, security, and delivery of personal, live video streams at full-motion rates without delay and jitter.

Tribal Fire's technology fully enables the core business, an Internet broadband service that offers a revolutionary way for millions of people to be emotionally and visually connected with their families and friends.

I've just begun marketing to venture capital, and I'm wondering whether you'd like to read and/or hear what I'm up to.

Best regards,

Luke Morrow
President/CEO & Founder
Tribal Fire Networks

∞

At 11 a.m. on Friday, Luke finally awakens, and soon, he is sudsy on cloud nine in the shower—until his cell buzzes in a vibrating circle on the floor. He leans out, answering.

"Luke, it's Ellen."

"Uh oh, what did I do now?"

His divorce attorney says, "Well, I just got a letter from Lisa's lawyer. I mean, it's ridiculous, right? You didn't really leave ejaculate on her toilet?"

"Not intentionally."

"Luke, this is serious. She wants a restraining order against you."

"Ellen, that's possibly the most outrageous thing I've ever heard. Lisa is a complete sociopath, trying to punish me because I don't want to be married to her anymore. And what I haven't told you is every time I go over there, she attacks me with uncontrolled anger. Her hostility toward me is scarring Trevor, so draw something up, because she needs to be gone at least ten minutes before I arrive."

"We'll have to file as well. Apparently she's willing to say anything."

"Take off the gloves. Who is the judge gonna believe— me or the pill popper?"

"Write down everything that she does."

"How about she's already feeding Trevor solid rice cereal mix against the pediatrician's warning. You should see Trevor's reflux reaction; his tongue immediately mouths it back out. He's bound to choke, but she couldn't care less."

"Whoa."

"See? You don't really know someone until they rip off their mask."

∞

Until there is a restraining order against her, Luke won't take Lisa's abuse, and it's not like Trevor will remember Luke didn't come by anyway. And since Luke still can't go into work at Nicaida & Knight because of his "food poisoning," it's time for R&R in Las Vegas. Within hours, Luke is relaxing in first class on American Airlines, having drained three green-can Heinekens over the 42-minute haul.

Later, in a Deluxe Augustus Tower room at Caesars Palace, Luke showers again, studding himself with Davidoff Blue Water. At 6 p.m., the escort is at his door. And she is dressed in jeans and a T-shirt with gold rhinestones—casually appropriate, per his request.

She joins him on the couch to get acquainted, and after one minute, they are. She leans over, frenching him down, saying, "Just like we're teenagers and our parents aren't home!" Two hundred seconds later, she is a nine, Forgot It

Was a Service, but that's just a prelude to the Once in a Lifetime backdoor ten.

Nut busted, Luke sends her on her way, because he has a dinner and can't be late. His reservation is for one at The Palm, where, bibbed in a booth, he dines on a mound of french-fried onions and a four-pound market price Maine lobster, which he wastes, since he wants to save room for his dessert: a half-pound slice of chocolate cake.

At 10 p.m., Luke is back in his room, ready for his next date. She is a straight-banged, almost-runway model who dresses in conservative Calvin Klein. But that's a minor detail on The Erotic Review blog; what's notable is that she squirts like a man.

But what gentlemen don't know is that's just her value proposition, and a 24-ounce tumbler of Crystal Light before each stint does the trick, allowing her to let her warm method crescendo go, earning her kudos and repeated business. Once she's performed and left, Luke calls room service to change the sheets ASAP. Downstairs, rolling to a $7,800 win at craps, Luke thinks her Erotic experience should be called an eleven—Transcendental.

The next morning, after a monumental brunch, Luke retires to his bathroom, where a third girl is waiting. In the

Roman tub, rich with foam, Luke delivers himself unto her, holding her ponytail from behind like a rein.

Luke spends the rest of the weekend recovering by the pool. He flies home to Los Angeles at 7 a.m. Monday morning, grabbing a Cinnabon and Wetzel's Pretzel for a nosh on the plane.

∞

Goble and Hoch hold court at 11 a.m., screening their newest spot: an industrial vise forging a two-ton diamond into a gleaming red truck. Attentive, Tom Nicaida and Doug Knight offer, "Good job," and "Very cool." But Luke simmers, disbelieving—haven't Tom and Doug seen this cliché before?

At lunch, still frail from the sushi virus, Luke heads to the doctor for tests. Only Luke is really on way to his apartment, where he can safely trail seditious mail. And when he reaches his home computer, his game is changed forever. On the screen are invitations from Sequoia Capital, Kleiner Perkins, and Accel to come see them immediately. Luke stares out over the ocean, ready for the impossible.

∞

Tom Nicaida and Doug Knight are sorry for the hole in Kit's heart and fully understand Luke's need to be with his family during her sudden, upcoming operation. But Luke promises to herd Goble and Hoch by phone, and he'll be back soon enough when his niece is out of the woods.

Hanging up, Luke wrestles with PowerPoint, paring Tribal Fire Networks into a three-minute pitch. Then he races for his plane, sprinting through the airport, ripping a seam in his black pants.

Hours later, in Kleiner Perkins' Palo Alto cathedral conference room, Luke sits with his laptop ready, torn pants hidden under the table. And his knees are shaking—an anecdote that will never be known. Soon, five partners enter, one dimming the lights. They've read Luke's white paper and now he must quickly make his case. Luke does, telling his story pure and true. The lights come up.

The managing partner says, "Are the algorithms patented? Because we could probably do this on our own."

Luke says, "I've already filed."

The men gut check. "We're in."

Five blocks down Sand Hill Road in his rental car, Luke slams on the brakes, skidding onto the shoulder. Shouting at his attorneys, he says, "Just get the patents filed. Whatever! …They can get it done! …Fucking give them half a percent of mine!"

∞

Byung-Jun's algorithms are priceless, but now they're Luke's, and it will turn out no one has registered facsimiles, and the formulas will earn multiple protections, remaining unassailable for twenty years, thwarting competitors and thieves. And it's not just Kleiner Perkins who is buying into Byung-Jun's bounty. Benchmark bids its way in the next day, and Sequoia too, with Accel begging for a piece.

Now word can't be contained; lore of the latest killer app spreads wild over Nor Cal, igniting powerbroker breakfasts at Buck's in Woodside, until venture capital's mold is uncarved from stone and obliterated. From shattered rules rises, unheard of, an investment federation of the big four, with late-stagers Silicon Valley Bank, Goldman Sachs, and Warburg Pincus piling on, flooding the deal with a third hundred million.

In return, investors receive 20% aggregate only, relinquishing voting control and 80% ownership of Tribal Fire Networks to Chairman and CEO Luke Morrow, who has never proven his market, let alone run a country store. As news of the extraordinary founding breaks the front page of *The New York Times* and *The Wall Street Journal*, Luke leases an entire glass tower on Howard Hughes Parkway in Los Angeles.

And while the First New Economy disintegrates around him, losing the planet's portfolio wealth, Luke's notional worth rockets to $240 million—without a sole customer. And how this could ever happen should be questioned, but it is simply the sixty-second of the infinite components of a miracle.

∞

Luke's ascendance rocks Tom Nicaida and Doug Knight and, wildly jealous of him, they play hardball, holding him to his employment contract. However, that's laughable, because he never signed it.

∞

The garage door churns upwards, revealing Lisa, who lets go of Luke's golf bag onto the driveway. She says, "Mariela's bringing him down."

Almost at the front door from his car, Luke says, "Thought the court said you're supposed to be gone."

"Don't worry, this will be my first and only time here. Because I want to move back to San Francisco—with Trevor."

"You think you can do that because...?"

"There's nothing left for me in Los Angeles."

"So my son will just see me on vacations?"

"If you let us go."

Luke says, "Fine. If that's what you want."

Lisa says, "Your heart is a chunk of glass." She gets into her Volvo and backs over the clubs before driving away.

∞

Luke stands on a vast stage in black jeans and T-shirt, leading thousands at Best Buy's world headquarters in Eden Prairie, Minnesota. To the national sales force, he says, "I've assembled the finest team in the country at Tribal Fire, and with my help, you're scaling broadband to unseen heights." Backlit behind him are his division heads.

"Let me introduce Nicole Pompa, formerly Executive Vice-President of Sales at Oracle, now Tribal Fire's President of Sales and Marketing. Johnson Ash, BSkyB's Executive Vice-President, now President of Tribal Fire International. Tribal Fire Chief Technology Officer Oren Sanger, past Senior Vice-President of Cisco.

"And former Wilson Sonsini Goodrich & Rosati partner, Julie Reynolds, now Tribal Fire's Executive Vice-President of Business and Legal Affairs. Last but not least, Laurie Dolan, formerly Chief Financial Officer of Dell, now Tribal Fire's Chief Operating Officer."

The rapt audience applauds, only now Luke is speaking to legions of Comcast cable operators at the Miami Beach

Convention Center. "I'm giving customers a better reason for broadband, because my service tugs at the heartstrings."

On giant screens behind Luke at Wal-Mart's headquarters in Arkansas, montages play of families having cameras installed in their dens and nurseries, so moms and dads can see their children on laptop screens at far-away locations.

In the great hall of the Jacob Javits Center in Manhattan, Luke addresses the national workforce of Verizon. "My company has grown from six employees overnight to more than 20,000 because my product, bundled with your existing service, has fueled broadband's explosive growth."

At the MGM Grand in Las Vegas, Luke steps forward as the keynote speaker of the Consumer Electronics Show. Before tens of thousands, Luke says, "You honor me, owing to the excitement I've created, and now, in less than three years, we have 30 million customers in all fifty states, paying $29.95 a month for gross revenues of $990 million. So I thank you for your support and I promise you—the best is yet to come!"

∞

Luke makes them wait twenty-five minutes at the day's end in the nineteenth floor conference room, though he could have descended from on high on time. But that is not indicative of power, as it's always better to enter a packed room at one's pleasure. Tense before him are his in-house marketing executives and the sharpest women and men from advertising powerhouse NNDO. Luke takes his Aeron chair perfunctorily, as if to say, This better be good.

A DVD whip-cut 30-second story rolls, depicting a gen-*Maxim* magazine businessman, who has, wherever he goes, computer screen views of: his garaged BMW, his Rhodesian Ridgebacks, and his Belgian model girlfriend, dressed in lingerie, who waves perkily at the ceiling cam from his bed. To the audience, the businessman says, "My world and welcome to it. Tribal Fire Networks.com."

Track two. A woman attorney—facing frantic phones and senior partners excoriating her to deliver briefs—smiles comfortably through it all as the point of view shifts, revealing, on her monitor, her dutiful husband at home bathing their toddler son in a toy-filled bath; both wave, "Hi Mommy!" up at the bathroom camera. The narrator says: "Your life under control. Tribal Fire Networks.com."

Luke swings his socks (no shoes) off the conference table and says, "I'm spending $50 million with you people and that's the best you can do?"

Someone chances, "We don't have to lock for a week."

Luke says, "What part of 'approved but boring' don't you understand?" To spare himself from further mediocrity, Luke exits to his private elevator, which whisks him to the tower's roof, where he lies down on the bull's eye of his helipad.

Into the deepening sky, he tells the universe, "I am neither half-creative nor half-businessman, I am a self-made whole of both. I have invented something that's going to print money. Bow down to me."

∞

Luke wants Mia, the 31-year-old Amerasian stewardess, whom he's never seen before. Only, he's flying the jet share Gulfstream V out of Santa Monica with his latest date, Meg, a leggy sales rep with sea glass-green eyes. That means fingers up in Mia will have to wait until the trip home, when Meg won't be on board.

Still, there's fun ahead. After a tedious pre-Initial Public Offering document signing in Palo Alto, there will be Sunday golf at Meadowood, St. Helena, Napa Valley—with Goldman Sachs paying the greens fees. And Meg is always available, arching on her side when he wakes up, suddenly lush for him.

For her part, Meg is cautious with this intriguing man. He's so damn comfortable in his own skin; dare she give him her heart? And she must be appropriate and independent and not harm her cousin-in-law's career, for Nicole Pompa, who introduced them, is Tribal Fire's third-ranking executive. Genuine, then, for Meg to pay her own way; a fashion convention in San Francisco next week is her business expense and her bosses will reimburse her for her hotel, meals, and business-class air.

So Meg insists on writing Tribal Fire a check for what she'll get, never wanting to take advantage, especially since other Tribal Fire officers are flying to San Francisco in the morning. So, even though she'll enjoy Luke's hotel suites, she'll make it clear that she is not after his money and that the man underneath is all that matters.

Luke and Meg take facing seats in the luxurious cabin, Meg kicking off her Keds, putting her feet up in Luke's lap, reinforcing herself as his girlfriend. And as Luke peers out the window, Meg becomes dreamy, certain he will give her a baby in time.

Soon, they're taking off over low-lying bungalows that remind Luke of Sara and Michael's brick shitbox in Chicago. Maybe he'll return their congratulatory calls one of these days, but it's their loss, not investing in Tribal Fire; let them have their dinky lives. And don't they know to stop showing up on his phone sheet? He's busy—so busy that he hasn't seen his son in two and a half years, since the Palisades' house sold and Lisa drove away, when Trevor was seven months old.

But tomorrow, Saturday, at 12:30 p.m., all that will change; Luke and Meg will attend Trevor's third birthday party at Lisa's Walnut Creek rancher. And Luke will make up for his time gone, bringing his son a plane full of toys.

Now, as the Gulfstream curls over the sea, Luke glimpses Santa Monica Community Gardens below, where a hobo missing a leg in a wheelchair shakes his fist at a man and a boy. Luke thinks that it's good to be above the riff-raff, because what is man—what has he got? If not himself, he has naught.

∞

As the morning's first photons appear, Trevor wakes up, excited in his bottom bunk. He tries to go back to sleep to make his mommy proud, but he can't. He sneaks into the dining room—the party room—and there is the sign hanging from the sky of the ceiling. Blue is his favorite color. The hanging sign is a shiny rainbow. It says *Happy Birthday!* Lisa says there are some smart kids who start reading at four, and maybe he will, too. Trevor's Mom & Me teacher, Miss Rey, called him bright and said that's something to feel good about.

Trevor tiptoes into Lisa's room. He goes into her closet, where his presents are high up on a shelf. He can't reach those presents, even with his tooth-brushing stool. The presents are wrapped in blue, shiny paper. What's in them?

Padding to the kitchen, Trevor climbs onto the counter and gets Froot Loops down from the cabinet. He pours some loops into a bowl and bends to eat the ones he spilled. Mom says they're not clean to eat off the floor. She's still sleeping.

He curls on the den couch with the cereal, eating circles one at a time, watching Barney. That boy on the show has something wrong with him. He can't hear; the thing on his ear is a hearing aid. Mom says a lady made up Barney in her head and that she is one smart cookie and very, very rich.

But she is not rich like my dad. He is owner of the fire company, and he is bringing me lots of presents today because I am important.

∞

Meg can't remember the last time she was so nervous, so she lowers the window of the chauffeur-driven SUV, desperate for air. Luke takes her hand, saying, "Don't worry, it's gonna be fine."

"Lisa knows I'm coming, right?"

Luke says, "Not a problem."

"What if Trevor doesn't like me?"

∞

Trevor is in the backyard squealing in a gated pen with other little kids, trying to pet the hyper, jumping puppies with the cowgirl who rents them. That crazy puppy just licked Sara R's eyeball. Sara R. has white-blonde hair. She is weird because she does not like apple sauce.

Domino's Pizza is coming. The pizza is cheese pizza. Pasta salad is for adults, but kids may have some if they like. Trevor may have Hawaiian Punch with his pizza, and his mom says it doesn't have Red Dye #4 anymore like when she was little. His favorite food group is sugar. She tells everyone in line at the grocery store. That is making conversation.

Then there is a big man standing over him with a girl-woman holding the man's hand. She is smiling like she knows Trevor all the time, but she is a stranger, and the man puts out his hand to shake and it is very, very scary.

Trevor runs to Mom—her legs are safe! Mom says, "It's okay, Trevor. It's just your father."

The couple have followed Trevor and are right there again. Meg says, "Hey Trev, I'm Meg."

Luke says, "How would you like your own yellow Hummer?"

Trevor tries to be a big boy and not cry. But he cries even harder, because it's his dad finally come, and he thought he would know his dad, even though Mom says a baby is too tiny to remember.

∞

They are all singing happy birthday, and Trevor's tears are long forgotten. Still, he feels funny, as if he's naked in front of them. He hears Aunt Becca shout, "Make a wish!" and he's heard that before at other parties and he knows what to do. He quickly wishes for a kitten like the neighbors have, even though he is allergic to domestic cat pelt.

Grandpa Stan says, "Blow out the candles!"

He will puff-puff, making smoke on them. While Grandma Pat starts putting cake on plates, he grabs the Tyrannosaurus Rex guy from the top of the cake, licking the frosting off of the dinosaur. Everyone laughs—even Sara R.—who his Mom says is very serious for a 3-year-old.

Plastic forks go around, and he hears Mom say crossly to Dad, "What's she doing here?" It feels bad, because he can feel that Meg is not supposed to be there at all, and he is suddenly ashamed of his special day.

But there are presents to open, everyone is clapping for him, and here comes his own electric mini-Hummer to ride in that the driver in the black suit has unloaded from Dad's important truck. Rip, tear—it's a rainforest Playmobil kit from Mom, and then a rubber suction-cup archery set from

Dad that Grandma Pat says doesn't look safe and could poke out an eye. Next is a play ambulance and fire engine with flashing red lights from Aunt Becca, and a sparkly, orange-colored BMX bicycle from his dad that his dad says is really copper-colored. But everyone says he's just a little kid, barely riding a tricycle, and that the BMX is too big.

Then there are pop-up books from Grandma and Grandpa, lots of Legos, a Buzz Lightyear from Meg, and a thing Aunt Becca says she loved when she was little, called Lite Brite, from Sara R. And from Dad, four GI Joes: an astronaut with a space capsule, a deep-sea diver, a soldier with mud on his cheeks, and a jet pilot with oxygen mask.

Now Grandma and Grandpa are folding up torn wrapping paper everywhere, saving it for "God knows what," Mom says, but they say it's still good and she says, "The Depression is over." And then suddenly, his dad is saying goodbye to him and Meg is saying goodbye to him, and Dad is bending over him with a high-five goodbye, before heading for that big, important truck.

Run to Dad at that opening door, grab around his legs—safe! Dad has important meetings at the hotel in the city, because he owns the fire company. Trevor crumbles and Lisa comes running, having to peel Trevor off of Luke. Luke acknowledges her help with a thank-you, and gets into the

SUV with Meg, who is at a complete loss at what to do, the whole thing far beyond her single-woman repertoire.

A tough two hours later, Trevor finally settles down in his bunk with Mom, his heaving sobs subsiding, his tears drying. And then the evening comes, and there is Chinese take-out with Becca, Grandpa, and Grandma, and Lite Brite with Becca until bedtime, and Mom tucking him in snug as bug, saying don't worry, your dad loves you.

7.

Tribal Fire stock will open at \$22, with Goldman Sachs hyping a \$75 close, predicting Luke's shares will be worth \$750 million. And even though he can't sell any options until the six month hold-back is past, another 10-12% climb per share at the initial public offering would reap another \$100 million on paper. Who would leave that much money on the table? A stupid businessman or someone insane.

Now Luke is told there's a Mr. Kim at reception, who has come all the way from Korea to see him. Only Byung-Jun doesn't have an appointment, and so what if he has been phoning and emailing for two years, asking for a role in Tribal Fire for himself, Francis, and Joey? Who even remembers those programmers for hire? Add on another call from Meg, who has been home from San Francisco for a week at least. But if he doesn't return her messages left on his voice mail, what makes her think she'll get through at his office? And he has already been with Mia the stewardess twice now, and is done with that, too.

In her Brentwood condo, Meg leaves Luke a voice mail, saying, "I didn't mean to pressure you at dinner, but there's nothing wrong with being honest. You know I can't waste one more year with a guy who doesn't want kids, and you already have your kid, so it's not exactly fair. Why can't we have one more? Don't you know when you have a second child, you grow a second heart?"

But Luke won't speak to Meg again. For him, it's just math: the average vagina is six inches long before expansion; there are a minimum of 20,000 beautiful women in Los Angeles and New York that he could date, so why commit to a half-foot of known road—with two miles of bush still out there?

Especially when Luke must focus. There are only sixty days left before Tribal Fire's stock debut, and what if Luke's former Croesus colleague is right? What if Kevin McNally speaks the truth—that Nicole Pompa and Laurie Dolan are underwhelming The Street? McNally tells Luke, "It's a damn shame you recruited them from companies like Oracle and Dell. Your IPO would have much more sizzle if Tribal Fire had both its president and chief operating officer stolen from Apple and Google."

The correct course of action? Luke didn't give Unite and Conquer Tribal Fire's advertising account, remembering how years ago, McNally distastefully abused Century City strippers. And only a clown could miss McNally's Machiavellian loop—McNally skis Ajax mountain with the Credit Suisse players; if he can get Luke to ditch Goldman Sachs and deliver Tribal Fire to Credit Suisse for banking, then Credit Suisse will recommend Unite and Conquer to their Fortune 500 portfolio. And if Credit Suisse creates greater value for Tribal Fire, Luke might feel an obligation to turn over his huge advertising budget to McNally, after firing Tribal Fire's current agency, NNDO.

Still, Luke is a bottom-line tactician; if initial public offerings are all about perception, and Luke can boost his management ranks to goose Tribal Fire's share price, why not? Luke gives McNally and Credit Suisse his tacit okay; they may have premier management, recruiting firm Korn Ferry, ask around.

Only, secrets get out and people talk. In American big business, proprietary information is capital for trade. Over smart phones, founded rumors fly, enlivening drinks and meals, nourishing enemies and counterfeit friends.

It doesn't take long then for the venture funds to hear: Luke's about to ax members of their own handpicked Tribal Fire team with only thirty days left before the IPO! Inside the halls of the underwriter, big shots wring their hands: "He's listening to bad apples, replacing oranges with oranges!" and, "Reckless firings can only signal chaos inside of Tribal Fire, torpedoing the offering."

Within hours, Nicole Pompa and Laurie Dolan demand to see Luke; they've heard the rumors, too. But, he reassures them, "You guys are my guys; all that talk about your being replaced—it's clearly coming from people with too much time on their hands."

In the meantime, Luke secures the services of Carolyn Mannes, Senior Vice-President of Sales and Marketing at Apple, and Denny Walenczyk, Chief Financial Officer of Google, luring them into Tribal Fire as President of Sales and Marketing and Tribal Fire COO respectively, with $2 million dollar salaries, 5-year contracts with mega-bonus formulas, and 500,000 stock options each.

What can Luke's investors do about it? Nothing. They gave him control of the company, and now he's blowing off his toes on the national stage. But they should have known:

Ninety percent of Luke Morrow's ideas are naïve and half-baked, and the megalomaniac is barely half-right half of the time.

Only The Street loves Apple and Google, instantly embracing Carolyn and Denny. So, even with a massive shake-up during the quiet period countdown, Tribal Fire stock soars on opening day, choking Chicken Little's clones, rocketing 16.66% above projections, personally garnering Luke $125 million more on paper.

So screw his partners for their lack of faith. To hell with their knives whistling in the wind.

"I am Luke Morrow, 9.9/10ths right, 9.9/10ths of the time. And ideas spring from my mind, straight to God."

∞

On the balcony above the NYSE trading floor, amid a raucous sellout of executives, Luke closes the session, pounding the gavel.

∞

Waiting for Luke at Tribal Fire's Los Angeles headquarters the next day are gifts of champagne and wine, tins of caviar, and a Davidoff humidor filled with Cuban cigars. Written on the humidor card: 'Congrats on a stellar IPO. Glad to have helped! XXO, Kevin McNally. P.S. I'll call to schedule a dinner.'

Luke thinks, dinner? With McNally? A man who goaded me into firing my first two key employees at the last minute? He can't be trusted.

But McNally, shameless, emails when ignored: "hey dude, me and credit suisse can commandeer your fave G-V any weekend u want. waimea or mauna lani course?"

Except Luke no longer likes cramped Gulfstream Vs; he's already commissioned his own Boeing Business Jet X-10000—the new Maybach of the sky. And Luke has house shopping to do on weekends, so he emails his new president, Carolyn Mannes, to tell Kevin, "Don't call us; we'll call you," telling Carolyn, "Imagine his balls, thinking we're in the same league with Mattel—on their death knell."

∞

Luke borrows against his stock to finance his plane, then does the same for land high above the Pacific Palisades. On Sestri Levante Lane on the Riviera's exclusive rim, Luke purchases contiguous three-acre lots, paying both properties' heirs 34.5% above market price to leave posthaste. Within weeks, he tears down a Cliff May architectural masterpiece on the first lot, then bulldozes a restored Paul Williams traditional on the second. Up goes a 60,000 square foot East Hamptons ocean view manor with rolling lawns and olive groves. A dozen protected California live oaks must be chopped down, though, even if they are centuries old, to make way for the 100-foot infinity pool, guest houses, and tennis complex stadium, which border the cliffside driving range—where Luke can tee golf shots into the Santa Monica Mountain Conservatory.

Inside the house: three ASKO dishwashers; a lighting control system for nearly one-half mil; indoor regulation basketball court; a basement AK-47 firing range; and a Crestron controlled screening room, with spots for 200 guests below his presidential recliner on Armani Casa Grevy's zebra skin couches (mid-1970s hides "legally" obtained).

But none of this construction happens overnight. For a long time, Luke comes and goes from the site, at odd hours at his whim, approving this and that, still living modestly at Shoreline Towers.

And it's not until he spends his first night inside Morrow Mansion West on Sestri Levante that he glimpses his neighbor—a young woman diving naked into her pool in the dark.

A surprising development, given that the pink chandelier in her backyard is gay.

Now he must solve the puzzle: Who is this fuckable, big-boned, brown-skinned beauty taking a dip alone, without her husband? She towels herself off after a few laps, then disappears inside her house, only to reappear at bedtime in Luke's imagination, begging him to enter her. Luke obliges, before drifting into sleep in his monumental master.

∞

Luke is up at 3:50 a.m., having trained himself to require a mere four hours of sleep per night, so he can bludgeon his underlings with their failure to keep up.

Once his trainer arrives at 4:15 a.m. for a workout in the 4,000 square foot gym with surround sound, Luke inserts earbuds and listens to his iPod; the African-American body builder trainer may instruct between songs when acknowledged.

After the trainer completes the hour and departs, Luke smirks to himself on the commode, *Keeping it real—still wiping my own ass.* Between 6:00 and 6:19 a.m., Luke dials twenty-seven employees, barking voice messages for all. *How come they are never at their business phones timely?* At 6:20 a.m., Luke walks his long driveway to retrieve *The Wall Street Journal*, knowing his soon-to-be-hired staff will retrieve the paper in the future.

But Luke is not alone in the murky light. Clanking an envelope into his mailbox is Alina, the swimmer from the night before. With her—the Marron twins, who are fussy in their double-stroller.

She says, "Sorry, just mailing that note for my boss."

Luke says, "Cute kids."

Alina beams at the homely girls. "I've been with them since they were three days old." Then she nods to the estate just below Luke's. "But sometimes I house-sit for Mr. Bram."

Referring to the twins, Luke says, "Where do they live?"

"Just next door." This is the estate just above Luke's. "Their parents went to Santa Barbara for the weekend, but they coming home soon—don't you guys worry. Anyway, Mr. Bram roll down his car window and give me the note, so there it is. And I better be going. My babies getting mad at me!"

She nudges the stroller down the grade. Luke reaches into the mailbox, thinking, Nice ass, body almost like a stripper. Opening the note, he reads: "Dear Luke, met you on a flight from New York and have been watching your house go up with great interest—I didn't know you were the owner until recently! And we're Tribal Fire customers, no less. My wife and I would love to have you over and maybe we can do some business after all. Cheers! Bram Brask."

Except Bram Brask never returned Luke's calls or emails when MyWorld.com needed an angel investor, and Luke thinks, That asshole? Next door? When he least expects it, I'll even the score.

∞

Luke reaches his office tower desk at 6:53 a.m. His number three assistant swiftly plates supplements, serving them with a quart of Rainforest Acai protein shake. Alone with his breakfast, Luke watches CNBC on a 65-inch screen, where the top of the news is: *Tribal Fire up another five points in heavy trading, bolting for a no-brainer split.*

Yes, his stock is a dollar shy of $200 per share and will break two for one, driving Luke's wealth beyond $2 billion— good for a middle slot on the Forbes 400. One anchor says, "Amazing how Tribal Fire Networks came out of nowhere."

The second anchor adds, "Every fund is rating it a Strong Buy."

The first anchor says, "Look for them to beat estimates by ninety cents."

Luke steps to his window, overlooking the Los Angeles basin and beyond. Investors of the nation, he thinks, tuck in my jet stream; draft in my destiny.

∞

Luke thrusts his Mercedes McLaren into third gear, raiding the road with 600 horsepower. Turning down Chautauqua, the car whines through a red light onto Pacific Coast Highway, catapulting him and his latest conquest—the next door nanny—to dinner at Bibione, where the best table appears with a bribe.

Having received a reprieve from the Marrons, who, at the last minute, took the twins with them, Alina is sprung and starving to boot. But what should she order?

Luke says she is "fucking sexy," and she should have her heart's desire; then he orders four appetizers, along with a bottle of 2001 Biondi Santi Brunello, which is the same price as a business-class ticket to Hawaii.

By the time Luke and Alina have finished their quail lasagnette, guanciale gnocchi, calamari fritti, and fried shiitake mushrooms with sauce of gorgonzola, they are looking forward to dessert—the restaurant's signature Amedei Porcelana chocolate soufflé. Only there are still three main courses on the way: whole charcoal Volterra lobster, veal chop with blizzard winter truffles, and a pan-seared chicken breast with lemon reduction. Luke and Alina can barely make a dent, and the leftovers go into boxes.

Over coffee and soufflé, Alina accepts Luke's decision to buy her implants. It took but two dates for him to pinpoint her insecurity—a gnawing New-Girl-in-LA Small Breast Syndrome. And as long as she's "Gonna go for it," she might as well "Go big."

After Luke pays for dinner on his rhodium American Express card, he and Alina link hands outside, where the McLaren is parked front and center next to the valet service sign. Luke tips the valet just as One Leg rolls up. Alina acknowledges One Leg with a gentle smile, offering the leftover boxes.

Lowering himself into his Corbeau racing seat, Luke thinks, that's my midnight snack, bitch. Then One Leg wheels away in the opposite direction as the McLaren, which, thrown into second gear, disappears in a cloud of racing fuel.

∞

At Luke's great-room bar, Alina teaches him how to make mojitos. By the time the moon has disappeared, bashful, the billionaire and the nanny have reached several times the legal limit. This makes for a fertile, erectile twist; Alina, fully not in control, takes Luke's dare to exhibit live on the Internet, courtesy of the Tribal Fire camera above his bed, which is linked to the Internet.

Assured that the lens position prohibits facial identity, Alina discovers herself *excitada*—wet for danger. Luke rips off her two-ounce dress, firing up his computer with his toe. Entering Tribal Fire's anal sex chat room, Luke opens the gate for voyeurs, letting them click on the icon next to SECRET CEO, his participant name.

Within minutes, fourteen separate parties are watching, making orderly requests through their home microphones to Luke's speakers: "Ram her with that big cock!" "Shove that dick up her fat ass!" Over the Internet the streaming goes— Byung-Jun's full-motion video seamless and glitch-free, delivering Luke doggie over Alina to the world.

And if anyone thinks this show is just for sickos, know that half of those exhorting are women. And though such a fact may be impossible to believe, it's true; women's fantasies can be disturbing too, not to mention that the ladies linger longer, emotionally drawn to the couple's plot—beyond the money shot.

∞

Watchful against others more desperate and mobile, One Leg tries to savor the leftovers in the dark, far from parking lot lights. He hasn't had lobster for half a lifetime, since the one he had steamed with lemongrass on his Navy shore leave during the Vietnam War, when he was an enlisted submariner in the South China Sea. He takes care to suck all of the legs, trying to get every morsel. Except it's nearly impossible for him to pick the meat from the shells, with his hands swollen from wheeling around without gloves. But that's life. Besides, the veal and the chicken filled him up nice. Feeling good, he shoots the empty boxes into a boardwalk garbage can, thinking, Better free-throw average than Shaquille O'Neal!

Then One Leg is off in search of shelter from the biting wind, which causes beach-bum raccoons to squint, lest sand stick in their eyes. Luckily for them, all they need is their sense of smell, which tonight is sensing lobster. Soon, the mother raccoon, cubs slinky behind her, finds One Leg's leftovers. The raccoons all climb into the can at once, snarling over their splits until their arguments tip the barrel onto its side.

The barrel's BANG! on the boardwalk is a shot heard around the bay, waking Luke on Sestri Levante. Beside him, sound asleep, is Alina, put away wasted. Luke climbs out of bed, removing the gun from his nightstand. Though his security system has not been tripped, he cases each room in boxer briefs, gun held in front of him with deadly aim. Finding nothing, he slips out a French door and onto his land—a Commando among lemons dangling in the dark. Nothing is there but singing frogs.

Down goes an ammo clip on the coffee table, with Luke on guard in his baronial living room, where he will spend hours waiting for assassins. For Tribal Fire has become America's homepage of choice, supplanting Google and Facebook—and all of the other clever portals that will come and go. Billions of dollars of click-through trade is now flowing through Luke, trickling down to others, who will have the lion's share no more—a simple reason to want him dead. But if those men had just been sensitive—creating a business that solves longing and pain—they could have been him.

∞

Above Santa Monica Mountain Conservatory, the sun rises, incandescent, and pours onto Luke, asleep with his gun. But when the sun's rays move across Alina, they become a hot surgery spotlight flaring over her—at a Beverly Hills clinic, where she's under anesthesia having augmentation. One more stitch in time and she is standing before her plastic surgeon, who unties her gown post-op, revealing her swollen breasts. "Everything looks good. They're healing right on schedule."

Alina says, "You think I went too big?"

"You made the right choice; they're perfect."

"I'm happy with them. I think my boyfriend will love them too."

Wearing sweats, Alina emerges into the waiting room, where her South American mother and 16-year-old sister wait, in town on temporary visas to care for her—courtesy of Luke's loving generosity and grafting attorneys. Mother and sister beam for striving Alina, proud of her bold foothold in America. And with supportive kisses for each other, the women set out into Beverly Hills for their greater destiny—*gracias, La Santísima Trinidad.*

∞

Jill Marron invites her reclusive neighbor to Jon's birthday bash, and she hopes that the man will cherish Alina forever and lift her from poverty. Alina has become like a daughter to Jill, and wouldn't it be great if Luke Morrow—Number Four on *Vanity Fair*'s "New Establishment List"—became Alina's knight in shining armor? Even if it means Jill losing her nanny.

Luke accepts the invitation through Alina. He will put in an appearance and meet her at the Marron's house after she puts the twins to bed—still her responsibility on the big night. Luke considers driving his Bentley next door, in case he and Alina decide to leave early and head for Club Prey. However, driving up the street contributes to global warming, so Luke decides to walk instead, conscious of his carbon footprint.

Luke heads down the driveway to his guard house and security man, who accompanies him in lockstep to the Marron's circle driveway, where the security man halts, his protection completed. Luke proceeds past valets, up the stairs, into the foyer. There, Kevin McNally, in a Brioni suit, spots him—but Luke, better-dressed in Enzo D'Orsi, strides past, saying, "Nice to see you," as Kevin does not serve Luke's interests at present.

Outside, Alina waits by the balustrade for Luke. She is dressed in an elegant black dress, simply adorned with a diamond teardrop necklace and matching studs—all gifts from Luke. She gives him a tender kiss hello, and he says, "You look beautiful on my arm."

"You're pretty handsome yourself."

"Girls asleep?"

Alina shows Luke her Tribal Fire phone view of the twins, who are down for the count. Luke and Alina descend the staircase onto the lawn, all eyes upon them: they are a fairy tale in the making. As a waiter offers them flutes of Cristal, Bram Brask rises from his table.

"Luke—Bram Brask. You remember Peter Wessler."

Luke offers a distracted hello.

Bram says, "You got my note?"

Luke says, "How's your empire?"

Bram sighs, acknowledging that Camden Capital took it on the chin. "Actually, I'm back in the hard money business—I had to dissolve the fund after unforeseen losses."

Luke says to Peter, "No more million nine?"

Peter admits, to his wife's unresolved dismay, "Unfortunately, it was all on paper."

Bram says, "But Peter is still a terrific salesman and a big fan of Tribal Fire. Maybe he could meet with you sometime and be an asset to your team?"

Marnie looks down in further humiliation—her husband out of work after buying a new house, her rich friend begging for them. But Luke is understanding. "Sure, I'm always looking for good people. Call my office and we'll set something up."

Peter's spirit soars, encouraged by this great man. "Wow, thanks! I'll email you tomorrow!"

Luke takes Alina's hand, leading her deep into the property, where a lush lemon grove borders the Marrons' land. Nodding toward Bram's mansion down-ridge, Luke says, "Got a key?"

"You crazy."

Eyeing her mixing bowl breasts trapped in her tight dress, he says, "It's time we christened those."

"You gonna get me in big trouble!"

∞

Alina retrieves a key from under a flower pot. She unlocks the guest wing to the Brasks' house and disables the alarm. Moments later, Luke is stiff inside her on Bram's media room floor. Switching for spice of life, Luke sticks Alina onto him, while he lies across Bram's mahogany desk. On Bram's side of the master bed, Luke dolphins Alina, before handing her a ricotta chinstrap. After a repose, Luke says, "You'd better get back to the party, in case the girls wake up."

"You still haven't met Mrs. Jill."

"Next time. Tell them about my big day tomorrow."

Alina looks at the cooling mess dripping to her chest, not believing what they've done.

∞

Luke's big day is: his Boeing Business Jet X-10000 is finally certified, ready for delivery. What grown man wouldn't behave like a birthday boy? Who is so rich and jaded that he'd sit still and apply himself at work, responding to emails from Peter Wessler?

Luke stands on the tarmac at Santa Monica Airport, shielding his eyes against high noon as he watches his plane land in wavering heat.

The doors to a ten-story hangar part and *The Defensible* backs in, pushed by a tractor tow. Disengaging, the tow skedaddles away as the hangar doors shut the plane inside. The jet's cabin airlock unseals with a weighty *whoosh*, allowing Luke to enter the aircraft from a retractable skyway. In the Vegas casino-styled sports book, TV screens show thoroughbred race tracks live coast-to-coast—with overlapping announcers proclaiming, "And *heeere* they come!"

Luke steps outside the jet onto a hydraulic lift, into black silence. He raises himself higher until he can climb onto the top of the plane, where he sits straddling the jet, the X-10000 extending massively between his legs.

Rising on a lift at the aircraft's fore: Byung-Jun Kim, Francis Oh, and Joey Wook, who are wearing tuxedos under a showman's spot. Francis and Joey pop bottles of champagne, while Byung-Jun announces into a microphone, "Ladies and gentleman, the beguiling Princess Amalia of Denmark, the Princess Elena of Luxembourg, and the Princess Desiree of Liechtenstein." Francis and Joey pour champagne onto the plane for the pleasure of the princesses, who swallow the froth from the nose cone.

"Sir?"

Luke is now in flight on the X-10000, lost in thought, unaware that the steward is at his side, tipping a bottle of flowing champagne. But then Luke takes the offered Dom Perignon, while glancing at Alina, who is busy writing in her journal in Spanish. Luke stares out his window again, knowing that he will never do something pointless like journaling, although he has hired archivists to preserve his doodles for posterity.

Alina looks over at Luke and thinks about her words—how they're capturing his sadness. How cruel of his ex-wife Lisa to move 500 miles away, when Luke was under so much pressure building his company. How caring and self-sacrificing of Luke to forgo seeing Trevor for the past two years—to spare the little boy the stress of being shuttled back and forth between cities. But since Luke has his own plane now and Trevor is older, maybe Trevor can begin to spend weekends in Los Angeles with them—and the three babies she is planning.

∞

Lisa received Luke's email a day ago, and she does not know what possessed him to want to see Trevor again. He has not phoned since Trevor's third birthday, and she has never expected more from the man who abandoned her son. And there's never been a reason for her to communicate with Luke; she has provided for Trevor all these years, after opening a successful mortgage brokerage with her sister Becca ahead of the California boom.

It's better that way, anyway. Lisa wants Trevor to grow up normal, not become a billionaire's brat. So she has never asked for money from Luke, and he has never offered so much as a Tribal Fire subscription. And since she never asked him for child support, cash for Trevor has only vaguely crossed Luke's mind. Yet he still sends Trevor $2,000 every year for the boy's birthday, weeks or months late.

Lisa is torn. This inexplicable man, who fought for the right to visit his newborn, left custody unconcluded, never caring to hammer out Trevor's vacation visitation, religious upbringing, or school approvals. But a boy has a right to his dad, and Lisa wants Trevor to have a dad. And even if there were a stepfather in the picture, it wouldn't be the same. Lisa, for Trevor's sake, writes back, lowering the drawbridge, paving the way for Luke to check in. After all, a man can change his spots before it's too late.

∞

Trevor's tummy feels funny on the foggy field at 10 a.m.; his shiny blue shorts and blue spotted jersey with #2 on the back are like slimy pajamas, and his feet are squeezy in his black Lotto cleats. His shin guards are itchy over his sweaty wool socks, and there is the shouty dad coach and ten other 5-year-olds kicking at the ball with him on the grass, and the boys are dressed like him because they are a team: the Blue Leopards.

Today is the first American Youth Soccer Organization soccer game of Trevor's life, and everyone is sure it is a big deal, as he has only kicked the checkerboard ball in practice at Walnut Creek Park with the other guys. But now he's told he's going "to start" and play the first quarter against the red and white guys with red shorts who are the Volcanoes. They seem bigger, older, and mean, and Trevor is not sure about what to do when the referee dad, in a yellow jersey and black knee socks, blows the whistle.

But Trevor will play soccer because that's what he thinks his mom expects, and his father is coming all the way from Los Angeles to see him play, so Trevor knows he must not do bad for Dad, important owner of the fire company.

And just as the game is about to begin, there is a giant man in sunglasses over him saying he looks great in his uniform, but the man is not with the girl-woman from before but a girl-woman named Alina in big bug sunglasses with sparkly stones, who embarrasses Trevor by saying, "He so cute!" and kissing him on the head—yuck! Why did she do that?

Then the yellow-shirt dad says, "Everyone on the field," and the shouty dad coach is saying, "Let's go, Trevor," but Trevor cannot move because he is panicking, because he is only a 5-year-old and he does not know what running around on the ball field to do, to know his dad.

He buries his face in Mom's shoulder and cries, and despite the shouty coach saying, "Don't worry, you can do it!" Trevor's whole body and legs are fearing and will not go. He is very ashamed because his dad is very mad and disappointed, even though Dad doesn't say any mad words. All the other kindergarten guys are running around on the field together in scrunchy circles, kicking at the ball, and it is easy for them, making their dads proud.

Trevor peeks toward Alina, who says, "It's okay!" Why is she saying that to him; why does she act like she knows him? Lisa sits Indian-style and comforts Trevor on her lap. She seems like she's not mad at all, and that he can play whenever he's ready.

And then the Blue Leopards score a goal kicked by a kid nicknamed Bear, whose proud dad is telling everyone that

Bear is "very competitive with his older siblings." The blue-spotted boys jump around in celebration, and Trevor starts to feel excited for his team, and he is planning to play soon. He would have played anyway, even if his important dad hadn't kneeled at Mom's lap, telling him, "If you play the whole second half, I'll give you a model of my brand new plane."

Trevor does play the second half, until a Volcano kicks the ball into his stomach. He is suddenly on the ground, on his back, with the trees and sky above him spinning past a cawing crow, and he cannot breathe with his body stuck. He hears, "Everyone take a knee," while he dies.

Except he's alive, and the referee dad is at his side, saying, "He just got the wind knocked out of him," and as the wind comes back into Trevor with short, stopped-up breaths, the dads help him up. He feels like he will barf, but he doesn't, and he sees all the blue and red guys sitting down on the field in worried silence.

Then the families on the sidelines start clapping for him, and he is a brave boy after all. His dad comes over to give him five when he returns, a hero, to the sidelines and into Mom's lap. It feels good, and it's even better when the time is up and the Blue Leopards have won 3-0 on Bear's "hat trick," though no one is supposed to keep score when the boys are only five years old.

After the Blue Leopards do a cheer—"Two, four, six, eight! Who do we appreciate? Volcanoes! Volcanoes!"—and all the families and the girl-woman Alina make a people tunnel and yell the boys through, there are orange slices and Krispy Kreme donuts and strawberry Gatorades for the celebration snack. And if that weren't enough, Trevor gets to go to the private plane airport and play on his dad's new jet.

∞

Trevor is a little peanut, looking up at *The Defensible*, a fifty-ton albino Brontosaurus. And as he climbs onto the jet's first step, Dad says, "Feel free to explore, but don't touch anything." Trevor scampers up in his blue socks. Alina follows behind, toting Trevor's muddy midget cleats.

In the main front cabin, Trevor leaps onto a swiveling lounge chair. "Is there a pilot guy?"

Luke says, "Two. Knock and say hello."

Fortified from Dad, Trevor knocks tap-tap, while Luke and Alina head deeper into the plane. The cockpit door opens and the captain says, "We've been expecting you, c'mon in!" The co-pilot leaves his chair saying, "Here, take my seat."

The captain says to Trevor, "Now you're the co-pilot."

Trevor can't see out the windows, but who cares, with all the millions of colored lights and Air Force switches.

The captain says, "Now to the North Pole—to see to the penguins!"

Trevor says, "Penguins are only at the South Pole."

"Then the South Pole it is." The captain pushes the throttle forward, pretending.

Trevor grins, "Here we go!"

In the quiet, mid-cabin den, Alina pursues her journal in Spanish, with her need to document how other soccer dads were on their phones throughout the game, answering calls with subdued hellos. But not Luke, he left his phone behind in the limo. And now Alina, unlike other controlling wives, understands Luke's post-game need to return some quick calls. Because soon enough, business will be over, allowing him to play with Trevor, her future stepson.

Trevor exits the cockpit, closing the door behind him as instructed. He runs down the aisle past the steward, who peers around with a doting smile. Reaching Alina, Trevor says, "We just landed on the ice! The plane has skis!"

Alina laughs at his grand happiness. "*Muy excelente!*"

Trevor slips into Luke's suite, where Luke is on the phone having important conversation. Trevor climbs onto the bed and begins jumping.

Luke wags a strict finger, sending Trevor on a new adventure to the galley. There, the steward says, "How about a 7-Up?"

Trevor says, "Not now. What's this?"

"The stairway to the cargo hold."

So excited, Trevor takes the stairs like a marionette, his legs stumbling out from under him, tumbling him—ashes, ashes, we all fall—down onto the cargo hold floor. In the dark, picking himself up, he discovers a spooky land filled with beverage cases, luggage, and a wood plank crate marked *Hazardous*. Trevor goes right up to the crate, but he would not if it said "Danger"—a word he knows. He tries to peek through the cracks, but the white light is blinding, making him see pink Dubble Bubble splotches on his mind that fade to toad-green.

He clambers up the stairs quadruped and scampers back to Luke's suite, where he jumps on the bed again. Luke concludes his call on the cabin phone and says, "Okay, settle down. Time for a family meeting." Luke daddy-steers Trevor to a couch, where Alina joins them. Then Luke tells him the bad news. "I just got off the intercom with my pilots.

Unfortunately, heavy fog is heading in from the bay, and if I don't take off now, my plane will be grounded. And I'm offering the CEO of Virgin Media the opportunity of a lifetime tomorrow—in Washington, D.C. Did I tell you I'm putting Tribal Fire in Great Britain?"

He did not.

"I want everyone there to enjoy it, and I'll be making a deal over breakfast, so 40 million English customers will have access to it, including The Queen."

Trevor says, "But I don't want you to go, and I'm hungry for lunch."

"Don't worry. You like Mickey D's?"

Trevor does.

"Okay, I'm giving you this $100 bill. Dean, the driver, is going to take you there on your way back to your mom's, and you can have as many Chicken McNuggets as you like and a McFlurry for a special treat. And I also have presents for you." Luke opens an overhead compartment, removing a model of *The Defensible*, along with a man's soccer shoe in a Plexiglas case. "This is for playing the whole second half—a cleat that once belonged to Pele. Do you know Pele?"

Trevor doesn't.

"Pele was the greatest soccer player of all time. An African-South American Brazilian. Do you know where

Brazil is? Next to Venezuela, not far from Alina's favorite beach. Only they don't speak Spanish there; they speak Portuguese. Can you say Portuguese?"

"Pour chew geese."

"Pele signed this cleat, which he wore when he kicked his 1,200th goal. I paid $14,000 for it at a charity auction for teen pregnancy, so we know the money went to a good cause."

Trevor tries to understand the shoe, feeling Luke sternly eyeing him. "Thank you, Daddy."

"Good boy. Now give me a hug."

∞

Lisa is doing paperwork at her home office when—something's wrong—she sees the limo returning hours early. Out of the house she goes. Dean opens the back door to reveal Trevor, tears running over his ketchup-messed cheeks. Beneath Trevor's feet: his midget cleats in a plastic bag with McDonald's trash.

∞

Sad, abandoned boy. Trevor stares at his ceiling until a rapping at his window rattles the blinds. He lifts the slats and there is Becca, wearing a scuba mask, snorkel, and flippers. Through the snorkel she gurgles, "C'mon already!

Ya can't stay inside forever!" Waddling backwards, she pauses at the pool before one-stepping backward—*kersplash!*

Trevor runs around to the lanai doors, where Grandma Pat is ready on the diving board in her 1952 University of Oregon diving cap. She says, "Go Ducks!" and executes an All-American half-pike.

Then Grandpa Stan jumps from behind the barbeque, bellowing, "Cannonball!" He leaps, bowlegged, into the air, becoming a grey-bearded fetus until he lands in a towering splash.

Trevor doesn't want to be sad anymore. He peels off his soccer jersey and races for the deep end, going flying squirrel over the pool, hollering, "Belly Flopper!" before hitting the surface with a stinging slap.

∞

At a gazebo table under a spanning umbrella, the Hudsons and Trevor, cozily wrapped in beach towels, scoop up guacamole. Lisa finishes grilling chicken and hot dogs. "Dad, hot dog?" She puts one in a bun for Stan, who does his best to fart-squirt mustard on it, for Trevor's pleasure. Then Stan raises the hot dog to sun-streaked canyons. "Good people of XinJiang, I love Trevor Morrow!"

∞

On the X-10000, south of the middle Platte, Alina tries to square Luke's hasty departure from San Francisco with her disdain for phone-addicted dads. They spend time with their children, and the man she reveres does not. But his rough patch as start-up entrepreneur is long past, so it's time for her to speak up, as the new Morrow matriarch.

"Luke, may I talk a moment?"

If she must.

"I know you're working for meetings, and that you're under pressures, so please don't take these the wrong way, but I thought you were going to ask Trevor about spending weekends with us. I thought that's why we gone."

Busy on his laptop, Luke says, "We 'gone' so he could see my plane."

"Okay, but I feel bad for him, because the other boys' fathers—"

"The other boys' fathers what? Do you understand I'm changing content for mankind, that I run a mega-billion dollar company? Those fathers you hold in such high esteem—"

"I don't—"

"You do, and guess what? At best, they're lawyers billing their lives away. And while you're traipsing around Paris this week with my credit card, I'll be bringing Tribal Fire to the French people, because they want it."

"I didn't mean it that way."

"You don't have a clue who I am."

"I do."

"No. Tell me. Who am I?"

She's trying.

"C'mon, tell me!"

"You're President—President of Tribal Fire!"

"President? That's all?"

∞

In the diesel dusk on a deserted tarmac in Des Moines, the steward conveyers Louis Vuitton suitcases down to Alina, who is no longer welcome aboard. The stairs retract into *The Defensible*, before thrusting engines direct the aircraft away. Alina throws her diamond earrings and teardrop necklace at the plane. But then she must pick Luke's gifts up, because they are all that she has.

∞

On the final approach to Ronald Reagan National, Luke checks his email, receiving another from Peter Wessler. Luke reads, "Hi Luke, I know you're incredibly busy, but I just wanted to say again that I will be a relentless, hard-charging salesman for your amazing company! For your review, I've attached my resume, and I look forward to your consideration. Sincerely, Peter."

Luke opens the attachment and sees how Peter has been Vice-President of Sales for ESPN, Telepictures Syndication, and The Disney Channel. With an MBA from Northwestern. But if Peter isn't to blame for Bram's failed venture capital fund, why hasn't he been offered another job?

Luke replies: "while you have experience at companies i admire and though it is good to have someone smart as part of one's sales team, i'm not going to bullshit you and need to tell you i think you're out of the loop. thanx.' He closes his laptop. Sighting the capital below, Luke's heart is full, thinking about how much he loves to fly. 'The High Blue Yonder. Yes! No dirt, no deceit, no slander up here.'

8.

How do you sell Tribal Fire to the peoples of the world, making monthly subscriptions a necessity like food or water? A Homeric task, spurring millions of Tribal Fire manpower hours, with global product domination a clamant quest. But not to Luke. He will have Tribal Fire in every hut and home, even if gross pressure to win costs him an employee like Johnson Ash, President of Tribal Fire International, who drops dead from stress in a Salzburg sanitarium.

And how to explain the way Tribal Fire superstructs? A detailed case study for a Wharton Business School course would fill a seminary with single pages stretching to Saturn. But when four fast years are done, Tribal Fire Networks is partnered with France Télécom, British BT, Deutsche

Telekom, Cetegel, Tiscali Italia, and all of the providers' successors and competitors to come. The result is millions of broadband customers ponying up for Tribal Fire in the United Kingdom, France, Germany, Russia, Italy, and Sweden.

Except Tribal Fire's millions of subscribers are hundreds of millions short, as far as Luke is concerned, and he will not rest until 100% of all broadbanders are on board. This leads him to his breakout scheme, and who says having oneself nominated for the Nobel Peace Prize is far-fetched? Jerry Lewis and Hitler are former nominees; all a man has to do is get someone caring to write on his behalf. True—from 150 yearly nominations, only one is honored, and obviously, Luke is not going to win, but how can anyone not grasp the fantastic, free publicity for Tribal Fire? What the fuck does he pay Carolyn Mannes for? She needs to go home and nap her lack of imagination, because her career is over.

For his third Tribal Fire President of Sales and Marketing, understand that, in Scandinavia alone, townships will someday erect bronze statues of Luke, even if it means raising taxes, as more than 50% of families there enjoy raising children out of wedlock. How the heck is a Denmark dad working sixty hours a week in Allerød supposed to see his daughter, who lives with her biological mom in Vester Lem?

Answer: with married parenthood a minority phenomenon, Tribal Fire is the video tie that binds. No wonder that Agneta Jagellonica, Chairwoman of The Centre for Mind in Nature at the University of Oslo, composes a Nobel recommendation for Luke. After all, Luke's mantic thought has shored up the family, preserving love.

However, becoming a global game changer is not without pain. Luke, at forty-one years old, is wracked with arthritis in his wrists and in his neck, through his ankles and knees, from traveling 270 days a year twisting through time zones, hopping back and forth between hotel suites and his jet's boudoir twenty-seven times a month, and having to go nuclear at his employees' incompetence nine times per day on average. And what will be the toll on his liver and kidneys with all the Vicodin?

But being rich and fairly famous has its benefits. Principally, Luke has willing beauties ready-bedded wherever he goes—in apex apartments from Paris to São Paulo, and whistle stops in between. It costs a pretty penny—all those secret rents, with morning-after pill prescriptions. And endorphins released during sex are short-lived. So Luke's physical pain never wholly subsides and, in fact, builds to a crisis.

After a speech extolling Tribal Fire to an adoring audience at the Royal Institute of Technology in Stockholm, he strides his swelling spine offstage, whereupon he collapses. Aides help him to a chair, but by the time paramedics strap on a blood pressure sleeve, Luke's vital signs are normal.

Weakened, he takes his Volvo limo to *The Defensible* for a flight to Lausanne to see Dr. Georges Charcot, rheumatology specialist to Andorra. Nothing's new, according to the doctor. Luke's joints show no further enhanced degradation, so he should see an internist as soon as possible; losing consciousness may be related to another serious condition.

Mindful of his importance to interdependent economies, Luke flies to Geneva to visit Dr. Édouard Moulle-Berteaux, a renowned physician to oligarchs. The EKG, X-rays, and CAT scans all come back normal. But if the specialist may be so bold, the trouble could be psychosomatic. "Don't kid yourself, Mr. Morrow—running the hardest-charging company on the planet would be tough on anyone. It might not hurt to get some coaching."

Luke considers one of Wall Street's worst kept secrets: that Bill Gates, Warren Buffett, and Steve Jobs have all needed Tony Robbins' private phone number. Maybe if Luke had Tony cheering him on, his disease would end. And though Tony would sell his children to name-drop Luke, Luke instead chooses an advisor with international cred.

That expert is the 82-year-old Fédération Suisse des Psychologues Emeritus Dr. Staufenbiel, who cured Pervez Musharraf of stage fright. In a yellow velvet chair with a Lake Lucerne view, Staufenbiel posits to Luke: "Can money really buy happiness?" "Does the person with the most toys win?" "Is the purpose of life to be the richest man in the graveyard?" "Dare we not stop and smell the roses?" And: "On our deathbeds, will we really say, 'I wish I'd spent more time at the office?'" These are *The Chestnut Rhetoricals*, but Luke will not surrender to them; philosophies rarely weather capital analysis, and who does Staufenbiel think he is, judging Luke's worthy wealth? Luke leaves uncured and $500 poorer.

But back at the Hotel Lucerne, with rack-of-lamb room service, Luke thinks that maybe the shrink is right; he should work to live, not live to work. And in that moment, a thought passes over him, the same as one from years before: I have a son.

∞

Her son is her life, but how can she always know what's best for him? He's nine, and his dad is calling from a $200 million jet, offering the boy a vacation in Hawaii, after not having seen him in 1,416 days. Lisa will have to phone Luke back; she's racing to get loan documents out. "Really, Luke? You just appear out of the blue after four years? Beyond the pale!"

Luke says, "Sounds like you need some sun, too. We'll overnight tickets and pay for your hotel next door. In or out?"

Luke presses the next line, rolling calls.

∞

Lisa sets an emergency appointment with Harriet Herman, a therapist in her sixties, whom Trevor has never seen. Lisa has visited Harriet over the years, and the two have continued to address the question of how to build a happy boy when his own father has rejected him. Presently, if Lisa doesn't tell Trevor that his father has inquired, Trevor will find out someday anyway. And her son will hate her for keeping him from his dad. Only, a visit with the father could cause more harm than good, and should Lisa make excuses for the father's lack of interest? It's a tough, real-life question, even for a seasoned professional.

Inevitably, won't the boy, when he grows into a man, see his father for who he really is? Can any mother really shield her child from the truth?

"Take the trip, Lisa," Harriet says. "Trevor won't forgive you if you don't, and maybe—just maybe—Luke is finally ready for his son. And if not, pick Trevor up, dust him off, and love him all over again."

∞

Luke flies Lisa and Trevor to Maui on American Airlines, where Lisa fights old anger toward Luke in first class, since drinking fresh-squeezed orange juice from a champagne bucket en route to paradise is uncommonly festive. Moreover, the humidity in the Kahului Airport terminal after landing is heaven, and there's a peppy, lemon-yellow convertible waiting for her, pre-paid.

With Trevor's boogie board stuck in the back seat, Lisa and Trevor turn onto Pulani Highway and Sugar Cane Row, heading toward a man they barely know. For Trevor, the last-minute trip is thrilling, and since he is a bigger kid now, his fears about seeing his father are formless and frightening only in the dark.

And this is Hawaii, after all—land of smoking volcanoes and the Grand Wailea water park pool, which is finally within Trevor's reach. When Trevor came here as a 3-year-old with Lisa, Becca, Grandpa, and Grandma, he was too small for the Grand Wailea's world-class waterslides—irresistible, magical adventure for fortunate children. But this time, he's four-foot something—big enough.

And what is his dad to him anyway? A very famous man, making Trevor secretly proud to be that dad's kid. Trevor has heard strangers' whisperings—that he is the son of Luke Morrow, the billionaire. And that envied man made a big point of coming to see his only son in a big black truck on the boy's third birthday with many toys. And now that man, even though he is especially busy, has invited Trevor for a vacation at a very, very expensive hotel. In Trevor's heart, he knows it is best to be quiet about his good luck, so other kids don't think he's spoiled.

∞

Lisa brings Trevor to the Four Seasons Maui, and she is holding his hand tight for both of them. There, inside the lobby shallows, shirtless in board shorts, is Luke. With midmorning sun glinting off the sea, backlighting an aura around him through open porticos, he steps forward.

Lisa holds Trevor's hand harder, only Trevor is now bolting for his dad, leaping into his arms, draping his head on his chest—his dad has come. Luke grins at Lisa as if to say, 'Under control, as if there were any doubt.' Trevor hugs onto his dad, eyes shut, and Luke carries his son away. A bellman loads Trevor's suitcase and boogie board onto the luggage cart and follows. Lisa stays until they're gone, a castaway with rental car keys in her hand.

∞

Lisa glides on her back in the Kea Lani's adult pool; she is the sole swimmer there in turquoise waters. And set in her singlehood, the emerald palm fronds glinting above in cathedral winds, she finds her peace, as always. I have Trevor, she thinks, and he is enough for any woman's life.

Over lunch at the pool café, Lisa observes newlyweds sharing baskets of fries. And she wishes them the best, knowing that at least 50% of them will end up divorced someday. Making her way offshore onto the lava reef shoal, she turns back to face the jade mountains. And without her engagement ring, which once dazzled under a daytime moon, she breathes, "Thank you, God, for bringing me here."

Soon, the hotel's evening porters are lighting the resort's pathway torches, making way for Jupiter and Mars. Lisa eats by herself at an outdoor hotel trattoria, finding the simple pleasure in hot cracker crust pizza made with local goat cheese and fresh, highland tomatoes. For dessert, she stops at the boisterous gelato place on the lower level, joining joyful families who don't notice her polishing off small, decadent scoops.

Back in her top-level, ocean-front room, she relaxes on a king bed, enjoying her travel guide to Maui. But there is no flashing red light atop her room phone. The phone will never ring that night, and Lisa will try hard not to cry, alone in the South Seas.

∞

Trevor can't wait; he digs through his suitcase in Luke's presidential suite, piling up undies until he finds his favorite Hurley jams. On they go, and he is ready, Freddy—but Luke is on the Internet in the second room.

"C'mon, Dad!"

Luke complies, closing The Erotic Review's homepage.

Trevor takes Luke's hand and drags his dad on a hurried time-trek through the Four Seasons, out to a volcanic rock path leading to the Grand Wailea Hotel pools. But a tourist can't just use the Grand Wailea's half-acre water park; everyone needs a neon bracelet telling the lifeguards that he is a Grand Wailea hotel guest, and no Four Seasons hotel customers next door can buy a water park bracelet on a daily basis if they're not guests at The Wailea, no matter who they are, because the Grand Wailea has restrictions.

But policies shift with grift, and if the bronzed lifeguards at The Wailea think the founder of Tribal Fire Networks isn't gonna get his kid into their pool, their heads are up their a-holes. On goes a neon-pink strap with a security snap, and Trevor is can't-believing with the unattainable band actually on his long-awaiting wrist. But Trevor may not leap into the pool just yet. Luke says, "Stop being a wiggly worm and hold still already," as even a guy like Luke is pre-wired to sunscreen his son.

Off goes Trevor on his own, super-swimmer skipping over pool parapets to the Lava Slide, 238 feet long with a three-story drop. And when he plunges into a splash at the bottom, it is a big-boy triumph for his life. Soon, Trevor is lost in an imaginary world: the park's tropical river and artificial rapids snaking past nine pools on six levels could take Don Gaspar de Portolá weeks to explore.

While Trevor is gone, Luke has the resort staff ready lounges with towels, but Luke does not pull the concert-shell umbrella over him for shade. Instead, he basks in the high noon sun to dry his damp joints. A sun bath is good for mending one's mind too, and maybe Luke should rest on his laurels for once.

Only, Luke cannot stop thinking about his pricey division heads, who might mismanage Tribal Fire into the ground within hours. So what's the point of watching aquamarine waves break over opalescent sand?

Trevor, wet from the pool, pounces Luke's flank, blocking the sun. "C'mon, Dad—time for our adventure!"

Luke, regarding himself in an outermost thought as an unparalleled dad, rises for the cool of the pool. There, he takes several turns swinging off the Tarzan rope before trailing Trevor to the park's peak, where they slide Ana Puka 115 feet to the bottom with a 360-degree turn.

Then it's a ponderous wait for a wet ride in the world's only water elevator, built for a mere $2 million. But that's a good way to reach the Rapids Slide, which rushes riders downward 16,000 gallons at a time.

Starving afterward, Luke and Trevor eat giant grilled hot dogs, Maui chips, pickle spears, and iced Coca-Colas in the concert shell umbrella's shade, and it is their first meal together ever. And it is the best hot dog and chips Trevor has ever had. It's so cozy eating them cross-legged with Dad on starchy-smelling towels in their bear cave by the sea.

∞

Trevor returns to the slides for the rest of the afternoon, and Luke naps under his umbrella. It's not until nearly sundown that Luke jumps into the water again, joining Trevor's journey through jungle pools to a secret waterfall grotto.

There, the guys take stools at the swim-up bar—for bountiful banana smoothies.

Back in their suite, Luke and Trevor shower and dress for dinner, en route to the open-air HumuHumu Restaurant, where the trade winds buffet Trevor under a merry moon. And when it's finally time to settle into sleep after spiny lobster tails and macadamia bread boudins, Trevor feels in love with life, for he has had a perfect day with Dad.

∞

Trevor wakes at 4 a.m.; after all, it is 7 a.m. in northern California, where there are photons of light. But he will have to stay in bed, excited for the day ahead, until Luke gets up at 6:30. At breakfast with his dad at the terrace restaurant, a raspberry-headed bird lands on their table, pecking at Trevor's muffin. But the crazy bird doesn't like bacon. There are all kinds of muffins besides blueberry at the buffet, and they keep them in Plexiglas cabinets with doors kids can open. Luke says that keeps the moisture out so the pastries stay fresh. The omelet chef asks what ingredients Trevor would like in his omelet, and Trevor asks for egg. Dad laughs and says, "Omelets are eggs!"

∞

Trevor and Luke ride a 50-foot catamaran to Molokini, an extinct volcano tip off the Maui coast. On board are five other families, plus two sunglassed men who share the lounges near Luke's. Big-muscled, they hardly speak during the sail, and when it comes time, they choose not to snorkel. But that passes over Trevor, who just wants to swim, and he will never know that the men are Luke's bodyguards. Reaching Molokini, Trevor and Luke slip from the back of the boat into the Pacific, floating above red dragon wrasses and purple-tipped tangs. Bobbing in the swell, Trevor yells to his dad, "Did you see that lightning stripe guy?"

Luke shouts back, pointing below, "Huge school of snapper!"

"C'mon!" Trevor pops in his snorkel and frog-legs with Dad. Together, they swim above elfin eels and swaying, malachite-colored maninis. And when a bale of sea turtles paddle by, the scheduled time for the outing is suddenly up. Luke and Trevor can't believe how quickly the time has passed; they've barely taken breaks with the winded rest of the group, who hang on the catamaran's keels. Trevor and Luke's trip through Hawaiian waters has been miraculous, and the voyage home under skin-salting seas is Shangri-La.

Back at the Four Seasons, Luke and Trevor spend the rest of the day boogie boarding with other mainland families in affluent fellowship. Later, on their way back to the suite, Luke checks his watch and suggests that he and Trevor make a quick stop at the hotel lounge for Fiji water.

In the lounge, Luke bumps into Logan, a beautiful businesswoman who just happens to be staying at the hotel for a conference. Luke tells Trevor, "Logan is an important executive with Verizon."

Then Dad says to Logan, "Well nice to see you. Enjoy your stay."

After Trevor eats chicken fingers for dinner at Spago, it's time for bed. But Trevor is still on Northern California time, and wakes again at 4 a.m. The TV flickers in Dad's room, so Trevor goes there to snuggle. Except Dad is asleep in bed with the woman Logan.

On the TV with the sound low, a naked girl with bologna-slice nipples is moaning, while a tatted pirate sexes her vagina. Frightened and ashamed, Trevor presses the picture off. Then he crawls back under his comforter, and it's not until sunrise that the suite door softly opens, before carefully clicking closed.

At breakfast with Dad, Trevor feels sinful and destroyed. When the raspberry bird lands for his blueberry muffin, Trevor scares the bird away, and when it comes time for an omelet, Trevor will not near the chef's station, because a boy should know an omelet is egg, not made from pancakes. Instead, Trevor has Froot Loops, but he cannot finish them.

Down at the water slides, Trevor is done, the mountain holding no more magic. He returns to the concert-shell umbrella and sits on the edge of Luke's lounge, braving back tears.

Luke stares into the dead day, wondering what's missing. But then, he remembers he wants a yacht.

∞

Lisa and Trevor fly first-class on an American Airlines red-eye, their return tickets open-ended from the start. And it is an Airbus bound for the blues, after Luke needs to get to the German shipyard, cutting the play date short. On her best behavior with Trevor present, Lisa can only accept the boy back at the Four Seasons. Scolding Luke would only harm their son.

Trying to comfort Trevor after his dad's departure, Lisa says, "We'll stay the weekend at the Kea Lani, just you and me." But Trevor's unresolved relationship with his father has done its damage; the little boy just wants to go home. So Lisa and Trevor flee for Nor Cal rain and Trevor's boogie board no-show at the mainland claim.

9.

The Defensible lands smoothly on a military strip in barreling Bremen winds. *Heil* to the X-10000's design; the Lürssen Shipyard salesmen would have toasted the plane even if Luke hadn't wired a $160 million deposit for his new frigate.

Luke's private yacht will be leviathan—the biggest ever—built in secrecy on a warship platform. The bark will have: aft cannon guns with a carrier deck for an attack helicopter and programmable drones; stadium seating in the movie theater; a pool grotto formed from a Playboy Mansion mold; 7,000 separate alarms monitoring 6,000 systems; and two onboard submarines for undersea excursions. Luke also adds some upgrades: missile detection antennae and torpedo tubes—just in case—along with advanced Dutch mine-sweeping technology. The master state room has a bedside, hand-fed, central vacuum suction port for the instant removal of loaded Jimmy Hats. Final vessel cost: $900 million USD.

But the ship will take twenty-eight months to build, no matter how many dollars Luke throws at it. And given the scarcity of slots for the construction of mega yachts, coupled with the world's richest men clamoring for them, the craft will be worth at least 25% more upon completion. Leveraging $900 million in yacht futures today will realize a $225 million gain in just over two years.

Still, Luke is somber on his comped Maybach ride back to his jet. He wanted to sail soon and now he must wait, after buying his way to the head of the line. It makes his wrists flare.

Back in Los Angeles, Luke stands on the lawn of his Sestri Levante mansion before a modern art pavilion—a Renzo Piano-designed, 30,000 square foot sphericon of achromic steel. Luke steps inside the epic hall, where a Damien Hirst panda bear pair mating in formaldehyde only reminds Luke of its $46 million price tag, and the animals' dead bafflement stirs nothing in his heart.

Beyond the bears, a two-story Leon Golub mural of beaten, bloody men at the feet of penniless police is pointlessly soiled linen. Even a Jeff Koons piece—a $29 million life-sized gilt porcelain of Britney Spears baring her beat-up catcher's mitt slit holds no whimsy.

Luke climbs to his mountaintop, where he achieves clarity. I am too isolated up here, he thinks. I need to be down below with the people.

∞

Those who have everything want what none think possible, and Luke will do anything to get what he wants. Including spending 23% of his escalating eleven-figure fortune to buy Billionaire's Beach in its entirety, from Carbon Canyon to the Malibu Pier. And how each and every entrenched lot god would be craven enough to sell their south-facing sand to Luke at three times its value is but the twenty-third of the infinite components of a miracle.

And don't think that Luke will have trouble with the Coastal Commission when he tears down 100 homes and businesses. Save for his Cape Cod compound, formerly owned by an entertainment puppetmaster, who always sells ephemera for crazy numbers. No, the commission likes the deal, and Luke will return the shore to its natural habitat, opening Carbon Beach to the public—so long as the public remains 500 yards north and south of him, despite the mean high tide line. This earns Luke civic sainthood, and his gift to Los Angeles shall never be topped.

Nonetheless, owning the coast doesn't end the chase. Lately, Luke has been having incidental notions about granting a young wife to himself. If he were to die someday, a new wife could schedule eulogies at his funeral and spread his ashes over the capitals of the world.

Moreover, with his travel demands, it would be good to have a doting person to help him pack. Besides, he's tired of having to wait for women to show up—it can be hours before they're in place. But a grateful wife who is always open for business would be better. And dating women casually makes them starved for attention, causing them to prattle on; wouldn't it be better to have a wife who is confident enough not to talk, who will happily let him open a newspaper in her face at breakfast?

Plus having girlfriends creates other aggravations, like they're always high-maintenance, wanting him to put them on a pedestal—when a smart wife will put him on a pedestal once and for all, where he belongs. And enough of girls getting angry at him for not understanding their feelings or being considerate of what they're wanting all the time. Enough of having to be their mind reader; a younger, new, grateful, smart wife will read his mind first.

And so it happens on a summer evening that Luke meets the woman who will become his new wife. The encounter takes place after he spends Sunday afternoon with his division heads, whom he summons on a 96-degree day to fix their fourth quarter proposals, which disappoint him, despite his clear instructions to come up with better ideas before he's made to come up with them himself. He makes the employees stay until 6:50 p.m., and if they don't like missing dinner with their families, they can wear orange aprons at Home Depot.

Excused execs leave, lifeless, for burning hot cars and the beach traffic grind. Luke leans over his deck with a tumbler of 1937 Glenfiddich, enjoying his private surf. But the space just north of his home is not bare; there, a woman in her early thirties with a little girl of about five are shelling, the woman singing sweetly in the lapping tide. Luke descends his staircase to the sand. "Kids—this is a private beach."

The mom looks up, shielding her daybreak-blue eyes and autumn-brown hair with Ray Bans and a Mizzou Tigers baseball cap. "Oh, sorry. C'mon, Max—"

"Didn't you see the guards?"

Somehow, she missed them.

"On an ATV 500 yards that way and another toward the pier. There are No Trespassing signs every thirty yards on the fence."

"Apparently we can't read today."

Her daughter says, "I can read every day."

The woman says, "Beth and Maxine."

"Luke Morrow. Maybe I need signs every fifteen yards."

"Max, the beach belongs to this man and he has warnings I ignored and that's wrong." She says to Luke, "We went to the Santa Barbara flower show and stopped to cool off."

"Talk your way out of speeding tickets, too?"

Maxine says, "I got an orchid for my room."

Luke says, "It must be beautiful."

"It's mauve."

"Wow, your mom really loves you. When you're ready to go, there's a shower at the stairs."

Beth says, "We'll rinse here."

Luke heads for his deck. "Big girl, Maxine, knowing how to read."

"I'm only five!"

Beth leads Maxine into the surf, washing the sand off her legs. Only, once Max heads to the tide line, the breeze blows grains back onto her ankles. Beth leads Max to the stair shower for a second rinse, where Luke checks Beth's ringless finger from above, imagining Beth soaping herself alone near nightfall, her yellow sundress hung on a nail on a whim. He says, "You can take the shortcut through my house."

Beth says, "We don't have passports."

"Next time."

Beth helps Max up. Luke shows them the way across his deck through his great room to the highway gate. There, Luke says, "Give me your email. I want to send you something."

Beth says to her daughter, "A bill for footprints."

"Your mom is silly."

Max holds onto her mom's hem, proud. Beth gives Luke her email and says, "Thanks for not pressing charges."

"If I did, you wouldn't come over for dinner."

Beth looks worried at the proposition. "What do we say?"

Max says, "Very-nice-to-meet-you."

Luke says, "You, too. Maybe next time, you'll build a castle on the sand."

∞

Beth clicks Send/Receive time and again, night after night. But one week later, Fed-X Ground delivers a box to her Ocean Park bungalow. Inside the box is a thick packet of press on Luke, extolling his accomplishments. And, handwritten on his Tribal Fire Chairman's buck slip is, "Enjoy! Yours, Luke."

Beth emails back: "Have received. Will there be a quiz?"

Luke responds, "When you're on my plane to China."

Beth types, "???!"

Luke writes back, "Call you in five."

But she never gave him her number. Never mind—her home phone rings minutes later.

"Beth, La Chanteuse," Luke says.

"When have you heard me sing?"

"On the beach to your daughter."

"Before we got kicked off."

"Rules are made to be followed."

"We're not riff-raff, and what's all this about China?"

"I'm headed for Shanghai, and I thought you might like dinner—there."

"How do you know I'm not married?"

"I don't."

"Divorced three years."

"Boyfriend?"

"If he's kind."

"This is a platonic date, at the most. I've only met you once, and I'll be on my jet working, so you'll need to bring a book along—the flight is fourteen hours."

"I could say yes, if my ex-husband will take Maxine. But where will I stay?"

"In your own room. I'm a complete gentleman—ask anyone."

"Okay. Not to be insecure or anything, but why me?"

"If you were me and you saw how beautiful you were and what a great mom you are, you'd want to get to know you, yourself."

"I'll have to call back. It's a lot to consider."

"My plane leaves Santa Monica airport at noon Thursday, returning Monday."

"You don't even know what I do."

"You'll tell me over the Sea of Japan."

"A half-blind date halfway around the world—the whole thing's crazy."

"True, but I only live once."

∞

Beth and her friends try to figure out the invitation: Is it destiny or a really bad call? Stay at home with a tub of ice cream, or regret the adventure for a lifetime?

∞

Beth is late for the flight. She miscalculated the time it would take for the last-minute dash to pick up her cute black dress at the cleaner's. At ten to noon, she bangs over a speed hump in her dented white Mercedes, with an urgent spin into the hangar parking. But the ground steward is still loading bags and the Tribal Fire stewardess is ready at *The Defensible* door, saying, "Welcome aboard."

Beth says, "Sorry I'm late, but my car suddenly won't go in reverse, and I had to wait for a neighbor to push me down the driveway." Which is her way of admitting that the car hasn't gone in reverse for months, and that she can't scare up the money to fix it.

"Right this way." Beth follows the stewardess through the main lounge, where businessmen downing cocktails eye her. "Your private cabin." Beth takes her seat, buckling a Jack Spade restraint. "Champagne?"

"Just some water."

The stewardess removes a card. "The water menu."

Beth says, "How many people are on board?"

"Twenty-six, plus eight crew."

"Where's Luke?"

"In the conference room on the rotunda—he won't be down for hours. But you're free to move about the cabin after takeoff." The stewardess produces a second card. "Map of the plane."

∞

Beth reads the bottled water list and selects the Aix les Bains.

The stewardess says, "It pairs well with ice made from Mont Roucous or Puits St. Georges."

"Room temperature is fine."

Soon, Beth is drinking water, wanting to love this incredible flight. But she is nervous that she doesn't belong, and the sea below is stark, and she suddenly needs a martini. Just a tiny one with a splash of pomegranate and a twist of ginger.

∞

Beth rises to explore the plane. In the bar, British Telecom execs show off, battling their Chinese co-venture team at foosball. In the casino, U.S. Congressmen hopping a ride to the Far East play Texas Hold'em against reporters from Bloomberg and Nikkei Interactive. The dealer offers Beth the last seat at the table, but Beth tells the gang that she does not know card games beyond Go Fish and Mahjong. This earns her a charity chuckle from the men, as she's fuckably hot.

Beth heads toward the rear of the plane, where she finds an elevator. Just as she's about to push the up arrow, a hand presses it from behind, parting the door.

Luke says, "Come see the view with me, Ma Chanteuse." Luke and Beth emerge at the plane's top deck, where Luke offers her one of two hydraulic chairs. The chairs whisk them upward into a tetrahedral glass dome, giving them a panoramic vista of the world outside. "Pretty fantastic, huh?"

Beth says, "Amazing!"

Luke says, "Now imagine Mars, Venus, and Jupiter." Luke and Beth imagine, and sure enough, the window slices through pitch black until the brilliant planets are right there—candy-red, yellow, and green. Then Luke says, "How about a sudden storm?" Immediately, the X-10000 soars into detonating thunderheads, with lightning ribboning the plane. Frightened, Beth reaches for Luke's arms. He whispers, "It's okay. Once the rain passes, we'll see the Milky Way." Again, there is silence and night, but this time it is filled with stars.

After a moment, the view blends back into blue. Luke says, "Homework is waiting for me downstairs, but stay. I've arranged for a driver to show you around Shanghai while I'm tied up. He'll bring you to dinner Saturday night." Luke's seat descends, leaving Beth alone with the company of space and sky.

∞

Wei Ping will chauffeur the American VIP around Shanghai, showing her the most interesting sites. But she's so tired from the time change that she slumps in the back seat of the BMW.

"Visit famous white jade Buddhas, then return to hotel."

Beth says, "No, no I'm fine. I can sleep next week!"

"Then Sun Yat-sen residence next. George Bernard Shaw get ideas at tea ceremony there, very notable historical."

"In your hands!"

Wei Ping grins. Now fifty-one, his greatest pleasure is guiding interested people through the booming city. But when he drops Beth off for dinner at Ten Kingdoms Restaurant several days later, he worries because she is trembling at their goodbye. Wei Ping doesn't know she's been waiting for her date, and that she's scared she's being used. And that suddenly, she's feeling panicky in a frantic land, when she could be home in Santa Monica with her daughter, safe, with toasted cheese sandwiches and sliced tomatoes.

Ten Kingdoms seats Beth in a rosewood booth, carved in 1890. There, with a glowing oil candle, Beth quavers tea to her mouth until Luke finally shows up thirty-five minutes late. He says, "My assistant should have texted."

Beth says, "It's okay. It's the weekend; she's probably tired!"

"She overbooks me, but I had her order ahead. Hairy crab is the specialty."

"Whatever you like." Then Beth gasps, because two 5-foot alligators are roving the floor with roped jaws.

Luke says, "The local delicacy."

"They let them loose!"

"Prized free-range caiman."

"My therapist wants me to be adventurous, but—"

"Therapists should talk—they're more fucked up than their patients. I have arthritis, and since the doctors at USC couldn't fix it, they sent me to this European Jungian grandpa-dude, who tells me I'm under pressure running the hottest company on the planet. Really—ya think?"

"Sorry about that. You're so young."

"If you keep ice bags ready for me, you'll earn a girl scout badge."

Beth says, "I'll do it for free."

"You're too good to be true."

"Maybe, except there's something I need to tell you. I don't have Tribal Fire; my daughter is with me all the time."

"Your ex-husband could have cameras in his house."

"Apartment, and he'd never allow it."

"Jerk."

Beth looks down, remembering the rule to never discuss her divorce on a date.

Regardless, Luke says, "My ex-wife won't allow cameras either, and I own the company! Then again, my son isn't really my son—DNA tests."

"Oh, that's terrible."

"Result of her many one-night stands. But I fully support him."

Ditching the rule, Beth says, "My ex-husband had an affair with my partner. She and I had an interior design business together. He was a contractor, until it turned out he never got his license, which he never told me or anyone else. After a year in jail, he's working at Home Depot—in the garden shop!"

"Karma."

"And the whole betrayal thing by a girlfriend and my husband... Anyway, I've been sober for two years, and I'm stronger for it now. And working at Pottery Barn isn't so bad!"

"You'll get back on your feet soon enough."

"It's fine, really. I'm doing just fine. And now I've met you."

∞

After a meal of crab, prawns, and aromatic duck, Luke and Beth take his chauffeured Rolls back to the Four Seasons. In the elevator on the way to their separate floors, Beth says, "Next time, I'll try the caiman."

"Calling ahead—reserving the cheek meat."

The elevator reaches the twentieth floor—time for her to go. She steps into Luke with a hand to his chest, giving him a slow kiss goodnight, so that he will know she wants more when they meet again. Stepping out, she says, "Wait till I cook you dinner."

Luke says, "I'll call you," with the elevator door closing.

∞

Beth does not see Luke again in Shanghai, nor on the flight home to the U.S., though he is on the plane in meetings. But he suggested that he'd see her again in Los Angeles at his first opportunity, and he does have a big job, after all. Beth returns to her single-mom struggle, picking up Maxine from camp after her daily 6-hour shift at Pottery Barn. But the job is decent enough, earning her some thousands selling occasional chairs and canopy beds. Still, Beth wipes tears away on a display towel, thinking, Hey, China trip—no harm, no foul.

Luke calls ten days later, saying, "According to *The Rules*, 'If he doesn't contact you by Wednesday, you must put him off until the following week.'"

Beth says, "Well, it's Wednesday."

"What are you doing tomorrow night?"

"I'm with Max, and I'm not a Thursday girl. I'm a Saturday night girl, and only a Friday through Sunday girl, if there's already been a previous Saturday night date."

"I have a board dinner Saturday. I'll cancel it."

"That's not necessary."

"I want to see you."

"I want to see you, too, and I know I shouldn't be saying this, because I know you've been slammed, but I haven't heard from you since Shanghai."

Luke says, "Maybe I want to take things slowly."

"Did you get my thank-you note?"

"I did. But my not rushing things—it should give you comfort."

"It does; it's great."

"So just let it breathe. On my father's grave, my intentions toward Ma Chanteuse are honorable."

∞

"What can I bring?"

"Just yourself."

Luke drives from Sestri Levante to Beth's bungalow in an armored Mercedes; she thought he would have come with a driver, even though the trip from Pacific Palisades to Ocean Park is only ten minutes. But now, he's a regular guy with a bottle of Brunello, and Beth doesn't mind if he drinks it all by himself in the course of an hour.

Over crackers and brie, Beth explains how her business broker father helps her with the pricey lease of her two-bed, one-bath 940-square foot home, built in the 1920s. Luke agrees that she's made the place very cute with Pottery Barn accents—30% off for the sales staff. And it's nice having original wood floors, even though they need refinishing, and it's not death without a dishwasher; eventually racked dishes dry on the countertop. While serving Vongole alla Napoletana, Beth says, "Do you think you want to get married again and have more children?"

"Wow, getting right to it."

"I don't have to know right now or anything, just that you're open to it—to the possibility."

"To the possibility, yes. I liked being married and I love kids. But right now, Tribal Fire comes first."

Beth says, "Just so you know, I wouldn't even consider marrying you for at least a year."

∞

Beth and Luke walk to Ben and Jerry's, and she pays for the ice cream cones from her pocketbook—the least she can do for a generous guy. They walk out onto the public beach, where the question comes up, as always.

She says, "What are you thinking?"

"Nothing."

"Promise; you can tell me anything." Luke holds her tighter and she is glad for it. She thinks, Here I am at last, with a good man who isn't broken by his divorce or job.

Later, back at her bungalow, Beth lights a warming fire and begins shedding clothes. But before she surrenders, she says, "Can I just tell you this dream I had last night? I mean, I'm not religious or anything, but somehow I ended up dancing with Jesus in the pews at Brentwood Presbyterian, and he was saying that everything's going to be okay in the end. Then after I woke up, I took this Rabbit vibrator thing that I bought last week and I threw it in the dumpster behind the church—in broad daylight! Isn't that crazy?"

"No shame in having a vibrator."

"The first one I ever bought. Too much going on with it!"

"It's okay, c'mere."

Beth lies next to him. "I'm scared."

"Don't be."

"Are you gonna make me a princess?"

He puts a finger to her lips. "Shhh." Beth lets him fill her, stretching her to just enough, beyond ever before.

∞

Beth rises with the sun, her relationship with her new, caring man a source of peace. And the early morning start is beatitude too, now that she has meaningful work.

True, her boyfriend got her the mid-level marketing position at his company without her having direct experience, but it's her idea to offer Tribal Fire subscription scholarships to families in schools around the world, in exchange for Tribal Fire publicity.

Plus, additional gifting to private schools for fundraising events keeps Tribal Fire front and center internationally, expanding the company's customer base.

So that Beth may be safer and feel more confident, Luke has his business managers lease a new white beginner's Lexus in her name. The car will also help her build credit: she will make thirty monthly payments all by herself after the first six months. After Beth signs the paperwork at Luke's Carbon Beach estate and receives the hand-delivered car, Luke texts her, "go to bev hills and get some new clothes. whatever you need, just put it on your visa, i'll reimburse you." When they meet for lunch at Spago, Luke surprises Beth with diamond studs and a teardrop necklace from De Beers. In return, Beth floors Luke with her orgasmic superabundance.

But she knows their connection is more profound than just sex. She knows Luke sees her goodness, and not just when she's bringing him ice bags. Plus she holds her own at business dinners. Now all that's left is the tension over trust; once betrayed, a woman searches for guarantees, with the hope that she will find a good man someday. So Beth works hard to forget her fears—actions speak louder than words—and if Luke's opening his Palisades Riviera home to her and Maxine while he's traveling isn't love, what is? And what mother and daughter wouldn't want to have tea parties with Luke's garrulous chef, who bakes them lemon squares from estate-grown fruit.

But Beth cannot beat back dread; what if the man she loves is not faithful and shares himself with other women? Only, Luke leaves his phone about and his email open—which would never happen if he had tracks to hide. So Beth believes a girlfriend should do unto others and not snoop, unless she's starving for a self-fulfilling prophecy.

And if she finally cracks, checking his browser history—just for a second, in a moment of weakness—she still won't find peace, even though all he's reading are sites on private enterprise rocketry. Because if another woman falls under him while his girlfriend isn't around, the other woman surely makes a sound—waking the entire resort. Maybe half a Xanax near noon wouldn't hurt, and a small glass of Syrah at dinner, and another, because it's really vodka that's a wolf in Absolut's clothing.

Several months into her doubt, try as she might, Beth can't silence suspicion; on nights when Maxine is with Beth's ex-husband, Beth drives short of Luke's gated estate where darkness hides. And it only takes six stakeouts and seventeen vodka miniatures over the course of a week to prove that she's right: one morning when Luke is supposed to be in D.C. in front of the Federal Trade Commission, a Czech model leaves Sestri Levante in his Audi limo at 7 a.m. with her window down for a last trace of night jasmine.

Beth tails the car to the suspect's domicile in Beverly Hills, and eleven hours later, to the Four Seasons on Robertson, where the woman valets her 330i BMW on her way to the bar. She joins a leggy Bulgarian, who uses the same untalented colorist. Soon, the women are teasing a fifty-something who buys them Bellinis.

Ten minutes later, the Czech girl accompanies him into the elevator, returning an hour and fifteen minutes later to give her parking ticket to the valet. Within minutes, the woman is back at her apartment, letting herself in.

Incall to outcall—call girl confirmed. Beth drives home to her Ocean Park bungalow. Dizzy, she races to lie down on her bed in the dark. But the room is spinning mayhem.

Beth bolts through her front door for the sidewalk and blacks out on the cold concrete—directly in the path of a man in a wheelchair. One Leg doesn't know she's just a good person from St. Louis; once he's seen one wasted whore, he's seen them all, and why stop and help when his own life burns? One Leg diverts his wheelchair onto the grass, pressing on toward the dawn.

∞

What doesn't kill Beth will make her stronger. She can live like a Kennedy wife, if she can just have the inner grace to look the other way and agree that, biologically, a man needs all the illicit sex he can get once in a blue moon—especially if he's a good man 90% of the time.

∞

Beth looks forward to dinner at Pezzo Grosso in Ocean Park; the restaurant is one of Los Angeles' most expensive, and she has never had the money to try it. Tonight, though, the tab is on the Provost of Harvard University, who encourages her to order Japanese Wagyu steak, rare or medium rare according to restaurant rules; Beth will have Prosciutto Capri to start. The fêting company makes the appetizer even better, and the Harvard development team is bright and engaging.

It's a welcome time for Luke, as well, even if the group is coasting for his money. The dinner is only a favor to his Harvard-trained attorneys back East, who fight for Tribal Fire Networks before the United States Court of Appeals. There, Tribal Fire sues Broadview and ADT for patent infringement, because the home security giants are offering similar Tribal Fire full-motion video suites under the brand names We See and Family Tree, using Tribal Fire algorithms, claiming the underlying codes are generic and open.

But Luke will not grant the future to his competitors, who join together in a legal partnership to defend their theft. If the rooks win, Tribal Fire's market lock will pop. No wonder Luke downs glasses of Barbaresco with every course—Wall Street is awaiting the court's decision at 9 a.m. EST tomorrow. And that he doesn't notice once-sober Beth drinking right along with him fuels her rage. While the Harvard stories grow—of tricky times at the World Bank in Burkina Faso, or the possibility that the Kennedy School of Government has Al-Qaeda sleepers—Beth seethes. After dinner at a red light three blocks from the restaurant, she abruptly gets out of Luke's Murciélago.

No one gets out of Luke's car unless he tells them to.

Beth says, "Too bad, so sad. I don't fucking care," and throws her necklace and earrings at him, like so many women have done before. She backs into the shadows, beginning a haunting run through beachfront alleys.

∞

Four hours later, near 2 a.m., One Leg spies Beth's diamonds under a gibbous moon. He bends to get them, just as a Prius taxi comes to a halt at the yellow light. The hybrid's kinetic energy vibrates the curb, releasing the potential energy of the jewels, which slip into the storm drain; a trickle of water carries them to sea on their way to the Tonga Trench, where they settle for eternity.

∞

Luke stands before his wall-sized LCD TV in his upstairs home office near dawn. Luke sets the screen for CNBC, where coverage begins from the Appeals Court. And the breaking news is: Broadview and ADT are infringing on Tribal Fire's patents. They must cease and desist and pay Tribal Fire all profits earned. Upon the court's decision, Tribal Fire stock rocks up to $19 at the closing bell.

Luke steps through the TV screen onto a palm tree planet beneath towering 24-carat gold glaciers. Rising above him is a 100-story scale of justice.

Ex-MyWorld Chief Technology Officer Byung-Jun Kim emerges from beneath a sunflare, aiming an 80 mm Avalauncher air cannon at the mountain. *BOOM!* The great peak rumbles into an avalanche, piling a golden glacier onto the right side of the scale, slamming the acre-sized dish to the ground. Luke notes the motherlode and says, "God's money."

From behind Byung-Jun, Francis Oh and Joey Wook train a larger 120 mm air cannon. *BOOM! BOOM!* The second golden glacier, three times the mass of the first, roars down, slamming onto the scale's left side, pounding the dish into the earth, punching the lighter, right side of the scale into the sky.

Luke regards the greater pile of gold on the ground. "My money. Now I have more money than God." Luke suddenly feels so much better that he can hardly feel the pain in his neck and wrists anymore.

Stepping back through the screen and his reverie into the home office, Luke observes Beth on a Tribal Fire video link, slurring at Luke's gatehouse, demanding to see him.

But Luke's security men will not let her pass. She swears toward the second floor window, "Let me in, you bastard!" while her nails claw the guards' faces in an ensuing scuffle.

The guards tackle her, just as an urgent LAPD car skids into the driveway.

Luke considers how Human Resources has her discussing his quirks on company time with her former boyfriend, as well as spilling Tribal Fire secrets to others—when she signed a non-disclosure agreement. There's a legal difference when a boss hires and fires a girl who got her job because of the boss's kindness, versus a boss entering into a relationship with an established employee, whose career tanks when the affair ends. At most, he'll give her six months' severance. For a mere moment more, he wonders, *What about her car lease and credit card payments?* concluding, *Not my problem—they're in her name,* and, *How dare a woman drive drunk?* She could have left her own daughter motherless or killed innocent children at play. And who has the time for a new wife anyway, when his own 13-year-old son needs him?

Beth sobs, head down, shackled in the back of the squad car. At the second floor window, Luke draws the drapes, snuffing out her light on the hill.

∞

Trevor's mom loves him so much, and so does Grandma Pat and Grandpa Stan, and Becca loves Trevor to smithereens, along with his uncle Case, her sandy-bearded husband, a very fine architect and surfing compadre, who bought Trevor a sweet Sex Wax sticker for his board when he was only ten.

And Emma and Emily, Trevor's 4-year-old cousins, are beautiful twin crazies for him, chasing him around in rainbow tutus. And Trevor has lots of friends in his class at the Catholic school, and his mom says Our Lady of Ygnacio is a happy place because it teaches that God made a good world.

And Alec, in Trevor's grade, is a Grand Theft Auto addict and a good buddy, and it's ridiculous how his mother gets him whatever fish he wants for five different tanks—three freshwater and two salt. His jewel cichlids had like 500 babies and the male hatched the brood in his mouth; to protect his fry, that male chased the Panaque pleco and the Cuvier African bichir so much that they died from stress.

Sloan, next to Trevor in natural science, is smart and tops with him for First Honors, and she has Dr. Wass for an orthodontist like Trevor, and she's athletic like a boy, so Trevor has to be careful when she's on the opposing flag football team, because she can be highly vicious.

Sam and Wynn are girls too; they passed a note with "shitbag" written on it to each other, then threw the note away in the computer lab trash, where Mrs. Babcock found it, and now the girls are on probation because Mrs. Babcock is a douche.

William is so funny. He always yells that Trevor and the other boys are "Perverted!" and whenever someone accidentally makes a squiggly noise in class, he shouts, "I just made a girl fart!" and then Father Weber bans him from recess. He makes William stay cooped up in the classroom, which is a bad idea, because of all the kids, William needs to run. What happens is William goes crazy in class later because he has autism just like Trevor's cousin, Kit.

Now William has to have this Cal State East Bay college girl sit with him part-time in the back row to control him. He sorta does okay in advanced math, but he always forgets his homework. And blurting, "Bitches!" at the kids in class when they're just minding their own business is funny, but it gets him bad attitude marks for being obstructive.

Trevor's mom says he has to have empathy for William because William can't make his thoughts come out clean, and the world is frightening and jumbled to him, and it's hard for him to be a normal seventh grader like Trevor.

But Trevor needs to have the most kindness for Danny, because his best friend was his dad, and his dad died last month, at only forty-five years old, from cancer. Danny has two little sisters, too, and his mom and dad were already divorced when his dad got sick. His dad spent the last two years away from Danny going to Mexico for a special cure that didn't work.

Then his dad died alone at Danny's grandparents' home, 700 miles away in San Diego, because there was no one else to take care of him when the hospital couldn't help anymore, and he thought it would be too painful for Danny to see him dying.

So Trevor tries to help Danny when he gets stuck on his homework, but it's hard for Trevor to feel bad for Danny all the time, because he has a living dad who doesn't love him.

∞

What if Trevor wanted to die?

∞

A mother's love is not enough. A 13-year-old boy, imagining his father, lays waste to her self-sacrifice and years of unflinching care.

∞

"You made him go away, I hate you!"

∞

How would a boy feel inside if his father—a once-in-a-generation visionary—created Tribal Fire Networks for millions of families, becoming a famous billionaire written up in *People* magazine, and every kid at the boy's school and all the parents and teachers believed the boy was his bastard son.

∞

He's gone from As to failing.

He used to enjoy his classmates.

He put a pair of scissors to his throat.

∞

Trevor's self-hating pain forever remains in the devil's grip. But Lisa and Dr. Herman fight for the boy through the terror. For Trevor, in despair, is reading blogs on suicide. And it doesn't take an intuitive mom or a good therapist to understand misplaced rage.

∞

Lisa says to Luke, "He can't wait another year. He needs to see you here."

∞

Luke lands in San Jose at 10 a.m. He will meet with Lisa and Dr. Herman at 4 p.m., after his scheduled Tribal Fire meetings in the valley. At Reverse Engineering, Luke views an application enhancement for Tribal Fire: Kickstart Media's servers store ninety days of live feeds, which a Tribal Fire subscriber, for an upsell charge, can access and edit on an interface. So baby's first steps captured live on a Tribal Fire home camera can be saved, ready for email forwarding.

From Sunnyvale, Luke heads down to Apple iTunes for a revenue-sharing contract signing; iTunes will now be available on Tribal Fire's interface, so music can be added to subscriber video feeds. Then there's lunch for all in Palo Alto at Caffe Riace, chosen because Luke must head across the bay after the meal. But bottles of wine flow like the bronze fountains, and the next thing Luke knows, it's 3:20 p.m.

From his limo, Luke texts Lisa: "Running behind. Start without me." But the purpose of the session is for Luke to hear from Lisa and the therapist—in the hopes that he will awaken to his son's suffering. Lisa and Dr. Herman can only wait, until Luke shows up fifty minutes late.

But that still leaves ten minutes to discuss the matter, so, "Shoot."

Dr. Herman says to Luke, "Simply put, Trevor's crying out for your love."

Lisa says, "You can't just check in every four years. He's your son."

Luke says, "You summon me here just to persecute me, like it's my fault, like I'm all bad? You don't have a clue what it's like to be a 13-year-old boy, and what's really going on is he's just playing the victim. And to be fair, he could call me once in a while, although he never does.

"He never cares how I am, and if he wanted, he could easily make plans to see me when I'm in town. There is an opportunity each and every day to call my secretaries to find out where I am or where I'll be. So this whole kangaroo court thing—"

"It's a discussion, Luke."

"No Lisa, Trevor's just being manipulative, and you're trying to blame me for his behavior. But it's you who's been giving him whatever he wants, whenever he wants."

"How would you know?!"

"Dr. Herman, tell me the Fifth Commandment."

"Why don't you tell us?"

"It's honor thy father and thy mother. Note the order, and it's not honor thy children. There is no commandment to honor thy children because children should honor their parents if properly raised." Done, Luke leaves.

Tears plunk onto Lisa's blouse. Dr. Herman says, "I'm sorry. Trying to make Luke see—to reason with him—it's like spanking a cat. The cat doesn't know right from wrong; it doesn't have the capacity, so it lashes out instead."

"Trevor has such high hopes for their reunion."

"You'll be waiting on the curb when Trevor comes home. You'll comfort him all night if you have to."

"He just wants a dad."

"But he's got an awesome mom, instead—a fortunate stroke of great good luck."

∞

Luke's limo arrives at Lisa's ranch house. Trevor steps outside with his back to the street, securing the porch door. Luke steps out of his limo, saying, "Maybach—the most luxurious ride known to man."

The boy, with his mouthful of braces, turns to face him.

Luke says, "Maybe you wanna lose the earphones."

His son lets one iPod earbud go.

"I'm taking you to Portola Valley for dinner. We're going to sit outside under some California oaks. They've been there for hundreds of years; by law, you can't cut them down."

The driver opens the rear car door for Trevor, who joins Luke in the Maybach's soundproof cabin. Luke nods at the center console. "If you plug in, you can listen to me." Trevor, so anxious with his all-powerful dad, steals a look at the man. Luke says, "I think you'll enjoy it—it's my authorized biography. I agreed to narrate, but since I don't have time to speak the whole book into a microphone, they record me reading random pages. The technology clones my voice, capturing my cadence and punctuation. It's genius."

Trevor thumbs his own iPod volume higher—a kid's knee-jerk, shaky shield. No matter—Luke reclines in his ivory leather throne, saying, "Time for a nap." Luke closes the back curtains, listening to himself narrating his own biography, into a super slumber.

∞

Zott's restaurant—a one-time, clapboard gambling hall—is now a Stanford burger joint tradition. Luke and Trevor sit in Zott's gravel courtyard under live oaks at a picnic table. Luke thumbs through his email while Trevor listens to his iPod. Over the loudspeaker, the Morrow order is ready.

Luke nods—*fetch*. Trevor leaves his iPod and goes inside for rectangular hamburgers on rolls. He balances the dinner baskets back to the table, spilling a few fries. Luke pours a Rolling Rock into a paper cup for Trevor, saying, "Enjoy. It shouldn't be forbidden fruit." Trevor has never tasted beer. He likes it, especially since his mom would never allow it. Luke says, "So the rumor is you're not happy at school."

Trevor says, "Mrs. Babcock, she's such a bitch. Her class is so boring, if we sway just to be funny, she yells 'Hold still!' And if we move again, because it's hard to control your legs sometimes, she shouts, 'I told you to stop moving!' and then she docks points. Once I was looking out the window at a squirrel, and she's like, 'Stop looking at that squirrel! That's it, I'm docking points!'"

Trevor puts his cup out for more beer and Luke pours. "Then Dad, you know how our school is so poor, we don't even have hot water?"

"C'mon."

"It's freezing when you wash your hands, but there's hot water in the teachers' lounge. At recess, Tino scraped his arm, and in math, Mrs. P. said to him, 'You need to go to the boys' room and wash that with hot water,' and I said, 'We don't have hot water, we're too poor!' and she said 'That's it, I'm docking points!' Then at lunch break, Mrs. Babcock sent me to the principal."

"For looking at the squirrel?"

"No—me, Tony, and Tino, we were trying to push each other into lockers and she caught us."

"Just you?"

"I was the one pushing when she found us out. And she said I could have suffocated Tony, and that children who climb into refrigerators and washing machines die all the time. But the lockers have these air stripes, so it can't happen. And the principal said because I don't know what a locker is for, and because I had 'an uncontrolled vitriolic tongue' about no hot water, he was giving me detention."

"Sounds like they have it out for you."

"I want them fired."

"Ah, except the problem with teachers is that they're the bosses, and bosses can't easily be fired. But let me give you some advice that most fathers won't make time to explain: you don't want to spend your life working for any boss, because eventually, they will abuse you, cheat you, and make you suffer. Trust me—the only way to really be happy in life is to make sure you're The Big Kahuna, so you can call the shots.

"And don't think for a second because I have a lot of money, you're gonna be handed my company or made CEO. No, my friend. Warren Buffett—he's not leaving corporate control or his fortune to his children. He's vocal about that, because children must make their own way in the world to have purpose. So I'm going to follow his advice in spades and not leave you anything, because whatever you haven't earned yourself will only make you sad.

"But you don't need to worry about your financial future, because every person on earth can become rich and happy— if he will just make and sell a product or thing that no one has thought of that everyone needs. I believe you can do that, becoming the boss of the workers you hire to produce your invention, and if you start trying to create that product now, you'll have a jump on everyone else. I did exactly what I'm saying creating Tribal Fire Networks, and now 100,000 employees *have to lick my balls*. That's right! I see you smiling!

"So whatever is impossible for people to do, create something that solves that impossibility and make millions for that something, and then you can be like me. Did you know that Harvard University didn't accept Luke Morrow when he applied, and that Harvard people look down on Stanford people, even though Stanford is heaven on earth? And now Harvard is begging me for buildings!"

"I want to go to Harvard!"

"If I buy them one measly auditorium. But I'm not going to because they rat-fucked me thirty years ago. Now, one last thing. Since you're thirteen, it's time you knew the truth about the past, which is that your mom and I got divorced because she decided to stop trying. Whatever else she tells you is a lie."

∞

Having straightened Trevor out, Luke returns him by bedtime, en route to the X-10000 and Vaitape, Bora Bora, where the Lürssen Shipyard, for a $1.25 million service charge, has delivered the greatest mega yacht ever, for all foreseeable times and beyond.

Named the *North America, Dub Edition*, the boat floats because he who has the best toy wins. Docent details: final length, 900 Shaquille-sized feet; $919 million to complete; fourteen decks; crew of ninety; captain's salary, $1,450 per ship foot, per annum; ship christened with Krug Clos du Mesnil 1995, market price.

And who cares if The Great Housing Bull Run after the First Great Internet Age is over, and the world is on life support after the Dow-Nasdaq death? Because populations, reeling, will cut out Starbucks, trips to the Apple Store, and mani-pedis before they'll think of cancelling Tribal Fire. So while cities suffer and countries collapse, Luke makes more money than ever. And why not enjoy?

Through French Polynesia he goes, sailing the warm climes. And what fun, flying a black-market Russian KA attack helicopter from the *North America*'s prow, skimming the waves with 30mm GSH 30 cannons and Vichr 40 mm missiles. And who wouldn't spend millions for a made-to-measure skeet shoot sling, to launch clay Sikorskys into the sky—for Luke to blast into the swells for shits and giggles?

And if he accidentally hits a whale, or two, and they sink in bursts of blood, Go Tell Aunt Rhodie; their calves whistling after them got milk, and it's high-time the kids were weaned on the krill.

Back on deck, life improves with eleven Ukrainian girls, and when two aren't with Luke at the same time, they're with each other for love—that's how wild the world. And if this seems dark, living in Kiev is darker, if a woman is starving, pretty, and poor. It's a step up onboard the *North America*.

For Luke, dreams do come true, and what's a kid like him from Highland Park, Illinois doing with so much pussy, all tasting like French vanilla. 'Props to you Mao Tse-Tung, but it's quality over quantity, and your 4,000 dirty little concubines? Not on my good ship.'

And to those who think docking in St. Barts or Cap Ferrat gets old after a while—it doesn't. Money can buy happiness, and anyone who doesn't think so ain't got money.

10.

The boy marooned overachieves, on a quest for self-worth, missing the rest of childhood.

Trevor's frantic faith: if he can't get straight As in seventh and eighth grade, setting the standard, he can't get straight As throughout high school. He underscores his obsession by entering every one of his quiz and test scores into Excel, in columns of 90-95, 96-100, one mark at a time. For this kid—so hard on himself—believes that getting into Harvard will show up Dad.

Improving grades are a relief to Lisa. Trevor's return to the top of his class is welcome; surely he's turning the corner. But he stays a loner, studying for hours when he knows his subjects pat, and when he's assigned five pages for a science report, he writes nine, with extra pictures, detailed footnotes, and a glossy folder cover.

His old, good friends become ball scores from summers past, and when it comes time for his eighth grade graduation party, Trevor, second in his class, doesn't want to go. Instead, he'd rather celebrate with a slice of pizza and an orange soda at Marco's Pizza, with just Lisa.

And maybe Lisa has set the wrong example, because she's become a loner too. Yes, there have been suitors and midterm relationships, parceled. But listen to the foils, and every woman will understand: boy toy Mt. Tamalpais Academy tennis coach; Morrison & Foerster corporate attorney, 24/7 for covered bonds; and a ne'er-do-well heir to a child's portion of the Rice-A-Roni fortune. And countless other dates on Match.com, the kind where she meets at a hotel bar for a drink, engages in wordplay, and then comes to the realization after sixty minutes crooked on the couch that there won't be a second date.

Still, family and friends think a single mom needs to be remarried, but that idea is from a yonder era. Ask any number of divorced, working moms and they'll assure anyone that two dinners with a man per month can suffice, if concluded with PIV. As in, Penis in Vagina.

And nowadays, who wants to combine broken families, anyway? Radio show therapists say don't do it, and 80% of all second marriages end in divorce, despite greater commitments to make them work the second time around.

But more than that, kids are just little for a short time, it seems, and before a parent knows it, the kids are on their way to college, California, or New York. If a woman is divorced with children, she's really not alone, and her time with her kids is the last of her springs, so why muck it up?

Despite her family's worry for her greater happiness, Lisa remains single. For she listens to the real Book of Luke, and she knows that where her treasure is, her heart will also be.

∞

With his boat in a Brisbane berth, Luke flexes his power from the Tribal Fire tower. But what to buy with the company's cash? Or would a corporate merger measure more money? For Luke's stock is a singular star, and no Apple or Google or any iteration of either will ever be able to buy Tribal Fire at any price. However, maybe Tribal Fire should combine with them to grow even bigger.

But Luke knows business history, and he's thought about his place in the story; why gamble his Hall of Fame fortune? Henry Leland sold Lincoln Motors to Ford in 1922 with a promise to run the company he founded. Later that year, he was shown the door. And who wouldn't learn from Theodore Turner, who lost TBS and CNN to the AOL/Time Warner wasteland, and now must spend his last days miserable, tramping through buffalo pie on 2,000,000 pristine acres?

No—Luke won't put himself in a position to be fired from that which he created. Because how much money does he really need when he'll be the richest man in his own ten square mile graveyard, which he's willing to the State of California as park land? And what about a spending spree? Could Luke not buy Verizon, DirectTV, or Samsung himself, or their inheritor chameleons? Would this not make him one of the greatest businessmen ever?

Luke spends five years kicking tires, considering acquisitions. But then he quiets; Tribal Fire is his, and he will not make it pregnable. There are other frontiers beyond industry to conquer, and should he dare to be the first private citizen to walk in space?

∞

The boy with gold-flecked blue eyes becomes an emergent man. By eighteen, Trevor is strong and lean, bobbing on his surfboard, alone in the sea.

∞

The word is out and the gospel is: college admissions committees are now searching for achievers with genuine grace, not The Pre-Packaged Pervasive, with padded resumes and prepped pursuits. Lisa gives 14-year-old Trevor his choice between a privileged private school or his local public high, and he chooses the normal latter, to her relief. There, he excels among solid peers, finding camaraderie on the water polo team, which he leads to the state finals his junior year.

Gaining confidence as a recruitable collegiate athlete, Trevor turns to his surfing passion, leaving at 5 a.m. on Saturday mornings for the foggy San Simeon coast, where he joins a collective of adventurers who aim to conquer Maverick's 50-foot waves.

But Maverick's waves are unearthly and can lead to certain death if mortal and unlucky, and Trevor will take on Maverick's only once. Paddling out to become a legend, he catches a 30-foot curl and rides the tube for one glorious moment before it buries him under 4,000 tons of water.

For the next twenty-six seconds, the force of the wave carries him under water toward jagged rocks, which will kill him. But then he pops up at the last moment, allowing a Jet Ski-lifeguard to scoop him from danger. Only, Trevor isn't okay. His eardrum is ruptured and his shoulder is dislocated, and Lisa is devastated when she gets word from the emergency room that he could have died.

Hanging up his board for a year, Trevor finds a new journey, endearing himself to a craggy surfboard maker, who has been famous since the late 1960s for solid wood longboards, hand-worked. Trevor becomes the artist's apprentice, learning the simple pleasure of sweat and toil in a 1940s Quonset workshop.

However, the money Trevor earns part-time is barely enough to pay for Subway sandwiches, and Lisa says, "See how tough it is for ordinary people to get by? We're lucky we can afford a nice home and live near good schools."

That gets Trevor thinking. Mom and Becca have been industrious all along, investing their profits buying local apartment buildings, sheltering their mortgage business from an unforeseen meltdown. But what if they would agree to house one underprivileged family in each of their buildings, so the families' kids could receive an excellent neighborhood education? And what if the tenants of each building joined in, each contributing to the family with matching dollars from the landlords?

Lisa and Becca agree to support his charitable plan, helping Trevor found Sharing for Shelter, a non-profit organization that leads apartment owners and their renters to subsidize one low-income family per building. The empathetic effort makes *The San Francisco Chronicle*, and soon, Trevor has twenty-six buildings committed to the cause.

Now all Trevor needs are Advanced Placement As and 99th percentile SAT scores. He gets both and applies to college ranked third in his class. And his application essays soar: he writes about how he wrestled a mighty wave and lived to tell the tale; how he learned to work wood for pennies, finding fulfillment in craft for craft's sake; and how people in America will open their hearts to other families and share their homes to help sixty-seven kids.

With his applications filed in the fall, Trevor relaxes for the first time in seven years, slacking off the second semester of his senior year. Half-assed efforts earn him Bs, but no matter—he'll still graduate with a low A average.

And for the first time, Trevor frees his schedule for a girlfriend of sorts—a junior spirit team gymnast who is serious about her grades and future too. So, like many 16-year-olds of her time and place, the last thing she wants is a serious boyfriend messing with her emotions, forcing her to act all committed and couply. So she casually hooks up with Trevor once a week until he graduates, and if that means oral or occasional sex for both without love, let it be.

∞

Eight schools accept Trevor, including Harvard. Six months later, Trevor heads across Harvard Yard under a crisp eastern night—with disdain for his dad, whom Harvard rejected.

Trevor's destination is the fall's first mixer for the Harvard International Business Club, where he meets Daria Morton, the club's vice-president by way of San Jose society. And she is smart-girl magnetic, with flashes of beauty and the goal of becoming the United States Ambassador to France.

Morrow, Morton—they almost have the same last name, and when their eyes lock during the faculty sponsor's opening remarks, the lustrous brunette wants to reach up to his broad swimmer's shoulders and kiss him under a tree, while he thinks, frisky heavy naturals under her sweater, ready to be handled.

Only he's a freshman, and she's a senior on track to graduate a semester early, but it's hardly a May-December romance; he is the son of Luke Morrow and a three-year difference doesn't matter when they're making out later for the first time on Widener Library's steps.

The next day they find each other under a soft rain after morning classes, and during a cozy Cambridge lunch, they turn into a stunning preppy couple—patrician California kids in the Ivy League, falling in love. But how can kids have forever feelings for another so fast, and how does everyone on campus know Trevor's rich?

Daria says, "They just do, surfer boy. What does it matter, anyway?"

"People just want to be my friend because of my name."

"Except you'll always know who's fake. But I just love you for you. I wouldn't care if you worked at McDonald's."

∞

"Ambassador Morton?"

"Surfer boy."

"Check this out."

She leans in, reading. "Oh my God."

"The first email he's ever sent."

∞

Trevor accepts Luke's email invitation to use his $42 million penthouse on Central Park West for the weekend, while Luke is at Cape Canaveral; the keys will be with the doorman, with $750 cash left in the fridge for food.

Trevor and Daria take the early train to New York on Friday and a cab to the condo, where the home's luxury thrills them. Inside are: 360-degree views; a life-sized Giacometti Walking Man bronze in the living room; 15-foot-high walls bearing originals by Francis Bacon, Lucian

Freud, and Gustave Courbet; and pre-Columbian treasures on bookshelves.

Holding fearfully onto Trevor before an encased nineteenth-century Jivaroan shrunken head, Daria asks, "Why exactly would he have this?"

"No idea."

"Can we please be tourists now?"

Off the students go, to Liberty Island to see the statue up close. Then they take a brisk walk through Wall Street, before a late afternoon lunch at a Greenwich Village patisserie.

Later, at the penthouse, Trevor and Daria have an extended romp in the 3,000-square foot master, before enjoying an evening at the New York Philharmonic.

There, in Tribal Fire's corporate seats, she nestles her head on his shoulder through Beethoven's ninth symphony. After the concert, they have a wild cab ride to Little Italy for a late night dinner at Benito's II. Finally home at 12:40 a.m., Daria lights candles next to the hot bath. In the dark waters, she slow-kisses her boyfriend.

"I love you."

"I love you, too."

∞

The couple spoons under covers with the sun stuck behind blackout blinds. Eventually, their long sleep leads to low blood sugar, and it's time for a quickie steam shower together before deli brunch.

After preposterously huge omelets and an unnecessary side order of lemon blintzes, Trevor and Daria hold hands against the blue, blustery day and walk to the Guggenheim Museum. Inside, the sophisticates enjoy Cézanne, Gauguin, and Pissarro. Window shopping later under a somber sky, the couple dips into a boutique jeweler, where Trevor admires white gold earrings set with aquamarines and pinpoint diamonds.

Daria says, "They're too extravagant."

Trevor says, "I've been saving $2,000 a year since I was three. Finally, I can use it."

"No."

"We'll take them."

Daria's eyes glisten in the jeweler's mirror with the earrings on. "Thank you."

Trevor holds her from behind, admiring her grace in the reflection. "Wow, beautiful Harvard girl."

The couple returns to the penthouse, where they dress for dinner—Trevor in a suit and tie and Daria in a simple black dress. Off they go to Daniel Boulud's Bistro Moderne, for Super Green Spinach, Pommes Frites, and DB Burger Royales, layered with 10 grams of shaved black truffles.

Then they embark on a subway adventure to Brooklyn Bridge Park, where they gaze at New York City from the river's black edge. Trevor says, "By the time I'm forty, my private equity firm will rival Apollo and Kohlberg Kravis."

Daria says, "You'll get there; I know it."

"I'll launch a successful leveraged buyout of Tribal Fire Networks, then fire my dad."

"Don't say that."

"He's a bad human, so it's pretty much okay."

"I wish he could make it up to you."

"Disappearing for eighteen years? That would be a challenge."

"Deep down, he loves you."

"Really? How about the last time he came to see me in junior high? After he left, I tried calling him, but I always got his secretaries or his answering service, and they would say, 'He's actually in a meeting, or he's actually traveling, or I actually don't have him right now.'

"So I would leave word, only to get messages on my voice mail from him in the middle of the night while I was sleeping. I'd call him back the next day and the same thing would happen all over again.

"Many nights, I waited up until two, three, four in the morning, hoping he would call so I could hear his voice. I could barely keep my eyes open. But during those times, he never called—so I finally just gave up. He played an epic game of phone tag with his own son."

"I'm sorry."

"Don't think twice; just understand that my mom is paying my tuition because we won't take a penny of it from him. And if the X-10000 crashes, I won't care. But you and I will leave him a thank-you note for reaching out."

∞

Wearing crimson- and white-striped mufflers, Trevor and Daria lie back on Luke's master bed, recording for the Tribal Fire camera on the ceiling. Trevor says, "Thanks Dad, for your pad and the cash. And it's my honor to introduce Daria Morton of Harvard's Adams House. Remember her name, because she will be famous one day."

She says, "Thank you, Mr. Morrow. I had a great time. Your art is fantastic!"

Trevor ends the taping with a bedside button, moving to the LCD screen on the desk. With Daria learning over his shoulder, he attaches the recorded video to an email for Luke.

∞

In the penthouse den, Daria stands before a masterful painting.

"Titian, take care." In the living room, "Giacometti, goodbye." By the shrunken head, "Scary—see ya!"

∞

On a train hurtling home, Daria sleeps—sublime, curled in Trevor's arms.

∞

Beautiful girl, radiant girl: Daria. In his daydreams, it is them bravely against the world—to beat out Dad, and if she should be disfigured in a car accident, Trevor will remain at her side her whole life; that's how much he loves her.

Only Harvard is hard, and Beyond is already upon him, and how can he get into Harvard or Stanford Business School on the way to a Wall Street empire if he doesn't get all As freshman year and after? So Trevor must ace: Uncertainty and Statistical Reasoning; Principles of Economics; Introductory Humanities Colloquium; Calculus and Differential Equations; and Comparative Literature 257—Trauma, Memory, and Creativity.

An ambitious class load for any first-semester athlete, who would be wise to skip acute love, as the aforesaid makes it really hard to concentrate. When Trevor gets a C+ on his first Econ quiz, freshman panic follows—he can't see Daria every day anymore. To her, if that's how he feels, fine, but it's kind of immature since the score only counts for 10% of his final grade.

Maybe she'll just focus on her own personal goals; graduating summa cum laude is still possible, and her senior honors thesis, "Patronage vs. Exceptionalism in American Ambassadorship Selection," could contend for a Poli Sci prize. So Daria spends Saturday afternoons in the library alone, instead of cheering for her boyfriend and the water polo team at the pool.

Now, when Trevor sees Daria across campus flirting with senior lacrosse players, he feels a dagger, because it's obvious he can't hold onto her, and maybe he and Daria will not have that rambling house in Connecticut after all.

Still, she says she loves him and why discuss the future now? It's only the second week in November. And she's sorry she can't meet his mom for Thanksgiving in Walnut Creek; Daria is not even going home to see her own family, because she has a job interview with the Rockefeller Foundation in Manhattan on November 26th.

And don't worry about her on Thanksgiving Day; she'll be volunteering at the Salvation Army in downtown Boston. But they can always text and say hi, though her phone is off for most of the weekend while she concentrates on her thesis.

Trevor tries to understand, but when Thanksgiving break is over, he senses he's somehow unwanted, like she's pulling away. But they watch *The Daily Show* in her bed together night after night, and she always reads him pages of her honors paper for objectivity.

But then it's suddenly the second week of December, and should Daria interview at Bechtel International in McClean, Virginia on the 28th, or split the holiday with her family in Snowmass and Trevor's in California? Except, who would turn down the interview? Especially when she knows from her research that the fastest way to an ambassadorship is having great wealth, or directing that wealth. Excelling within a famous global corporation like Bechtel could pave her way to the jet set.

For Daria's father is merely a millionaire commercial real estate contractor, who rode the Silicon Valley building boom with his homemaker wife. If Daria's dreams are to come true, she must become far richer—as a benefactress to political parties and American Presidents, who will appoint her to Paris.

After a kiss for Trevor, she flies to Colorado to meet her parents and younger brother. December 27th, she takes a flight back east to Bechtel, then returns to Snowmass, where she holes up in the lodge to complete her paper.

Home in California, Trevor is cheerless as a coroner, even while his twin cousins, Emma and Emily, bake him sugar cookies and braid his hair with chopsticks. Trevor longs for his girlfriend, and what is all this bullshit that she doesn't want to talk about her interview because she doesn't want to jinx it, and that she's too stressed to even snowboard or text because she needs time to write?

On a 1 a.m. walk around his hometown cul-de-sac, under siege, Trevor warns himself, You're letting her fuck you up, and, She wouldn't have bought you Dirty English aftershave for Christmas if she didn't care...even though she got it for you after you gave her an iPod Nano.

But then all is well after she calls, saying, "I miss you," on New Year's Eve, and follows that conversation with a Hallmark Happy New Year Internet greeting card to him the next morning. So enough with all the doubt—she is his.

Trevor flies back to Cambridge January fifth, sure he will see Daria in the early evening. Home in his Wigglesworth dorm, he opens his laptop to update his email, and suddenly, there is a new note from Dad.

The subject line says, "Enjoy!" and there is a Tribal Fire video attached. Trevor opens the video, and on it is a 10-second clip from the New York penthouse ceiling camera of Daria naked under Luke.

Before Trevor can fully comprehend the participants, he shouts, "NO!" but he cannot reverse time.

He replies, "YOU FUCKING MONSTER!" then grabs the phone, barely able to dial. But Daria doesn't answer. He tries to text but his fingers stop working and just then, Luke emails Trevor back: "email mistake, meant for ambassador morton. but she's too young for me, so I got her a job in paris!"

Trevor runs through the snow to Adams House, charging up the stairs to Daria's room. Only she's gone and all her possessions are moved out. Trevor races home to Wigglesworth, emailing Dad, "BURN IN HELL!" before collapsing on the floor.

But there's no reason to write back, nor time. Luke is strapped in his own advanced space plane atop a new-generation Atlas V Heavy rocket at NASA, with less than minutes to go: he is about to be the first civilian to fly into orbit alone. And if anyone is shaking her head saying, "Not possible," it's only a matter of some billions, paid to the free-market brain behind NASA: United Space Alliance, LLC.

And astronauts can fly at night these days, weather permitting, and never underestimate United Space Alliance capabilities: Mission Feasibility, Space Plane, Extravehicular

Activity Planning, Rapid In-Flight Anomaly Resolution, and fine food procurement for the trip.

For Luke has been training over three years now for his brave journey—flying T-38 Talon jets out of Edwards Air Force Base, blowing chow in the Vomit Comet umpteen times, and maneuvering in a weighted space suit underwater for eight hours at a time.

Now, with the world watching on his Tribal Fire cockpit cam, he runs through his final checks. At mission control, a protective computer calculation sets off alarms, because the orbiter is somehow thirty pounds heavier than normal. Only it's too late to abort, so: "Three, two, one, liftoff of *Tribal Fire One*, the first single-manned joint mission between NASA and private enterprise adventurer, Luke Morrow!"

Only Trevor is not glued to the Internet or TV watching his dad blaze into history; Luke forgot to invite him to the launch or the celebratory return landing party on Luke's fiftieth birthday. Instead, Trevor is buying an unregistered gun and .45 caliber shells in a South Boston back alley, contemplating patricide.

And how an Ivy League student-athlete with a kind heart could be headed in despair to kill his billionaire father is painfully plausible, and Trevor just has to lie in wait in the Park Avenue penthouse for him to return in thirty-six hours.

Trevor kept the keys because Dad never specified their return, and he'll surely need some downtime (before his morning media tour victory lap) on his own bed. There, point blank, he shall be shot in the face—surprise, enjoy!

∞

Luke circles the earth, piece of cake. And finally, after his first day away, he conjures the right words to describe his humbling experience for the little blue marble below. "My world, by my efforts, revolutionized."

But that's not all; mankind also receives his free gift: an Eco Spacewalk to capture a fried Google Maps satellite from polluting the void, using the $245 million Manned Maneuvering Unit—a Morrow Aerospace rocket propulsion backpack. As for Luke's life, should the MMU fail, he posts on Facebook, "The only risk is the one not taken," which he copyrights.

Out of the hatch he floats, the MMU's thrusters guiding him toward the space junk. With the people of the planet on the edge of their seats, Luke captures and feeds the failed Google satellite into the space plane's trash compactor bay, where it's pressed into a recyclable ingot.

With showboating somersaults, Luke returns to his spaceship a reality TV star, and with cameras off for some private time, he enjoys a vacuum-packed, poached Le Cirque lobster dinner. After espresso and bombolini for dessert, it's time for bed, but instead of strapping himself into his bunk for the night as directed, Luke dons the MMU again and lets himself outside for an unplanned second walk.

At mission control, there's startled disbelief. "What the hell is he doing?" "Only one kilogram of propellant left!" "Return to ship, OVER!" But Luke is a happy person without fears, and he will savor his time in his universe. He ignores the crackling radio and bobs beyond NASA's view, free and unfettered.

Then, into the continuum from his thigh pockets, he lets go of thirty pounds of gold coins—requisitioned at the last minute from the Franklin Mint and forged with his chiseled profile, name, and website. Off his monuments go, glinting in the sun, flipping end-over-end into faraway worlds, where new civilizations will learn of his feats.

Then all is quiet, save for his labored breathing, for Luke is suddenly afraid. Because he is not yet master of his imagination and desire, and he does not possess the wood plank crate that suddenly, inexplicably hovers just out of his reach, blinding him with white light.

He puts a hand over his visor bubble to further shield his eyes, using the other hand to accelerate toward the light. But like a mirage, the box shimmers and disappears, mere feet away, above him, below him, to his left, his right. He can't grab it, to his enraged frustration.

Moseying up, wearing his own space suit and MMU, is Hershey Resnikoff. Hershey says, "It's just a vision and a trap. Why are you always wanting what you can't have?"

The box yaws, revealing a digital clock on its side with tenths of seconds flying backward, evaporating time. Hershey says, "The contents of the box have an expiration date. I meant to mention that when we first met."

Luke draws a titanium screwdriver from his pocket, threatening to use it once and for all. "What's inside?"

"The contents are only good till 1:24:47 a.m."

"My birthday!"

"Exactly—on your fiftieth year, down to the second."

Luke lunges for the box again, but it scoots away, vanishing.

Hershey says, "The actual one is still in the hold of the X-10000."

Luke shoves Hershey aside, sending him tumbling away. Receding into the cosmos, Hershey says, "There's a storm below! Don't risk your life!"

∞

Luke claws through the airlock into his seat. He punches his keyboard, positioning *Tribal Fire One* for a rapid descent.

Except that's not the plan; mission controllers whip heads to screens.

Soon the space plane is plummeting, rumbling through the atmosphere, engulfed in molten fire. Until it's suddenly not, soundless on a glide above deepest navy blue, before stratospheric winds slingshot the ship over the earth's bend into a ferocious tropospheric storm.

Luke fights the controls, but the trouble is beyond his talent. *Tribal Fire One* rolls into blasting lightning, spelling Luke's end. Except Hershey roars past in the rain on a WWII B-24 Liberator bomber, shouting from the gunner's turret, "Eject, *mon capitaine!*"

The space plane's canopy explodes upwards, and Luke's seat violently trampolines beyond the weather, discarding him. Luke's high-altitude chute opens gracefully against a full moon. Down Luke floats in winter silence, till his feet crunch virgin snow. He sheds the chute as Hershey nears on a musher's sled.

The barking dogs halt and Hershey hops off, placing the wood plank crate with the blinding white light from the sled onto the ground. Hershey tosses Milk Bones into the air for the dogs, who clamp the bones and about-face, springing with the sled into a partition in the sky.

Luke discerns the mountain range around him to every dark horizon. "Where am I?"

"On a starry pinnacle in Northern California, eighty-four miles from the crash site." Hershey nods at the crate. "But since I knew precisely where you'd land, I got to thinking out there. And I worked really hard to see your point of view, and I decided: Why should a man suffer for one foolish goal? But I forgot the key to the box's lock. So everyone goes home disappointed, never getting to see what's inside."

On the crate, numbers on the timer fly by—down to ten seconds, zipping to zero. Luke runs for the box with his titanium screwdriver, driving the tool into the lock—a fool's errand, with six seconds, four seconds, three seconds, less.

Except there, leaning against a snow-laden Spruce, is a lumberjack's ax. Two seconds, one second, Luke seizes the ax, and *whack!* shears the lock.

A loaded spring pops the top, revealing a toy-sized Patriot missile, which fires from a mini-launcher carrying its blinding white marble ball warhead tip into Luke's space suit, into his hidden heart. Luke drops to his knees from the impact. Hershey says, "Your soul, back inside you. You lost it by the ditch in upstate New York, but luckily, the hand of

God found it and put it in the crate for safekeeping—in case you might need it again one day."

Luke keels forward onto his stomach, no longer dressed in the space suit; instead, he's wearing his dark jeans, a black linen shirt, and black boots from days past. And his hair that was once shorn short for power is now back to russet waves. His Panerai watch—gone.

Flushed thick with sweat, Luke says, "I'm burning up!"

Hershey says, "The effect of empathy re-rooting, melting the ice in your veins." Hershey tosses a down jacket onto the snow. "Soon you'll be cold; the coat will keep you warm during the crucible."

Sure enough, Luke begins quaking with shivers. Willing himself up, he dons the jacket as a silver IMAX curtain drops from the sky, dwarfing the men. On it are Luke's former secretary Tracy, Daniel the Intern, Johnson Ash, Carolyn Mannes, Nicole Pompa, Oren Sanger, Julie Reynolds, Laurie Dolan, their hundreds of loyal employees, and the Tribal Fire executives from the Sunday at the beach.

Hershey says, "The men and women you betrayed, dismissed on a whim, or abused. A handful were set for life, but what about the others who never regained their footing? Your hand in their lives was tangential, footnotes in your history—you never even knew their names."

The men and women take one last look over their shoulders at Luke, before vanishing as ghosts, near the feet of Byung-Jun Kim, Francis Oh, and Joey Wook. Hershey says, "The co-creators of Tribal Fire that you cheated. How different their lives might have been is anyone's guess. But why think about it?"

The wives and children of Byung-Jun, Francis, and Joey join them, all taking a final glance at Luke, before they disappear, behind the forms of Amber, the call girl; the Caesar's Palace hookers; Li Po, the Ginza Spa masseuse; Saryn from Carat USA; Alina, the nanny; Meg, the sales rep; Mia, the Amerasian stewardess; the Erotic Review call girl from Hawaii; Beth, the mom from Ocean Park; the Ukrainian yacht playmates; and the 494 other women who went to Luke's bed.

Hershey says, "Your women. Some had better lives after you, but most did not. However, they were big girls. They knew what they were getting into; no one twisted their arms."

The women dematerialize into dust, making way for Sara, Michael, and Kit. Hershey says, "Your sister, brother-in-law, and niece. They could barely make ends meet, so what good were they?" Sara, Michael, and Kit fade into the frost.

"And your son, Trevor."

In Luke's New York penthouse—Trevor—despondent in a chair, unshaven and sleepless, spinning the barrel of a gun. But Trevor will not kill his dad. Instead, Trevor places the gun on the table and rises, stepping behind the Giacometti Walking Man sculpture.

Dug in with his shoulder against the bronze, Trevor drives the statue toward the floor-to-ceiling windows, until *wham!* he rams the Walking Man through the glass. Trevor steps back from the shattered pane, placid. Then he leaps out into the sky.

On the mountaintop, Luke screams, "NO!!!" but he cannot stop fate. Trevor falls through time and space until he lands next to the impaled sculpture on a Manhattan pavement, momentarily as an 8-year-old boy with little entrails spilling out from a tear in his tummy.

Luke sees himself coming to cradle Trevor, but there's nothing to be done. His child dies in his arms.

Then on the IMAX curtain is Lisa, alone in a canoe, in the center of Skinny Bear Lake—where Don Gaspar de Portolá's overland expedition passed in 1769. She pauses under a cold winter sun, before falling out of the boat and sinking like a stone.

Empty in the canoe's stern are two bottles of Ambien and one bottle of Absolut Citron.

Hershey says, "Your loving wife Lisa, who cherished your son and could not bear his loss."

Sirens near the New York sidewalk, where authorities abruptly step in and take Trevor from Luke's arms, sealing Trevor, now an 18-year-old college freshman again, in a body bag—just as the Northern California funeral for Trevor and Lisa begins. Beside adjoining graves with imponderable grief: Stan and Pat Hudson, Case, Emma, and Emily, and their mom, Becca, destroyed amid the roses.

Watching, Luke flushes with sweat once more. "I'm burning up!" He rips off the jacket, throwing it at Hershey. "Keep it! It's been fun to meet my father's best friend, but this isn't for real!"

Hershey says, "Oh it's real, alright."

"Right! Real enough for a dream! But soon this will be over, and I'll be with Trevor in our garden. He's only eight, you know—I've got a pizza coming and we're going to eat it under the stars."

Hershey peers into the wind. "No Luke, that's not how it's going to go. You won't be seeing Trevor ever again, either way."

Luke fights to breathe; it cannot be, what he has wrought. *"THIS IS NOT MY LIFE!"*

Hershey says, "It is your life—your life in hell—because you destroyed everyone you touched. But what of my life?"

Suddenly, Luke is in a German field under a warming sun. A B-24 Liberator bomber on fire, Hershey in the turret, slams into a nearby apple orchard and explodes. Hershey says, "It happened so fast. I didn't have time to see the world."

At Jefferson Barracks National Cemetery in St. Louis, Luke and Hershey stand among 160,000 headstones. Hershey says, "I'm not sure which one is mine, where I am; we'd have to check the grave locator. But what about your former life—the one you didn't want?"

Back on the starry pinnacle, a second IMAX curtain slams downward, revealing the landlady pounding on Luke's apartment door. Luke is slumped over the kitchen table at The Pico South Seas, bits of his brain on the dinette tabletop from his self-inflicted shot—the first step on his journey to his own funeral at Forest Lawn.

There, Keri, Bram, Marnie, Peter, and their boys clasps their hands in sorrow, while Lisa and Mark try to comfort 8-year-old Trevor.

But Trevor breaks free when the casket goes down, throwing himself over it, hugging on. *"DADDY!"*

Hershey considers the two funerals: Lisa's and Trevor's on the first screen, Luke's on the second. Then Hershey says, "Two destinies ruined. But as we only get one life in the end, which will you choose? The man who took his own life, leaving his boy fatherless? Or the billionaire who drove his son and ex-wife to take their own lives?"

Luke tries to speak.

"Here or there?"

Luke looks to the first screen. "You stacked the deck! I could have had a heart!"

"No, Luke. You wanted to be filthy rich—you had to play the part."

Luke looks to the second screen, where Lisa and Mark, sole guardians of Trevor, tuck their boy into bed. Luke lowers his head, tears spilling to the ground. Finally, he says, "The past, where his mother and stepfather will love him forever."

Hershey says, "Eternally without you."

"My life for his life."

"You'll be giving up great riches. Your yacht, your jet, your homes—it will be like they never existed." Luke accepts his death, making the sign of the cross. The wind-whipped

IMAX screens come unmoored and instantly disappear, suctioned backward into the sky.

Role complete, Hershey turns to his friend. "One last thing: How did you know your choice would earn your reprieve?"

"I don't understand."

Hershey believes him. "Go home, Luke. Take whatever rain. And do right by a little boy."

∞

Luke's head is down on his Pico South Seas apartment dinette table. He awakens, unsure why he has fallen asleep right there. And his gun, once on the table by his hand, is gone.

Luke rises, climbing onto his chair, opening the safe on the closet shelf. He removes his tackle box and inside it is his gun, unloaded. He secures the gun and box back in the safe, and as he steps down from the chair—is that the last remnants of Sharpie-scribbled code, vanishing from the ceiling and scattered papers? He looks to the side; did he just see fragments of calculations bleeding white into the walls?

Luke goes to the Shaquille O'Neal memorabilia shoe, but it is untouched, in perfect condition in its Plexiglas box. Luke steps back to the table, and there, where it was not moments before, is the oil portrait of Hershey Resnikoff.

Luke picks up the painting, and under it is an airmail letter, circa 1944. The letter reads: "I turned back the clock. One day till your fortieth birthday, one last chance to fulfill your destiny with the algorithms you sought. Share them with the creator who misplaced them and you will have riches. Sincerely, Hershey."

On the table is One Leg's tattered composition book, filled with algorithmic code written in blocks of red, blue, green, and black ink.

∞

Holding One Leg's book, Luke stands before Plot #23 in Santa Monica Community Gardens. The seedlings are not kicked over or destroyed; they've grown into sturdy plants, bearing rapini, peas, lima beans, and Brussels sprouts.

∞

Luke rings the doorbell of a Park La Brea tower apartment until Joey Wook answers, wiping Mr. Sandman from his eyes.

∞

Byung-Jun Kim, Francis, and Joey are at the card table in the apartment, with One Leg's journal open before them. Byung-Jun says to Luke, "The computations are pristine; it's the code we couldn't crack."

∞

Luke, Byung-Jun, Francis, and Joey are in a darkened glass cathedral conference room at venture capital firm Kleiner Perkins in Palo Alto. With One Leg's journal on the table at his side, Luke presents Tribal Fire Networks' business plan on PowerPoint to world-renowned venture capitalist John Doerr.

The lights come up. Doerr looks to his executive team, who confirms his instincts. He says, "We want it. We'll give you $500,000 up front with 200,000 shares of stock each, with $95,000 salaries to start to get the company launched. Congratulations, Founders of Tribal Fire Networks."

∞

Luke stands before One Leg on a Venice street near Gold's Gym. Luke holds out the composition book and says, "I found it by the community gardens. It must have fallen from your bag while you were caring for my plants. And at first, you know, I couldn't figure out where I'd seen it before, so forgive me, because I first took it to my friends, who are amazing programmers in parallel processing just like you.

"And they made a copy of it for safety, and then they showed that copy to the big money guys in Silicon Valley, who think your algorithms, coupled with our humanistic applications, can be a brilliant business for all of us."

Luke removes a check from his pocket. "This is for $200,000 made out to me, but $100,000 of it belongs to you, and I thought maybe we'd use some of it to find you a place to live with some proper care, where you can have a warm bed and plenty to eat.

And then when you're better and your hands have healed, you can join us at the company, where it will be a great honor to have you on board."

One Leg nods okay, blinking back tears.

∞

In a courtroom, Luke stands with his divorce attorney, Ellen, below a woman judge in her forties. At a table on the other side of the room is Luke's ex-wife Lisa and her lawyers, with Mark Morello II seated in the row behind them.

The judge says, "In light of the evaluation, and given Mr. Morrow's gainful employment as well as his payoff of Rainforest, LLC's legal judgment against him, I find he has sufficient means to support his son, as well as to settle other pending debts.

"And as the parties' son, in the opinion of the court psychologists, has an enduring bond with the father, it's my ruling that the mother and stepfather may not remove Trevor from the state of California without Mr. Morrow's consent. Mrs. Morello, you are free to relocate to Martha's

Vineyard, with visitation rights to your son to be worked out between the parties."

∞

The titanium Aston Martin whines into the reflection of Luke's Ray-Bans and halts in front of The Pico South Seas. Trevor climbs out of his seat to Luke. Luke gathers his son up in his arms as the car departs.

Trevor says, "I get to be with my dad on his birthday!"

Luke says, "And I have some very good news for you. I have a new job that I'm passionate about. And we're gonna celebrate that accomplishment eating day-old lobsters cold with mayonnaise."

"What is that passionate new job?"

"I will tell you while I'm preparing the rapini."

∞

Luke ties a lobster bib around Trevor to match his own, then serves chilled Maine lobsters, along with garlic bread and bowls of hot, buttered vegetables from their garden. But before they dig in, Luke says, "Remind me. What's your job again?"

Trevor says, "I forget."

"Your job is to be a kid. What's my job?"

Trevor shrugs.

"My job is to love you. And you know what I say? The two easiest jobs in the world." Beyond the boys, out the barred window, the lemonette still hangs from its branch. And on branches all around it: eight new, white blossoms, fragrant under the moonbeams. And how this could be on that spindly tree is but the first of the infinite components of a miracle.

About the Author

Todd R. Baker grew up on the North Shore of Chicago and somehow ended up on the shoal of Los Angeles. During Todd's film industry career, he produced and developed movies for 20th Century Fox, Paramount Pictures, Disney, Miramax, and Universal Pictures, starring Kevin Costner, Leonardo DiCaprio, Tom Cruise, Jack Nicholson, Robert Downey, Jr., Adam Sandler, Elijah Wood, Robert Duvall, Anjelica Huston, Whoopi Goldberg, Raul Julia, Daryl Hannah, Chris Farley, Steve Buscemi, Brendan Fraser, Christopher Lloyd, and Kenneth Branagh. He licenses two of his U.S. patents for one of his inventions and is a Phi Beta Kappa graduate of Stanford University. Todd lives in Playa Vista/Silicon Beach, California.